KINGDOM OF SILENCE

KINGDOM
OF SILENCE

Lee Wood

 MINOTAUR BOOKS ✿ NEW YORK

KINGDOM OF SILENCE. Copyright © 2009 by Lee Wood. All rights reserved. Printed in the United States of America. For information, address St. Martin's Press, 175 Fifth Avenue, New York, N.Y. 10010.

www.minotaurbooks.com

Library of Congress Cataloging-in-Publication Data

Wood, N. Lee
    Kingdom of silence / by Lee Wood. — 1st ed.
        p.   cm.
    ISBN-13: 978-0-312-34031-5
    ISBN-10: 0-312-34031-1
    1. Police—England—Fiction.   2. Animal-rights activists—Fiction.
3. Leeds (England)—Fiction.   I. Title.
PR6073.O613K57 2009
    823'.914—dc22

                                                        2008036247

First Edition: February 2009

10   9   8   7   6   5   4   3   2   1

AUTHOR'S NOTE

While many of the places in this novel are genuine, with the exception of well-known historical and political figures, all characters are imaginary and any resemblance to real persons, living or dead, is coincidental and unintended. All events portrayed in this work, historical or current, are a product of the author's imagination and are completely, totally, and absolutely fictitious.

Well . . .

. . . except for those bits that aren't.

For Simon Street. I just write words. You live them.

ACKNOWLEDGMENTS

I am grateful for the invaluable assistance of many people who generously gave of their time, expertise, and support during the writing of this novel.

I'd like to thank Andy Fisher, head of the Wildlife Crime Unit, New Scotland Yard, and Angus Nurse, investigations coordinator for the Royal Society for the Protection of Birds, Bedfordshire.

In West Yorkshire, my warmest thanks to Derek and Joan Green, Cowling; and to the Yorkshire Dales Falconry and Conservation Center in Settle. Many thanks to Police Constable Colin Waddington of Bridlington, Mercyside Police, and his wonderful wife, Jill, for opening doors—in every sense of the word.

In Staffordshire, a special thank-you to Sergeant Simon Street, his wife Sharon and son Daniel; and to Police Constable David Eivers, his wife Denise, son Tom, and daughter Amy "the Worm." You guys rock my world.

In Somerset, my thanks to Quita Allender, who edited and self-published *Fields of Fire,* a collection of letters, poems, and prose written by farmers and vets, housewives and schoolchildren, journalists and policemen and ordinary people whose lives were touched by the FMD outbreak. Find it, buy it, read it, it'll break your heart.

In Northumberland, thanks to gentleman farmer Arnold Harrison; and Sarah Miller of Newcastle Radio. Thanks to Robin and Andrew Birley of Vindolanda, for an unforgettable summer excavation experience in one of the finest Roman archaeological sites in the world. My thanks to veterinarian Jim McLellan and a special thank-you to his colleague, Frank Decaluwe, for the extraordinary gentleness and compassion he showed to my much-loved best mate, Robinson the Cat, at the end of his life. Much love to those in my old village, Keith Benbow and Diane Baxter, Kim and Michael Palmer, Christine Liversedge, and June and Rollie and Anne and Big Dave and Little Dave, you all were and will always be my family. And, as always, with love to all-around good guy and windmill-tilting knight in Haflinger armor, Jon Barron.

In the United States, my thanks to Mev Camozzi, retired Santa Barbara County Sheriff and good friend. In Canada, my warmest thanks to Dr. Anthony Barrett, Professor Emeritus of the University of British Columbia, who allowed me to join his archaeological excavation at the Lunt Roman Fort in Coventry at the last minute, and to his Amazonian-goddess grad student, Jennifer Boyd.

In New Zealand, much thanks and love to so many who came to my rescue after my world unexpectedly caved in: Gotham and Ellie Bhatia, the Brosnan family, Paul and Sonya Burgin, my dear friend Raewyn Cozens (and Luke and Emily and Jack and Alex and Peppi), Jonothan Cullinane, Mike and Vicki Gedye, Sue Gee, Grahame Lee, Rae McGregor, Connie Parkinson, Ian Russell, Dave Scott, Jenny Thomsen, Sue Underwood, Shelley Underwood, Vivianne Vagt, the members of my writers' group Seven Kiwis and a Yank, and all my wonderful, caring friends from South and East Ceroc. Proof—when I needed it the most—that the vast majority of Kiwis are among the most generous and compassionate people on the planet.

My thanks also to those people who do the hard bit of making books a reality: my literary agent, John Silbersack at Trident Media, and to my editor extraordinaire, Kelley Ragland at St. Martin's Press, and her assistant, Matt Martz. They don't come any better.

This is the silence of disbelief.

The next silence is the worst silence.

This is the silence

Of the steaming kitchen at three A.M.

When half the cattle lie stiff in the yard

and half are still waiting.

This is a silence with no name.

—excerpt from "An Ill Wind," a poem by Katrina
  Porteous, commissioned by BBC Radio 3 and
  first published in *Fields of Fire*

KINGDOM OF SILENCE

PROLOGUE

FEBRUARY

On a chilly, wet Monday morning in February 2001 a young vet in Essex named Craig Kirby made a discovery which would trigger a chain of events that would devastate the entire country. He had been routinely examining animals being unloaded from livestock lorries into the Cheales Meat Company when he noticed three groups of lame pigs being herded into the abattoir for slaughter. He lifted their hocks to check and, on one pig after another, found large weeping blisters lacerating the pads of their feet. These pigs had been in agony for quite some time, a wonder they could walk at all.

He'd never seen anything quite like it before, at least not outside of a textbook. But although he hadn't even been born during the only outbreak in Britain in 1968, he knew with a sinking heart that he was looking at the classic symptoms of foot-and-mouth disease. He immediately brought the abattoir to a standstill, and conferred with a visiting veterinary officer from the Ministry of Agriculture, Fisheries, and Food who came to the same diagnosis. They sent the tissue samples taken from the twenty-eight ailing pigs off to the Pirbright lab for express testing. Less than twenty-four hours later, MAFF's chief veterinary officer, Jim Scudamore, officially corroborated the young vet's suspicions: this was FMD—a viral disease that is rarely fatal to animals and not transmittable to humans, easy to vaccinate against, but potentially lethal for the regulation-bound British meat export industry.

A bull on a farm next to the abattoir had also been infected with the virus. It, along with forty-nine other cattle, was immediately destroyed, while arrangements were made for all the animals at the abattoir and on every farm within a five-mile radius to be killed. But with a fourteen-day incubation period before the first symptoms even appear, MAFF officials knew they needed to track down the source of infection and any other animals the pigs may have contaminated—*fast*.

A frantic inquiry traced the pigs back to Burnside Farm in Heddon-on-the-Wall, a quiet, picturesque village in the Northumberland countryside that—up until now—had been notable only as a minor tourist stop along Hadrian's Wall and for the excellent beers produced by the Wylam microbrewery tucked behind the stables at Houghton's Farm.

Local people had known for some time all was not well at Burnside Farm, neighbors complaining to MAFF and the RSPCA, Newcastle Trading Standards, environmental health inspectors, the local council—anyone who would listen, really—about the grimy "hillbilly outfit" run by its surly owners, brothers Bobby and Ronny Waugh. Six months before, the Waughs had been warned by the local state vet, Jim Dring, that the standards on their farm were unacceptable. Lame and crippled pigs wallowed through muddy yards, dead animals rotted in the open for days, and the stench of unprocessed pigswill the Waughs concocted out of waste collected from schools, hospitals, and the rubbish bins of local restaurants could be smelled from a fair distance off. But rather than officially reprimanding the brothers, the vet had agreed to "pretend" his visit had never happened if conditions were tidied up.

They weren't.

The state vet issued a final warning in December, which was ignored. The Waughs themselves knew their pigs were in dismal health two months later when the animals were shipped off to Essex for slaughter, but they didn't call in the vet to treat their livestock or notify MAFF when their pigs began showing symptoms of ill health—in the hope the pigs might pass through the chain unnoticed.

By that Friday, the disease had already spread from the Waughs' farm to contaminate a neighboring farm's sheep. But these animals were long gone themselves; auctioned off through Hexham's cattle market and the Longton market in Cumbria to wholesale traders. They had then been sold and resold and shipped along with hundreds of thousands of healthy animals for a few weeks of fattening before slaughter in the fields of Anglesey and Wales, Hereford and Gloucester, Warwickshire, Northhampton, Somerset, Devon, Cornwall, Essex, Kent, the Cotswolds, the moors of Dartmoor, and even Ireland, France, and Spain. Contact with the contaminated sheep had already expanded the range of the virus, like shock waves radiating from the epicenter of an atomic bomb blast.

One of these infected sheep had shared a holding pen in the Hexham cattle market with a dozen other healthy animals. A pair of sturdy, soft-fleeced Northumberland Blackface ewes from that lot were sold to a dealer, who then transported them down into Yorkshire and sold them on to David and Margot Dean, a young couple who had decided to sell up their flat in London and escape the City rat race. The Deans had invested every penny they had in a whopping mortgage on a farmhouse with twenty acres in the green rolling hills of Ilkley, and set up their own *Good Life*–style freehold, raising organic vegetables, free-range chickens, and two small daughters. This would be their first venture into breeding their own sheep, and Margot had bought an old-fashioned spinning wheel off one of their neighbors, fellow farmer's wife Joanne Kestleman, already imagining the jumpers she could knit for her girls from their very own homespun wool.

On the twenty-seventh of February, local authorities issued with emergency powers ordered the closing of public footpaths, woodland walks, coastal routes, and horseback trails, even roadside lay-bys, all throughout Britain. It wasn't only farmers who suffered: as tourists canceled reservations, country hotels, B and Bs, and pubs stood empty. Bicycle shops closed down when no one bought bikes they couldn't ride anywhere. Caterers and conference centers sent home their staff as companies withdrew their contracts. Canoeing and fishing and hang gliding and rock climbing and Girl Guide camping and children's pony trekking vanished overnight. The backbone of the rural economy was being systematically broken.

By the time MAFF ordered an indefinite nationwide standstill on all livestock movement, it was already several weeks too late. That same day, Nick Brown, the Labour minister for agriculture and MP for Newcastle and Wallsend, where the epidemic arose, publicly announced to the incredulity of British farmers who knew better, "The outbreak is now under control." Rejecting the advice of dozens of veterinary surgeons, farmers, and scientific experts urging ring vaccination as a firebreak to stop the spread of the disease, the government decided to cull domestic livestock on a holocaustic scale no country on earth had ever seen before.

The animals of Britain began to die.

February's Death Toll: 1,981 cattle, 9,877 sheep, 1,781 pigs, and 4 goats.

Because of their proximity to the Waugh farm, 350 pigs and a handful of sheep and cows on Jimmy and Joan Brown's farm in Heddon View East are slaughtered, then burned on their land, ending the elderly couple's livelihood of thirty-five years. "They didn't even check our stock," Mrs. Brown said. "He [Minister for Agriculture Nick Brown] said our stock was infected—well, it wasn't." They were angry, but added, "All we know is that they've got to stop this disease, before it does to someone else what it has done to us."

MAFF officials supervise the slaughter of 80 cattle, 140 pigs, and 360 sheep at an abattoir in Witton-le-Wear, County Durham, the firm's entire livestock. John Thompson and son Mark have owned and run the family business over forty years. John Thompson was too distressed to talk about the crisis after the cull, but son Mark is uncertain of the future of the business, or the jobs of the twenty-two employees who have been laid off. "We are closed for business," he said. "I can't see a way out of this."

Blizzard conditions cause widespread power failures and shut eighty schools in North Yorkshire and County Durham, while accidents rise on roads normally kept open by farmers during bad weather conditions and which have remained closed as farms shut down due to foot-and-mouth.

Representatives with the Farmers Union warn that gusting winds in the Northeast could not only hamper efforts to contain the outbreak but spread the virus even further as well.

Government officials fear the death toll could rise to as high as 25,000 animals.

1

MARCH

Icy thunderstorms pushed up clouds as hard as bricks over the Atlantic Ocean. The captain apologized for the turbulence in an exquisitely bored English accent, adding the local time and current temperature with equal indifference as red-eye British Air flight 176 from Los Angeles to London finally began its descent into Heathrow. The morning sky had lightened to turquoise above a bright fairy-tale landscape of clouds, fading as the plane slid into gray soup. Droplets scrawled against the outer window as pinpricks of light appeared below, car headlights and storefront neon illuminating the distant ground like the Peter Pan ride Kim vaguely remembered from a family trip to Disneyland.

Unlike the dreamy pretense of that long-ago make-believe, U.S. Marshal Kimberly Prescott had always hated flying. She'd ended up dribbling most of her coffee down her chin when the airplane lurched like a truck driving over a pig. The wings outside her window flexed alarmingly and she could hear the creak of luggage shifting in the racks overhead. Her stomach clenched against the turbulence as logic told her nothing that *big* could possibly stay airborne. And it didn't help to be handcuffed to Eunice Gordon Connor, British national, pregnant mother of two, convicted felon, and whining pain in the butt. All that the fat bitch had done the entire flight was complain and go to the toilet every hour, dragging Kim along to the accompanying stares of fellow passengers.

Kim's partner on this extradition trip, Elliot Redburn, had been less than helpful. She'd had four days to develop a permanent and abiding loathing of both her prisoner and her partner, any satisfaction her colleagues' envy about transporting Connor to London quickly soured.

As one of the department's most experienced marshals in transporting difficult prisoners, Kim Prescott had developed a reputation for being a tough, unflappable officer disguised as a rosy-cheeked grandmother. Connor was far from the most dangerous prisoner she'd ever had to transport; the flight to Vancouver with the serial killer who believed himself the reincarnation of Jesus Christ had certainly been trickier. She'd simply lavished him with praise and flattery for providing them such lovely weather to fly in the entire trip, which kept him sweet enough if it nauseated Redburn, at least until they'd landed and a half-dozen Canadian police officers had to wrestle him to the ground before they could get him into the transport wagon.

Connor was neither a dangerous nor a violent criminal, but her numerous escapes and bail skips, as well as being the longtime girlfriend of a man wanted in Britain for far more serious crimes, made her a valuable prisoner. Her lawyers in Britain were already hammering out a deal for a suspended sentence in return for her guilty plea and cooperation in apprehending her lover and the father of her three children, along with her testimony in court to convict him once he'd been caught. So much for true love. The extra attention had lent Connor a misplaced sense of self-importance, with a sizable dollop of smug pride Kim found tiresome.

Nor was Redburn the most annoying partner she'd ever put up with, either. She'd learned to handle male prejudice in the job in all its nasty forms since she'd been a twenty-two-year-old rookie on the Santa Barbara City Police; Redburn was no better or worse than the average.

With only four months to go before retiring, Kim tended to let her mind drift more often to the future, a future of not having to get up at five in the morning ever again, never wear another uniform in her life. She and Ted, her husband of thirty-two years, had managed to save up enough to put down the deposit on reservations for that long-planned Alaskan cruise. She was looking forward to spoiling her new granddaughter—she was halfway through crocheting a lacy christening gown with adorable matching little booties—and to taking her seven-year-old grandson to Disneyland for his birthday this summer. Her future would *not* include extraditing the dregs of society in the company of arrogant Boy Scouts barely out of diapers.

She'd nearly lost her renowned composure when the flight attendant had handed out their in-flight meal and Connor predictably whined, "I gotta go to the loo again."

"Oh, for . . ." Kim bit back her irritation and ignored Redburn's muffled snicker. Connor sat between the two marshals, Redburn having snared the window seat. "Can't you at least wait until after we've eaten?"

"You nivver been pregnant?" Connor sneered. "Ten pounds of baby pressing down on me bladder, I gotta *go*."

So once again, Kim had unlocked Connor's wrist from her own and locked the woman's hands together, draping her own sweater over the cuffs to hide them from the gaze of the curious and the sensitive. She shifted their meals onto Redburn's table and escorted the pregnant woman down the aisle to the restrooms. They had to wait for an unoccupied cubicle along with another woman and her young son. The young mother smiled at Connor with a glance at the prisoner's swollen stomach, and patted her own.

"When are you due?" the woman asked amiably, with the confidence of one pregnant mother to another.

"End of May," Connor said, smiling back. Kim watched the exchange, indifferent but not inattentive. She noticed the boy's interest in the glint of metal under the sweater Connor held in her hands.

"Your first?"

"Third. Two boys. Hoping for a girl this time."

A cubicle opened, releasing a whiff of talcum powder, airline disinfectant, and shit. An elderly man smiled apologetically before squeezing past. The young mother watched puzzled as Kim quickly inspected the inside of the lavatory, checking that the old man hadn't secreted a weapon for their prisoner. Once clear, she allowed Connor inside and waited. The woman and boy had taken the second toilet when it came vacant, done their business and gone back to their seats before Connor managed to finish her pee. The attendants were collecting empty dinner trays as Kim escorted Connor back to their seats. Connor scowled at the plastic-wrapped meal on the seat tray in front of her.

"I can't eat this," she complained, and pushed the tray back resentfully. "I told you, I'm vegan—nothing with a face."

"So don't eat the chicken," Kim growled, suppressing the temptation of making a sarcastic remark about the prisoner's own face.

"There's cream in it, it's slopped on everything else. I'm not eating this crap . . ."

Kim bolted down her own now cold food as quickly as possible, gritting her teeth as Redburn burped contentedly and asked for a second cup of coffee and Connor argued with the flight attendant to bring her another meal.

Connor's hyperactive bladder also ensured that Kim missed the ending of the in-flight movie, and—after Redburn had been roused from his own after-dinner snooze to keep an eye on their prisoner so Kim could take a nap as well—woke her up every half hour when the lights had been dimmed to allow passengers a few hours' sleep. Predictably, just when Kim had managed to close her eyes for a few moments of peace and quiet, the lights went up to the bustling of flight attendants passing out breakfast which, just as predictably, Connor refused to eat because it had eggs in it. They made two more trips to the toilet before the captain's announcement of their descent, the seat belt signs binging on.

Kim wasn't fond of flying, no matter how many times she'd done it. She was even less fond of landing. She avoided looking out the window past Redburn when rows of brick houses with neat gardens suddenly rushed up from below, unnervingly close. She gripped the arm of her chair, taking slow breaths until the tires hit the tarmac with a jolting crunch, wings shuddering ominously. Airbrakes folded over jet exhausts and screamed. On the other side of the aisle, a large group of men in red turbans burst into enthusiastic cheers and applause. The landing hadn't seemed that smooth to her. She eyed the deliriously happy Sikhs, wondering what they knew that she didn't.

She was more than happy to have the security of solid ground under her feet as they disembarked. They followed along behind other passengers into Heathrow's maze of corridors until Kim spotted two plainclothes officers waiting for them. They stepped out of the mass of people funneling into Customs and Passport Control.

"United States Marshal Kim Prescott," she said, holding up her identification.

"Deputy Marshal Elliot Redburn," her partner echoed.

"DI Vic Sanders," the older of the two Brits said, and displayed his wallet opened to his ID in return, then nodded at his colleague. "DS Llew Kenlay. Welcome to Great Britain." He smiled at Eunice Connor, the expression coldly amused. "So nice to see you again, Eunice. Been a while since we've had the pleasure of your company."

"The pleasure is all yours," Connor retorted.

Sanders chuckled. "And we plan to make sure it stays that way." He turned to Kim. "Customs is handling your baggage. Not to worry, it'll be sorted for you." He swept his hand in a courteous gesture. "If you'd like to come with us?"

They were led into a small, barren room where Eunice was searched and her handcuffs swapped over from Kim's to those of the British police. The exchange and signing of paperwork took less than fifteen minutes, before Sanders and Kenlay escorted both their prisoner and the two marshals out a back entrance to a private parking lot.

"You staying on in London long?" Sanders asked Kim as his partner unlocked the back door to an unmarked police car. Outside, it was unpleasantly cold, a fine mist and a whiff of ozone hanging in the air.

"A few days. We've got a rental car booked." Kim grinned. "Don't know how much I'm going to like driving on the wrong side of the road, though."

Sanders flashed a quick smile back. "Here, the wrong side is the right side, and the right side is the left side. Dead easy. We can give you a lift over to the airport car hire, save you a hike. What company is it?"

The thundering roar of a departing plane suspended any reply

Kim could have made, as well as covered the sound of a small motorcycle as it pulled out of a parking slot, the rider wearing an airport employee yellow reflective jacket and a mirrored motorcycle helmet. The motorcycle slowed as it reached the five people standing around the car, and Kim idly glanced over her shoulder.

Years of experience and training made her reaction more instinctive than deliberate, her eyes barely having time to register the short, black machine pistol being pulled out of the motorcyclist's jacket before she pushed Eunice Connor behind the open door of the car. "Take cover!" she yelled. Her voice was barely audible over the jet engines above them.

There wasn't much cover to take, really, nowhere to go, Kim's mind observed dispassionately, as bright flashes of light flickered out of the barrel of the pistol, pocking a row of dimples along the car. The two startled Brits dove in front of the car while Redburn ducked down on the opposite side, the car between himself and the motorcyclist. Kim felt a one-two punch hit her hard in the chest, knocking the breath out of her. Beside her, Eunice Connor kicked Kim hard in the leg as she scrambled into the backseat of the car. Off balance, Kim sat down heavily on the wet ground, gasping for air, blinding pain squeezing her chest like acid.

Oh, shit. She watched the motorcyclist race away from them, the back tire smoking as it spun against the tarmac. It wobbled slightly as the rider thrust the machine pistol back inside his jacket, then turned a corner and was gone.

It was over in seconds, Kim leaning back against the cold metal of the car and looking up at the belly of the British Air plane still climbing laboriously into a gray sky above them, leaving behind a backwash of jet engine exhaust and a vibration that rumbled clear to her bones. She started as an arm thumped across her shoulder, thin strings of blood lacing through the fingers, wrists still handcuffed together.

She turned her head to glance at Eunice Connor and knew from the woman's startled unblinking stare at nothing that she was dead. Kim opened her mouth to call out for Redburn, and suddenly coughed, her throat spasming, choking her. A bright spray of blood spattered across her lap. Her lungs were burning, but she managed to pull enough air into them to clear the rushing noise in her ears.

One of the Brits had gotten to his feet and was running after the motorcyclist, yelling unintelligibly into his police hand radio. The other, Sanders, sat hunched over on the ground with one leg under him, the other straight out with both his hands clamped around his thigh, a dark stain spreading on his trousers, blood leaking through his fingers. Redburn scrabbled around the back of the car and toward her on hands and knees, his face pinched white with shock.

"Jesus Christ!" Redburn was panting. "Jesus fucking Christ. Are you all right, Kim?" He had to shout to be heard over the now receding roar of jet engines.

She coughed again, spitting the taste of blood out of her mouth. She glowered at him in irritation. "Do I *look* all right, dickhead?" The words came out in a wet croak. A stab of sharp pain knifed through her. *"Oww."* Then it subsided, rolling away like waves receding from a beach. The relief was nearly as intense as the pain had been. Redburn hovered over her, his eyes round and as scared as a child's. "Don't worry, I'll be fine," she whispered, trying to smile at him reassuringly.

Then she closed her eyes tiredly, exhaled a long, exasperated sigh, and died.

March's Death Toll: 164,626 cattle, 751,302 sheep, 61,742 pigs, 397 goats, and 314 unspecified animals.

Deputy Veterinarian Chief Richard Cawthorne says he expects the number of confirmed cases of foot-and-mouth to rise further before falling again as a "second wave" of the outbreak hits Britain, adding that this was a "relatively self-limiting disease" which could be kept contained with tight regulations.

Minister for Agriculture Nick Brown has stated that the crisis is of a "different order" than previously thought, but insisted it was under control. His announcement that 500,000 healthy hill sheep due to lamb may have to be culled prompts NFU Chairman Jon Rider to say, "It is a horrendous possibility. It is almost thinking the unthinkable."

Two Texel ewes, Bessie and Elsie, belonging to fifteen-year-old school-boy Jon Fraser, who had bought them with pocket money he had saved over that year, are culled along with the family's other 350 healthy sheep on their Wolsingham, Weardale, farm in County Durham. His mother sent him to stay with relatives in Tyneside during the cull, fearing he would be traumatized if he had to witness the killing and burning of his pets.

French border officials block a British lorry transporting essential sup-plies to Romanian orphans because it contained 500 Cadbury Crème Eggs, fearing the milk used in the production of the confectionary could contain foot-and-mouth virus from infected cows. Darlington schoolchild-ren on a bus trip to Arques-la-Bataille in France are banned from eating sandwiches containing butter, margarine, chocolate, meat, cheese, or any other dairy product during the seven-hour coach trip.

A pile of 1,400 sheep carcasses are left lying for five days in Wens-leydale, yards from where children play, prompting local councilor Yvonne Peacock to declare the "situation is totally unacceptable."

Six tame sheep, three pigs, and eight goats in the "Old McDonald's Farm" petting zoo for young children at Alton Towers are killed, as well as a heavily pregnant cow named Daisy on loan to the amusement park from a local farmer. An RSPCA spokesman expresses regret at the deci-sion: "I am surprised that Alton Towers was unable to isolate the ani-mals." Postmortem tests prove none of these animals had been exposed to the virus.

2

APRIL

Keen Dunliffe stood in the kitchen window of his farmhouse, half a cup of tepid coffee in one hand, gazing out at the darkness as cold rain formed glittering necklaces of droplets at an angle along the windowpanes. Clouds as black as coal hunkered along the hills, dry-stone walls dividing the pastures nearly invisible in the rain.

This had been one of the most miserable, cold, wet springs he could ever remember, the persistent smell of damp earth in the air. A thin gray streak of dim light along the horizon was all there was to indicate this was another grim Yorkshire morning rather than the middle of the night.

At least he didn't have to work night shifts anymore, he thought, sipping the last of the coffee. That was one small consolation for working in CID. He still had his uniforms in the closet, swathed in dry-cleaner plastic. But civvies didn't mean he could get away with wearing comfortable jeans and a plaid shirt, either—he looked more like an accountant than a cop in a gray suit, white shirt, lackluster tie. Which, he thought, with a faint pang of regret, was about all he was at the moment.

He downed the last mouthful of coffee, rinsed out the cup and set it in the sink, then reached for his mobile phone plugged in the charger on the counter by the door. And stopped.

The phone wasn't there, the charger switched off. Again. "Shit," he said sourly. Keen patted his jacket and, not surprisingly, found his mobile still in his pocket exactly where he'd left it the night before. The battery was flat. Oh, well. Damned things were more of a bloody nuisance; he'd survive without it for a day.

Thomas had finished his own breakfast and sat waiting by the front door, washing any last trace of cat food from his whiskers with a dainty paw. Keen plugged the mobile phone into the charger and flipped on the wall switch. It beeped in faint reproach. He shrugged into his mackintosh, set the house alarm, and opened the door, keys jingling in his hand as he looked down at Thomas.

"Surprise me and go kill some mice."

Thomas took one look at the rain hammering down outside and glared up at Keen.

"Don't blame me, cat," Keen said. "I don't want to go out in this muck any more than you do."

It took pushing the cat out the door with his shoe before Thomas would be convinced. With one last glower of resentment, the cat dashed for the shelter of the derelict cattle shed, slithering his fat little body through a gap formed under the door where countless decades of boots had worn down the stone threshold.

Heavy rain had washed away gravel at the end of his drive, and Keen's Vauxhall bucked as he drove over the corrugated ruts onto the main road. He'd have to get more gravel in soon before the lane to his house became impassable. The roads into work weren't much better; cars threw out fans of water as they plowed through puddles the size of small lakes. The police car park had also acquired a large artificial pond, and those lucky few who arrived early enough to park on dry land left little room for latecomers. Try as he might to tiptoe through the standing water, Keen's shoes and socks were still soaked by the time he reached the back entrance to the nick, a dark ring around the hem of his trousers.

He walked past the door connecting the front office with the anteroom. Brian was on the front desk, chatting with a man in dirty yellow City Refuse coveralls who'd come in to argue about his parking fine. Both of them looked tired, Brian ready to go off duty, the man leaning on the counter.

"You lads on Roundhay Park next weekend?" Brian was asking.

"Yeah," the skinny man said morosely as Brian scribbled on an excusal form. "Them nurses c'n drink more lager'n one afternoon than all the day-trippers in Blackpool inna month. Rain keeps up like this, right mess that'll be, too."

"Well, think of it as our own little Glastonbury; just wouldn't be right without the mud, would it?" Brian said. The skinny man didn't much appreciate Brian's humor, judging by his wry grimace.

The morning shift parade had come and gone, uniform already out on duty. Jasmine Farrell was pouring a cup of coffee from the coffeemaker in the corner of the CID office when Keen walked in. She smiled at him in greeting.

"Hey-up, boss."

"Jazz."

"Want one?"

"Ta."

At the far end of the long room, the detective chief inspector's door was open, but Glen Harper was absent. Mark Flaxton wandered into the CID office just as she had finished pouring, his eyes puffy and red, and took the mug out of her hands as she turned around. "Thanks, love," he muttered and downed about half of Keen's coffee. Jazz grinned in bemusement, shook her head, and poured another. Bill Edwards arrived with Matt Jenkins, the latter newly transferred from uniform to CID and still far too chipper first thing in the morning for Keen's liking.

"Mr. Mullard isn't here yet?" Jenkins said.

Flaxton leaned back in his chair, stretching his arms above his head as he yawned hugely. "Nope. Probably still over terrorizing Pudsey's lot . . ."

"Wrong again," the detective inspector said, striding through the door with a pile of report folders in his arms. Nigel Mullard glared at Flaxton disapprovingly. "Rough night?"

"My turn to bottle-feed. Between teething and colic, she never *ever* stops crying."

Mullard didn't appear sympathetic. "Got a couple lads in hospital, hit-and-run," he said curtly, and dropped a file onto Flaxton's desk. "Occurred around two this morning over in Chapel Allerton. The victims were at a bus stop when a dark blue estate car traveling on

17

the opposite side of the road swerved and mounted the pavement to drive straight into them. Car's possibly a Passat, possibly an Audi, possibly a Volvo, or possibly something else; witness is a dozy OAP, she knows bugger all about cars."

"Streets have been pretty slick. Accident?" It was a reasonable question, what with the bad weather keeping Traffic busy with collisions and cars sliding off into ditches.

"Not likely. One of the victims was pushed through the bus shelter Plexiglas, cut him up pretty bad. He's still in critical care. Car backed up and took another run at his mate trying to crawl away on the pavement. He was lucky—ended up with only both legs broken and a concussion. The driver was described by our witness as being dark, possibly Asian or a light-skinned black, wearing a black knit cap and a blue T-shirt with what she thinks is a Nike JUST DO IT logo on the front. Car also had one of those orange triangular air freshener things the RAC give out as freebies hanging off the rear mirror."

For a dozy elderly pensioner, Keen thought dryly, she was remarkably observant.

"Sez here they both got form for dealing class-A drugs. Think it's related?" Flaxton asked, flipping through the meager amount of paper in the file.

Mullard shrugged. "Victims regularly use that particular bus shelter as their own personal chemist's shop, so I shouldn't be surprised. If they do know who did it, one isn't saying and the other can't. CCTV camera picked up a car matching that description two miles south of the shooting. Registration plates H993 HBF, reported stolen two weeks ago. We need to find this guy, before someone who *doesn't* deserve it gets hurt."

He took a few steps farther along the row of desks and plopped another file in front of Edwards.

"Yesterday morning, a man described as being in his late forties, between sixteen and seventeen stone, with long, gray hair and distinctive tattoos, indecently exposed himself to the entire Sunday congregation of St. Chad's whilst waving a big red plastic Halloween scythe about and bellowing at the top of his lungs—and I quote: 'Naked came I out of my mother's womb, and naked shall I return thither; the Lord gave and the Lord hath taken away, blessed be the name of the Lord.' Sound like anyone you know?"

"Oh, bloody hell," Edwards grumbled. "Wee Willie Wilkinson's gone off his medication again. He's harmless enough, sir."

"He's a registered sex offender," Mullard retorted, unamused. "Pick him up. If you can find him." He dropped another file onto Jasmine's desk. "Got a nice one for you, Jazz. Kidnap and rape of a young girl. She's fifteen, been done for shoplifting and vandalism, lives in Crag Hill. Her mother reported her missing two days ago."

Keen watched Jasmine wince as she opened the file to the first of several glossy photographs. Mullard smirked sourly at her reaction. "Bin men found her beaten unconscious and left for dead behind a skip back of a chippie in Halifax early this morning. She's in stable condition, but she's going to need serious plastic surgery; her mother had trouble identifying her. The girl isn't up to being questioned yet—she may be suffering some brain trauma, so even if she isn't a vegetable, chances are she won't remember much anyway. There's previous allegations she's been sexually abused by her stepfather since she was twelve, but the mother says he went back to Cyprus last year, serving in the regular army."

Jasmine nodded, still looking through the folder.

"You'll act as the family liaison officer with Calderdale's Child Protection Unit. Mother's pretty distraught, they're not getting much out of her in interview. Maybe she could use the more gentle approach?"

Jasmine's mouth pulled into a thin line, but she smiled tightly up at Mullard. "Sure thing, guv."

Jasmine was the only CID officer without children, but Mullard seemed incapable of seeing past her gender, diverting any case involving rape or child abuse onto Jasmine's caseload. Keen wasn't sure if Mullard was unaware of his sexism or if it was deliberate.

But he was certain of Mullard's intent when the DCI dropped the last of his folders on Keen's desk. "Missing bird. Take Toffee here and supervise." Mullard jerked his thumb at Jenkins.

Keen didn't react to Mullard's smirk, simply opening the file as

19

the DCI stalked out of the room without another word—on his way to another nick in his division to make someone else's life a misery.

"Why does he keep calling me 'Toffee'?" Jenkins complained, mystified. "I'm not even Welsh."

Edwards glanced up at them both, amused, but said nothing.

"It's just the way he is," Keen said flatly. "Ignore him."

Sooner or later, someone would get around to explaining to Jenkins that Mullard wasn't calling him "Taffy"; Toffee was an acronym: TOFI. The Other Fucking Idiot. And Jenkins would then wonder who the first idiot was. Keen didn't feel like enlightening the naïve PC to office politics at the moment.

The lad was neither lazy nor incompetent, simply inexperienced. He could well enough have handled a case this straightforward on his own; supervising was more punishment Mullard chose to inflict on Keen than on Jenkins. Keen tossed the keys to one of the unmarked CID cars to Jenkins. "You drive. Pick me up in front."

The bird in question was a bird of prey at the East Beck Falconry Centre, off the A658 near Riffa Wood, owned by an ex-policeman and an old friend. Gerald Mitchell had lost both his job and the use of his legs ten years ago after a drunk driver fell asleep on the M1 and plowed into the family car. The only one not wearing a safety belt, the drunk, died instantly. Little Jerry and his mum escaped unhurt, but the engine block had driven the steering wheel into Gerald and snapped his spine.

The trip out took less than half an hour. Jenkins drove as Keen slipped off his shoes to dry his stocking feet on the car's heater and then quietly studied the file on his lap, neither man speaking during the ride. The rain had petered out now to a fine drizzle. The windscreen wipers on the car needed replacing, smearing across the glass in watery streaks that did little to aid visibility. When they pulled into the Falconry Centre, the car park was nearly deserted, the only other vehicle a red and white hire tour bus. As Keen shoved his feet back into his shoes and got out, he heard the shrill noise of children on a school outing, despite the cold, damp weather.

Jerry Mitchell waited with his hands in his quasi-uniform pockets, bony shoulders slumped, lank dark hair falling into his eyes. Keen shook his hand, still amazed at how tall he'd grown. It had taken an effort for him to stop calling the lad "Little Jerry."

"You've lost another bird?" Jenkins asked, taking the lead as he flipped open his notebook.

"Yeah. They took Sybille, one of our merlins." This was the second theft in as many months. "You'll want to talk to Bobby. It was his bird." Jerry glanced at his watch and nodded at the group of buildings on the far side of the site. "He's doing a show at the moment, shouldn't be long."

Keen gestured to Jenkins to go on ahead; they would follow behind.

"You're still doing shows, then?" Keen said.

"Not if it's raining hard or too cold. But the birds need regular exercise, even in winter. Oh." Jerry belatedly followed Keen's glance to the MAFF notice tacked to the front gates of the center, realizing. "Yeah, for the moment. It hasn't affected us too much. There's loads of rabbits and woodcock down along Riffa Beck right now, where we usually go hawking, but all the footpaths are closed. We just have to keep them happy with hand-feeding them chicks." The local poultry farm gassed day-old male chicks after they were sexed and donated the carcasses to the center. The center survived off such charity, along with various adoption schemes and hawking courses.

"How's your da?" Keen asked and smiled, changing the subject.

"Fine. Mad as hell, as usual. He's organizing a picket of the local leisure center." Gerald senior might have been confined to a wheelchair for the last ten years, but he'd lost none of his fiery temperament with his legs. His two favorite causes were harsher legislation against drunk drivers and the rights of the physically disabled.

"What for?"

"They won't let his longbow club on their fields. Says access ramps would cost too much and the wheelchairs cut up the turf." Gerald senior believed archery not only developed those muscles the wheelchair-bound needed in top form to chase down recalcitrant

MPs, but fought off depression and self-pity, two emotions Gerald senior had utterly no use for.

"Dad says if they took council money to pay for a new football field, then every taxpayer should be able to use it, not just those with two working legs."

Jerry grinned as a hundred high-pitched voices cheered "Hey!" in unison. "Bobby's flying Athena, our African horned owl. Sometimes she gets up in the trees and won't come down for the bait. Bobby has the kids yell, try to startle her out."

A second enthusiastic shout went up.

"Does it work?"

Jerry's grin widened, lopsided. "Not much." Another cheer met with a mix of laughter and applause. "But sometimes."

A few minutes later, a scattering of children heralded the noisy deluge behind them. Four harried teachers tried to keep order as children in grammar school uniforms jumped, ran, skipped, rolled, stomped in rain puddles, did everything but walk toward the bus. As they stampeded around him and Jerry, Keen wondered with a pang what his own boys were doing at that moment.

"Geoffrey! Getdownoffthatrightthisminute!" a teacher yelled as a boy balanced along the top bar of the car park's rustic wooden fence. The boy scowled and jumped, landing on hands and feet, barely missing skinning elbows already speckled with scabs from previous exploits. Unhurt, the boy darted toward the bus and pulled a blond girl's plait as he passed her. She howled more in protest than pain.

Behind the main building and the mews, the center's birds lived in zoolike cages: two Andean condors, a gyrfalcon, a breeding pair of African vultures building a nest of dry sticks. A young golden eagle sleepily stretched out six feet of wings, then scratched under its chin with a wicked set of claws.

Farther along, open artificial caves of concrete and limestone housed barn owls and tawny owls, kestrels and Barbary falcons, which Keen recognized only because they were so labeled. One hunchbacked black falcon stared with malevolent yellow eyes, a nylon cord looped through jesses anchoring the bird's leg to a perch, and shuddered to fluff up feathers against the chill, seeming bigger than it really was.

"That's Petruchio," Jerry said. "And he really is as mean as he looks. See his left wing? They hunt along roads right at sunset, skim close to the ground. Car comes along, headlights stun them. He got hit, wing smashed up too bad to fix properly. Found him in a lay-by like near starved to death. He'll never fly again."

Jenkins waited at the door of the workshed as Bobby climbed the hill from the enclosure toward him, a tiny fuzzy owl on one arm, gauntlet and what was left of a dead chick in his other hand.

Keen and Jerry reached the sheds in time to hear Bobby ask, "Sybille?" When Jerry nodded, the lad turned to Jenkins. "That were *my* bird," he said thickly, his face clouded with anger. "Two years old, trained her myself. Best I ever had." While the center took in injured wild birds, many of the hunting birds belonged to the boys who worked there. The Lanner falcon stolen the month before had been Jerry's.

Bobby showed them the empty shelter the bird had been taken from. Jenkins dutifully recorded the time, day, and date in his pocket notebook. Keen said nothing as Jenkins asked for names or addresses. He wouldn't have had to, as he'd known both boys for years, but he let Jenkins get on with it on his own. The owl on Bobby's arm swiveled its heart-shaped head halfway around its body and blinked orange eyes myopically at him. It lifted its tail and shat. No one paid it any attention.

"When do you think the bird was taken, Bobby?" Jenkins asked.

"Late last night, probably. Maybe early morning."

"No alarms, CCTV?"

Bobby shook his head. "The open aviaries don't have alarms, just the main house. I stay in the guesthouse, sort of like a night watchman, but I didn't see or hear anything." Clearly, he was upset for having failed to prevent another bird from being stolen. "But it were somebody who knew what they were doing. You can't just sneak up on 'em, grab a falcon and walk off with it. They'd have had a hood, a gauntlet."

"Any idea who might have taken her? Heard anyone talking about wouldn't it be nice having a bird of their own for a pet?"

"Every day. That's our job, try to interest the public in birds of prey." He fed the last of the chick to the owl, the bird gulping it down. "But they're not pets. Birds can be trained to work for food; they're not capable of loving you. You want a pet, get a dog."

"How about another falconer took a fancy to your birds?"

Bobby shrugged, unhappy. "I don't like to think so."

"We've had a few phone threats from those animal rights nutters before," Jerry said. "You know, think all wild birds should be set free, steal them, let them go. Don't realize maybe we're doing more good than harm breeding endangered species, keeping injured birds that would normally die."

"Like Gadget here," Bobby said, stroking the back of his fingers down the owl's wingfeathers. "He can't be released into the wild."

"Why not?" Keen said, curious.

"Fell out of a nest as a baby, had to be hand-reared. He's totally fixated now."

"Fixated?"

"Grown up thinking he's people, too. Makes breeding tricky." Jerry grinned. "Nothing like a romantic owl to have a crush on you."

Bobby didn't share his humor. "He also can't learn to hunt for himself. People think owls are smart, but they're not. Somebody steals him and lets him go, he'll starve to death."

"Either of the two birds taken unable to hunt for themselves?" Jenkins asked.

Bobby glanced at Jerry. "They'd do all right if they had to."

Jerry looked disgusted. "I'd rather it were animal rights nutters than some weekend falconer playing Robin Hood. A lot of birds die just because people don't know how to take care of them properly."

Jenkins closed his notebook. "We'll make a report and look into it," he said, trying to sound confident.

"Not much to go on, though, Jer," Keen added. He didn't want to encourage the boys' false hopes. "If they've been released, we'll do what we can, but it's not promising."

Bobby's face was still red, the boy fighting off tears. "Thanks anyway," he said, already resigned, and walked away, the owl on his arms beating its wings impotently.

Both men shook hands with Jerry. "Tell your dad hello from me," Keen said, "and good luck with this longbow fight."

"You should think about taking up the longbow yourself. It's great exercise. You might enjoy it."

"I'll think on it," Keen said, as close to a promise as he allowed himself to get anymore.

Keen had Jenkins drop him off at the front door of the nick before parking the CID car in the back, bang in the middle of the temporary lake. Keen's socks were still damp in his shoes as it was. As Keen walked in the front, Brian nodded at his wave hello. Behind him, Carrie Dalgren struggled to find room on the public bulletin board already crowded with an NSPCC Child Protection Helpline poster, a warning about Colorado beetle infestations, an RSPCA notice urging pet owners to register their flea-bitten mongrels, and the latest MAFF restrictions on livestock.

"G'us a han', skip?" the petite Special mumbled around the pins in her mouth, exasperated.

Keen pinned up her recruiting advert for the Special Constabulary, two leggy models pretending to be hobby-bobbies walking briskly and smiling over the blurb, "Are You Doing Anything As Worthwhile in Your Spare Time?" They looked infinitely more pleased about their job than Carrie. Keen had his reservations about Specials, but he'd seen Carrie calm down belligerent drunks pulled after a pub fight and reassure hysterical mothers of kids more likely bunking off in a video arcade than kidnapped by depraved sex maniacs. But Carrie had put in her notice she was quitting at the end of the month, back to university to become a solicitor and join the ranks of the enemy. What a waste, Keen thought.

"Thanks, love," she said with a brilliant smile. What she lacked in height, she made up for in looks, and knew it. Keen watched her walk away appreciatively. It lightened his mood, however temporarily.

Jenkins had started in on his report, spending over half an hour on it before he handed it to Keen to look over. Edwards stuck his head into the room, leaning on the doorframe. "You busy?" he said to Jenkins.

Jenkins glanced uncertainly at Keen.

Keen tipped his head in Edwards's direction. "Go," he said to Jenkins.

The lad grinned, happy to be out on real police business instead of shoving paper around on desks. But, Keen thought as he read through Jenkins's report, he'd be spending more time practicing his writing than he'd like if he continued in this slapdash fashion. Spelling errors were not a big deal, and even the "witness intimidated the theif might be an animal rights actavist" was more amusing than irksome. But Jenkins had made so many basic errors Keen was tempted to make the young PC do it over again.

He leaned back in the chair, bouncing his mechanical pencil on the file as he deliberated. Jenkins was impatient, still new enough to believe he could make a difference. Shame to waste that enthusiasm while it lasted; Mullard would do his best to throttle the lad's idealism anyway, no sense handing the bastard the ammunition to do it with as well. Keen filled in the missing bits of the report himself, signed off on it and tossed it into the out basket where, along with all the rest of the no-hopers CID routinely filled out, filed, and forgot, it would be stored away and vanish into oblivion.

Keen spent the rest of his afternoon on his own paperwork, the role of the CID sergeant about as exciting as that of a night watchman in a graveyard, for the most part. Not that he was complaining, exactly. He'd had enough excitement in his career, the previous year providing him with all the excitement he could handle. With nine years left to retirement, getting back to a quiet life was just fine, thank you very much.

At two, he heard the brief swell of noise through the station as the shifts changed, officers coming and leaving with a regularity he could set his watch by. An hour later, he looked up when Jasmine returned, the normally bubbly woman somber, mouth pulled down in a tight, unhappy line.

"I hate these cases," she said, flopping down behind her desk. She leaned on one elbow, fingers raked into her hair, short spiky strands poking up between her fingers. "I hate these cases, I *hate* these bloody awful cases."

"Not going well, I take it?" Keen said phlegmatically.

"What am I supposed to say to her? 'I know how you feel'? I *don't* know how she feels! So I sit there trying to get something coherent out of her, and all she wants to do is bawl her eyes out and talk about how horrible the world is, what kind of monster could do this, her sweet baby girl lying in hospital. If I sit there holding her hand and pretend, then she knows I'm lying so I end looking like an uncaring git as well as useless." She glared at Keen. "It's not fair. Why does he keep giving them all to *me*?"

She meant Mullard. Keen shrugged. "Same reason he keeps handing me all the badger-baiting cases, the hare-coursing cases, the fox-snaring cases, missing birds and slashed horses and dodgy Chinese medicine and selling wild frog spawn in pet shops, even though I'm not officially the designated wildlife officer. He looks at me and sees 'farmer.' He looks at you and sees—"

"A pair of tits," she finished for him acidly.

Keen frowned but raised his eyebrows, amused. "Not how *I* was going to put it, but something along that line. He's a tosser, but he's the boss. What can you do?"

She slapped open the file on her desk and bent over her report forms. "Well, I bloody hate it," she muttered rebelliously at the open folder and began to scribble.

Keen didn't bother to assess Jasmine's case notes, signing off on them with nothing more than a cursory scan through. He didn't have to: Jazz was a thorough, focused, and extremely competent officer, and her pique at being assigned as the family liaison officer was not an indication she lacked empathy, far from it. Her strengths simply lay elsewhere, but Mullard couldn't or wouldn't see where she was best applied.

He pushed back from his desk and wandered down the row to the desk DC Alan Cooper shared with Flaxton, picking up a folder from the untidy stack of files. He flipped through it briefly, then tossed it in front of Jasmine.

"Go chase up these two bonehead witnesses, and don't take no for an answer," he said. "I'm not having some scrote walking on a half-million-pound stolen goods charge because it inconveniences his solicitor's holiday in Ibiza."

She looked at him skeptically. "That's Cooper's case."

"He's not here. You are. It's my call, so go."

Jasmine grinned. "Thanks, boss."

If there was a problem, he'd take the fallout from Mullard later. The rest of the afternoon passed uneventfully, and at four, he booked off and headed for home.

The Vauxhall was low on oil, but Keen would just as soon buy a couple cans to do himself than pay to take it to a garage. He took the rat run up from Old Otley Road and pulled into an Esso station behind a blue Audi occupying the only diesel pump, the estate car packed to the gunnels with all the detritus of holiday-makers everywhere and towing a scruffy-looking caravan. The morning's rainstorm hadn't done much to clean the caravan's dust-streaked aluminum. Its worn tires could use a bit of air as well, he noticed, the caravan sitting heavily on its axle. That wasn't really any of his concern.

The air was chill and damp when he got out, the sky a glowering Technicolor of burgundy and lavender thunderclouds. As he walked by the Audi, he glanced inside. A sharp-faced woman with black roots under harsh blond hair tried to placate a two-year-old clearly unhappy to be imprisoned in a child's safety seat. She looked as out of patience as the baby, attempting to stuff a baby bottle into its puckered mouth. The child thrashed its head, wrenching off its oversized red woolly hat.

As a matter of reflex, he glanced at the car's registration plate so covered with dirt he could barely read it through the muck. His heart skipped a beat. He reached into his pocket for his mobile before remembering it was at home, plugged into the charger. *Of course it had to be today.* He veered toward a phone booth under the WC sign.

A note had been taped across the phone: OUT OF ORDER. Someone had prized open the coin box with a screwdriver and hammer.

Picking up the handset, he pretended to punch a few numbers, then held the handset next to his ear while he studied the fore-court. The woman took no notice of him, preoccupied with the now screaming baby, its back arching in furious indignation. Keen scanned the inside of the store. Streetlights and neon signs reflected on the window glass, and shelving obstructed what little he could see of the interior. He could make out only the cashier behind the counter. His heart hammered in his chest as he hung up the phone, palms sweating.

Oh, Lord, I'm getting too old for this, Keen thought. His legs felt rub-bery as he crossed the forecourt. A bell dinged as he opened the door and strolled as casually as he could behind the aisles, counting three customers other than himself. Two stood at the counter register, the third a pimply teenager with a battered skateboard sorting through a selection of Walker's crisps, apparently undecided between artificial Marmite–flavored and artificial pickled onion–flavored.

Keen took a single can of Coke from the cooler and joined the queue behind the two men. The man at the front was late twenties, a tall, muscular lad in a plaid shirt, about fourteen stone, clean-shaven, his mouse-brown hair cropped short in a severe military cut. His skin was the deeply leathered brown of someone who spent a great deal of time in the outdoors. He placed a packet of Winston Lights on the counter. The Asian lad behind him was shorter, several stone less, mid-thirties, stringy mustache matching dark hair pulled back into a ponytail with a dirty rubber band. Tufts of underarm hair stuck out from his sweat-stained sleeveless T-shirt. A blurry death's-head tattoo on his forearm grinned at Keen. He held a week's worth of junk food and a six-pack of Stella Artois. Neither of them looked up at him.

Which one? His policeman's gut also seemed to be inconve-niently out of order. He knew which he would have picked but took a chance.

"Lousy weather for towing a caravan," he said casually. The ponytailed man glanced at him in curious annoyance. But to his surprise, it was the big lad in the plaid shirt who nodded without looking round. The clerk rang up the sale, cash register beeping. The man handed the bored clerk a twenty, intent on his change. Keen's mouth felt dry. "Going far?"

"Suffolk," he said, then, "Thanks," to the clerk and put the change in his pocket. He turned, his gaze locking with Keen's. He squinted, puzzled, then his eyes widened with sudden comprehension. *"Shit!"* He dropped the packet of cigarettes and reached inside his shirt.

It took only seconds but felt like forever. Keen dropped the Coke and pushed the ponytailed man aside. *"Police officer!"* The man in the plaid shirt was still turning when Keen hurled himself onto his back. The momentum threw them both against the counter. Keen heard the man's *whomph* as the breath was knocked from him, and scrabbled desperately for a headlock. *Just my luck,* the disembodied part of Keen's brain was thinking, *it would have to be the big 'un.*

The man heaved his head back, punching hard into Keen's forehead. Keen saw a brief flash of white and blinked against the sharp pain. His grasp slipped. Then he launched every ounce of weight he had and sent them both skidding across the top of the counter. He scissored his legs around the other man's and hooked his ankles together. His fingers crab-walked past the man's ear until his arm pinned him down. They both lay there panting, immobile. Keen's head pressed against the man's cheek, pinning him to the counter. He could smell the man's wheezing cigarette breath.

From the corner of his vision, Keen could just see the clerk's astonished face, frozen with fear. He gulped in a few breaths before he could speak. "I'm a police officer," he rasped. His throat hurt, which puzzled him. "Ring 999 and tell them an officer needs assistance." The clerk stared as if he was speaking Martian. *"The phone!"* Keen screamed, and distantly realized this was why his throat was raw. *"Pick up the bloody phone!"*

For a sickening moment, he thought the clerk would faint. Then he heard a click, and the faint tone of three numbers being punched. "Uh, is this the police?" a reedy, teenaged voice said. "Yeah, hello. You know the Esso station on Tinshill Court, corner of Holt? Well, you got this police officer here needs assistance? Um . . . I dunno. I think maybe he's just caught a shoplifter or something . . ."

"What the hell are you doing!" Both Keen and the man underneath him flinched at a woman's high-pitched shriek. *"You let go of him!"*

He felt something whack into his already aching head, though not hard enough to do any damage or make him lessen his grip.

" 'Ey, lady," the ponytailed Asian man protested in a strong Cockney accent. "You can't 'it 'im, 'e's a copper . . ."

She did it again anyway. The plastic baby bottle ricocheted across the floor and spun to a stop, teat pointing toward Keen and his prisoner accusingly. Milk leaked out the end like teardrops.

"Let go of me, you bastard!" the woman screeched.

"Oi!" the second man yelped. *"Leggo my 'air!"*

The clerk still stood rigidly, his bulging eyes unblinking. Police sirens nee-nawed in the distance underneath the woman's hysterics and the scuffling behind them. Suddenly the man pinioned under him bellowed, *"Shut the fuck up, Angelina!"*

She did. In the sudden quiet, Keen could hear his own heartbeat. Outside, a baby wailed.

"You stupid cow," the man said wearily. "You left the baby out there by himself where any sick pervert could walk off with him. Get back in the fucking car and take care of him." Blue lights flickered facets in the glass cabinets behind the cash register.

The woman burst into tears. "You son of a bitch!" she said, choking. "I hate you!" and stormed out as several patrol cars pulled in, sirens and lights going.

The man relaxed underneath him. "Women," he muttered. Keen did not much feel like commiserating with him. He was wondering what the hell was taking so long when he felt hands grab both him and the man he had pinned to the counter.

"Police officer," he mumbled, sounding strange even to himself.

"It's okay, guv. We've got him. You can let go now."

Every muscle in his body hurt as he released his hold. He reached for his wallet with bloodless fingers and opened it to his warrant card just before his knees turned to water. He leaned against the counter to keep from sliding to the floor. Three PCs were busy handcuffing the man in the plaid shirt. He was no longer resisting, looking at Keen as if waiting for something. Oh, right. Keen swallowed against his sore throat.

"I'm arresting you on suspicion of taking a vehicle without consent, dangerous driving, and the hit-and-run assault in Chapel Allerton area resulting in grievous bodily harm to two victims this Sunday past," Keen said, sounding far calmer than he felt. "You do not have to say anything, but it may—"

The man's eyes widened as he jerked over at the waist, two PCs hanging on to his arms. Keen watched a lump slide down one leg of his jeans and drop out with a clatter. Everyone stared at the pistol lying on the floor. The man in the plaid shirt looked up at Keen sheepishly.

"And carrying a firearm with criminal intent," Keen added impassively. "You do not have to say anything, but it may harm your defense if you do not mention when questioned something which you later rely on in court. Anything you do say may be given in evidence. Do you understand your rights as I have given them?"

"Guess so," the man said, oddly meek.

"You lads want to make sure he hasn't got anything else down his smalls that shouldn't be there?" Keen didn't think his hands were up to it and watched as the man was searched. When they came up with nothing else, he was led out the door to the back of a waiting patrol car. Angelina sat with legs out the open door of the Audi, arms around her knees, her head nearly in her lap as she bawled inconsolably. A WPC leaned over her, patting her shoulder. The baby, still in his safety chair, sucked his thumb with wet-eyed fascination while snot bubbled around a forefinger jammed up one nostril. Officers emerged from the caravan, gesturing excitedly to one another.

"You ought to have an alarm system put in," Keen heard a PC behind him say to the clerk.

He turned in time to watch the clerk blink, look down and numbly press a button behind the counter. Immediately an earsplitting siren shrieked. Every police officer in the car park crouched in surprise. Keen sighed. His head hurt.

"Sergeant Dunliffe?" Keen focused on a vaguely familiar young PC; Horsforth station, maybe. "It's your nick."

Keen nodded, then realized that wasn't smart, the movement making his headache worse. "I'm off duty," he said, meaning he had no radio. They probably knew that. "See if we've a custody officer on at Weetwood." He wished the alarm would stop so he could think. "Shut that damned thing off," he said to the clerk.

"I don't know how," the clerk said, his voice barely a squeak in the deafening blare. Keen understood him more by the movement of his lips than by sound. He walked outside.

If anything, the alarm was louder there. "He's got more firearms than the IRA on a skeet shoot!" someone was shouting over the clamor. "Two dozen shotguns, semiautomatic rifles, drawers full of revolvers, night scopes, boxes full of ammo . . . *Jesus!* There's a bloody AK-47 in here!"

"Naw, that's no AK-47," someone else said, his bored tone not quite convincing. "That's a rip-off Chinese 57, see how the bayonet is fixed under the barrel?"

Keen walked over to his Vauxhall and stared at it, baffled. He couldn't remember now why he'd stopped in the first place. He jumped as someone touched his arm; the teenager who had rung the police, skateboard still tucked under his arm. "I did okay?" the lad asked. Metal braces on his teeth reflected blue light.

Keen attempted to smile in return. "Brilliant."

"I've kind of thought about, you know, maybe being a policeman after I leave school," the lad said, trying to pitch his puberty-cracked voice down into an adult range.

Keen cleared his raw throat. "Let me know when you do, and I'll write a recommendation for you."

"Really? Wicked!" The lad beamed. "Think we'll be on tellie?"

Bloody hell. He hadn't thought of that. "You keep an eye out for them, okay?" He gave the boy's shoulder a friendly squeeze. "I still have work to do."

He walked over to an inspector and a sergeant standing beside the panda. The prisoner sat in the back, head lolling indifferently.

"Weetwood?" Keen asked. When the sergeant nodded, he added, "I'll follow you, then. I have my car here."

When he pulled out of the service station, the alarm was still wailing. With the rain-soaked clouds darkened to a rich bloodred, the taillights of the patrol car in front stared him down like the amethyst eyes of some Hollywood monster. He touched his forehead gingerly. A swollen bump at his hairline was soft and painful under his fingertips.

It took another hour to get the prisoner processed through the charge room into a detention cell. Somewhere else in the station, Angelina wailed in two-part harmony with the baby's howl. Glen Harper waited for him, as did Davis. When Keen reached the part where he'd been thumped in the head, Harper frowned and asked to see the injury. Keen pushed his hair up from his forehead and watched Harper's frown deepen.

"Police surgeon should give you a look when he's done with the woman," Harper said. "You could have a concussion."

He didn't want a doctor. He wanted the job over with so he could go home. It was late; he was tired and cranky. Finally, he dotted the last *i* and crossed the last *t,* signed his name and was done. Davis walked him out to his car.

"Maybe you shouldn't be driving," Davis said. Keen gave him a hard look. Davis shrugged. "Be careful, then. And if you won't see a doctor tonight," he warned, "don't come in tomorrow until you do." He slapped him on the back. "Damned good nick, Keen."

He agreed, to both things, and went home. He was sure someone followed him as far as the turnoff at Leathley, to his irritation and covert relief.

Curiously, Thomas didn't rush out from wherever he was hiding to greet Keen as he pulled up in front of the house and got out. The rain had stopped, so the greedy moggie should have been making a nuisance of himself by rubbing Keen's legs and trying to trip him as he went inside, demanding his dinner. Keen dropped his keys on the counter, picked up the post from the floor, glared briefly at the mobile phone in the charger, then stood in the open doorway as he scanned the fields. Charcoal clouds slunk along the hills, the bite of ozone still thick in the air. Grazing sheep ignored the distant thunder. Wind ruffled the grass, undulating lines snake-dancing.

"Thomas . . ." he called out.

A few sheep looked up, black eyes inquisitive.

He pitched his voice higher. "Here, puss, puss, puss . . ." He stopped, feeling a complete fool. In all the years he'd had Thomas, he'd never called him "puss." Likely the cat wouldn't know what the hell Keen was going on about, if he heard him at all.

"Damn it, Thomas!" Startled sheep retreated, kicking up hind feet in protest. "I'm not in the mood!" Irritated at both the cat and himself, he went back inside but left the door open just in case.

His headache had settled into a knife edge of pain down his nose and a dull throb in the back of his head. He touched the lump not far from a small patch of white hair, a souvenir of another whack on the head in the line of duty. He knew enough from that experience not to make any sudden turns and not to give in to the temptation of a sip of medicinal scotch.

He wasn't hungry, although he'd missed supper. He had a cup of tea instead, washing down a couple of paracetamol he found in the back of a kitchen cabinet, and tried to stay awake as long as he could, in case he did have a concussion. He read his mail, tossing out the ads for cheap car loans and special offers at Kwiksave and anything addressed to "The Occupier." His American girlfriend— if that was what she was—had sent him a letter from Oregon, complaining again about his lack of a home computer and e-mail. It wasn't that he was a Luddite; he had enough of computers at work and didn't see the necessity of spending several hundred pounds on a machine so that he could swap vulgar jokes with colleagues and strangers for fun. Besides, he thought as he read her cramped handwriting, smiling despite his headache, it was nice just holding something Jillie had touched, about the only physical contact he had with her most of the time.

Long-distance love affairs sucked, he thought. But she'd be coming over in a fortnight's time for nearly six whole months, on some sort of archaeological dig up on Hadrian's Wall. If the grant money came through. If enough grad students had signed up for the course.

If the foot-and-mouth didn't shut down the site. If, if, if. He sighed as he folded her letter back up and slid it into the envelope.

By ten, the cat still hadn't returned and he reluctantly locked the door before slowly climbing the stairs for bed. He didn't even bother to brush his teeth, dropping his clothes onto the floor before he crawled into bed, wanting nothing more than to lie down and not move.

Keen found it as hard to sleep without an annoying lump of cat on the bed as it was with it. It took him ages, but once he'd finally dropped off, he slept deeply, dreamless.

3

Well before dawn, in the early morning darkness, Pete Phillips had been cruising this run-down estate on the edge of Gateshead for more than an hour and hadn't seen so much as a flash of yellow eyes in the bushes. He sighed, stifled a yawn, and turned right onto another nondescript street. His white panel van was unmarked, the two large magnetized plastic signs with their neatly lettered blue and gold PHILLIPS & ARDEN VETERINARY CLINIC tucked under the passenger seat.

Usually, nights were a good time for bagging at least half a dozen strays, plenty of domestic cats out massacring the wild bird population. But this month had been so cold and wet, even the most hard-hearted of cat owners were allowing their pets to spend their evenings lying by a cozy cottage fire—or at least next to council housing central heating radiators.

He wasn't overly concerned about being stopped by the police; if some paranoid insomniac noticed him canvassing the neighborhood and rang the cops, he would simply display his forged RSPCA identification, explain he was searching for a reported injured dog/cat depending on which sex the officer happened to be (men tended to prefer dogs, women favored cats), and that would be that. On one occasion, the officer had even helped him to catch the huge feral ginger tom he'd been trying to bag for three months. Between the pair of them, they'd trampled more than a few flower beds and earned several deep scratches before the spitting fiend had been looped and hauled into the back of Pete's van. The bobby had made a lame joke about Pete's job being more dangerous than his own, before answering a radio call and driving off.

Pete had driven around the block and parked, and within ten minutes, the malicious flea-bitten mog had been lightly anesthetized, shaved, and its testes whipped out. Inside another ten minutes, it had opened dilated, astonished eyes, hissing unconvincingly as Pete dumped it back out on the street behind a hedge of acacia bushes. Pete prided himself on the speed at which he worked. On his best night, he could catch and neuter a dozen males, but his average remained between three and four.

If his father, one of the partners of Phillips & Arden who co-owned both the veterinary clinic and the van, knew what Phillips junior had been getting up to over the past year, he never mentioned it. He also knew the animals Pete captured and altered were never likely to bring in any income to his or anyone else's clinic, their owners too poor, too lazy, or too ignorant to bother. And as Pete handled the accounts, the cost of any missing supplies was carefully buried in the books. The inflated prices charged by Messrs. Arden and Phillips to the regular clients willing to spend hundreds of pounds on neurotically unnecessary checkups and expensive drugs and even homeopathic acupuncture for their more cherished pets adequately concealed any minor loss of profit.

Pete had clipped all the outraged letters to the editor and articles in the papers denouncing the Rogue Vet—or a few more rude aliases the tabloid press preferred, such as Goolie Grabber and Jewel Thief—not exactly with pride, although that did come into it, how could it not? He wasn't a real vet, having never earned his degree; his dyslexia and stammer had put paid to that. But even at the age of ten he could castrate a bull and turn a breech lamb far better and faster than his father ever could.

"Aye, it's the young vet P-p-petey," the local farmers would all say, ruffling his hair to take the sting out of their teasing. But they listened to his advice, as respectful of his competence as they were of his da's.

Other lies the tabloids printed offended his sense of fairness, like the ludicrous claims he'd actually broken into people's homes to snatch their animals or had spayed obviously pregnant females close to their term and left the kittens to die. One particularly vicious letter from a local member of the Cat Fancy Association had accused him of neutering her pedigreed Ragdoll tom, causing her a loss of thousands of dollars' worth of stud fees. While the claim was spurious, he personally detested Ragdolls, genetically defective freaks insensitive to pain with no more personality than a wet sock.

But no one was printing much about him these days—foot-and-mouth had pushed him to the back of the papers, whenever he appeared at all. His da and Henry Arden had been kept so busy by the epidemic Phil hardly ever saw his father these days; every vet in the country press-ganged into either blood testing or the culls, so that the care of ordinary pets had become less vital. Even owners stayed away out of a vague sense of alarm, as if their dogs and cats and guinea pigs and hamsters were in danger of catching the disease just from association with a vet. His unofficial service was more important than ever.

It had been a crap night, raining most of the time, a stiff wind blowing. He'd snared two dogs and a cat by three A.M., both dogs already neutered and the cat a female with his small tattooed mark in her left ear to show she'd been fixed on a previous occasion. So all he had to show for the night was three bloody claw marks down the back of his hand where the cat had scratched him.

Now, with it almost six in the morning, people would be getting up and going to work, his duty for the evening nearly done. He glanced at his watch and, in spite of his best effort not to, computed how long it would take to get home versus timing it so he could "coincidentally" arrive just as his next-door neighbor would be getting in herself, coming off the A&E night shift. Myrna had made it crystal clear they were "just friends," meaning his chances of ever getting a leg over were less than his chances of winning the Lotto—less than zero now that Gerald Spalding had started in courting her. His teenaged nemesis, the hulking bully who had made his schooldays hell, was now a bobby with military-cropped hair and gym-toned muscles straining against skintight T-shirts, constantly around at her flat glowering possessively. But Pete couldn't help himself; even the briefest glimpse of her trim figure in her nurse's uniform filled his heart with an ache, an odd mix of unrequited lust and self-disgust making him feel like a parody of a stuttering Frankie Howerd chasing after the buxom Barbara Windsor in one of those silly *Carry On* films his mum was mad about.

He headed toward home, north along the A69, then, on a whim, turned off onto a back road to his favorite hideaway spot where he and his best mate Irwin Boyle had been young lads with cheap fishing poles and a pack of illicit fags and vague dreams of a future that had never materialized. He pulled into an isolated industrial estate and parked in the empty lots behind the corrugated tin warehouses and an abandoned Victorian chimney. In the sixties, this had been a prosperous brickworks factory, employing hundreds, including both of Irwin's parents. Half the houses in Northumberland were built of their bricks. The plant had gone bust before Irwin had even been born, and now the sign on the building read RICHMONT INDUSTRIAL STORAGE, with a rusting hulk of an old tractor parked at the roadside end of the estate. It wasn't a particularly picturesque spot, but it was tranquil and high enough up on the hillside to overlook the Tyne River and the graceful arches of a distant white half-moon bridge across the water, open now only to foot traffic, playing peek-a-boo in the early morning fog.

Pete braced his feet up against the dashboard and ate his packed breakfast—an apple, a boiled egg, and a jelly sandwich—content to sit in the dark and the quiet while listening to Radio Newcastle. He rolled down the window to toss peeled eggshell fragments into the weeds growing along the chain-link fencing, the outside air nippy as it gusted into the warmed cab, and quickly rolled it back up again, shivering.

He was laughing quietly at one of Paddy MacDee's sillier jokes when several hazy shadows broke away from the square black silhouettes of warehouse buildings, racing along the perimeter of the chain-link fence. For a moment, Pete simply stared, mystified, then his heart jumped into his throat with the wild notion he'd sighted one of the legendary big cats many had claimed to have spotted all around Britain, descendants of black leopards escaped from circuses, panthers from private zoos. Then a shadow stood up, with the quite unmistakable shape of a human being, to Pete's mix of relief and disappointment. And irritation that they had invaded his child-hood haven.

Half a dozen human shapes in dark clothing and hooded sweat-shirts furtively skirted the fencing along the industrial buildings before disappearing around the back of the estate, out of sight, no doubt the usual pack of adolescent toe-rags out nicking cars and thieving anything not nailed down. Pete methodically chewed the last of his jelly sandwich while he watched, then washed it down with the weak, milky tea in his thermos. A faint light wavered on the glass of the warehouse's high windows, someone shining a torch inside. Then it went out, the windows dark again.

Whatever mischief they were up to, he had no intention of try-ing to stop them; he was no have-a-go hero. He did briefly con-sider ringing the police on his mobile, an impulse that was quickly enough quashed by the inevitable questions as to what he himself was doing parked up in an empty industrial estate at six in the morning. Besides, it would be just his luck if it was Myrna's boyfriend took the call as well. Wasn't any of Pete's business, and he had enough grief in his life without asking for more. Best if he was going now anyways, he thought, with another glance at his watch.

He finished his apple and rolled down the window to throw the core in the same direction as the eggshells, and had started the en-gine when he stared at a small white object moving toward him er-ratically. It stopped, dead center of the car park, and shook its head irritably in the misty air, waving long floppy ears.

"Ya poor little bugger," he muttered to himself. "C-catch your death out in this cold." No doubt some kid had forgotten to latch the door of the hutch, and their pet bunny had escaped. This sure wasn't the best place for it to have ended up, far from any residen-tial houses or gardens. He hesitated, then sighed to himself, know-ing he wasn't going to manage to bump into Myrna coming in from work now.

Pete shut off the engine, reached around to the back to retrieve his loop and pole. He got out, walking slowly toward the rabbit. "Hello, little bun," he said softly. It stared back with pale red eyes, hopped uncertainly toward him, then sat up on hind legs, front paws folded neatly as it sniffed the air. "Come to Petey, nice juicy c-c-carrot in it for you . . ." He held the lasso out cautiously and paused, waiting patiently. Bloodred eyes bulging from its skull studied him solemnly, nose twitching. Then it twisted to thump hind claws against an itch on the back of one ear, and Pete had the loop around its neck and taut in a heartbeat.

"Gotcha," he said cheerfully at the rabbit thrashing at the end of the pole. "T-take it easy, I'm not going to hurt you—"

As he straightened with the rabbit securely in his arms, he stopped, baffled. Two more white rabbits hopped toward him across the car park tentatively. He watched as they hopped past him, followed by three more. Then several dozen skipped and leaped out of the morning shadows across the car park.

"What the f-f-f—?"

A trickle of white rabbits became hundreds pouring out from the bushes around the warehouses, red eyes gleaming like tiny demons. They streamed past him in a stampede of white fur as he stood cradling the one he'd lassoed, astonished. Where were they all coming from?

"What the fuck are you doing!" someone shouted at him. Startled, he turned around and recoiled from a huge man in a black balaclava and hooded sweatshirt bearing down on him. Two others identically dressed followed behind him waving their arms at the rabbits to herd them along. The rabbit in his arms squirmed in protest as he squeezed it against his chest. Back claws raked his arm, leaving long red scratches in his skin.

A boy—no, a woman—sprinted across the car park toward them. "Let's go, let's go, let's go!" she was chanting in a high, excited voice. She held a small camcorder, red recording light glowing in the morning darkness. She skidded to a stop, startled eyes pale in her black balaclava. "We gotta get out of here, *now!*"

"Leg it, it's the cops!" another voice shouted.

Pete looked around wildly. Relief quickly turned to dismay when he saw no one and realized they meant *him*. Two more masked people in black materialized from the shadows, sprinting away from the warehouses, toward the riverbank. They seemed to leap into the air and vanished down the bank, stones clattering down the steep incline.

The pair shepherding the rabbits toward the trees stopped flapping their arms and stood uncertainly, ready to bolt. Pete started walking backward toward his van, his arms still full of reluctant rabbit.

The masked man grabbed him by the arm and roughly jerked the pole out of his hands to free the rabbit from the loop. The rabbit kicked back legs in protest, but once dropped to the ground it bounced away with the remaining stragglers still milling about the car park. Pete turned to run, but the masked man punched him hard in the stomach, doubling him over, then shoved him against the bonnet of the van and held him there with one powerful arm braced on his chest. Pete heard himself whimper, in fear and anger, the heat of the engine against his back. He blinked through tears of pain, one arm wrapped around his stomach, the other held in front of his face protectively.

Pale blue eyes glared at him through the holes in the mask, the skin of his lids finely wrinkled, dark lashes as thick as a girl's. Steam from his breath seeped through the weave of the balaclava, smelling faintly of cigarettes. The man outweighed Pete by several stone. His arms were bigger than Pete's legs, oversized muscle taut against the fabric of his sweatshirt. He pinned Pete against the van as effortlessly as spearing a fish.

"Where are the others?" he demanded as he roughly rummaged through Pete's jacket pockets and inside his shirt. "Fucking goddamned filth!"

"Oh, for chrissake, he's not a cop!" the woman with the camera said. Her voice was familiar. The man in the balaclava twisted to stare at her. "Come on, *look* at him," she insisted. "Fat little git like that?"

"B-b-b-b-b . . . ?" He struggled to get her name out, his voice strangling in his throat. The man in the balaclava jerked his head back toward Pete, one eyelid spasming behind the mask.

"Where are your keys?" For a moment, Pete didn't answer,

thinking the man was still talking to the woman. Then the masked man bunched the front of his shirt in one fist and shook him roughly. *"Where are the keys, asshole!"*

"In th-th-th-th . . ." His stammer made the words impossible.

Several motorcycle engines coughed to life along the riverbank below, small cc engines whining like mosquitoes as they ripped through the gears, fading away. "We gotta go," the woman said urgently, dancing from one foot to the other in impatience. "We gotta go *now!*"

"Shut up," the masked man ordered. "Get him on the video."

"What?"

"Get him and the registration number of his van on the video!"

The woman brought the camcorder up to her face and pointed the lens at him for several seconds, then swept to the van with several white rabbits still hopping around the tires. "Okay, I've got it."

As she turned, a muffled boom exploded all the glass out of the warehouse windows and a bright light flashed across the car park. The woman and Pete flinched at the blast, but the masked man seemed to straighten, growing even bigger in the mounting blaze, his mouth open underneath the mask in exultation, his breath misting through the knit. In unison, the several dozen rabbits still lingering in the car park stood up on hind legs inquisitively, sniffing at the smoke beginning to roil from the shattered windows, firelight turning their fur orange, then they scampered into the brush.

"Bloody hell!" the woman breathed in awe. She turned the camcorder onto the burning building, a few straggling rabbits zigzagging away in panic. "Come *on*, Rory! We gotta get *out* of here—!"

The masked man who still held Pete by his shirt collar rounded on the woman in fury. *"Don't use my name, you stupid bitch!"*

"Fuck you," she retorted just as heatedly. "I'm off, you do what you want."

She tucked the camcorder under one arm and raced away in the same direction as the other four had gone, down toward the river embankment. Pete heard her crashing through the undergrowth, a couple of voices too faint to make out the words however clear the tone of urgency. Down by the river, several motorcycles coughed to life and whined up through gears as they sped away along the quayside below.

The man in the mask glared at her until she disappeared, seething with anger. "Cunt," he snarled before he turned back to Pete, propelling him around the van. He picked Pete up by the back of his shirt collar and waist of his jeans to toss him over the driver's seat into the passenger side as easily as he might a sack of potatoes. Then he climbed in, turned the engine over and rammed it into gear, tires spinning in the gravel for purchase.

Pete struggled to sit upright in the passenger seat, his heart pounding, feeling sick with the fear. He sat silently, staring straight ahead out the windscreen as the man in the mask drove out onto the road, and headed south, back toward Newcastle. Breathing hard through his nose, he let his left hand drop to his side, creeping toward the handle, trying to screw up enough courage to open the door and jump from the speeding van. As if the masked man could read Pete's thoughts, his arm shot out to grab Pete by the throat, squeezing hard enough to cut off his air.

"Try it," the man said, "and I'll break your fucking neck. Okay?"

Pete nodded frantically and forced himself to lace his hands together in his lap, fingers clenched together so tight they hurt. The man released him, shoving him away.

They came to a roundabout a few miles on, where a motorcycle overtook them, leaping into the front, brake light flickering.

"Good girl," the man murmured, and followed the motorcycle into a lay-by and parked along the deserted country road. Shutting the engine off, he pulled the keys from the ignition and tossed the keys out the open door like a cricketer pitching a ball. They flashed briefly and fell with a merry jingle as they hit the ground, spooking a small flock of sheep on the other side of the fence.

The masked man pulled Pete out of the van, kicked the driver's door shut, and hauled him to the far side, away from the road. Pushing Pete up against the van with one hand on his neck, the man fished his other hand into Pete's back pocket for his wallet. Pete squirmed in his grasp and got a hard knee in the bollocks for his trouble, agony shooting down his legs and out the top of his skull. Sensing any residual fight was gone, the masked man released him to let him wilt onto the graveled lay-by, Pete's hands tucked into his groin. He didn't care as the man rifled through his wallet, tossing out the money and the credit cards to flutter down onto the ground around Pete. The woman on the motorcycle sat twisting the handle, revving the engine, her head invisible under the motorcycle helmet.

"Peter Phillips," the man said, holding up his forged RSPCA identification card. "I got your name. I got your car number. I know where you live." He squatted down in front of Pete, speaking quietly. "You tell anyone about us, about what happened tonight, and I will find you, and I will hurt you. I will hurt your family. I will hurt your fucking *goldfish*. Do you understand what I'm saying?"

Pete nodded.

"I can't hear you."

"I underst-st-st-st . . ."

The man laughed, an ugly sound. "Whatever."

When he stood, the woman tossed him a motorcycle helmet. Walking away with his back to Pete, the man pulled off the mask before shoving the helmet onto his head, a dark curling mass of hair all Pete could see of his face. The woman relinquished her position as he straddled the bike, sliding back to ride pillion behind him. Without even glancing back at the road for traffic, the man pulled out of the lay-by, his companion wrapping her arms around his massive chest. Within seconds, they were gone, only the distant throaty growl of the motorcycle engine left behind.

It took Pete over an hour to find his keys, the morning light now a soupy gray but enough to spot the glint of metal in the muddy field. He squatted on the ground, rubbing the mud off the metal. As a police car pulled in behind his van, he straightened up guiltily, an action mimicked by alert sheep, heads popping up in the field behind him. Pete's heart sank as the two uniformed cops got out and walked to the edge of the barbed-wire fence, staring at him curiously.

"Hey, Petey," one of them called out to him. "What's up? Is there a problem?"

He couldn't believe his bad luck this night. Of course, it just had to be Gerald friggin' Spalding.

4

Without warning, no transition from dreaming to reality, Keen woke up, pain slamming into the back of his head and shooting out his eye sockets. He opened his eyes to the dark, rain tapping feebly against the window. He rolled onto his back with a groan, the mattress on the unslept-in half of the bed cold against his bare skin. It took all the willpower he had to throw back the warm duvet and haul himself out of bed.

Downstairs, he heard the faint yowl of a very annoyed cat on the other side of the locked kitchen door. Thomas glared up at him from the steps as he opened the door.

"Bloody hell, Thomas. You look worse than I feel."

The cat was more than just soaked. Tufts of fur had been yanked out of his hide, one eye swollen half shut, both ears tattered and bloody. A huge sore on his back oozed pus. Thomas licked his tongue over his scratched nose, then hobbled into the kitchen. Keen emptied a can of fresh cat food into his bowl, cracked an egg over it, and set it in front of the cat.

While Keen was happier than he could ever admit to see the damned cat, Thomas had never looked so bad. The cat ate less than half his breakfast before he sprawled onto the kitchen floor and licked frantically at the seeping wound on his back.

Although Keen wasn't hungry, he added milk to his coffee and drank the rest straight from the bottle to settle his stomach. Keeping an eye on Thomas, he finished his coffee, then rinsed the milk bottle and set it on the porch step. He shaved quickly, picked his clothes off the floor where he'd dropped them, and dressed. Then he waited until eight to call Mrs. Gobrey, and not a minute longer.

He wrapped Thomas in a bath towel before stuffing the cat into a cardboard box, prying determined claws from the edges. The cat yowled.

Bridget Gobrey ran her veterinary clinic from her home in Farnley, a town of half a dozen farmhouses, one pub, and a red phone box the other side of the river Washburn where it broadened into the Lindley Wood Reservoir. Her husband, Mack, ran a newsagent shop in Newall. As Keen turned up the drive, Mack pulled out, exchanging a sleepy wave with him. Mrs. Gobrey waited in the doorway, wiping her hands on an apron. She nodded at a wet black plastic mat in the bottom of a tray placed in front of the house, and Keen dutifully stood in the disinfectant tray before he crossed her threshold.

He carried the box into a house filled with the aroma of fresh bacon, fried eggs, and beans. His mouth watered, his appetite returning. Thomas howled, heartbreakingly.

Her clinic in the back gleamed, white tile and stainless steel, and smelled of mentholated spirits and disinfectant. Through the windows, he saw a small herd of yearling calves nibbling unenthusiastically at a bale of hay in a muddy paddock.

"You're lucky you called early," Mrs. Gobrey said as she led him through. "I need to be off in a half hour. Shortage of vets means we're working around the clock, seven days a week. I'm lucky to get four hours' sleep a night."

"Testing?"

Mrs. Gobrey snorted in disgust. "I wish. How do you test a couple million animals in one month? It's impossible; we don't have the equipment, never mind enough vets. MAFF is badly overstretched, half as many as there used to be before Thatcher's spending cuts, so they're desperate for any of us vets they can rope in. No, right now, we're just killing them all as humanely as we can, as fast as we can. I at least have a proper captive bolt, pith them, and do the job as it should be done. Half these so-called licensed slaughterers are using any rifle they have to hand, running about the fields like a bunch of mad Daleks shooting at pregnant ewes and lambs like it's some sort of sick carnival." She did look tired, her eyes red-rimmed in fatigue. "It's insanity. Amazing they don't shoot each other. Now there's talk about it getting into the deer population, as if we don't have enough animals to kill."

"I'm sorry to have to bother you when you're this busy . . ."

"Are you joking?" She laughed, her smile bitter. "I'm just happy to be doing something good for *any* animal right now. So let's be seeing him."

He set the box onto the examination table and watched as the veterinarian took the cat out, making consoling noises. "Nah, then, you poor thing," she cooed. Thomas stopped howling to glare at her hatefully.

"You've been in quite a fight, you have, m'love."

Her words might have turned into syrup, but the hands examining the cat were efficient and professional. Nearly sixty years old, as stout as her husband, Bridget Gobrey came from generations of Yorkshire farmers with an affinity for animals. "How long was he gone missing?"

"Just last night. He was fine when he went out yesterday morning."

She smiled benignly at the cat. "Toms get into territorial fights, that's what's happened here. Seems you took the brunt of it, din' you, kitlin?" Her voice dipped into the saccharine, then back to business. "Claws are dirty. Poked under the skin, it's like an injection of pure bacteria. Gets infected, ulcerated. This 'un's bad. Have to drain the abscess and clean it out thoroughly or it'll just close over and reinfect itself. I'll give him an injection of antibiotics, should help." She brought out a cloth-wrapped pan.

Thomas glowered as she filled a small syringe with a mild tranquilizer and a larger one with milky antibiotic, lifted the skin on the neck to inject the cat. He held on to Thomas while she snapped plastic gloves over her hands and picked up a scalpel. Wincing, he looked away as she lanced the abscess, buttery white pus spurting. He found the poster behind her illustrating the life cycle of fleas positively enthralling while she swabbed out the wound.

"That wasn't so bad, was it?" Keen wasn't sure if that was for

Thomas or for him. "You should have this animal neutered." That was definitely for him. His legs pressed together protectively.

"Fraternal empathy," he said.

She frowned reproachfully. "I strongly advise it. Were it female, you wouldn't think twice having her spayed rather than her going into heat and dropping a litter every few months."

"It's a sexist world," he admitted. "He's supposed to be a mouser." Although not a very good one. He rubbed the cat's ears. Thomas ignored him. "Wouldn't that ruin his hunting instincts?"

"No." She dabbed antiseptic on the cat's scratched nose. Thomas kept his eyes closed, only his whiskers twitching. "Hunting is a learned skill. If the mother doesn't teach her babies how to do it properly, past a certain age they never learn. I had kittens some years back so young I had to bottle-feed them, but to keep them warm, I put them in with the laying hens. They grew up thinking they were chickens. Quite a sight, full-grown cats letting baby chicks walk all over them and loving it."

He remembered Bobby's owl. "Fixated."

"That's right. Worthless as hunters, but they made nice pets." She picked Thomas up by the middle, his legs drooping, and laid him on his side, palpating his internal organs. To Keen's surprise, Thomas began purring, although the cat's expression was still one of complete loathing. She chuckled. "Some cats do that," she explained without his asking, "try to convince you everything's fine so you'll let go." Her voice went sickly sweet. "You li'l charlatan, you."

Thomas had his ears laid back, hostile eyes mere slits, but his purr went up another gear. Mrs. Gobrey grasped his head in the vise of one meaty hand to examine his scab-caked ears and swollen eye.

"So if he's a good hunter now," she said, tone back to a no-nonsense timbre, "he'll do just as well with his reproductive capabilities removed."

Now he knew why Thomas was such a wretched mouser. Dysfunctional family environment, it was. "I'll think on it."

"I'll give you some antibiotic pills for him, one every morning."

She managed to put Thomas back into the box with considerably less difficulty than he'd had. He rubbed his forehead, digging his fingers into the ache lodged behind his eye sockets. "You don't look as you're feeling all that grand yourself," she said.

He dropped his hand. "I bumped heads with someone last night. His was harder than mine."

"In the line of duty?"

He shrugged, vaguely embarrassed. "Occupational clumsiness."

She pulled out a bottle from a drawer and shook two pills into her palm. "These should do you. Acetaminophen with codeine. Just don't stop off for a morning snort."

"Aceta–what?"

"Extra Strength Tylenol."

They were so large he wondered if she was giving them to the calf outside. He choked them down with a paper cup of lukewarm tap water.

"He should be fine in four or five days. If he does have any more problem with that abscess, just gi'us a ring."

"Thanks."

"My pleasure," she said sadly. "Now it's back to the real world for me."

Although his headache lessened considerably, between last night's painkillers on an empty stomach, the horse pills and the coffee, his gut ached by the time he returned to his farmhouse. Thomas had claws anchored in the flaps of the cardboard box, and his nose between them. Keen pushed the cat's face back into the cardboard box.

"Just hang on a minute, you," he said to the cat, and got out to go around the car to the passenger side. Juggling the box under one arm, he unlocked the door to the house and opened it before letting the cat out. Thomas sprang out of the box in one fluid bound, hit the floor, and escaped under the sofa. From his refuge, the cat glared at him and hissed.

"You have a nice day, too, mate," Keen said to the cat, and closed the door. It would be close to ten before he got to the nick. He sighed. No time for a real breakfast and no supper the night before.

He arrived at the nick ten minutes to the hour, not that anyone would make mention of it. The suspect he'd arrested the previous day turned out to have absolutely nothing to do with the two lads in the hit-and-run; the CCTV camera had picked up the Audi completely by chance, and the driver turned out to be a notorious criminal wanted on illegal firearms charges in just about every county from the Scottish borders to the Penzance peninsula. Everybody seemed to want to congratulate Keen on his arrest, from the temp typists in upstairs administrations to the chief superintendent from Wakefield who just happened to drop by. The only person too busy elsewhere was Nigel Mullard, unsurprisingly.

Keen had not been present during the taped interview with the suspect; Mullard had leaped in with all claws extended, not about to let such a juicy case escape. He'd be lucky if he was even mentioned again as the arresting officer. The next time Keen expected he'd see the suspect was at the trial. That the suspect had immediately demanded his solicitor and responded to each of Mullard's questions with a frustrating "no comment" was a minor consolation. But the attention on Keen was both uncomfortable and gratifying.

"Mornin', Superman," Edwards said, grinning. "How's the skull?"

" 'Yorkshire born and Yorkshire bred.' "

Edwards laughed, knowing the rest of the doggerel. *Strong i' th' arm and thick i' th' head.*

He nipped down to the canteen for a quick snack and bolted down a stale Swiss roll with a thick layer of white icing. The combination of headache and sugar rush made him feel queasy. On his way back to the CID room, he ran into Graeme Davis in the hall. "Morning, Keen. You've been to see your doctor then?"

Keen stopped. Damn. He'd forgotten all about that. "Yes, sir," he said cautiously. " 'Bout an hour ago." It wasn't strictly a lie; a veterinarian was sort of a doctor, wasn't she?

"And?"

"Nothing to worry about, should all be fine in a couple of days."

"That's it?"

"Gave me some Extra Strength Tylenol."

"Good." Davis nodded, satisfied. "You'll be wanting to submit a report. Get it recorded as an injury on duty."

"Right." This was definitely another of his not-so-Keen ideas; he wondered how to explain Mrs. Gobrey's recommendation for neutering in his report. He rang his GP who agreed to sneak him in at twelve-thirty for a quick exam before Davis figured it out and decided hers might not be such a bad suggestion after all. He drove to the surgery in Ireland Wood on his lunch break where it took all of ten minutes for Dr. Arnold to take his blood pressure, choke him with a tongue lozenge, blind him with a penlight, whack his kneecaps, grope his head bump, and write him a prescription for the same Extra Strength Tylenol the vet had given him. But at least it would cover his arse as far as the medical report was concerned.

Half an hour before he was due to book off for the day, he'd been standing by the coffeemaker by the window, reading over file notes while waiting for a freshly brewed batch to finish trickling into the pot. Behind him, Jazz was tapping steadily on her computer keyboard with her phone jammed against her shoulder, still on hold to the Crown Prosecution Service.

Keen glanced out idly at a car pulling into the rain-swamped car park, smiled as the car door opened and a well-dressed man and woman hesitantly got out, futilely trying to avoid the puddles. He had his attention on the woman's legs, shapely and athletic under a short if severe skirt, before he glanced indifferently at the man. An unpleasant jolt of recognition ran up his spine, prickling his face. He stepped away from the window instinctively.

"Fuck me," he murmured, anger seeping into his voice.

Jazz looked up at him, startled by his uncharacteristic vulgarity.

This goddamned arrest. He would never, ever again stop at that bloody Esso station on Old Otley Road, he swore to himself. He tossed the file onto Jasmine's desk.

"Anyone comes looking for me," he said, "you don't know where I am."

"Where you going?"

"If I don't tell you, then it won't be a lie, will it?"

All he needed was to get through the next half hour and he

could leave. Feeling like a coward, he managed to dodge meeting anyone in the corridor and hide out in one of the admin offices on the second floor, with only ten minutes to go before Jenkins stuck his head inside the door and grinned at him.

"There you are, boss!" the lad said cheerfully. "Been looking all over for you. CI Davis wants to see you in his office sharpish."

"Does he, now," Keen muttered darkly. And decided that in future maybe Jenkins would spend a lot more time on writing up his case notes after all.

Graeme Davis, his chief inspector of operations, had his own tiny office to himself at the far end of the station. Like most of the desks in CID, his was equally cluttered, but in an oddly ordered manner: folders piled on his desk had their corners neatly aligned, books and binders on the shelves were organized with meticulous care, files in a steel-gray cabinet were shut and locked, but with a crayon drawing by his only granddaughter Cellotaped to the side of the cabinet. The walls were decorated with the usual police paraphernalia— oversized shields on walnut mounts and framed photos of Davis in dress uniform, smiling rigidly while shaking hands with various superiors as they handed him indeterminate awards, as well as one of Davis grinning from ear to ear with far more real delight as he stood in a boat holding up a huge fish. He kept a dozen framed pictures of his wife and kids displayed in matching frames arranged by size, and the Christmas cactus in a blue and white pot on the windowsill still had a few wilted pale pink flowers clinging to the tips.

The man and woman Keen had spotted in the car park sat on hard plastic chairs impounded from the canteen, a cup of tea each on the edge of Davis's desk in front of them along with a thin manila folder. They swiveled their heads around in unison as Keen stood in the doorway and said, "Boss?"

"Come on in," Davis said, his smile stuck in the same professional mode as in his photos. There wasn't another chair; nor room enough to put one if there had been. Keen sidled to the edge of Davis's desk, his own professional smile feeling like a dead weight on his face.

The woman appraised him with dark green eyes in a hard-set face, her expert makeup and blunt-cut blond hair doing nothing to soften her appearance. A small American flag pinned on the lapel of her tailored suit jacket glittered in the office's neon light, turning the blue to purple.

"Ynez Ross," Davis said. "Special Agent with the FBI. DS Keen Dunliffe." Keen knew he wasn't able to keep the surprise out of his expression, but the woman barely nodded her acknowledgment. "You already know Chief Superintendent Pete McCraig, from the London Metropolitan Police."

"Yes," Keen said, and folded his arms across his chest. Neither Ross nor McCraig made any proffer of a handshake, although McCraig raised an amused eyebrow at Keen. Ross glanced from McCraig and back to Keen, uncurious but astute.

"Right," she said, dispensing with any polite preamble to the conversation. "Last month, a U.S. marshal was shot and killed by an unknown assailant at Heathrow while transporting a British national extradited for trial in the U.K." Her voice was as hard as her manner, with an unpleasant twang to her American accent.

"A Metropolitan police officer was also wounded in the attack," McCraig added. "The female prisoner was killed."

Well, well, Keen thought. Guess they weren't here to congratulate him on his arrest after all. But whatever McCraig did want with him this time, Keen was sure he was going to like it even less.

"Saw it on the news," Keen said tersely. A dead American and an injured London cop explained why the FBI and the Metropolitan Police were involved. He glanced at Davis, wondering what any of this had to do with him. Davis sat with his chair tilted back and hands laced on his stomach, his expression bland but his shoulders lifting in a tiny shrug.

"Eunice Gordon Connor was twenty-seven weeks pregnant," Ross said.

Keen did the math in his head to translate it into English. Nearly seven months. "The airline let her fly?"

Ross glared, but Keen suspected it was more from habit than hostility. "British Air allows passengers to fly up to their seventh month. She'd been examined by the prison doctor and certified as healthy, no complications to her pregnancy."

"It couldn't have waited until after the birth?"

"Two weeks more, and the trial would have had to be pushed back. There was reason to feel some urgency in the matter," McCraig said.

"That, and any child born on American soil is automatically entitled to American citizenship," Ross added dryly. "A situation our government was happy to avoid. Eunice Connor was an expert at exploiting every legal loophole she could, no matter how small, to further her own ends. Having a child with American citizenship would have simply given her more ammunition."

Keen glanced between them, disgusted. Whatever the extenuating circumstances, a young mother and her unborn baby had still been murdered.

"Connor was a member of a small-time extremist group calling itself the Justice for Animals Defense Alliance. It started out about nine years ago as a student protest group at a liberal arts college in High Point, North Carolina. Then, it was a relatively insignificant special-interest organization which restricted its activity in the United States to the usual volatile rhetoric and protest marches, staying within the limits of constitutional rights of free speech and assembly." Her tone suggested an underlying frustration with the confines of the law. "When such methods weren't achieving the desired effect, JADA started up a campaign of graffitiing cars, vandalizing houses, throwing paint on people wearing fur—the sort of thing we've seen from ALF or PETA."

"Animal Liberation Fr—" McCraig started to clarify.

"I know what they are," Keen interjected, his tone bland enough to leach it of any insolence.

McCraig smiled, unoffended, ignoring Ross's narrowed look.

"Over the past year, though," McCraig said, "animal rights attacks have begun escalating beyond vandalism into far more deadly campaigns; Brian Cass—the director of Huntington Life Sciences—was badly beaten with ax handles last month and left for dead. His marketing director, Andrew Gay, had acid sprayed in his face and was blinded, right in front of his wife and little daughter." He shrugged. "Up to now, that was a British problem."

"While *we* considered JADA solely an American problem," Ross continued. "They operated like many amateur groups, a loosely structured collection of mostly leaderless underground cells, idealistic college students rather than any hard-core activists, more of a nuisance than a threat. Then about three years ago, that all changed. They went professional."

"Professional." It was a question, but Keen kept his tone flat, not liking where this was heading.

"Very much so. Someone came in and did a systematic restructure. The idealists were eliminated—along with any agents we had on the inside. Most of them were simply expelled; they didn't know enough to be any danger to the group. But a couple of FBI undercover agents were found dead when their car drove off the side of a cliff."

Ross shrugged and smiled grimly. "Winter, ice on the road. Ruled accidental, couldn't prove a thing. What was left tightened up into small cells run with military precision. They coordinate attacks with their cells through e-mails, coded text messages on disposable cell phones. They mostly employ strike-and-run tactics, and prefer property destruction or intimidation of their targets, regardless of any danger to innocent bystanders. Members of different cells never meet any others, except for training exercises. Everyone has aliases, no one knows anyone else's real name outside their own cell, and their actions have all the hallmarks of military training—bombs, guns, operations. The problem with these terrorist groups is that if one cell is compromised, you get maybe half a dozen suspects, but no one knows enough about any other cell to make any viable connections. We know there is at least one person, possibly two, pulling the strings, but we've never been able to identify any of the top leaders.

"Then we arrested Eunice Connor during one of their raids on a mink farm in Wisconsin six months ago. She and two of her companions were bitten by mink, and since the animals had been released and couldn't be retrieved to be tested, they had to be treated for possible rabies." Ross smiled, for the first time. It did nothing to warm her eyes. "Long needles, injections directly into the abdomen. Very painful."

"Connor's longtime lover is a particularly vicious activist named Lyle Harmond," McCraig continued, taking up the account.

He opened the file on the desk and slid a photograph across the desk toward Keen. He glanced at it, the man in the picture glowering with resentment and arrogance, dark hair shaved nearly bald, a gold ring in one nostril, and a teardrop tattoo at the outer edge of his left eye.

"He's an ex-squaddie, lasted eight months in the army before being kicked out after one too many drunken bar fights, broke a beer bottle on the face of a major in the Royal Marines. Went back to the East End as an enforcer for a dodgy nightclub and casino owner, then met Connor, and found his true calling in life: saving wee helpless lab rats. He's wanted in connection with the bombing of a biotech company in Preston with links to the animal-testing firm Huntingdon Life Sciences. JADA is suspected of having committed more than two hundred criminal acts worldwide. The Preston bombing was their first actual murder."

"*First* murder," Keen repeated.

"Three people—a security guard and two cleaners working late—were tied up and gagged and intentionally left to die in the explosion. Connor knew the security guard was their inside man." McCraig shook his head wryly. "He had huge gambling debts and expected JADA would give him enough to pay off his creditors. Technically they did; his widow benefited from his life insurance. Since then, JADA has been linked to the murder of more than twenty people in the last two years. Connor was willing to testify against Harmond for murder, and assist the police in apprehending him in return for a deal to drop charges against her as an accessory after the fact."

Keen let out a snort of incredulity. "And you think *he* killed her? The father of her children?"

"The autopsy determined that Harmond wasn't likely to have fathered her latest baby." Ross exchanged a glance with McCraig, the corner of her mouth again twisting with a dry smile. "Who-ever did, he was black." Her smile melted away as quickly as it had appeared. "Even if he had been the father of Connor's child, if it meant killing his pregnant lover to silence her and protect JADA, he wouldn't have given it a second thought. He's a cold-blooded, vicious killer and fanatically loyal to the cause. Harmond provides JADA with not just muscle but internal discipline. Step out of line, you're dead. So, yes, we suspect he's the one who may have carried out this attack."

"Okay," Keen said, eyeing Davis again. His chief inspector gazed back placidly, a hint of a smile at the corner of his mouth. "All very interesting. So what does any of this have to do with me?"

"Three weeks ago, there was another bombing," McCraig said. "This time up in Northumberland. Animal rights people broke into a small rabbit-breeding facility, released the animals and bombed the offices. No one was killed." Ross shot him a look. "In the explo-sion," he amended.

"Harmond?"

"Not likely. Harmond is a diehard Londoner, never been spot-ted that far north. But this time the bombers were observed by a young man who'd been parked up at the far end of the car park. He's the son of a local veterinarian, been running his own one-man cat-and-dog-neutering campaign out the back of his van. He's a sort of local mysterious celebrity, the papers labeled him the Rogue Vet."

That rang a bell, which didn't quite register until Davis clarified it with the police's own internal slang. "The goolie gonger." At Ross's look of incomprehension, Davis added blithely, "As in 'ging gang gooly gooly watcha, ging gang goo.'" The woman blinked, mystified.

Keen's effort to suppress his grin was made easier as McCraig said, "Yes, well. He's in a coma, not expected to live."

"He was assaulted?"

"Not exactly. He was roughed up, but that's not why he's in hospital." McCraig fished his pipe out of his pocket, more to have something in his hand to fidget with; the station was a no-smoking zone. "The rabbit breeder has experienced problems with animal rights protesters in the past. They've threatened his family, his employees. Bricks through the window of his house, set fire to his barn, cut the brakes on his wife's car, stalked his kids. It's standard operating procedure for these bastards, trying to drive animal suppliers out of business." McCraig shrugged. "The farm then found itself in the middle of the foot-and-mouth outbreak. So last month, our harassed breeder publicly announced he was going out of business, MAFF came in and slaughtered his remaining stock in a precautionary cull, and the animal rights people celebrated their 'victory.'" McCraig's voice was heavy with the irony.

Keen's eyes narrowed suspiciously. "'Remaining'?"

"This was a just small breeding farm that chiefly supplied cute fluffy bunnies to pet shops; they're the ones culled. But the breeder also raised very expensive specialty lines of genetically modified rabbits for medical research—pure New Zealand Whites, Watanabe, and St. Thomas, a few special hybrids." His smile was twisted. "Since these particular rabbits had been paid for by a government grant, they were considered far too valuable to destroy on the remote possibility that *maybe* they'd been exposed to the virus. So they were moved to a temporary situation, a small lab tucked away inside an unused warehouse in Northumberland. No one but the breeder, four of his longtime employees, and three researchers with University of Newcastle even knew the animals were there."

"What were the researchers doing with them?" Keen asked.

McCraig shared a quick glance with Ross before he leaned back and exhaled slowly. "You ever hear of MRSA?"

Keen shrugged his ignorance. "Another animal rights group?"

"No. It's an acronym for methicillin-resistant *Staphylococcus aureus*, more commonly known as a superbug. There's a number of staphylococcus bacteria which are resistant to conventional antibiotics. There's some evidence that certain essential oils commonly used in aromatherapy are effective in treating infections."

Keen stared at McCraig for a long moment. "Aromatherapy?" he said, trying to keep the incredulity out of his tone, and failing.

"The research was aimed at developing a type of soap and

shampoo to be used in NHS hospitals for patients with weakened immune systems. They'd infect the test rabbit with various strains of superbug, then cure it with a rinse and a set." McCraig chuckled wryly, as if he couldn't quite believe the absurdity himself. "Apparently, it does work."

"But not for our witness," Keen guessed.

"He handled one of the infected rabbits. We're not sure which one, since none of the test rabbits have been recovered."

"Hold on," Keen said with sudden comprehension. "Just how many of these rabbits you got out there running loose?"

McCraig grimaced. "A few dozen. We've managed to recover a couple of the control animals, they're all perfectly healthy. I'm told by the researchers that the infected animals can't survive longer than a couple weeks, max. By now most of them are likely dead. We've got people looking for them, dead or alive, but there's a problem: They're inside a blue box area for foot-and-mouth. With all the culling going on, a few sick bunnies aren't high on anyone's list of priorities." McCraig glanced at Davis. "And creating a possible public panic when it may not come to anything is best avoided, at such a particularly sensitive time."

"Jesus," Keen breathed with disgust.

"But before our witness's condition worsened, we took a statement from him. He got a name, 'Rory,' nasty piece of work, seems he was the leader of that little group. Other than a name, we have no idea who he might be. But our witness thought he recognized one of the bombers."

McCraig slid another photograph of a young woman paperclipped to a sheaf of arrest reports across the desk toward Keen.

"Beryl Rafferty," McCraig said. "Twenty-four, unmarried. Comes from a well-to-do family; father is a commercial property developer, spends most of his time in Hong Kong. Mother is a solicitor, specializes in civil litigation. Parents divorced when she was ten, mother and daughter moved into their country house in the Dales. Beryl has two older brothers, Byron and Brandon. Brandon is a gynecologist, private practice, married, lives in Kent. Byron works in the City as a corporate investment analyst. Not married, bit of a mummy's boy, apparently. Possibly gay, who knows?"

Who cares? Keen thought, but kept it to himself.

"Beryl, on the other hand, was the wild child, rebellious, always in trouble. Family has pretty much disowned her. A regular with the hunt saboteurs since she was fourteen; her main function with the antis has been as a sort of media specialist, fancies herself as a documentary maker. But she had several arrests for blowing hunting horns to draw the hounds out onto busy roads, smashing windows and slashing tires on cars belonging to the hunt followers, shooting at horses with BB pellet guns to try and spook them so they throw the riders. The usual nuisance. Because of her age, there wasn't much anyone could do. Once she turned eighteen, though, she promptly went 'legal,' no arrests. Pays to have a lawyer in the family—she knows the law. What with foot-and-mouth effectively shutting down hunts all over the country, she may be lending herself out to the more radical animal rights groups."

As McCraig spoke, Keen scanned the reports, flipping through the pages. "Including JADA?"

"Not that we've been previously aware of. But forensics determined this wasn't the usual makeshift petrol bomb; it was a sophisticated high-order explosive device, small but powerful enough to pulverize everything in a twenty-meter radius and burn the building down. Trace evidence says it was military, and we're certain the timing devices were part of a supply stolen last year from the Catterick Army Base."

"Anything to connect that to JADA?"

McCraig shrugged. "It's their style."

Which wasn't an answer, Keen knew. "She's not your bomber."

"No. She's just their media consultant. According to the witness, he's almost a hundred percent certain he recognized her."

"Almost." Which Keen also knew was code for "utterly unreliable evidence."

McCraig raised an eyebrow and shrugged, confirming it. "He's a hundred percent certain Rafferty works part-time in a pub in

Corbridge, where he occasionally drinks." He chuckled. "Guess making videos for hunt saboteurs doesn't pay the bills."

"Unfortunately for us, though, she's got an alibi for the time," Davis put in, earning himself a glare from the American, which he ignored. "Stayed with a mate after her car was booted for illegal parking at a club in Gateshead, where they'd been dancing with enough friends to corroborate her story,"

McCraig shrugged. "Not airtight, most of the friends were pissed as stoats, and several of those statements conflict seriously enough to merit closer scrutiny. But it's probably good enough to stand up in a court."

Keen studied him distrustfully. "Not to keep repeating myself," he said, "but again—what does this have to do with me?"

"Seems we're in luck; Rafferty went to high school with a woman named Rachel Colver, who is now a PC working in the west of the county, little station called Sandford. You know it?"

"Not offhand."

McCraig slid the last of his photographs toward Keen, this one of a young woman smiling brightly at the camera, painfully young in her uniform and cap. "It's not a big station," McCraig commented. "Very rural, in the Dales, not too far outside Skipton."

"That's North Yorkshire," Keen pointed out dryly.

McCraig shrugged. Yorkshire was Yorkshire, as far as he was concerned, Keen knew. "In any case, Colver and Rafferty knew each other. Smoked fags together in the girls' loo, drank Scrumpy Jack behind the local youth club, the usual teenage bonding rituals. Colver hasn't seen Rafferty since school leaving, so Rafferty might not know she's a cop. Our young PC is just finishing up a crash course in undercover work down in London."

"Good luck to her, then."

"She'll need a handler."

Keen simply stared at him for a long moment, the silence palpable. He glanced at Davis, who looked back blandly. The Yank simply watched, aware of an undercurrent but not its significance. Finally, Keen said, "You have *got* to be joking."

"Pete, I thought you said this guy was—" the Yank started.

"He *is*," McCraig cut her off. "Graeme, if you don't mind, I'd prefer having a private chat with the sergeant."

Keen would have rather he didn't, but didn't protest as Davis stood up leisurely, rolling his chair back. "Ms. Ross? Why don't I give you the grand tour of our little establishment?"

The American's mouth thinned into an aggrieved line and she exhaled unhappily through her nose, but followed. Once the door had shut behind them, Keen said, "Thanks anyway, but I'll pass."

"I don't think you quite understand the situation," McCraig said amiably, smiling although his eyes didn't match the expression. "It's not like I'm giving you the option."

At that, the anger that lay perpetually coiled dormant in Keen's gut stirred. "I don't work for you," he said. "And the last time I did, I ended up on suspension with a discipline complaint."

"Which didn't stick," McCraig pointed out. "I made sure of that. I've told you before—like it or not, I'm your guardian angel."

Keen smiled tightly, more in resentment than humor. "Right. Let's just make this clear; I don't owe you a damned thing. And whatever this is really about, I want *nothing* to do with it. Or you."

"Which is exactly why I want you. You don't take things at face value." McCraig shot a glance at the door, a gesture meant to indicate the American agent. "The Yanks are only involved because one of their marshals got shot."

"So what's Rafferty's connection to Harmond?"

"As far as we can tell . . . there isn't one."

Keen pinched the bridge of his nose, rubbing at his persistent headache and fighting losing his temper along with his patience. "Then what the hell do you need me for?"

"Our FBI lady here may act like she's Jodie Foster after Hannibal Lecter, but in reality, Ross is well down the pecking order. The big boys are all busy chasing JADA, Harmond, and whoever killed the marshal. This bombing up in Northumberland is most likely unrelated, but she wants to make her mark, willing to grasp at straws. Meanwhile, we've had a quiet, ongoing countrywide investigation for a couple years now—it's a big net, lots of fishermen, we're after lots of fish, all sizes. Rafferty may be a minnow in the bigger scheme of things, but she's a minnow who likes to swim with sharks. So we get two officers for Rafferty. That's it." McCraig held up his fingers for emphasis. "*Two*. One of them a green WPC whose luck has landed her in the shit, except she doesn't realize it yet. She's in desperate need of a guardian angel of her own, and while I know you don't give a damn about sucking up to the bosses, I know you *do* care about our toddlers out on the sharp end."

"No," Keen said, not to deny McCraig's assessment but in resistance. "You've got a lot of other officers with far more experience than I have, you don't need me."

"Well, if it makes you feel any better, you weren't my first choice. You weren't even on the short list. But after the marshal was killed, the Yanks stuck their oar in and tied up my first-line guys with other teams. I was starting to worry about who I'd put on with the girl when, lo and behold, what do I see in the morning reports but that our own DS Dunliffe has nicked himself a gunrunner, all on his lonesome. I'd almost forgotten about you up until that moment."

His previous vow never to buy petrol at the Otley Road Esso deepened.

"Anyone else would have done the same," Keen said flatly.

"No doubt. But I see you've also been doing a lot of animal welfare work, wildlife protection, that sort of thing. Fits in well with your experience." When Keen didn't answer, McCraig fiddled with his pipe, chipping at the edge of the bowl with his thumbnail. "From where I stand, you don't seem that happy with your current situation."

"I have no complaints."

"You're too good an officer to tread water until retirement." McCraig's sham humor had vanished. "And this time the offer comes with a reward. Sandford station is losing its acting commander end of the year, retiring. Do the job, and it's yours. With the promotion to inspector to match."

Keen tried to hide his reaction, unaware up until that moment how desperately unhappy he'd become being Mullard's obliging whipping boy, how far he'd suppressed any ambition of his own.

"A rural station, out in the tooliewamps?" Keen retorted. "Nice and quiet. Sounds like I'd still be treading water."

McCraig shrugged. "At least you'd own the pond. Or . . . the tooliewamps." One of Jillie's odd American words had sneaked into Keen's vocabulary, and sounded ridiculous coming out of McCraig's mouth. "Look, Sergeant. You and I both know Rafferty is more of a nuisance who keeps bad company rather than any real radical threat. Colver's drawn the short straw only because she has an in. But she's young, she needs looking after; keep her occupied and out of harm's way. Basic surveillance is all we need on this one, just until we nick Harmond. Then Home Office will be happy, the Yanks will be happy, I'll be happy. And you'll be happy."

Keen hated himself at that moment, mostly because he was tempted. "Last time I did a job for you, didn't all work out quite so rosy and neat."

"The difference is, last time you did a job for me, you volunteered. This time I'm asking. Nicely."

Keen felt the muscles in his jaw working. After a moment, McCraig said far too casually, "How is Dr. Waltham doing these days, by the way?"

"What?"

McCraig raised an eyebrow. "I'd heard you'd spent your holidays in Oregon last year; I assume you were visiting your girlfriend."

He didn't bother to protest she wasn't his girlfriend. "How do you know that?"

McCraig feigned innocence. "I tend to hear things in my position. For example, I hear Dr. Waltham is flying into London in a couple weeks, planning to spend the summer on some sort of archaeological project up in Northumberland. Be convenient for you, if you're on a job in the area. That's where you'd be going. Neither you nor PC Colver are known in the area, and you've got training and impartiality on your side to balance out her inexperience; you'll make a decent team. True, I can't force you to accept the assignment, but should you decide not to volunteer, I rather suspect Dr. Waltham might have a bit of a problem getting through Passport Control when she arrives in Heathrow."

"You can't—" Keen started to retort hotly.

"Oh, but I can. She has a criminal conviction."

"For student protests when she was eighteen!"

McCraig shrugged. "It's still a criminal conviction. It's up to the discretion of Home Office whether or not to refuse her entry." He frowned at his pipe and put it back into his jacket pocket. "You see, Mr. Dunliffe, I prefer to, but I don't necessarily *have* to ask nicely to get what I want."

Keen didn't answer, but McCraig seemed content to wait patiently while he stewed. To be honest, Keen thought, he hadn't been happy here for a long time. A change might be refreshing, what with a promotion and being in charge of his own station. He just didn't like it all being so thoroughly, and obviously, beyond his control.

"Sandford," he said finally. "And you make sure Jillie gets her visa, no pissing her about." When McCraig nodded, he added, "And when this is over, I never see or hear from you again, *ever*. This is it, we're done."

McCraig grinned. "Deal."

5

In a sprawling Victorian house at the far end of the village that had served as the Sandford Police Station since the First World War, Sergeant Maurice LaRue got a 999 emergency call from the distraught ex-wife of one Stuart Bellamy, who had apparently barricaded himself into his mum's cottage on the high street, where he'd been living for the past year and a half since his divorce. His mum, thrice-married Jayne Bellamy Nilsen Grey, a shriveled stick of a woman known as Lady Jayne to her regulars, owned the pub on the opposite side of the street. Sergeant LaRue could hear children crying and the clink of pint glasses and harsh laughter and Lady Jayne grumbling in the background as Sheila Bellamy sobbed down the phone.

"He's gone mad, 'e has, completely mad!"

"If'n 'e's gone mad," Lady Jayne snarled, "it's you driven 'im t'it."

"Shut up, just *shut up,* you miserable old cow!"

A chorus of cheers and jeers on the other end of the line threatened to drown out Sheila's voice altogether. "Sheila," LaRue was shouting into the phone himself. "Calm down. Just tell me what's going on . . ."

LaRue listened to an incoherent litany of complaints, accusations, insults, grievances, and the usual general bleating of domestic discontent, paying only half attention to the details until the word "gas" was mentioned.

"He's *what?*"

"He's turned on all the gas in the house, says he's goin' ta blow himself up, and the house with him!"

At the same time, some thirty-seven miles away, at the edge of the county, Rachel Colver sat in the passenger side of a patrol car with her partner, Sid the Yid. They were parked up along the end of a country lane to prevent any possible press or demonstrators from interfering while a pair of blundering MAFF officials chased ewes and lambs around a muddy paddock already littered with dead carcasses. The only so-called protester was the farmer's wife who stood outside the paddock with a videocamera, resolutely recording the cull and pausing only to wipe away her tears. One of the officials had been butted hard in the face by a fat Romney ewe trying to protect her twin lambs. He sat splay-legged in the mud, blood pouring from his nose, while his partner jammed the killing bolt rifle against the angry ewe's skull and pulled the trigger. She went down and lay twitching as the bloodied man staggered to his feet and gave the dying animal a vicious kick in revenge, her two terrified lambs skittering away. Rachel averted her gaze, her stomach clenched in a hard knot.

Sid the Yid wasn't watching; he was absorbed in catching up with his paperwork. He signed off on a file with a flourish and tossed it into a cardboard box on the back seat. "Another one down," he said blithely, "only two million more to go."

Rachel squinted at him, unsure if he was making some sort of macabre joke. She was spared from having to make any reply by the crackle of her personal radio, in unison with that in the dash of the car.

"Three-zero, can you make the Queen's Head pub Sandford High Street. Report of a disturbance, possible domestic assault at Lady Jayne's cottage. Stu Bellamy's apparently gone off his rocker, threatening suicide."

"Three-zero," she said into the radio clipped to the shoulder of her uniform. "Has he got any firearms?"

"Negative," she heard LaRue's phlegmatic voice drawl. "Just a cigarette lighter. Quick as you can, please."

"Three-zero, understood," Rachel said crisply, although she didn't really understand. "On our way."

Sid the Yid flipped on blue lights and sirens as they blasted through a mostly deserted countryside, little traffic this end of the

Dales. Even with thirty-seven miles to go, they were still first on the scene after Morry LaRue and the part-time hobby-bobby, nineteen-year-old Special Constable Ansell Ridley. LaRue had used a patrol car parked crossways to block the narrow road, and his own private car farther along as a traffic barricade. He'd given Annie the unenviable task of trying to keep the punters at the Queen's Head back from the road.

The village of Sandford wasn't much more than a loosely knit clot of rather dreary eighteenth-century stone buildings along the crossroads of a single-lane B road and an unmarked and barely paved single lane, all leading to nowhere in particular. Sandford's only saving grace was that it was the first village on that particular road leading into the Dales, the gateway for city tourists looking for the fairy-tale thatched-roof-and-cottage-garden chocolate-box version of England that had been extinct for decades. In the summer, Lady Jayne would bedeck the Queen's Head—the biggest building along the road—with huge hanging baskets and oversized planters of petunias and nemesia and geraniums and impatiens and lobelia and trailing ivy, as if that could somehow disguise the astonishing ordinariness of the village. It was always a contest between her pub and Lester Bird's antique shop, Annabelle Zeeman's souvenir gifts and teashop, and Lady Jayne's fiercest rival, Elliot Hildebrandt's bed-and-breakfast. The only building along the road that didn't look like an Easter Day flower parade float was a converted Victorian manor that now housed the Sandford Police Station. Even then, there would be the inevitable thick tourists who would stop and ask, sometimes in incomprehensible foreign accents, for a room with double bed and en suite, oblivious to the POLICE sign over the door or the men and women at the desk wearing uniforms.

Struggling for trade even at the best of times, Sandford had been exceptionally hard hit with the absence of tourism in the face of foot-and-mouth. So the chance of some entertainment in the offing meant getting the pints in and finding a spot that wasn't too wet to sit on at the tables outside the pub and watch the show.

Sid the Yid pulled up on the far side of the patrol car, cutting the siren but leaving the blue lights flashing as he and Rachel got out.

"What's up, boss?" Sid the Yid asked LaRue, scanning the smattering of broken glass and shattered bits of wooden window frame in the road, the remains of an old tellie now in bits, videos with unspooled ribbons of tape fluttering on the breeze. LaRue had the boot of the patrol car open and handed Rachel and Sid the Yid their riot gear. As Rachel shrugged into her fireproof overalls, shinpads, armguards, and protective vest, LaRue gave an abridged synopsis of the situation.

"Stu's four months behind on his child maintenance. Sheila got the hump, refused to let him see his kids till he pays up."

"And that's why he's gonna top himself?" Sid the Yid smeared a few drops of Fairy washing-up liquid over the inside polycarb visor of his helmet, then handed the bottle to Rachel. "Seems a bit extreme, dunnit?"

"He's been on a bender for three days, probably seems logical to him at the moment." LaRue nodded at the cottage. "It's a one-room flat, only one entry, exit, flight of stairs back side of the cottage."

"No access from his mum's?" Rachel asked, her fingers sticky from washing-up liquid. The Fairy soap would keep the visor from fogging up with her breath once she had it on over her face.

"Nope. Blocked off years ago, turned the upstairs into a rental flat."

From the second story of the cottage, Rachel could hear Stu shouting, his voice hoarse over the noise of a stereo cranked up full volume and blasting out Metallica and feedback squeal.

"Leave me alone! Come anywhere near me and I'll blow us all to hell!"

Sid the Yid sniffed the air, his nose wrinkling doubtfully. "Hmmm." Rachel caught the whiff a moment later—the unmistakable odor of gas. "We're not in any hurry to be breaking down doors here, are we, Sarge?"

"TRANSCO man's been called. He's on his way. Another fifteen minutes out."

"Well," Sid said, eyeing the upstairs windows. "Glass busted out—let's hope the gas can escape before Stu asphyxiates himself."

"In the meantime, why don't you two give Annie a hand convincing people they'd be a lot safer inside the pub, just in case?"

The young hobby-bobby's acne-spotted face was red with frustration, no one paying him any mind as he struggled to assert his authority. "Don't make no difference what I tell 'em," Annie complained bitterly, "they just won't go in."

"Uh-huh," Sid the Yid replied, not even looking at the boy. "Hey, gorgeous," he said to Lady Jayne. "You're gonna have to get all these folks inside, or we'll shut the pub, send 'em on home. And you might want to put out the fag, pet."

Lady Jayne sucked the last few centimeters off her cigarette before grinding out the butt under the toe of a stiletto shoe. Her face resembled old leather, tanned to deep ochre by too many holidays in Spain, wrinkles etched into her skin as if carved out by a chisel. She squinted through the haze of exhaled smoke and pushed a lifeless strand of bleached blond hair from her forehead.

"Right, you lot. *In,*" she growled, her voice as deep as a bullfrog's.

Meekly, the regulars picked up their pints and trooped into the pub without a grumble.

"And keep 'em away from the windows!" Sid the Yid shouted after her as she followed her customers inside.

"I could have done that?" Annie asked with awe at his tone. "Shut the pub?"

"No," Sid the Yid said laconically. "But I can."

From the upstairs window, Stu began heaving plates and bowls and coffee mugs like missiles from the window, all of them falling short. From the splattered remains of tea bags and cereal splashing out onto the pavement as well, he must have been emptying the kitchen sink of the washing up.

They were still waiting for the TRANSCO man when two more officers arrived, sirens and blue lights. They jumped out of the car, already half dressed in their riot gear, and hurried over. Their urgency diminished as LaRue briefly explained the situation.

"Hurrah, we're saved," Sid the Yid murmured scathingly under his breath to Rachel. "Our fearless leader has arrived."

Rachel tried not to grin in response as the station's command-ing officer, Inspector Bertie Trumble, strolled over, hands in his pockets, and squinted up as Stu flung the wreckage of what were once kitchen chairs at him, the pieces missing their target by several meters.

"TRANSCO man got lost," he said to LaRue without preamble. "Be another ten, fifteen minutes. Hopefully."

They watched as Stu continued chucking the remains of his furniture out the window, the pile of debris in the road growing. Metallica gave way to Iron Maiden.

"I wish he'd throw that fucking stereo out the window," LaRue groused.

"You kidding?" Sid the Yid said. "That's classic stuff, y'know. Takes me back to my carefree youth."

"Classic, my arse. Bloody headbanger crap."

The TRANSCO worker finally arrived, spending a few minutes looking for a parking space before the inspector walked over and had him park his van in the middle of the street. The gasman got out, hoisting his ponderous body out of the cab, every seam of his extra-large blue overalls stretched to their limit.

"Oh, joy. This is going to be fun," Sid the Yid said to Rachel. She shot a wan smile back at him.

The TRANSCO man inspected the cottage from a distance. "Right," he said. "What I have to do is cut the gas riser pipe, that thing under the window there, see, and stuff a bung in it. Then there'll be no more gas going up into the flat." He watched as a Dyson hoover wiggled its way out the window and smashed on the ground below in a gray cloud of carpet dust. "Just out of curiosity, how do you propose I get to the riser?"

"Not a problem," LaRue said with far more confidence than Rachel suspected he felt. "Three of us are going to make like a roof with the shields, we all walk under this roof until we reach the wall, you cut the pipe, we're done, back out again, and Bob's your uncle. All you got to do is just stay under the shields and you'll be fine, got it?"

The TRANSCO man looked doubtful. "Got it."

LaRue and Sid the Yid formed the front of the roof, holding the five-and-a-half-foot shields over their heads with the fat TRANSCO man sandwiched between them. Rachel held her shield sideways above her, her other hand on the gasman's back to keep the formation steady.

"Ready? Slowly does it, keep it together . . ."

They scuttled across the road like an ungainly turtle. As they reached the pavement on the other side of the road, Stu began hurling objects onto the shields. More cups and plates banged overhead, followed by a metal rain of silverware, dumped out of the drawer, followed by the drawer. It banged off the polycarbonate shields ineffectually, but it was obviously unnerving the TRANSCO man.

"Oh shit, oh shit, oh shit . . ." he murmured, balking.

"You're okay, we're doing fine," Rachel offered, and pushed against his ample rear to keep him going.

They reached the cottage and braced the shield roof against the wall while the gasman began to frantically hacksaw his way through the riser.

Rachel inhaled sharply as water began running off the shields, boiling hot as it trickled onto her backside. She winced as the kettle followed, bouncing off the shields. Behind her, she could hear the crowd from the pub cheering, and a few drink-roughed voices chanting, "Stu! Stu! Stu!"

"How's it coming?" she asked, unable to see around the fat TRANSCO man.

"He's about halfway there, nearly done . . ." Sid the Yid said over his shoulder.

The crowd's cheering intensified, alerting Rachel. She looked up through the shield to see something large and white and square teetering over the edge of the window frame. Just as she realized what it was, it began to drop.

"Tilt it, tilt it, tilt it!" Rachel yelled, pulling on the TRANSCO man's overalls. LaRue and Sid the Yid reacted automatically, raising their end of the shield roof without questioning why.

"Missile above!" the inspector belatedly called out from where he stood, safe and sound, on the far side of the road. "Brace yourselves!"

Several pounds of microwave hurtled down onto fourteen-millimeter-thick polycarb shields. The angle of the shields deflected the impact, and the microwave slid off onto the pavement. All the same, it hurt, the blow jarring her arm all the way to the bone.

"Gee, thanks, Inspector, don't know what we'd do without you," one of the men in front of Rachel grumbled under his breath.

The TRANSCO man had gone to his knees, his breath sobbing in his throat with fear and exertion as he cut through the last of the pipe. He dropped the saw, jammed the bung in the raw-edged gap, and started scuttling backward on his hands and knees.

"Hey, hold on!" Sid the Yid protested. "Easy there, big fella. Keep together now, and we'll back off this wall—"

"Sod that," the frightened gasman wheezed, and scrambled out from under the cover of the shields. "I'm off!"

Rachel made a futile stab at grabbing at him, fingers catching only a handful of overall fabric before the gasman pulled away. He stood up, turned, and promptly tripped over the microwave, landing facedown in the road. The crowd roared with laughter. He pushed himself up on his arms just far enough for a glass milk bottle hurled out of the window to collide with the back of his head. The milk bottle exploded, spraying its contents—not milk, but rather a pint of rancid piss. This time, the gasman's eyes rolled up into the back of his head and he collapsed, knocked out cold.

"Oh, fer fuck sake," Sid the Yid muttered darkly.

Two more makeshift urinal bottles smashed down on the shields as they slowly retreated backward, awkwardly stepping over the microwave and covering the unconscious gasman. Rachel held his legs up by both his trouser hems with one hand while LaRue and Sid the Yid each grabbed him under the arm. He was still heavy, even for three, and his belly dragged across the paving as they pulled him away and out of range. He groaned as they dropped him, rolling onto his back, his hair slick with blood and urine.

The inspector crouched beside the fat gasman. "You okay?" he asked, and waved his hand in front of the man's eyes. "How many fingers am I holding up?"

"Fuck off," the gasman mumbled.

"Close enough." The inspector glanced up. "Would you lot get the bosher, knock his door down, and drag that bastard out of there now, please?"

The two belated cops had finished donning their riot gear and hoisted the battering ram by the handles between them. Still winded, Rachel and Sid the Yid followed behind, their sergeant taking up the rear, as they crowded up the narrow stairway to Stu's front door.

The battering ram swung in an arc between the two men and thudded into the door hard enough to splinter the wood. The latch and door handle popped out of their sockets, and one hinge ripped away from the frame. But the door didn't open. Using their shoulders and brute force, the two men at the top tried again, without success. Something on the other side toppled over and broke, with the tinkling musical sound of breaking glass.

"He's barricaded the door!" Sid the Yid's voice could barely be heard over the pounding heavy-metal music inside the flat.

Like a rugby scrum, all five—Rachel still with the job of pushing on men's rear ends—used their collective weight to shove back the motley assembly of drawers, armoires, bookcases, armchairs, and settee and anything else Stu had in the flat that he could pile up behind the front door.

"One, two, three, *go!*" They pushed the barricade back a few more inches. Slats from a bedframe had been braced against the door panels, and one cracked with a sound like a gunshot under the strain. "Again! One, two, three, *go!*" This time they made enough room to clamber over the jumble of furniture and into the living room.

LaRue promptly kicked the stereo, as if he was Rio Ferdinand aiming for the back of the net, the silver and black machine exploding with the force of his punt. The sudden silence was nearly as deafening as the music had been. Rachel's ears seemed to hiss in the quiet. But Stu was nowhere to be seen. The door to the kitchen was closed, but when LaRue tried the handle, it was unlocked but didn't move.

"Bloody hell, he's got this one blocked as well."

This door, however, opened out—simply knocking it off the

hinges wasn't going to work. Nor was it a cheap hollowfill door, either. It took a good ten minutes of battering the heavy Victorian wood door with the bosher before it splintered into enough pieces to be removed, one by one. Behind that, however, was a large refrigerator wedged into the space.

Outside, the crowd cheered again. LaRue looked out the window as something small and dark dropped from above to shatter on the pavement below. He glanced down, then twisted around to stick his head out just far enough to look up. "I don't believe it," he called out to the others. "He's up on the roof now!" He ducked back inside as another dark object tumbled past the window. "He's chucking the roof tiles down!"

They tried to push the refrigerator back but, after several attempts had failed, decided to drag it through the doorway. Gripping onto any purchase they could find, they pulled. And again. And again. It gave an inch at a time, then jammed.

"Pull it down from the top," Sid the Yid suggested. This worked marginally better, although the door to the fridge opened to spill out its contents. A jar of Branston pickle broke as it hit the floor, along with loose potatoes, cans of lager, a carton of yogurt with a cap of blue fuzz, and several oily white cartons of half-eaten Chinese takeaway, making their footing even more difficult.

"Pull!"

They pulled.

"Pull!"

They pulled.

"Pull!" A bright shower of sparks shot up from behind the fridge, the electrical cord still plugged into the wall.

"Shit! Stop pulling!" They stopped pulling and hastily retreated to the other side of the room, glancing at each other nervously.

After a moment, LaRue said slowly. "Well, since we didn't all just blow ourselves into the next county, I guess we can assume the gas has dissipated."

Sid the Yid blew his breath out through puffed cheeks in relief, then eyed the refrigerator still stuck in the doorway. "Now what?"

Rachel undid the strap to her riot helmet and took it off. Her uniform clung to her skin with sweat and her muscles were twitching with fatigue. "Sarge? I think I can squeeze through there, if you give me a hand up."

Her first attempt was unsuccessful, her protective gear making her too bulky. As she began to strip off down to her shirtsleeves, LaRue said, "It's too risky—"

"Just keep him occupied, so's you know where he is," she said, undoing her utility belt.

Sid the Yid leaned out the window to look up. "Hey, Stu!" he shouted. "You're a bloody nancy, y'know that? You throw like a girl!"

"Fuck you!" came the predictable response, followed by a heavy barrage of more slate roof tiles. Sid the Yid laughed as he ducked back inside. "I think he's occupied."

Rachel stepped into LaRue's laced hands and grabbed onto the other side of the refrigerator to squirm through the tiny space, sliding ungracefully out the other side and landing on the floor on her hands and knees. She scrambled to unplug the cord from the powerpoint, and flipped the switch to OFF. "Okay! Clear!"

Now that it had been unplugged, the refrigerator took only a few more tries before it tumbled over, facedown, onto the living room floor. The four other officers climbed over it into the kitchen, where Rachel stood with her hands on her hips, head tilted, staring up through the square access panel into the loft above. The roof had been completely stripped of tiles, Stu silhouetted by sky as he sat on a naked joist above her, swinging his legs back and forth, wood creaking under his weight.

"Hi, Rachel," he said meekly.

"Hi, Stu. You about finished?" she asked. She squinted in the daylight, unable to make out his face with the light behind him.

"Yeah, I guess so. He said I throw like a girl," the man said sullenly, voice still slurred with drink.

Rachel shrugged. "So what? *I* throw like a girl." After a moment, she heard the man laugh quietly. She glanced at LaRue and covertly waved him back.

"Ever'body's well and truly cheesed off at me, aren't they?"

"Nothing that can't be worked out. It's over now. Come on down."

"You gonna arrest me?"

"Kinda have to. Nothing personal, it's just my job, y'know?"

"Do I gotta have handcuffs on?"

"Yeah, 'fraid you do. Tell you what, though—I'll do it, nobody else, deal?"

"Promise?"

She made a childhood gesture across her chest. "Cross my heart." She held out her hand as Sid the Yid passed her a pair of Quikcuffs. "See? Got 'em right here. In your own time, love."

After a long moment, Stu hauled himself off the joist and dropped down onto the crossbeams in the ceiling. Grabbing onto the ledge of the access opening, he levered himself out and landed on his feet in front of her. At well over six feet tall and seventeen stone, he towered over her like a penitent bear. He gazed down sadly and said, "Me mum's gonna kill me," before he turned and held his hands out behind him, fingers wriggling. The cuffs barely fit around his wrists as she pressed the ratchets into place.

Stu went quietly down the stairs, grinning sheepishly as the crowd now spilling out of his mother's pub cheered raucously. His grin quickly faded as Lady Jayne stepped out of the doorway to glower. He climbed into the back of the patrol car almost eagerly, more than happy to be getting away from his mother's wrath.

Sid the Yid helped Rachel pick up her discarded riot gear and followed her down the stairs to the street. Inspector Trumble waited for them. "Good job, all."

"Thanks, gov," the group murmured back in unison.

Rachel was knackered, every muscle in her body ached, but she still felt amazingly good, the adrenaline buzz not yet melted away.

"I'm putting you all in for a commendation for bravery, especially you, Rachel. I want to see you in my office when you get back to the station."

"Yes, sir. Thank you, sir."

They watched as he strolled away, heading back along the high street toward the station but stopping to shake hands with bystanders in the way politicians do, Rachel noticed, with both hands and a big smile.

"It was just Stu being bloody Stu," she said to Sid the Yid. "He doesn't need to go making a big deal out of it."

"Yup," Sid agreed, tossing the riot gear into the boot of the car. "All in a day's work." He slammed the boot shut. "Still, makes for a cracking story to impress the ladies with. Mind if I'm the hero this time, Rach?"

Lady Jayne stomped across the road. "Who the hell is going to clean up this mess?" she demanded.

Sid the Yid gazed around at the wreckage placidly before he smiled at her. "Your son. Your cottage," he said. "Your problem."

Back at the station, the usually quiet building now rang with overly loud laughter and conversation. "Good on ya, Rach!" Molly, the civilian dispatcher, called out as Rachel passed her tiny call room. She waved back cheerfully and headed to the inspector's office on the next floor, knocking on his open door for attention.

He was on the telephone to the press, she gathered by listening to only his end of the exchange, and gestured to her to take a seat. "No injuries to any of my officers, and the TRANSCO worker is being treated in hospital for a minor concussion." He paused to listen. "That's correct. T-R-U-M-B-L-E. Inspector. Right, see you then. Thank you very much. Goodbye." He put down the phone, laced his hands on his desk, and beamed at her. "Good job today."

"Thanks, gov."

"There's going to be a photographer out tomorrow from the papers." But as Rachel was wondering if she could get her formal uniform dry-cleaned in time, the inspector added, "I'm sorry to say, you can't be in it."

Startled, she said, "Why not?"

"I got the green light from Home Office this morning—you start your undercover job tomorrow." He raised his eyebrows at her. "It's what you just spent the last fortnight of training down in London for. You still want to do this, don't you?"

"Yes, sir, of course." She felt a pang of disappointment, then chastised herself. It was just Stu being bloody Stu, she reminded herself. No big deal. While this job *was.*

"Right, then. You can't be doing undercover with your face plastered all over the local rag, now can you? Home Office has assigned you a handler; he'll be here first thing in the morning. So be here eight sharpish, in civvies," the inspector said.

She stood. "Yes, sir."

"Oh, and Rach? Tell the rest of 'em to stop calling Shinkowicz 'Sid the Yid.'"

"But . . . *you* call him 'Sid the Yid,' everyone does. Even his mother calls him 'Sid the Yid.'"

The inspector grimaced. "Your handler, this Sergeant . . ." He shuffled through a file on his desk for the name. "Dunliffe. Keen Dunliffe. He's been handpicked by some higher-up in the London Met. We know nowt about him, other than after I retire, he's filling my shoes here. So until we know whether he's some Home Office flunky or a real cop, let's keep it neat and proper, all right?"

Pots and kettles, she thought, but said, "Yes, sir."

She spent the last half hour of her shift filling out the paperwork, then shrugged on her jacket and started the walk home. The air had chilled, and although the days were getting longer, the sky had already started to darken. She stopped at Claire Vale's house, ringing the bell, and heard Laddie whining with anticipation behind the door before it opened. As soon as Claire opened it, he bounded out and ran in eager rings around the front garden, overjoyed to see her.

"Has he been a good boy?" Rachel asked, as she always did.

"Of course," Claire said, and handed Rachel his lead. She stuffed it into her jacket pocket and pulled out a package of dog treats from the other. As soon as the dog heard the crinkle of plastic, he plopped his rear end down, tail whipping the grass. She fed him a treat, thanked the dogsitter as she handed her a tenner, and let him out the gate.

He was an odd-looking dog, with a white head that belonged to a Staffordshire bull terrier grafted onto the lean brindle body of a boxer, long legs bouncing like pogo sticks as they walked along the public bridle path. She threw the odd stick for him, smiling as he leaped through the fields to chase it, always losing it—distracted by a bird or a blown leaf. The euphoria of the day's excitement wore off almost as soon as they turned the corner of the tree line and Rachel's home came into view.

Well, Rachel thought sourly, not exactly "home." Cowsgill Bank Farm had never been prosperous, even when her father had run the place. Her grandfather had been the last real farmer, and by the time he'd died of cancer and drink, well before Rachel was even born, he'd lost interest in the place as well as life. The whole farm reeked of old manure and hopelessness. The farmhouse hadn't seen a new coat of paint in decades, the wooden window frames flaking away with rot, the roof developing a perceptible swaybacked slump. In the winter, it was bitterly cold, what little warmth the ancient woodstoves could radiate sucked out through the drafty cracks in every corner, even the ancient wallpaper shivering. The only stone barn had long ago tumbled into a roofless pile of rocks, while the wooden outbuildings had collapsed, leaving the rusting skeletons of metal supports behind. But the land was good, rolling green fields down to the distant boundary line of dark trees, still leafless, marking the oxbow bend in the river and the woodland copse where fox and badgers and the occasional roe deer made their homes. Although Rachel had lived there all her life, she never could quite think of the place as "home." It all belonged to Nana, Rachel allowed only on sufferance.

She couldn't afford to buy a house, not that there were many left in the Dales that hadn't been snatched up by London townies who used them for summer holiday homes and weekend retreats. And on a PC's salary, any hope of ever being able to move out of her grandmother's house into a flat of her own looked increasingly un-likely. She felt a twinge of guilt; the old woman had looked after Rachel since she was eleven, when Rachel's father had died and her mother had promptly remarried a man with five kids of his own, moving away to Canada and leaving her only child behind with her mother-in-law. Growing up under Nana's roof had been difficult enough, being the surrogate target of the old woman's blame for the loss of her son and hatred for the woman he'd married. Rachel had grown up unloved but not abused—at least not in any legal definition that would have mattered. It had only been in the past few years that Nana's health had worsened, and her temper with it.

Rachel let herself into the house by the back door, Laddie heading straight for his bowl by the dishwasher, nails clicking on the cracked vinyl tiles.

"Did you clean that filthy animal's feet first before you let him in?" Rachel heard her grandmother rasp from the front room.

"Yes, Nana."

She poured an old ice-cream container's worth of dry dog food into his bowl and scratched his ears as he munched through his meal enthusiastically.

"Heard on the radio there was a bit of bother in town."

"Just Stu Bellamy gone off the rails with too much drink, nothing serious."

Rachel put the kettle on and began making her grandmother's tea—always the same thing, day in and day out: half a dozen cold slices of processed turkey, instant mashed potatoes from a box and watery Bisto gravy, plain white bread with margarine, and an entire packet of digestive biscuits, all washed down with a large bottle of Diet Pepsi. Never any vegetables; the old woman refused to eat them, and no amount of coaxing from her granddaughter or stern warnings from her doctor would persuade her. Nor could they discourage her voracious sweet tooth, the old woman devouring a Cadbury Milk Tray of chocolates a day.

"I'm going to be away for a while," Rachel said loudly. "I've got the social arranged to come out on weekdays, and Mrs. Armstrong will look after you on the weekends."

"You know I can't stand that woman," her grandmother argued, as Rachel knew she would. "She steals things. You shouldn't be working in the police anyway. I want you to quit before something terrible happens to you."

Rachel knew the old woman didn't care if she was hurt or not; she just hated strangers in her house and resented losing her live-in slave.

"It's important, Nana. Temporary assignment—y'know, because of the foot-and-mouth. Everyone in the police has to help out, it's just my turn. I won't be gone too long, maybe a few weeks at most. I'll be back before you know it." She tried to make her voice sound regretful, but she was secretly relieved to be getting away from the tyrannical old woman.

Laddie made the mistake of peeking through the open doorway and was greeted by the old woman throwing her cane at him. Rachel winced as it clattered to the floor, and the dog skittled into the safety of his bed, head on his paws and ears down with fear.

"You're not leaving that damned animal here!" her grandmother yelled. "Dangerous bloody thing. Saw on the news the other day one of those pit bull dogs ate the face off an old man while he was asleep, ripped his throat out to drink the blood. I'm warning you, you should have that rotten beast put down before it hurts someone."

"He's not a pit bull and he's not dangerous," Rachel protested, but her voice sounded defeated even to herself. "And he'll be staying with Claire while I'm gone, you don't have to worry yourself about him."

Rachel set the food out onto a tray and took it through into the sitting room, stooping down to retrieve her grandmother's walking cane as she passed. Her grandmother sat in the overstuffed easy chair in front of the tellie, her bandaged legs propped up on a footstool, a two-bar electric heater glowing by her slipper-clad feet. The bandages needed changing, brown stains where the lesions had wept through the linen. The old woman was beyond morbidly obese, reminding Rachel of a termite queen, little head and arms attached to a huge body, fat sagging in rolls. She never moved from the chair except to go to the toilet and to bed. No amount of scolding would convince her that she needed exercise as well as a better diet, either, content to sit in the gloom with the curtains drawn and watch television from morning to night.

As Rachel set the tray down on the folding table by her grandmother's chair, she sniffed the stale air suspiciously, her heart sinking. "Oh, Nana, not again . . ."

"It's your fault," the old woman said testily. "You bought the

85

wrong Bisto. I've told you before, I can't handle anything with gar-
lic in it." Her grandmother picked up a slice of bread with yellow-
taloned claws and glared at her. "I'm hungry. And I want to watch
Blind Date. It can wait."

So Rachel retreated back into the kitchen and smiled at the dog
reassuringly. His tail thumped against the side of his wicker basket.

"Shut that bloody animal up!" her grandmother shouted.

Rachel sighed, her eyes smarting with frustration and guilt and
anger as she poured a can of Baxter's vegetable soup into a bowl to
heat in the microwave for her supper, while her grandmother sat in
her own diarrhea and ratcheted up the volume on the tellie.

6

Many thousands of miles away on another continent, Jillie Waltham sat at her kitchen table in her bathrobe, drinking coffee and steadily working through a pile of student essays. The sound of running water from upstairs turned off, and she listened to the squeak of old floorboards as footsteps crossed from the bathroom to her daughter's bedroom. It was the music of the morning, she thought; all the familiar noises as predictable as the chimes of the grandfather clock ticking away in the hall.

Fifteen minutes later, Karen came down the stairs, bleary-eyed, her skin still flushed pink from the heat of the shower, the ends of her dark, curling hair glittering with moisture. She had Jillie's wild hair and brown eyes, but her lean athletic build she owed to her father, as yet untouched by time or worry. She'd dressed in her bright green work uniform top but wore her usual scruffy jeans and running shoes. The photocopier shop was lax about dress codes, so close to a college campus and catering mostly to students who dressed even more casually. But, Jillie noticed, Karen had on her jade earrings this morning, as well as a touch of lipstick and mascara, a sure sign that someone had quickened her daughter's interest.

Karen poured her own cup of coffee and sat down with exaggerated heaviness in the chair on the opposite side of the table, slouching over the steaming drink. "Why are you up so early?" she demanded.

"I like getting up early."

"No one likes getting up *this* early." Karen took a slurp of coffee, then stretched and yawned hugely. She started as a newspaper hit the front door with a thump.

"Not that early," Jillie said without looking up. She made the last comment on the essay, signed her name, and added the student paper to her "finished" pile before picking up the next. "Seven twenty-five, on the dot. You can set your watch by Roddie Mildford."

"Roddie Milford is a creepy little twerp who lives in a bizarre Disneyland bubble world with his zombie parents who still think it's the nineteen-fifties," Karen groused, and shuddered dramatically. "People who smile that much should be locked up for their own good."

"You just don't like Roddie because he kept knocking over your AL GORE sign in the front yard."

"And lying about it. 'Gosh golly gee whiz, Mizz Waltham,'" Karen sang in a parody of a thirteen-year-old boy. "'Wasn't me, musta been a dog or the wind or the divine hand of the Lord God Almighty bringing His judgment down upon all you sinful heathens and liberal Democrats.' And what kind of sadistic parents name a child 'Nimrod,' anyway? Kid doesn't stand a chance of being normal."

Jillie looked up with a rueful smile. "What do I care? As long as the paper is delivered on time. Speaking of which . . . ?"

Karen made a face, then went to retrieve the paper from the front porch. It was a ritual between them, Karen always reading the front page news while Jillie took the local section. Every once in a while, each would read snippets to the other.

"Oregon schools are going to lose two hundred and eighty million a year as part of Bush's budget-cutting plan," Karen announced.

"Big surprise," Jillie retorted. "Sheriff Mark Frye is asking county commissioners to pass an ordinance to require every household to have a gun."

Karen looked up. "'Require'?"

"Mm-hm. Says he believes that will scare away criminals, like a BEWARE OF THE DOG sign on your gate." Jillie glanced up with a grin. "Thinks it will make us ladies feel safer. Aren't you so glad chivalry isn't dead?"

"Don't worry. If it isn't dead yet, someone will shoot it. You done with the comics?"

Jillie handed over the comics. "Not that funny today."

"I only want to read *The Far Side* and *Calvin and Hobbes,* anyway."

Jillie smiled to herself. She and her daughter shared so much of the same tastes that sometimes she felt more like a sister than a parent.

It had been hard, very hard, raising Karen on her own when Robert had walked out on them. At the time, she had felt like it was the end of her world, panicked with dread and resentment and anger. But somehow, to her astonishment, they'd survived, she and her daughter drawing strength from each other neither knew they'd possessed. Now, Jillie couldn't remember too clearly even being married any longer, Robert hazing into a series of unpleasant memories, like old holiday photographs long yellowed and left to molder in cast-off luggage at the back of a closet. *Speaking of which,* Jillie thought . . .

"Can I borrow your red carry-on suitcase?" Jillie said, draining the last of the coffee in her cup. "The lock is broken on my black one."

"Mom, you don't leave for another two weeks. You've got plenty of time to buy a new suitcase."

"Why buy one, when you've got a perfectly good set of luggage you're not using?"

Karen grinned wickedly. "Who says I'm going to be house-sitting here the whole summer?"

"I do," Jillie said. "Tuition isn't cheap, and your father is being his usual miserly self. You get *one* wild party while I'm gone, as long as you leave no incriminating evidence behind for when I get back. Otherwise, you go to work, you behave yourself, and you save your money for next semester. Got that?"

"Yeah, yeah," Karen said, unconcerned. But Jillie knew her daughter's desire to finish university was stronger than any irresponsible impulse to enjoy herself. Karen flipped over the last page and glanced at the clock on the kitchen wall before she got up to pour herself another coffee. "You want one?"

"Please."

As Karen set Jillie's cup back down in front of her, she picked up one of the student essays her mother had been grading. "The *theory* of twelfth-century kingship? How is being a king 'theoretical'? I would think you either are or you aren't. What's 'theoretical' about that?"

"It's about the mechanisms of control, different ways of analyzing systems of government; the exchequer, the chancery; and royal courts. This essay is on the loss of Normandy, and how that crisis triggered the Magna Carta."

Karen gave her a look as credulous as if Jillie had grown a third eye. "And how many students are you supervising?"

"Fourteen."

Karen scanned the postgraduate student's essay. "Jesus, this stuff is gibberish. All these guys are writing about the same thing?"

"Yup."

"Doesn't that get boring?"

"Yup." Jillie grinned. "But it pays the bills. Speaking of which, you'd better get going or you're going to be late for work."

Karen leaned over to pick an apple out of the fruit bowl in the middle of the table. "I've got plenty of time. Shop doesn't even open till nine anyway." She bit into the apple and lifted the first of a pile of books Jillie had half-hidden in the chair that was pushed under the table beside her.

"*Boudicca and the Revolt Against Rome.*" She read the title aloud, speaking around the fruit in her mouth, and glanced at the top in the pile. "*Bronze Figurines of Romano-British Military Communities.*" Jillie felt her face glowing with heat. "*The Erotic Art of Roman Britain*? And all of them by a certain Dr. Angus Sheridan." Karen grinned wickedly, snapping her fingers in a parody of faulty memory. "Hmm, Sheridan . . . Sheridan . . . Tall guy, dark hair, looks a bit like Jane Austen's Mr. Darcy after a bad couple of decades? You really have a thing for English guys, don't you?"

"There's nothing going on between Dr. Sheridan and me, our relationship is strictly professional. He's a colleague, that's all."

"Sure, Mom. You plan on introducing Keen to him when you're on this fantastic dig of his on Hadrian's Wall?"

"Keen's only got two weeks' vacation coming up in June, and I plan to spend it visiting him in Yorkshire. He's a very busy man, so I doubt he'll have much time to visit the excavation."

"That's a good idea. Best if you keep your boyfriends apart."

"Karen," Jillie said, more sharply than she intended. "Knock it off, you're not being funny. Keen and I are just friends, he isn't my 'boyfriend.' I'm a little too old to be having 'boyfriends,' don't you think?"

Karen swallowed her bite of apple and gazed back shrewdly. "Whatever." She glanced at her watch. "Speaking of boys who aren't friends, I'd better get going or Eric'll start wondering if I've run off with the photocopier repairman." She shrugged into her down jacket, snagged a banana from the bowl, and shoved it into the pocket. "Have a nice day . . . and Mom?"

"Yes?"

Karen pecked her cheek with a quick kiss. "You're *never* too old for boyfriends." Before Jillie could answer, her daughter had laughed and gone through the door, out into a world where boyfriends fell out of trees by the dozens—if you were a gorgeous, vivacious, twenty-year-old without a care in the world.

7

Isabella Mathers leaned against the middle slat of the old wooden gate at the bottom of her back garden, small body wriggling halfway through to hold out a clump of grass in one mittened hand several inches away from a large white rabbit.

"Come on, little bunny," she coaxed. "Have some yummy treats."

The rabbit had hunkered down under the hedge, eyes half shut and white fur glistening with the chill damp. It didn't react to the child's coaxing, inert but for the constant twitching of its nose. Isabella gave up on the grass, then squirmed backward to sit on her haunches and gravely consider her next course of action. She'd badgered her parents for months for a rabbit, always put off with excuses and vague half-promises that even a seven-year-old knew weren't really promises at all. And now one had magically appeared in her back garden . . . well, nearly the back garden, if she could just entice it a few more feet where she could lay legitimate claim to it. She mulled over her tactics and decided that she needed better bait. Brushing a strand of baby-blond hair from her eyes, she decided to take the risk of leaving the rabbit for a few minutes, hoping against hope it wouldn't decide to run off before she got back.

As stealthily as she could, so as not to spook the animal, she tiptoed backward until she reached the path leading up to the back door, a crooked strip of concrete slabs her daddy had set into the grass to make it easier for her mum to walk down to the whirligig clothesline without getting her feet wet on the grass.

At seven, children preferred running to walking, and Isabella was no exception. She banged through the back door, gave a cursory wipe of her bright red Wellies on the doormat, and rushed into the kitchen.

"Mummy! Can I have a carrot?"

Mrs. Mathers was in the lounge, ironing her way through a pile of clothes on the settee, while watching early-morning chat shows. At that moment, Isabella's mother was more engrossed with whether or not the six children of the sobbing fat woman had been fathered by her scrawny git of a husband or by his brother who worked the transsexual cabaret circuit in Blackpool than with her own child's demand for her attention.

"What, darling?"

"Can I have a carrot? Please, Mum, can I?"

On the television, the interview had devolved into a foulmouthed brawl between fat woman, skinny bloke, and brother in full drag-queen regalia while the talk show host danced out of the way of her bouncers. But at least the peculiarity of the request tore her mother's interest away from the screen.

"A carrot? What do you want a carrot for, Izzie?"

"Umm . . ." Isabella thought furiously. If she said it was for a rabbit, before she'd managed to actually catch it, her mother would surely scotch her plans before they'd even started. "I'm hungry."

Her mother raised an eyebrow, amused. "For a *carrot*?"

Steam hissed from the iron as her mother ran it over the sleeve of one of Mr. Mathers's work shirts. Isabella pulled at the zipper tab of her neon-pink My Little Pony anorak, feeling hot with both the effort of subterfuge and the warmth of the house.

"Carrots make you see in the dark," she said weakly, because she couldn't think of anything else.

Luckily, her mother supplied all the rationale her daughter was unable to imagine. "Ah. Roannah's been winding you up again, has she?" Roannah was the daughter of her mother's best mate who lived on the end of the street, the nine-year-old a constant source of both companionship and aggravation to her younger friend. "Let's get you some delicious carrot sticks, then, shall we?"

Isabella did her best to hide her impatience as her mother first scraped the skin off a carrot, then neatly cut them into a dozen child-friendly slivers. "There you go, sweetheart." And because Isabella knew it would be expected of her, she bit the end off one carrot stick and chewed with as much enthusiasm as she could muster.

"A miracle," her mother murmured. "She eats vegetables!"

"Thank you, Mummy!" Isabella chirped brightly and banged out the door again, heading for the end of the garden with a fistful of carrot sticks. As soon as she was sure her mother couldn't see her, she spat out the horrible mouthful of carrot and rubbed the back of her hand across her tongue to scrape away the taste, even the taste of woolly mitten better than carrot. But as she reached the gate and the end of the garden, her heart sank; the rabbit wasn't under the hedge anymore. It had all been for nothing.

Now someone else would find her rabbit, maybe even mean old Roannah. Her eyes welled with frustrated tears, and she kicked the locked gate resentfully. She wasn't sure which of them was more startled—the rabbit or herself—as the white rabbit shot out of its hiding place farther along the hedge, where, to Isabella's delight, the undergrowth had interwoven with old chicken wire to effectively trap the animal on *this* side of the fence. But now, rather than eight inches from her grasp, the rabbit was only two inches—no matter how she stretched out her arm, dangling a bit of carrot in front of its face.

"Lovely carrot," she cooed softly, "nice juicy carrot, c'mon, little bunny . . ."

Its fright over, the rabbit had again huddled into a tight miserable ball of fur, ears flattened against its back, and pale red eyes half-shut. Just as Isabella was about to give up in despair, however, it seemed to shake itself, roused, and sniffed the carrot stick hesitantly. She felt it nibble on the end of the carrot stick and drew back just a little to entice the rabbit forward. A few more tentative nibbles and—at last!—her rabbit was within reach. As the rabbit shuffled closer to the carrot stick, extending its head, Isabella grabbed it behind the neck as tightly as she could.

The rabbit immediately struggled, and it took all the little girl's determined strength to keep tight hold on the animal, pulling it this way and that, until she could drag it through the space between the undergrowth and twisted trunks of hedge. Triumphantly, she sat down on the damp ground, cold seeping through her corduroy trousers, and hugged the rebellious animal to her chest. She didn't even care as its back claws scratched her arms and face, doggedly squeezing it to her until it had quieted down.

She put her face into its fur and breathed in the warm, damp smell, felt the muscles still quivering. When she thought it had relaxed enough to venture standing up, she cuddled it in her arms and slowly got to her feet. The rabbit abruptly lashed out strong back legs, but a determined little girl was an invincible force.

A mother, on the other hand, could be an immovable object. As soon as Isabella staggered into the house with her precious discovery, Mrs. Mathers gasped, and not with delight.

"Look, Mummy!" Isabella said quickly, hoping to divert any objections she knew were inevitable. "I found it! It came into the garden and I gave it some of my carrot sticks, and it likes me. Can I keep it, please, Mummy? Please?"

"It's *filthy*!" Mrs. Mathers said in disgust. "Look at you, Izzie! You're covered in mud, and you've torn your sleeve, too, oh for . . ." Her mother's voice trailed off into the incoherent sounds of dismay. Then she frowned knowingly. "So that's what you wanted the carrot for."

Isabella didn't answer, simply holding the rabbit and doing her best to look pathetic, tears welling in her eyes, her chin wobbling— a trick she knew would have worked far better on her father. But after a moment, her mother sighed, softening.

"Izzie, a rabbit needs a hutch. We don't have anywhere to keep it."

"Daddy can make one."

Her mother's snort was commentary enough on her father's carpentry skills. "He can sleep in a cardboard box by my bed, and maybe Roannah's daddy can help make a hutch. *Please,* Mummy?"

"Maybe somebody else's little girl is missing her rabbit, did you stop to think of that, Isabella?"

The tear that rolled down Isabella's baby-fat cheek was no

pretense. "You promised," she said huskily. "You promised I could have a rabbit, you *did*."

"Now, that's not true, we said we'd think about it when you were a little older."

But her mother's voice had weakened. Isabella smelled victory and pressed her advantage. "I am old enough. Maybe the other little girl didn't take good care of him so he ran away and he got lost and I found him and fed him carrots and he *likes* me . . ."

Finally, Mrs. Mathers threw up her hands in defeat. "Ask your father," she said, to Isabella's delight. Her father would, of course, say yes, which her mother also knew.

But by teatime, Isabella knew that something was dreadfully wrong with the rabbit. It had crouched in the towel-lined bottom of the cardboard box lethargically, and no amount of stroking or enticement with bits of lettuce or carrots seemed to rouse it. By the time Mr. Mathers drove up, dashed up the short distance from the drive to the front door in the rain, and shook his way out of his jacket, Isabella already suspected her father's answer would make little difference. The rabbit lay on its side, eyes nearly closed, and panted shallowly.

"Hey, hey, what have we got here?" Mr. Mathers said cheerfully and gazed down into the box. "Oh. My. Well. Look at that." He glanced up at Mrs. Mathers, the two of them sharing a meaningful look. "It's a rabbit."

"She found it in the hedge this morning."

"Did she now."

"It's . . ." Her mother grimaced. "Not doing so well," she finished.

"Ah. I see." Mr. Mathers sat down cross-legged on the floor beside Isabella and scratched the rabbit's head between its ears. "He's a big fella, isn't he? You thought of a name for him yet?"

"Snowball," Isabella said, barely audible.

"That's a good name."

"Daddy? Snowball's really sick. Can we take him to a vet? They fix rabbits all the time on *Animal Hospital*. Maybe he just needs a shot or something?"

Her parents looked at each other, the way they always did when they were uniting against their daughter.

"It's too late in the day, sweetheart, all the vets would be closed now." As Isabella began to quietly cry, he added hastily, "But tell you what; if he's not better in the morning, we can take him then, all right?"

Mrs. Mathers promptly rolled her eyes and stamped off into the kitchen. Mr. Mathers watched her go, then put his arm around the little girl, drawing her against his chest. She wiped the tears from her face and sniffled. Her father's work shirt smelled like old oil and burned rubber, the odor of the tire shop indelibly impressed into the fabric.

"Snowball is going to be okay, isn't he, Daddy?"

Mr. Mathers sighed, helpless, and kissed her on her forehead. "We'll just have to wait and see, darling."

They didn't have to wait long. Sometime between Mrs. Mathers covering the top of the box with a towel to keep the rabbit warm and in the dark, and the family finishing a tea of cheese pasta and tinned sausages, the rabbit died.

Isabella cried as hard as if she'd owned the rabbit for years, heartbroken, and insisted on a funeral with full honors. So, in the wan evening light, in the rain, while Mrs. Mathers and her daughter huddled under an umbrella, Mr. Mathers dug a shallow grave at the end of the garden, by the same hedge where the rabbit had been found. He lowered the rabbit's body, shrouded in an old tea towel, into the hole, and filled it in again. The three then sang an inept version of "Jerusalem" and when Mrs. Mathers had led her grieving daughter away, Mr. Mathers furtively stamped the mound of sodden earth flat with his heavy Wellington boots and hoped he'd buried the carcass deep enough that no passing dog or fox would decide to dig it up for a snack.

Mrs. Mathers made sure *Animal Hospital* or any of the myriad other animal programs weren't on the schedule before they turned on the tellie that evening. The day's excitement and loss had taken its toll on Isabella, the little girl unusually quiet as she cuddled on the settee between her parents.

"Bedtime, darling," Mrs. Mathers said at eight, and brushed the hair back from her daughter's face. Isabella's cheeks felt hot under her palm, but that wouldn't be so unusual; the little girl had gone through a lot for one day. Tucked up in bed, Isabella quickly fell asleep.

"Maybe we should get her a rabbit," Mr. Mathers remarked a few hours later as he and his wife got into their own bed.

"You must be joking, Harry. You're not the one who's going to have to clean heaps of rabbit poo out of the hutch, chase it every time it gets loose, or take it to the vets to get its teeth and nails clipped every month, now, are you?"

Mr. Mathers grimaced. "Think she'd settle for a hamster?"

Mrs. Mathers didn't answer, listening to the sound of her daughter's hoarse coughing in the bedroom next door.

April's Death Toll: 265,930 cattle, 1,878,671 sheep, 67,642 pigs, 1,373 goats, and 145 unspecified animals.

Two hundred rams, ewes, and lambs of the rarest breed in Britain are slaughtered as their owner is served with the order at her home in Lothian and Borders six miles away and detained. Several police cars blockade her home to prevent her from leaving until the cull is completed.

At the Hall Hill show farm in Lanchester, MAFF officials slaughter 1,400 sheep, 5 cattle, 2 pigs, 3 llamas, 12 goats, and 3 deer, all pets that attract thousands of visitors a year. The horses, donkeys, rabbits, and ducks are spared.

In Danby Wiske, Northallerton, prize-winning mule sheep are among two hundred slaughtered after the rotting carcasses of several hundred other animals culled on neighboring farms had been left in piles, only forty yards from the village, for four weeks due to delays in constructing pyres or transportation to mass burial sites.

Agricultural Minister Joyce Quin blocks the dumping of a consignment of 330 Scottish pig carcasses at a landfill site in Cleveland situated only yards away from where healthy, disease-free animals are being kept. Biffa Waste Services, which owns the landfill, has insisted the dead pigs were not contaminated, all healthy animals slaughtered because they could not be sold at market, and posed no risk of infection to livestock in the area.

Susan and Brian Finch watch as their 130 sheep and 113 cows are slaughtered and burned in pyres on their Buckshead Farm in Evenwood, County Durham. All of the cattle prove to be disease-free but are culled as a precaution as they might have had contact with the sheep.

MAFF is considering exhuming the decomposed bodies of 1,100 cattle buried on High Hedley Hill Farm as regulations require cattle over the age of thirty months to be burned for fear of spreading BSE or mad cow disease. An Environmental Agency spokeswoman confirms 55 burial sites across the country contain the remains of over 10,000 older cattle and that an environmental risk assessment of any exhumation to public health will have to be made.

Villagers in High Etherley, County Durham, have complained of smoke from burning 400 infected cattle brought in from elsewhere blowing into local disease-free farms, raising fears of infecting healthy animals.

A videotape made of a Monmouthshire council employee chasing sheep in a field while taking random potshots at them with a rifle is shown on national television. The council refuses to discipline the employee. The farmer who made the tape, however, is threatened with prosecution for allowing his sheep to "stray."

The diary of eight-year-old Jessica Cleminson touches the nation with the little girl's distraught record of the killing of her fourteen-year-old pregnant pet cow, Caroline, the healthy animal slaughtered in a contiguous cull after a neighboring farm is confirmed with foot-and-mouth. After finding his daughter's diary, in it two smudges circled with the words "my tears," Jessica's father writes an open letter to Tony Blair, begging the prime minister to consider "a major restructure of agricultural policy as never before. All we want to do is make a living." The prime minister sends his condolences.

MAFF officials attempt to confiscate the videotape recording made by David Own of Leighton in Wales of slaughtermen shooting pregnant ewes only yards from his house, as frightened live animals scramble over the pile of bodies.

In Mouswald, Dumfriesshire, a pet goat named Misty belonging to Kirstin McBride is killed by a MAFF official who broke into the padlocked stable and shot the goat while the owner was confined to her house by a policewoman. The owner's distraught daughter is told by the MAFF official, "Your mother is going to be arrested, and the police will soon sort you out." Miss McBride then allegedly bites the policeman guarding the dead goat, is handcuffed and arrested and held for three hours before being released without charge. The 200 rare-breed sheep and Misty were all later found to have been free of the virus.

8

MAY

The evening before Keen's appointment with Sandford's station commander, he rang Laura in London, explained as much of the situation as he could to his ex-wife—who had been a copper's wife long enough to know which questions not to ask and which she already knew the answers to anyway. She wasn't too happy with the sudden revision to his access schedule with his sons, twins Colin and Simon, but understood he was even less so. He'd see more of them, she reassured him yet again, once they started the new school in Harrogate. Keen still wasn't sure if he approved of it or not but had to admit that if Laura and her poncy husband were going to pack the boys off to a boarding school, better it be closer to their father than somewhere in Scotland or Cornwall or, God forbid, bloody Switzerland. The boys seemed happy with the arrangement, looking forward to it as if it were a strange sort of summer camp. But they wouldn't start until September, and he'd seen precious little of them over the Christmas holidays as it was.

Then he rang Jillie in even farther-away Oregon, explaining it all over again but this time having to answer more questions than he normally would have been comfortable with. He wouldn't be getting those anticipated two weeks off, he told her, but reassured her that it might even work out better this way; since he would be up in that area for longer than he'd expected, and he could even drop by to see this archaeological dig of hers. He listened politely and made the proper noises as she, in turn, did her best to interest him in this aforementioned wonderful archaeological dig, a rare double-barreled site with a medieval town built on what was suspected to be the ruins of a major Roman villa. She described the myriad finds discovered so far, speculated on what might still be in the ground, rattled off names and dates he couldn't follow even if he'd wanted.

But it would bring her back to Britain, where he would have a chance to see if there was a future for the two of them after all. Why all the people he cared about seemed to live so far away from him was a source of constant irritation.

He packed the oversized rucksack the boys had decided he absolutely had to buy before he could spend three weeks in comfortable suburban Oregon rather than the wilds of the Australian outback, a black monstrosity with zip-away shoulder straps he'd never used and a huge Union Jack on the top flap that shouted "I am a tourist." But it was either that or the battered suitcase he'd inherited from his late father that he'd finally had to accept was too old and too small for anything more than weekends with the twins. He resisted the urge to fill the rucksack simply because he had a surplus of room. Then, because the rucksack looked so forlorn half collapsed in on itself, he stuffed in one more heavy pullover and a handful of books—a battered Ian Rankin paperback and a rather academic-looking tome on Roman Britain he'd bought in a second-hand bookshop, figuring that he'd better at least take a token stab at having some idea of what his not-actually-a-girlfriend would be doing on Hadrian's Wall. He remembered the little undercover work he'd done when he'd been a fresh-faced and naïve DC in the CID as consisting mostly of long periods of stultifying boredom punctured by brief episodes of disorganized mayhem, and knew that one or the other of the books would come in handy.

As an afterthought, he tossed in the copy of *The New Politics of Crime Control in the Community* he'd borrowed off Jasmine, one of her old textbooks from an OU course he'd been deliberating on whether or not to take himself. She'd liberally underscored the pages with pink and yellow highlighter pens and made little notations in the margins of the book with that cheerfully loopy script he thought more characteristic of much younger girls. At least she didn't dot her *i*'s with hearts or smiley faces. But Jazz was smart, very smart. She would soon enough earn her bachelor's degree, with honors, to leapfrog her way to promotions over less academically inclined colleagues like himself, Keen knew, and scamper up that careers ladder faster than you could say "affirmative action." Not that she wouldn't make a good boss . . . he just didn't want her to be *his* boss, not now. Not with the sugarplum of his own station dancing before his eyes.

At seven-thirty, he bundled a protesting Thomas into the car and drove the short distance to the Kestlemans' where the cat would board while Keen was on this assignment, and stayed for tea. Joanne Kestleman talked nearly nonstop, which while it wasn't unusual for the naturally gregarious woman, it did pique Keen's attention—she seemed almost anxious, fretting unnecessarily about plates and wineglasses and the food. What ordinarily would have been just another laid-back dinner with old friends seemed to have grown out of proportion to the amount of effort she was putting into it: fussing over a roast chicken, worrying about lumps in the gravy, explaining the trivial details on how she made her own applesauce. Thomas, looking slightly better and doing his best to appear gorgeous in the hope that he'd be rewarded with bits of stray chicken, sat next to Keen's chair with chest fur puffed up into a regal collar and eyes half closed in the illusion that he didn't really care if he was noticed or not.

At one point, Joanne had gotten up for the tenth time for something or other in the kitchen and stopped, her face completely blank as she stood as inert as stone. Keen glanced at Derek, puzzled. The Yorkshireman simply raised an eyebrow in return, a sign he was aware his wife was behaving strangely.

Joanne shook herself and smiled. "Forgot what I got up for," she said with a strained laugh. "Gettin' old."

"Spoon for the custard," Derek said placidly.

"That's right." She bustled into the kitchen to retrieve a serving spoon. "Now, you don't have to worry about Thomas, he'll be fine with us."

"I know," Keen said, repeating himself for the third time that evening. "He's in good hands."

"Yes," Joanne said, her eyes suddenly liquid and reddening. "Well, you lads enjoy your pudding, no, no, don't get up, you two just stay there and I'll get the washing up done . . ." Thomas, knowing his luck would be better with Joanne than with either of the two men, followed her into the kitchen, tail straight up with the tip flicking like a small pennant.

"Fancy a wee drop with your pud?" Derek asked and slid his chair back, legs scraping on the old wooden floorboards. He retrieved a bottle of Laphroaig from the side cabinet and poured them both more than merely a "wee drop." Keen accepted his with a nod of thanks and said nothing, having known Derek long enough that if he was going to explain his wife's odd behavior, it would be in his own time.

"Y'met the Deans?" Derek asked.

"Who?"

"David and Margot, young couple bought old Geordie Winterman's place."

The names clicked. "Just in passing once or twice."

Derek said nothing for a long moment, seemingly concentrating on the taste of his whisky. "Townies," he said finally. "Not that they're bad soarts, just wannabe farmers."

Keen nodded. The countryside seemed to be attracting more of those escapees from the cities who arrived with all the best intentions and none of the expertise that making a living from the land required. But he didn't blame them for wanting a better life, even if it meant they increasingly bought up farms and houses and left the young locals with nowhere of their own.

"Margot bought a spinning wheel off Jo."

Keen smiled and sipped his own whisky, trying to relax while knowing this might be his last chance to unwind for a while. "Sure it'll look grand in her sitting room."

"He's bought himself a couple Blackface ewes t'go with it." Derek looked up at him, his expression stiff. "Not local animals, got 'em off a northern dealer."

The penny dropped. "Oh. Damn."

Derek shrugged. "Don't seem to be showing any symptoms. Been a good couple months since they bought 'em. Blood tests've all come back negative, paid the vet themselves to do it." He went back to inspecting the liquor in his glass. "Not that that means owt. Man from MAFF wants 'em culled anyway. Deans are fighting, got themselves a fancy solicitor, keeping the livestock locked up in their own house—got 'em in an upstairs bedroom, can you believe that? Won't let anyone on the property."

Keen sighed and swirled his whisky, studying the amber color. "What about your stock?"

"The Wintermans' place is exactly point three miles outside the exclusion zone from my property line."

"Point three miles."

"Yup. Point three." He swallowed a gulp of whisky, his throat working. "Man from MAFF telling us the virus can only live for thirty minutes after slaughter. Then he says it's caused by weeks-old contaminated meat in pigswill. Lies just pouring out both sides of his mouth." Derek's tone was thick with anger. "Say they haven't made no decisions yet, but they've got JCBs digging pits other side of the weir. Stacking railroad sleepers. Getting ready. They've already made their minds up—don't matter what the tests come back like."

"What about your stock?"

Derek grimaced. "I moved the lot of 'em into the center field well before the outbreak, better grazing there, leave the far fields to rest a bit afore summer. They've had no contact a'tall with the Deans' animals, never did have. Thought that would make 'em safe enough. Man from MAFF says don't matter. Says it's airborne, coming out birds' arses, crows and gulls and the like, this bloody virus can't survive half an hour outside a body. So what's their cunning plan? Burn the infected carcasses and let the wind blow the smoke into the next county. Daft bastards."

In the kitchen, pots and pans rattled a bit too energetically in the sink. Derek glanced up and lowered his voice. "None of my stock goes for export, all goes to British markets, so I says, 'What about vaccination?' Man from MAFF says no, wouldn't be able to tell which was vaccination and which was just natural immunity. We'd lose our 'disease free' status with the Yanks and the Japs. Not that

anyone is buying British meat now anyways." He sighed in exasperation, the normally taciturn man struggling to get his words
out. "I got two hundred fifteen ewes, half of them due to lamb.
Jo's got a reject in the bottom drawer of the Aga keeping warm,
bottle-feedin' it. All the time it's in the back of yer mind—what's
the point of bothering to keep the poor thing alive? Taken me
thirty year to build up this line, best bloody sheep in the county.
Jo's worried sick we're gonna lose them all. And for what?" He
drained his glass of whisky, and Keen doubted he tasted a thing.
"So soft buggers in London never seen a sheep outside chops in a
Tesco's can kiss Brussels's arse, that's what it's about."

Derek stood and poured himself another glass of whisky, then
raised the bottle in a question. When Keen shook his head, he
put the cork back into the bottle and stood next to the lounge
fireplace.

Neither spoke for a long moment, the only sound in the room
the crackle of wood in the fire and the insistent complaint of a
hungry orphaned lamb in the kitchen.

"It's coming, Keen," Derek said glumly. "It's coming here, and
there's nowt we can do to stop them."

Keen went home that night sober, not enough whisky in Scotland to take the ache of dread out of his chest. When he woke the
next morning, already missing Thomas, the day seemed absurdly
cheerful. The sun had broken out and turned the sky a pale china
blue, the first good weather he'd seen in weeks. Some of the sheep
had already dropped their lambs, he knew by listening to the high-
pitched bleating of young animals and the lower, throaty answers
of their mothers. He showered and dressed, went downstairs and
poured a cup of coffee as he did every day, and took it out onto the
stone step of his house to breathe in crisp spring air still heavy with
moisture. A bright sliver of sunlight moved down across the fields
toward him as the sun rose over the hills and the roof of his house,
a wispy gauze of steam rising from the grass. In the distance, Keen
could hear the low grumble of Derek's tractor, and the fields he
leased to Derek were dotted with white sheep, lambs gamboling
through dewy grass, full of joy just to be alive. Robins and wrens,

thrushes and tits all sang volubly in the line of trees, already squab-
bling over nesting territories. A small, juvenile fox skulked along
the stone wall, looking for a breakfast of mice, its back just turning
a brilliant red, but its face and tail still a grayish brown. It froze,
stared at him for a moment, then slipped back into the undergrowth and vanished.

This was where he'd been born and bred. This land was in his
blood, in his bones, watered with the sweat of his father, and his father's father, and the long line of farmers stretching back to the peas-
ants tallied by their Norman Domesday conquerors, to the Viking
settlers before them, to his pagan ancestors here long before the Ro-
mans. Hardy people who'd wrested their livelihood from these lush
green hills with stone axes and wooden plows. This Yorkshire countryside was as eternal as life itself; everything here moved with a time-
less rhythm he understood in the same way that he understood his
own beating heart—it just existed, without having to think about it.

But today it all seemed just a shade too normal, too strained. And
on the horizon, like a dusky crack in the fine porcelain of the sky,
a thread of black smoke rose. It could have been an ordinary fire,
just another farmer burning off the scrap of winter, readying his
fields for the spring sowing.

Or it could be a harbinger that might soon bring this safe little
world crashing down around him, ripping away the fragile façade
of the landscape and exposing the underlying helplessness of both
animals and people.

Gloomy thoughts, he reproached himself. Wouldn't do to start
off the day with such a miserable attitude. He tossed the rucksack
into the boot of the car, drove over the ruts of his drive, and turned
out toward the main road. It would be a lot longer commute every
day from his farmhouse to Sandford than it was to Weetwood, but
the roads were good, west at Otley and a straight shot along the
A65 over toward Skipton. He half expected to see lorries full of
dead sheep or burning funeral pyres along the roads, but the countryside on either side of the motorway was serene, green fields and
the bare branches of trees reddish with new buds. The sunlight was
deceptive, the air outside still icy with the wet, lingering winter.

The Vauxhall warmed up quickly, making Keen feel slightly drowsy with the heat.

He followed Davis's directions but still got lost, missing the turnoff from Eastby, and was halfway to Appletreewick before he figured it out. He doubled back and only found the junction more by chance than logic, the white and black metal sign reading SAND-FORD, 12 M having been spattered to a nearly illegible brown by a farmer's slurry spray. The main road in was barely wide enough for a single car, and the paving cracked and buckled. So he was late by the time he drove down the single high street of Sandford village, noting the bright sparkle of shattered glass in the road in front of a cottage stripped of roof tiles, plywood nailed over the windows and doors, and a hire skip in the side yard brimming with broken furniture. The village seemed totally deserted, with the melancholy sort of atmosphere left behind once a carnival has packed up and left town.

He drove around the side of the Sandford Police Station and parked on the curb, a couple patrol cars on the other side of a chain-link fence between them. The front door was unlocked and the glassed-off reception area unoccupied. A hand-lettered sign next to an old-fashioned brass hotel bell on the countertop read, RING BELL FOR ATTENTION. BE PATIENT, PLEASE! So he dinged the little bell and waited patiently. After a few minutes, he dinged it again. When his watch had ticked away another ten minutes of his life, he tried the door. It was unlocked. Around the corner of the tiny reception area a narrow staircase led up to the second floor where he could hear the faint sound of someone typing rapidly on a keyboard. So he held the door open as he dinged the bell a third time. The typing continued unfazed.

Convinced no one was likely to answer the little bell, Keen went through and up the stairs, following the sound of typing. In a small room just off the landing, a middle-aged woman with bright ginger hair piled into a haphazard chignon sat in front of a computer terminal and typed with phenomenal speed and phenomenal vigor, heavily bejeweled fingers pounding the keys with such brutality that Keen suspected she'd been trained on an old manual typewriter and never made the transition to the more delicate keyboards of computers. She had a dictaphone earplug in one ear, squinting at the screen through a pair of half-rim glasses on a chain around her neck. Behind her, an old photocopier wheezed, light sliding across the gap, and spitting out pages into a collated rack. Keen had to knock gently on the doorframe to gain her attention. Startled, she glanced up at him over her glasses and put one hand against her ample chest theatrically as she laughed.

"Oh, my goodness, you gave me a fright there!"

"I did ring," Keen said, pointing over his shoulder to indicate he'd been downstairs.

"Yes, I know, I did hear. And no one came to the front desk?" She seemed aggrieved. "Well, is there anything I can help you with?"

He took out his wallet and opened it to his warrant card. "DS Dunliffe, Weetwood Station. Your DI is expecting me."

"Ah!" she said, scoldingly. "There you are! You're *late*."

"Sorry," he responded automatically, with the bemused deference he'd have given a particularly strict headmistress, which he suspected was exactly what she insisted on from everyone in the station. "Took a wrong turning getting here."

"Easy enough to do," she said, letting him off the hook, "especially for those not from round these parts. They've all gone out. Photographer, from the paper. Big to-do yesterday. Should be back shortly, but let's see if we can raise anyone."

She unplugged herself from the dictaphone machine, reached down on either side, and rolled backward in a wheelchair that he hadn't noticed before. Which explained why she hadn't come down the stairs, and made Keen wonder how she got onto the second floor in the first place. Her body seemed to be mismatched: from the waist up, she was a plump, sturdy woman with wide shoulders, a well-armored bosom, and strong hands. But her twill gray skirt was smoothed immaculately over bird-thin legs, silky tights reflecting light in a way that made them appear even thinner. She wore, inexplicably, high-heeled shoes, bright green to match the green of her blouse and the jeweled pins holding her hair in place.

The tiny control room had once been a rather cozy bedroom,

ornate marble fireplace at one end, not used now, with a large bouquet of dried flowers in a brass coal bucket rather than logs and fire in the hearth. Ruffed drapes with an old-fashioned William Morris design framed a window with immaculately clean Georgian panes of glass. A large print of Charles Barber's *Naughty Boy* hung in a gold-leaf frame over the mantel, the sentimental painting of a solemn Victorian girl reading to a sad-eyed Great Dane perfectly suited to the control room's décor. Dozens of framed photos of smiling relatives in bridal dresses and tuxedos and graduation gowns, rosy-cheeked grandchildren in holiday snap poses, and a variety of dogs and cats and horses festooned the mantel and her desk and the windowsill, stamping this area as her sovereign domain. But there it ended, and the rest of the equipment had been designed for her use, everything in arm's reach and tailored for someone in a wheelchair. Instead of a foot pedal for the desktop radio, she had it bolted to one corner of the desk where she could easily lean her elbow.

"Five-eight-seven-two, over."

Keen listened to a brief hiss of static before a painfully young woman's voice said, "Five-eight-seven-two, go ahead."

"You in station, Rach?"

"No, I'm at Lady Jayne's. Over."

The woman keyed the mike again. "Is himself with you?"

"He's gone with LaRue and Sid th—" A cough, and a break in transmission as the woman shot him a quick glance.

"Sorry, love, you're breaking up. Say again."

"The inspector's with the sarge and PC Shinkowicz doing the photo shoot. Have you tried his mobile?"

"Will do. Out."

She picked up a little mobile phone far newer than Keen's and punched a single button on the speed dial. "Bertie," she said to whoever had answered. "The Eagle has landed. Finally." She smiled at whatever reply had been made and hung up without saying goodbye. "He'll be ten minutes. Would you like a cup of tea or coffee while you wait?"

"I'm all right," he said. "Don't go to any trouble."

She pursed her lips in a disapproving way that made him think of the strict headmistress again. "No trouble a'tall, love. I'm having one meself."

Again, even the Tea Maid had been arranged to suit the wheelchair-bound woman, set on a worktop just high enough to make it the perfect height to roll a wheelchair under. She poured hot water from the kettle once it had boiled into a delicate china teapot, then settled a tea cozy crocheted to resemble a cat over it to allow the tea to steep while she arranged shortbread biscuits on a matching plate. He took the proffered plate and balanced it on his knee before she poured two cups of tea, scenting the air with the flowery smell of Darjeeling, and handed him a cup on a saucer.

"Thank you," he murmured, although he really hadn't wanted any tea. He drank it anyway and managed to wash down one shortbread biscuit as well, hoping that would be enough to placate her.

"I haven't even properly introduced myself," she said with false contrition. "I'm Molly Owens."

"DS Keen Dunliffe."

She laughed quietly. "Oh, we know who you are, Sergeant. You're going to be our boss here soon enough, so we've been told. If there's anything at all you need, you just let me know. I pretty much run this station, nothing gets by me."

I'll bet it doesn't, he thought, sipping his tea to hide his expression.

"There you are!" Mrs. Owens said brightly. Keen nearly choked on his tea trying to swallow and look around at the same time. Inspector Trumble entered the small room with one hand extended, dressed in full formal uniform as if welcoming a head of state rather than a lowly sergeant. Keen hastily looked around for somewhere to put his plate of biscuits and teacup and ended up setting them on the floor before he could stand and shake the man's hand.

"Herbert Trumble," the inspector said, adding unnecessarily, "Inspector Herbert Trumble. Sorry to be late, bit of a folderol with the photographer from the local paper. Getting our lads some well-deserved publicity, job well done and all that." The inspector pumped Keen's hand with both his own as he spoke, his grip slightly too firm and damp as he held Keen's wrist captive, then let him go with a quick pat on the shoulder. No doubt the inspector had practiced this innumerable times and would more than likely be running for some elected office after he'd retired. Keen suppressed the urge to rub his palm on his trousers.

"Anything I should know about, Molly?"

"No, sir. Everything's quiet at the moment."

"Good, good." The inspector turned his smile back on Keen. "If you want to come with me?"

Keen followed him down the hall to a room that had once served as the master bedroom in this large and sprawling house, with a well-polished brass plate on the door: INSPECTOR H. TRUMBLE. But the inspector's office seemed the antithesis of Molly Owens's control room fiefdom: whitewashed walls with only a map of the county for decoration on one side of the room facing the obligatory oversized portrait of the Queen on the other. Utilitarian venetian blinds on the windows cast slatted shadows over a gunmetal-gray desk, its surface devoid of anything but an immaculately clean blotter and pen set, a telephone, and a rather small picture of a pinch-faced woman Keen assumed to be Mrs. Trumble in a cheap Ikea frame pushed to the farthest corner of the desk. Even the bin by the chair was empty.

Trumble shook himself out of his uniform jacket as he said, "PC Colver is waiting for us to join her at the Queen's Head, pub just down the road." He swapped his uniform jacket for a tweed coat on a hook on the back of the door and fished a ring of keys from the pocket to unlock the filing cabinet. From the quick look Keen had of the contents, Trumble kept his files as neat as his desk, folder edges as crisp and neatly arrayed as if the man ironed them. Trumble took out a single file, closed the drawer and locked it again.

"It's only a few minutes' walk," he said and gestured toward the door.

"Fine," Keen answered and followed him out again. As they passed the control room, he returned Molly Owens's farewell smile with a quick, impersonal one of his own. She was a formidable woman; he recognized the sort—the kind that despised pity in any form, tolerating none within herself as well.

"I'd give you a tour round the place, since it'll be yours soon enough," Trumble said as they walked down the road toward the pub. "But there's not much to see, no one's about anyway, and Rachel's been waiting for us a while."

Keen said nothing, ignoring yet another reproach about his tardiness. He glanced at Trumble, taking in the man's exaggerated stride, the tweed coat a shade too affected, the austerity of the man's office and his seeming passion with neatness and punctuality. This was a man who wouldn't miss the job in the least—nor it him, Keen suspected.

The inside of the pub was surprisingly chilly. A fake log fire in what looked to be a perfectly functional hearth sparkled garish cellophane embers, an electric flex snaking from it to a powerpoint behind the fruit machine. A dour woman scarcely acknowledged their presence as they entered, although Trumble greeted her as genially as if she had. The only other customers at that time of day were an elderly man in a corner reading *The Guardian* and a young woman at a table at the opposite end of the room, huddled in a thick gray wool jumper and nursing a half pint of Coke. Keen and Trumble sat down at her table, without having ordered any drinks for themselves, Keen realized.

"PC Rachel Colver," Trumble said briefly. "DS Keen Dunliffe."

"Pleased to meet you, sir," Rachel said, extending her hand for a cursory shake.

"Pleasure."

Formalities dispensed with, Trumble said, "Right," and opened the file on the table. "Contact details, background information, photos, authorization forms, the lot." He slid a couple of paper-clipped bundles toward each of them. "If either of you have any questions?" Trumble's pause wasn't long enough to wait for an answer. "Right, then. Good luck to you both. Rachel . . ."

"Boss." Her response was automatic, her eyes scanning through the brief.

"Sergeant."

"Inspector."

Keen watched as the inspector exchanged a quick word with the woman at the bar, then shook the elderly newspaper reader's hand with both his as he had Keen's, one wrapped around the other man's wrist, followed by the condescending pat on the shoulder. Neither the woman nor her customer seemed overly impressed.

"Hands-on type, is he?"

PC Colver glanced up, obviously unsure whether or not Keen was making a joke. He was, but his deadpan delivery confused her.

"He likes to think he is." She glanced at her half-empty glass meaningfully. "Did you want to . . . ?"

"No, thanks." Keen gathered his pages together, tapping the ends into line, and stood. "Apparently, we're running late as it is. You parked here or at the station?"

"I don't have a car."

Keen's eyebrows rose in surprise. "You do know how to drive, don't you?"

The young PC flushed. "Of course I know how to drive," she said testily. "I just don't own my own car."

"Fine," Keen said amiably and handed his copy to her. "Solves that problem, then. You can brief me while I drive, two birds, one stone."

It didn't mollify her by much, he could tell. She drained her glass, stood, picked up a sports bag he hadn't seen before from under the table, and followed him out the door with a casual wave at the woman at the bar.

"Would you like me to carry your bag?" he offered.

"I'm all right, thanks," she said tightly, hoisting it onto one shoulder.

He feared it was going to be a long drive to Newcastle.

9

The drive up wasn't *that* bad, Rachel thought later in retrospect. Oh, sure, she felt rather nervous sitting for a couple hours next to the man who would be her new boss, trying to make a good first impression while sizing him up at the same time. He seemed completely at ease, which only made her more aware of her edginess. DS Dunliffe had to be at least as old as Inspector Trumble but seemed somehow younger, friendlier in a sort of offhand way. Trumble was always inquiring after everyone's family and personal lives, but she as well as the rest of the station knew he didn't give a jot about the answers; it was just something he practiced on them, readying himself for his political career. But she got the impression that DS Dunliffe actually listened to her, asking her questions and considering her opinions. Maybe he was trying to make a good impression on her as well, she had suddenly thought, the idea startling her.

He had had her read through the file aloud, not because there was anything new in it but just to make sure they both knew the players and the situation.

"You're just back from the training course in London, I've been told."

"Yes, sir. Two weeks. Well, ten days, really. Not a regular course, just modified whatever I need specifically for this job."

"They teach you anything useful?"

She couldn't tell if he was making a joke or not, his expression completely poker-faced. "I hope so," she said earnestly.

At that he did at least turn his head briefly to flash her a quick grin. "So just how well do you actually know this Beryl Rafferty?"

"Not that well, really." She thought that might not be a good answer, since it was her connection to Rafferty that had got her into this in the first place, and amended it. "I mean I *knew* her. The school wasn't that big, and we got on okay. She hung out with a different crowd."

He kept his eyes back on the road as he spoke. "How so?"

Rachel hesitated, trying to formulate a response that would be accurate without making her sound pathetic. "Beryl was one of the popular girls. Pretty, smart, good in sports. Teachers liked her, even when she was giving them stick. Boys were always trying it on with her, but never getting anywhere. She was just . . . one of the cool kids."

"And you weren't one of the 'cool' kids?"

She glanced at him, seeing the edge of his smile even though he didn't look at her. "Not exactly, no." She didn't want to go into her long, sad family history, not wanting anyone's sympathy—especially the new gaffer's—but found herself saying, "I had family responsibilities, so I didn't have a lot of time to spend bunking off or sneaking ciggies in the girl's loo, like the rest of them."

At that, he did look at her, gauging her astutely, and she averted her own eyes, uncomfortable.

"Her parents had money, but she didn't flaunt it," Rachel continued, determined. "At least not on clothes or shoes or things like that. She was more into video cameras, always had the latest kit, the very best that Mummy and Daddy's money could buy." Rachel inwardly winced, recognizing how jealously bitchy that had sounded. "She fancied herself a budding documentary filmmaker, always making short films about school, trying to make us seem like we were all a bunch of tough kids off a troubled London estate instead of just another ordinary rural comprehensive. She'd send short films in to the BBC or ITV, but she never got anywhere." She paused. "Except once, when a news crew came out and did a little feature thing on her, got about three minutes on the local news. She didn't like it—said they twisted it to make her look like a silly kid instead of a serious filmmaker."

"You ever feature in any of her student films?"

Rachel shrugged. "Not really. If I am in any, it's as part of a crowd scene."

"Think she'll even remember you?"

It was said offhandedly, and Rachel couldn't read from Dunliffe's tone if he thought he'd been stuck with a complete waste of time.

"She'll remember me," Rachel said flatly. "My grandmother owns Cowsgill Bank Farm. It's not used as a farm anymore, not since my dad died. We let the land out as summer pasture to people with horses. One of them was the honorary secretary for the local hunt and asked permission for access to our land for a foxhunt. My gran said yes, for a price." Rachel shrugged. "Nana's on a fixed income; without me working we couldn't keep the farm at all."

Not that Rachel labored under any illusion she'd inherit anything when the old woman died; Nana had made that quite clear. She'd willed it all to the local church, despite the fact the last time the old woman had even seen the inside of a church was her son's wedding over a quarter of a century ago. Rachel didn't mention any of this to Dunliffe, though.

"Beryl was with the hunt saboteurs, videotaping everything, running around like she was some Hollywood director, doing her Errol Morris impression." She added, as Dunliffe glanced at her questioningly, "Y'know . . . *The Thin Blue Line*. Not the comedy thing with Rowan Atkinson, the American documentary." When he still didn't respond, she said, "It's about the murder of a cop in Texas."

"Right."

She knew from his tone he'd never heard of it, never mind seen it, and wondered if she also heard a hint of impatience.

"Beryl started out with the League Against Cruel Sports people. They're into monitoring blood sports, and nonviolent campaigning—legally, for change. Not that I think she cared all that much about hunting or animal welfare, to be honest. It just wasn't exciting enough for her videos, all too tame for her taste. Not enough blood and thrills. So she got involved with the balaclava squad from the Hunt Saboteurs Association."

"Balaclava squad." The sergeant was smiling again, but she decided he wasn't asking a question.

"She never bothered with one because she was barely fifteen then. And she pretty much stuck to making videos. Anyway, the local sabs found out that the hunt club was planning to cross my gran's land. Beryl talked me into leaving one of the access gates at the lower end of the fields unlocked. She said it was just so her mate could park his Land Rover by the treeline so she could sit on top with her video cameras and get a good view of the hunt when it went by. I believed her. I was fourteen, and she was one of the popular kids. I was desperate then to fit in."

Rachel heard her own anger leaking into her tone and tried to sound more matter-of-fact.

"Except it wasn't just Beryl and her mate with the Land Rover; we had nearly two hundred hunt saboteurs come through that gate, with a dozen or so of the balaclava squad. They're the real problem, not the ordinary demonstrators. It's not like most of them are really criminals or anything . . ."

"They're not?"

Again, Rachel glanced at him, unable to read his ambiguous tone or impassive profile. "Well . . . trespass isn't technically a criminal offense. Most of these people go after the hunts with horns and whips and everyone yelling 'holloa' to confuse the hounds and the hunters."

"Whips? Seems a strange thing for people trying to protect animals to be carrying around, if they aren't really criminals."

She was beginning to wonder if she was being tested or if he really was this completely clueless. "They don't use them on the horses. Or people. Not normally. They're not trying to hurt anyone. Hounds are trained to be afraid of the sound of a whip cracking, it's a way to keep them from straying where they shouldn't or going after the wrong animal . . ."

"Sheep being so easily mistaken for fox."

That at least made her smile. "Some dogs are smarter than others. Hunting hounds when they get the blood up tend to be pretty stupid."

"Along with some of their owners, I suspect." She glanced at him warily, but he shrugged. "Never much cared for foxhunting," he explained.

"So you're on the antis' side?"

At that, he did laugh quietly. "I'm on the side of the law."

She studied him, confused and uncertain. She couldn't figure him out. "Anyway," she continued, "some of her more hard-core sab pals decided that my gran was a sympathizer, letting the hunt onto her land. So they broke all the windows in our house, rocks, bricks, chunks of firewood, anything to hand. Someone left a bottle full of liquid with a rag stuffed in the top with a note that said, 'Next time it's for real.' It was only water, but it was still scary. The Hunt Association paid for all the damage, and Gran got the better of the deal—we got double-glazing in the house for the first time. But I wasn't too happy with Beryl or her sab mates."

"You were frightened?"

It sounded more like a comment than a question. Rachel said, "I was fourteen."

The conversation faltered, Rachel staring out her passenger side window moodily.

After a few minutes, Dunliffe said, "You sure you're really up to this?"

She glanced over at him almost resentfully. She'd had to fight hard enough for the blokes at the station to take her seriously over her past four years in the police. Inspector Trumble was no problem—he treated everyone with benign contempt; age, sex, or race made no difference to him. But she'd be damned if she'd let the new gaffer start off with any impressions of her as either some delicate flower to be protected or the type to use her sex as an excuse.

"It's my job, sir," she said firmly. "I can do it."

He merely grunted noncommittally in reply.

1 O

They lapsed into companionable silence after that, broken only briefly when a huge rust-red statue appeared on the right-hand side of the motorway, a human figure with outstretched wings more appropriate on a jumbo jet—the Angel of the North.

"Do you like it?" Rachel asked him.

Keen could see where one would either love or loathe the gargantuan statue.

"I suppose it might grow on you."

That was the last of the conversation until he pulled into a side street in the city center, looking for a spot to park. After nearly twenty minutes of futile hunting, Keen finally found an empty gap behind a seedy warehouse, barely wide enough to jockey the car into, inch by inch.

The address he'd been given was still six blocks away. There was nothing on the outside of the ugly concrete and glass office building to indicate this was a government department of any kind, although two CCTV cameras aimed at the front doors at a conveniently vandalproof height and the locked entrance was unfriendly enough. Keen pressed the buzzer under a grilled speaker on an unembellished polished-brass plate.

"Can I help you?" a disembodied female voice asked politely, giving nothing away.

"Keen Dunliffe and Rachel Colver—we have an appointment to see Mr. Kramer." He felt under the circumstances adding their ranks might be unwelcome.

The door buzzed without further reply from the voice. Keen pushed the door open and held it for Rachel. She hesitated for a moment, obviously both unaccustomed to and dubious of old-fashioned male courtesy, before entering the building.

Inside, the disembodied voice turned out to belong to an attractive middle-aged woman with auburn hair pulled up into a French twist, silk tailored suit, and polished nails matching shining lipstick, as far removed from looking like a cop as Keen could imagine. She smiled as she stood and slid back a security glass.

"If you'd both like to have a seat, I'll let Mr. Kramer know you're here."

They sat on a long slab bench made of freckled granite, as uncomfortable as it was cold. Piped bland music played with nearly subliminal softness, the only other sound being the faint clicking of a keyboard. They mercifully didn't have to wait long. The single lift at the other end of the foyer opened with a musical ping, revealing a muscular man in a tight-fitting black polo shirt scowling at them. He placed one hand on the side of the lift to prevent the doors from closing.

"You two, come with me," he said brusquely, by way of a greeting.

No one spoke on the ride up to the fourth floor. When the lift doors opened, an even more muscular man with a severe military haircut stood several feet away, waiting with hands on his hips, glaring with ill-concealed impatience. His eyes flicked disapprovingly from Rachel to Keen before he snorted.

"Bloody hell," he muttered in disgust, turned on his heel and strode away.

As Rachel glanced at him uncertainly, Keen gave her a quick wink. Their escort jerked his head toward the retreating back of his colleague.

"Come on, then," he said.

They followed him down the corridor into a large office, six desks in pairs at opposite sides and a large situation board at the far end of the room. Two studious young men who looked more like college students than cops, stood conferring over various photos and squiggled notes on the whiteboard. An unshaven man in dirty denim jeans and T-shirt, leather jacket slung over the back of his chair, hunched over a file, scribbling notes. Conversation died as they all looked up when Keen and Rachel walked into the room. The second man had already entered a private office in the opposite corner, a room made nearly completely of glass. Now seated behind a massive desk overflowing with files and paperwork, he was lighting a cigarette, blew out the smoke and gestured curtly at them to come inside.

"DI Kramer, I'm assuming?" Keen said, once he and Rachel had reached the open doorway, and glanced at the NO SMOKING sign displayed prominently on the wall behind the man's desk.

The man squinted through the haze of smoke at them. "Yeah, you assume right. And you two must be the fucking pair of idiots Home Office has foisted off on me."

As they sat down in one of the plastic office chairs in front of the man's desk, Keen could sense Rachel stiffening beside him with indignation. "We are indeed," Keen said wryly. "DS Keen Dunliffe and PC Rachel Colver."

"So you're McCraig's blue-eyed boy." From the man's tone, Keen gathered Kramer and McCraig had more than a passing acquaintance, and from his expression, Kramer's dissatisfaction. "I expected someone . . . younger."

Keen smiled but didn't rise to the bait. Kramer studied Rachel for a moment, then demanded, "And just how old are *you*?"

"Twenty-four, sir."

Kramer grimaced. "Twenty-four. Bloody hell." He shook his head in disbelief. "Can you believe this shit?" He raised his voice, addressing the room in general outside the open door. "They've sent us Grampa Simpson and Lisa."

One of the lads at the computer looked up briefly with a smirk, then apparently thought better of it.

"You ever do any undercover work before, Constable Colver?" Kramer asked.

"No, sir. This is my first CID assignment. But I've just done the course in London—"

Kramer grunted his laugh. "Of course you did. Top of the class, too, no doubt. I'm sure that'll come in real handy, darlin'." He turned his attention to Keen. "Let me guess—you taught it."

"Not in London," Keen replied.

Kramer's eyes narrowed, unsure if Keen was being insolent or not. "Well, now that we've got the pleasantries out of the way, let me just run it down for you. This is my team. I own it. I put it together three years ago, and we've been busting our balls on getting these animal rights wankers all by ourselves just fine, thank you very much, without needing any assistance from McCraig's private little A Team."

Keen leaned back, fingers laced together across his stomach, deliberately disengaging from the man's tirade in order to observe impassively. He noted that while Rachel hadn't reacted, her cheeks had flushed with blotchy humiliation, the knuckles of her own clasped hands in her lap whitening.

"Now because some poxy-arsed Yank gets killed, the Americans are putting pressure on Home Office for results. They're buggering up our operation, furkling about with changing our course of action, demanding results *now*. We don't want you, we don't need you, but we're fucking well stuck with you. But while you're here, you'll be doing things *my* way, no bullshit, no argument. Got that?"

"Got it," Keen said evenly.

While Rachel had been busy researching her animal rights activists, Keen had done a quiet background check on Detective Inspector Marcus Kramer with a few discreet phone calls. Kramer was ex-army and ex-SAS, serving in Germany and Kosovo, before his final tour in Northern Ireland in covert intelligence, where he'd become somewhat of a minor legend, although Keen wondered just how reliable the stories were. Kramer had been married four times and was now on wife number five, this marriage purportedly failing as well; judging from Kramer's charm offensive on Rachel, Keen wasn't unduly surprised. But the answers also had a uniform quality: Kramer was a hard-ass; territorial and aggressive, loud, foulmouthed, belligerent, and a consistently drunken embarrassment in pubs—and, without exception, the one man every single person to whom Keen had spoken would trust with his life, unconditionally.

With that in mind, Keen stepped back mentally to watch Kramer's tirade, recognizing in it an element of amateur dramatics to what he was certain was genuine resentment with their intrusion into his team.

"*You,*" Kramer said, jabbing a finger at Rachel, "are so wet behind the ears, you're more of a menace to my team than an asset. The kind of ability you need for this job isn't one you're gonna get out of some fucking book in some fucking seminar run by a bunch of *fucking* pencil pushers who've never done a day's work in undercover intelligence. You're going to get a crash course in the real world here, flower, and I'm not putting any of my people at risk if you can't hack it—I'll bounce your pert arse back to whatever shithole they found you in, you got that?"

"Yes, sir." Rachel's voice was low, thick with barely repressed emotion.

Kramer scowled irritably. "And if you're going to get your pretty lace knickers in a twist and cry because the mean old boss yells at you, boo-hoo, you can piss off now and save us all a lot of time and trouble."

"*That* won't be something you have to worry about, sir," Rachel replied. Keen repressed a smile, hearing the veiled threat behind her words. Kramer apparently heard it as well, his eyes narrowing in a shrewd reappraisal.

"Good. And *you*—" The finger jabbed at Keen. Kramer stopped, considering Keen contemptuously. "Get a haircut."

Keen's eyebrows rose in surprise. "Excuse me?"

"And stop shaving. You look like a fucking cop. You'll stick out around here like an eighty-year-old nun in a knocking shop. Tomorrow morning, I want you in here looking more like one of the Mitchell brothers. And for chrissake, wear something that doesn't come out of a Lands' End catalogue."

"I'm not the one doing the covert work, I'm just supposed to be her handler."

Kramer laughed, a short, ugly bark. "You'll do whatever I bloody well *tell* you to do, and if I tell you to make the coffee, Priscilla, then that's exactly what you will do."

Oh, joy, Keen thought wearily, beginning to miss Nigel Mullard, wondering if next Kramer would be ordering him to get an ear-ring or HATE and LOVE tattooed on his knuckles.

Kramer's eyes shifted between the two of them before he leaned back in his chair, apparently satisfied he'd established his dominance in the pecking order. The hostility diminished markedly. Kramer took a last drag off his cigarette and stabbed it out in an ashtray with more force than necessary to extinguish it, the butt crushed to bits.

"Right. We've got a flat not too far from where this Rafferty bint lives. Since . . . what's your name again, petal . . . ?" He continued before Rachel could even open her mouth. "Rachel, that's right, got it now. Since Rachel here knows precisely jack shit about covert work, we're going to set the two of you up there together. We've had to give up one of our best safe houses for you two, I want you to know. Not best pleased about that, so don't break anything. You'll be more babysitter than handler." Kramer flashed a spiteful grin at Keen. "And you get to play landlord, not boyfriend."

Thank God for that, Keen didn't say. He had enough trouble with his real girlfriend.

Kramer turned his malevolent attention back on Rachel. "And you'll be restricted to surveillance, albeit a bit more up close and personal than I'd like for any agent with as little experience as you've got. Your job is relatively simple: just do the girl thang. Drink, chat, shop for shoes, swap lies about blokes you've shagged. I don't give a shit. But you never, *never* involve yourself in any of the animal rights groups she's connected to. You stay the hell away from them." As Rachel drew in a breath to protest, Kramer cut her off. "You're not trained for it—I don't give a rat's ass what bullshit they taught you down in London—and I don't have the time or patience to teach you. All you are is one more pair of eyes and ears out of many, many pairs—and ours have had a lot more practice than yours. We're less likely to end up with a bullet between them. You got that?"

This time Rachel simply nodded, the muscles along her jaw twitching.

"You report back to . . ." Kramer waved a hand at Keen impa-tiently

"Dunliffe," Keen supplied tonelessly.

"Dunny-boy, whatever, every night. You write up a detailed statement of everything you and Rafferty did and talked about, every detail. Except maybe for the shoes. If there's anything interesting or anything that correlates with any of the information my officers already have, we'll handle it from our end. *Danny!*"

Both Dunliffe and Rachel started at his full-throated bellow, as did the lad who had stifled his smile behind his computer screen. He jumped to his feet and obediently trotted the few feet into the open door of the office.

"Yes, boss?"

Kramer rooted around in the top drawer of the desk, then tossed a set of keys at Danny. The lad caught them one-handed.

"Give these two the grand tour, then take 'em to the safe house."

As Keen and Rachel stood, Keen steered her to the door ahead of him. "I'll be right with you," he said. "Just need a quiet word with the DI."

Kramer remained behind his desk but clasped his hands in front of him and leaned over aggressively while Rachel followed Danny out into the computer area.

"Well, well, Priscilla. Are we going to have a problem with you already?"

"Not yet," Keen said calmly. "I would just like to remind you that that 'poxy-arsed Yank' was a U.S. marshal murdered in the line of duty and that DI Sanders is a British police officer, still in hospital wondering if he'll ever walk again."

Kramer's eyes narrowed, but his feral snarl lost its sarcastic edge. Keen kept his gaze locked with the other man's, not giving ground. Finally, Kramer snorted and leaned back in his chair. "Point taken, Sergeant." He indicated Rachel with a glance directed at the woman being shown around the incident room. "Just try to keep that little girl of yours out of trouble long enough for McCraig to lose interest and ship you both back to where you belong. Are we clear on that?"

"Crystal."

"Good." Kramer lit another cigarette and opened a file on his desk, dismissing Keen without another glance.

Keen walked out of the man's office to where Rachel stood waiting for him with Danny. The office had emptied, only Danny and the scruffy man in the jeans still in the room. The younger man extended his hand, shaking Keen's with more force than necessary, but his grin seemed open and genuine.

"DC Danny Mayfield," he said, introducing himself. "I'm the team's technical and data collator."

"Our resident geek," the scruffy man in the jeans said laconically. He finished writing in the file, signing it with an illegible flourish, and closed it before looking up and flashing a smile. One gold-capped front tooth glittered with a diamond insert. He leaned back in his chair, the faded Phil-n-Time rock band T-shirt a size too tight and pocked with sweat holes, and rubbed the back of his fingers against the thick stubble on the edge of his jaw. His gaze traveled down Rachel's body and up again insolently. "Sweet," he drawled.

As Rachel stiffened, the man's grin widened. "That's his name," Danny hurriedly explained. "I mean that's what everyone calls him. It's not his real name. It's actually Christian Fletcher, like *Mutiny on the Bounty* and Pitcairn Island, and all that, except that was Fletcher Christian and his is the other way around, but he doesn't—"

"Danny?" Sweet interrupted without taking his eyes off Rachel. "Shut it."

"Right," Danny said sheepishly.

But the computer tech's babble had annoyed him, the interest in his expression fading. He stood up, shrugged into his leather jacket, and brushed between Rachel and Keen, intentionally close, forcing Rachel to step back out of his way. "Hope to see you around," Sweet said to her, then glanced at Keen. "But some of us have real work to do."

As Sweet backed his way out the door with a wry wink toward Rachel, another man passed him on his way in, a shabby cardboard evidence box in his arms. He walked past Rachel and Keen with a curious glance, then dumped the box on an unoccupied desk. He was in his late twenties, dark haired and dark eyed, with a razor-sculpted goatee on a bronze-skinned face, long hair pulled back in a short ponytail, and dressed casually, if with slightly more style than Danny.

"Hey, Sin. These are the two new guys. Rachel . . . um . . ."

"Colver."

"Sergeant Keen Dunliffe," Keen said, offering his hand.

"St. John Hawkins," the dark-haired man said, pronouncing it "Sinjin" as he shook Keen's hand perfunctorily. "And no, I'm not Asian," the man said tiredly. "It's like Saint John, except that's just the way it's said."

"I've read *Jane Eyre*," Rachel said.

St. John looked at her quizzically. "Good for you," he said, as if she was not quite rational, looked at Danny, and shrugged his obvious ignorance.

"It's the name of a character in the book by Charlotte Brontë," Danny said, and smiled supportively at Rachel, still trying hard to impress, Keen could see.

"Uh-huh," St. John said, unimpressed. "Me mum was an *Airwolf* fan. Just glad she didn't name me Stringfellow. Anyway, I got three more boxes of this shit in the boot of my car," he said to Danny, dismissing them. "These all need to be logged in and cross-checked by end of day if we want to get them to the pathologist for tomorrow morning."

"What are they?" Danny asked as he took the lid off the evidence box and removed a plastic-shrouded object. He held it by the top and let it unroll to reveal a splash of bright-colored feathers inside the bottom of the bag—green and red, blue and pink.

"Dead parrots."

"Eww." Danny said, dropping it onto his desk and pulling away, then reddened. "Actually, I think this one's a lovebird."

"I don't give a shit what it is, Sherlock. Just tag it and bag it and get them out of here before they start to stink, okay?"

"But the boss said I'm supposed to take these guys over to Holcroft Street."

The muscular man in a black polo shirt had returned. "We'll take care of it," he said. The belligerence he'd shown in the lift had gone, Keen noticed, but not been replaced by anything friendlier. All the same, he extended his hand to them both. "DC Pete Smythe," he introduced himself shortly.

Keen's relief they'd be spared any further etymology on names was short-lived as Danny added, "Smythe, with a *y* and an *e*." But Smythe's glare was enough for the computer tech to focus his attention back to the box of dead birds.

"You two have your own mobile phones, right?" Smythe asked.

Keen simply nodded as Rachel said, "Yes."

"Hand 'em over."

"Excuse me?" Keen said.

"Sin's got what you'll use while you're on the job."

St. John held out two identical mobile phones. "We'll reroute any of your private numbers to ring through on these from here. If these phones are stolen or lost, or the bad guys take a peek, there won't be anything on these to compromise friends or family. Or us."

"They've also got a tracker device," Smythe said. "It's dormant, can't be detected unless it's active, and it won't activate unless you punch in the code, or unless someone activates it from this end. Just in case anyone checks it."

Rachel handed over her phone without protest, while Keen gave his mobile to the tech with only token reluctance; half the time he forgot the damned thing anyway, and the only call he cared about missing would be from Jillie. If Laura ever needed to ring him about the boys, she knew enough to be able to contact him through Weetwood—they'd get a message through to him. In return, St. John gave them each an expensive-looking silver flip mobile. Keen struggled for a moment to figure out how to open it. Rachel, on the other hand, had opened hers with an adept flick of her wrist Keen could only admire.

"It's the latest Sharp J-SH05," Danny said eagerly and pointed to a button on Rachel's phone. "Hot out of the factory."

"Hot meaning new, not stolen," Smythe added dryly. Then he

raised his eyebrows. "Although who knows where the lads we took 'em off got them in the first place."

"It's got a dual SIM card, so we can split the calls. And it's also got a cool camera in it," Danny said, pointing to a spot on Rachel's phone. "Integrated 110,000 pixel CMOS imaging sensor, color TUFT LCD screen. Takes digital photos."

"Isn't this rather flash?" Rachel said, already playing with the device, while Keen stared at his distrustfully. The tech noticed, reached over and gave the thing a quick tap to turn it on. It beeped.

"Yeah, and so?" Kramer said from behind, visibly startling Rachel, who blushed with embarrassment. The DI glowered at her.

"So, how are either of us supposed to afford something like this?"

Kramer snorted. "You're a disgraced and disgruntled ex-cop." He jerked his head toward Keen. "He's a marginally house-trained sociopathic thug. That's the sort who always have the latest gear, and don't usually go about explaining to all and sundry how they got it. Got it?"

"Yes, sir," Rachel said quietly, fiddling with the phone to avoid eye contact with the DI.

"Well, then. If you girls are all finished cooing over your nifty new toys, why don't you get the fuck out of here?"

"We're going, boss," Smythe said and walked toward the exit without looking to see if Keen or Rachel were following behind. No one spoke on the way down in the lift, and it wasn't until the DC had led them outside and into a small fenced-off car park that Rachel said, "Is he always like that?" Keen wasn't sure if she was asking or just speaking to herself.

"Only when he's in a good mood," Smythe said. "Sometimes he's downright vicious."

They stopped in front of a line of battered aging cars. Smythe tossed Keen a set of keys attached to an unmarked green plastic tag. "You get the Escort." He chose to hand Rachel a second set of keys with a red tag. "You get the Polo." Both cars looked as if they'd been in more than a couple collisions, barely roadworthy.

"We get top-of-the-line mobiles, but crappy cars?" Rachel groused.

Smythe smiled. "We'll do our best to nick a couple of villainous scrotes with better quality motors for you, shall we? We use what we get." He turned to Keen. "Park up in here, you won't be needing your car while you're here—and you won't risk someone with a mate inside running the plates through PNC."

"You suspect there is someone?" Keen asked.

"We *always* suspect there's someone. You want to follow me."

They tossed their respective luggage into the cars as Smythe got into a late-model Rover in considerably better nick than the others. Smythe led them out of the car park, the engine of Keen's lime-green Escort knocking rather ominously while, in the rearview mirror, Keen could see puffs of black smoke behind the little red Polo every time Rachel changed gears.

Thankfully, Smythe drove slowly enough that neither of them was in danger of losing him as they drove through town, urban redbrick estate housing and kebab shops and rundown greengrocers left behind as they turned west onto the Scotwood Road, over the bridge, and soon enough were in the countryside, a few villages clustered along the horizon.

The safe house was in a cheerless estate on the edge of an even less prosperous village, the plain brick terrace house identical to every other terrace house along the row. Clouds of white steam billowed from a factory in the industrial park bordering the back gardens of the terrace, the rumble of heavy goods vehicles and the beeping of forklifts competing with birdsong. The house to the left had a faded FOR SALE sign stabbed into the weedy front garden, neglected flowers in the pots withered and brown. On the right, the sill of the front window of the house was overrun with hideously bright china dogs, heavy drapes behind the lace curtains drawn to block the sunlight.

As they parked along the curb, got out, and walked toward the front door of the safe house, Smythe nodded at the one for sale and said, "That's been empty for a few months. Bloke died, left three ex-wives and a bunch of kids. Family's still fighting over who gets what. Unlikely it'll be sold anytime soon." He nodded at the other. "Old dear in there is nearly ninety, stone-deaf. Doesn't get out much. Plays her tellie at top volume, tends to fall asleep in front of it, goes most of the night. You'll get used to it." He unlocked a newer dead bolt before rattling an antiquated oversized key into the lock, and pushed open the heavy wooden front door. A faint musty smell wafted out, inside colder than outside, as Symthe led them into the house. "Home sweet home," Smythe said wryly, and handed Keen the set of keys.

Inside, the short hall ended at a staircase. Smythe gave Rachel a second set of keys. "Your rooms are upstairs." As Rachel went upstairs to inspect her new lodgings, Smythe opened a door leading into the downstairs lounge. "This is yours," he said to Keen.

Inside, the carpet was a lurid green and pink paisley, worn near threadbare. The walls hadn't been papered since the 1960s, oversized brown flowers and grape leaves peeling at the corners. The furniture was a hodgepodge of charity shop rejects: a sagging sofa not matching the overstuffed armchair, a coffee table dappled with water rings. An empty pizza box sat on top of an old, oversized television, cardboard darkened with oil blotches. The three-bar electric fire had been badly fitted into the 1930s green tiled fireplace, and a faded print of some obscure Scottish loch hung over the mantel, the room's only attempt at decoration. An archway divided the lounge from the kitchen: drab pressboard units, worktops scarred and stained, a battered electric cooker buried under a thick layer of old grease. A smear of rust marked where the tap dripped into the porcelain sink. The fridge hummed asthmatically, with the occasional rattle of ice falling somewhere inside. The floor tiles had cracked and peeled, and a small collection of mouse turds had accumulated in the corners. Overhead, Keen could hear Rachel walking around, floorboards above his head creaking worryingly.

A small doorless area off to the side of the lounge that might have once fancied itself as a dining room now boasted only a single bed with a bare mattress, blue-striped ticking stained with suspicious yellowed rings. It was at least en suite, a toilet in a room barely big enough to contain it, and a shower with a plastic curtain with black mold filigreed along the hem.

In the far corner of the lounge, a desk sat catercorner, facing outward, with just enough space behind for the worn office chair. A large beige monitor and keyboard perched atop the desk, the twin computer towers tucked underneath. Smythe turned it on. It hummed to life, in better condition than anything else in the house.

"You're linked directly into the PNC," Smythe said, tapping the keyboard. "And everything else is pretty state of the art. Tweaked a bit, for security. You'll have to memorize some passwords, but there's a default button—hit that and it goes straight into a game of solitaire; you'll need to enter two passwords to get back in again. Just in case."

"Just in case what?" Keen said dryly.

Smythe shrugged. "Just in case."

Keen had lived in a variety of section housing in his younger days, most of it cheap, most of it cheerless, but nothing ever quite as dismal as this. He heard Rachel on the staircase, and both men turned as she entered the lounge. She was smiling. "Nice." Keen squinted. She wasn't being ironic. Smythe raised an eyebrow but didn't react.

"We've had Rafferty on our radar before, but up to now she's been pretty peripheral to any of our investigations," Smythe said, turning to Keen. "Most of the idiots she hangs out with are a bunch of disorganized, untrained, destitute student types with no special skills or knowledge but with big mouths and grandiose schemes. Other than getting drunk and gobbing off in student unions, these people aren't any more important than stink on shit, not worth the bother. A few of the hunt sabs she's run with before we do consider medium risk—some of them have military training and covert abilities. But because most of them also have a history of protesting in demonstrations or getting themselves nicked for vandalism, we know who and where they are. We keep an eye on them, but we don't have the manpower to waste on active surveillance. We're more interested in higher-risk cells, well funded, well trained, and covert—no history."

"Like JADA," Keen said.

"Yeah. Although we've never had any trouble with them this far north."

"So you don't think they're behind the warehouse bombing?"

Rachel said, refusing to allow him to exclude her from the conversation.

Smythe shook his head, the corners of his mouth pulled down. "Nah. JADA are pretty new kids on the block, at least in this country. ALF and PETA are our biggest headaches. As far as Rafferty goes . . ." Smythe shrugged again. "She's done some propaganda videos for PETA but nothing illegal. Clean as a whistle for the past six years, knows exactly where the line is with her sab pals and never crosses it now. Anyway, the Blue Bull in Corbridge is about five minutes down the road," Smythe said to Rachel. "Rafferty works there most evenings except Tuesdays and Sundays, that's probably your best point of contact."

"Okay." She glanced at Keen. "Should he go with me?"

Smythe stared at her, opened his mouth to speak, shut it and simply shook his head. He turned to Keen. "Just . . . try to stay out of trouble, okay?"

"Right," Keen said.

Smythe left without any further farewell.

"They all think I'm stupid, don't they?" Rachel said darkly.

"No," Keen said, and smiled at her. "They think you're young."

She glared at him, red flared high on her cheeks. "And what do you think?"

Keen shrugged. "I think you're young." Before she could protest, he moved to the desk and tapped the computer keyboard cautiously. "Which is probably a good thing for me because you're more likely than I am to know how this damned thing works."

1 1

Elaine and Harry Mathers sat together on a brightly upholstered sofa in a waiting alcove of the hospital wing, saying nothing, their hands entwined tightly. Piped music played over a muted intercom, instrumentals of bland eighties pop songs. Every time anyone walked by the open door of the waiting area, Elaine looked up with a start of hope and fear, then sagged against her husband again as no one spoke to them.

"Maybe I should go ask someone . . ." Harry murmured.

"You just did," Elaine said, her tone deadened. "Twenty minutes ago."

Several more minutes ticked by.

"Just to remind them that we're still here," Harry said.

Elaine sighed. "They know we're here." Now she sounded angry. "They've known we're here for the past six hours."

Another fifteen minutes elapsed. "I'll be right back," Harry said and stood up.

"Oh, Harry . . ."

"I have to pee," he said apologetically.

They smiled at each other, trying to be reassuring and only managing to look sad. And, of course, while Harry was in the bog, a nurse stuck her head around the corner of the alcove.

"Mr. and Mrs. Mathers?"

Elaine stood up hastily. "My husband's just gone to the toilet, he'll be right back." *Please don't leave, don't make us wait anymore . . .*

"That's fine," the nurse said. "Just to let you know, doctor will be with you shortly, won't be much longer."

The nurse left, Harry came back, and they were still waiting for the promised doctor forty minutes later. When the doctor did arrive—an immaculate white lab coat over an immaculate suit and silk tie, stethoscope draped around his neck like an insignia, and a metal-jacketed file under one arm—they both stood up automatically, clutching each other in dread. Elaine's nerves finally snapped, and she burst into tears before he could even speak. The doctor didn't even attempt to look encouraging.

"How is Isabella doing, Doctor?" Harry said, his voice shaking.

The doctor smiled but in the evasive way that conveys no particular warmth or confidence. "She's a very ill little girl, Mr. Mathers. We've put her in isolation, and we're still running tests, but to be honest, we haven't seen anything quite like this before. We're giving her several antibiotics, but she's not responding as expected." He looked back and forth between them. "We've decided that our best course of action for the moment is to slow down her metabolism as far as we can, so we've put her into an artificial coma, dropped her temperature. Give us some time to work out just what it is we're dealing with."

"Is she going to die?" Elaine could barely get the words out.

The doctor opened his mouth to speak, his expression uncertain. He exhaled in frustration. "We're doing everything we can, Mrs. Mathers," he said, which both parents knew was medical-speak for "I don't know."

The doctor referred to his metal-bound chart. "Now you said she got those scratches on her arms from a rabbit?"

"Yes, but it wasn't a wild rabbit," Harry said. "Just some stray bun that got loose from a hutch somewhere. She found it out in the back garden, soaking wet from the rain. Died a couple hours later, poor bugger."

Elaine Mathers was a step ahead of her husband.

"Could Izzie have caught something from that damned rabbit? Is it rabies?"

The doctor didn't meet her eye as he made a notation on the chart. "It's not very likely, Mrs. Mathers, and it's definitely not rabies, no. But until we can diagnose exactly what Isabella *does* have, we're exploring every possibility, no matter how improbable." When he did manage to look up, Elaine inhaled sharply, seeing the lie in his eyes. "If you feel up to it, there are a couple people in my office who would like to ask you a few questions about that rabbit . . ."

1 2

"I'm bored," Rachel said.

From where he sat behind the computer, Keen smiled at her over the top of his reading glasses on the bridge of his nose. "Yup. So you've said." *Repeatedly*.

Beryl Rafferty, no one had bothered to mention when busily rushing Keen and Rachel up to Newcastle, had gone off on a fortnight's holiday while the Blue Bull was shut for renovations. According to airline records, Rafferty had flown back to Britain from Hong Kong two days ago, and according to a phone message on the pub's answering machine, the Blue Bull would be open again for business at seven that evening. Rachel checked her watch again, sighed and dropped her arm. Keen reflexively glanced at the time in the corner of the monitor screen. One twenty-six P.M.

They'd been in the safe house for over a week, but there was nothing left for her to clean, he knew. She'd found musty linen in an upstairs cupboard, taken it all to a launderette, and turned his sordid bedsit into somewhere at least bearable to sleep. She'd scrubbed and washed and polished and hoovered and done the lot; the place hadn't been so spotless in decades. Now she lay sprawled on his lounge sofa, head propped on a cushion at one end, feet over the other, an open book turned facedown on her lap, one of his, he noticed. *The New Politics of Crime Control in the Community*, Jasmine's OU textbook. She'd already devoured his Ian Rankin novel, as well as the book on Roman Britain. She sighed, propped the book on her stomach, and doggedly read another page before turning it with a bit more force than necessary.

"Is it always this boring?"

"Mostly," Keen said, trying to concentrate on his screen. He typed in another number off the list Danny Mayfield had given him, searching for records of the dead birds from their leg bands. So far, he hadn't been overly successful. "There's a charity shop in the village. They should have some secondhand novels."

"I haven't finished this one yet."

He looked at her again over the top of his glasses, this time skeptically. "Interesting, is it?"

Rachel shrugged. "It's okay. Better than the one on Roman Britain."

That's what he was afraid of, he thought.

Next door, the old woman turned on her tellie, the volume up loud enough that he could identify Bruce Forsythe's voice, if not make out the actual words. Rachel groaned and dragged the cushion over her head to block her ears. She only held it there for a few moments before plopping it onto the floor in disgust. "Christ, she's like my nana."

"Should make you feel right at home, then."

"That's the problem," Rachel said darkly. "It does."

She didn't elaborate and he didn't ask. She picked up the book again, read another page, then let it drop on her lap. "What about you?"

"What about me what?"

"You're divorced, live by yourself, right?" When he looked up at her over the top of his glasses, she shrugged unapologetically. "You're going to be our new gaffer. You think we wouldn't check you out?"

He smiled, cleared his throat, and leaned back in his chair. "Yes, I live alone, if you don't count the cat."

"You have a cat?" She seemed surprised.

"Guess that wasn't in your investigative report. One tabby cat, Thomas. Fat bugger, crap at catching mice."

"I wouldn't have taken you for a cat person."

"I'm not a 'cat person.' He belonged to my wife, before she left us both. He's a country cat, didn't think he'd be too happy as a London moggie. So I inherited him."

"You don't mind living by yourself?" Her tone seemed almost wistful.

"It's not something I dwell on," he said. Or at least not as much as he would ever openly admit to. "At the moment, it's not an option."

"I wouldn't mind living on my own." She looked momentarily unsure. "Not that I ever have. But it would be nice, having my own place. Do what I want, when I want, not have to answer to anyone."

"Mm" was his only comment. After several years of doing what he wanted when he wanted and not answering to anyone, he was finding it rather monotonous.

"You don't have a girlfriend, then."

He hesitated. How to describe Jillie? "I'm . . . seeing someone." On very rare occasion, he didn't add. Even though Jillie had arrived four days ago, staying at a bed-and-breakfast near the dig in the quaintly named village of Twice Brewed—less than an hour's drive away—they'd only had a few phone calls and had yet to meet. Even with her inside the country, their relationship still seemed as long-distance as it was with her in faraway Oregon.

"What about your kids?" Rachel asked.

He knew that would also have been in any information the Sandford nick had dug up on him but suspected she was just making conversation to dispel the tedium. "Twin boys, Simon and Colin. They live with their mother in London, but I see them as often as I can. They'll be going to a boarding school in Harrogate next year, so I'll have every other weekend with them."

Despite himself, he couldn't help talking about his boys, as if just saying their names brought them closer to him. The awareness, though, made him uncomfortable. "How about you, got a boyfriend?"

She sighed. "No. Not anymore." When she said nothing more, he chuckled. "What?"

"You started this. You've wheedled out my deep dark secret about me having a cat. You want to talk, fine. It's your turn."

"I had a boyfriend," she said, a bit aggressively. "In high school.

140

He went off to university, I stayed home taking care of my nana. He got married. I got a dog. And a job. That pretty much sums up my entire life. The end. Roll the credits."

"You're only twenty-four, loads of time yet."

"For what?" she said sullenly. "I'm lucky I'm allowed to have a job and a dog. Because as long as my nana is alive, I sure as hell am not going to be allowed to have a life." She winced, as if embarrassed by exposing the sheer nakedness of her resentment. She rolled off the sofa. "You want a cuppa?"

"Sure," he said, although he didn't. But it would at least give her something to do, he understood.

When she brought it through and put it on the desk in front of him, she leaned over to inspect the computer screen.

"You're still working on Danny's bird case?" She was back to being all business. "I thought you'd finished with all that."

"Nope, loads more where that came from. This bit's mostly scut work he's cooperating on with Custom and Excise, nothing too exciting." He flashed her a quick grin. "Never hurts to ingratiate yourself with the low-ranking team members, though. They're usually the ones who *know* how to get things done, rather than the bosses, who just tell you to get it done."

Her eyes narrowed at him. "But . . . you are one of the bosses."

"Not here, I'm not." He shrugged. "And it's something to do to pass the time."

She sighed again, looked at her watch, then back at his computer screen dispiritedly. "So, what are you doing now?"

"Mostly simple data entry. Checking ring tag numbers from the information in our files against all known police and Custom and Excise databases to see if we come up with a match. I only have the British lists, although a lot of these birds had foreign tags, those that had any. But forensics is showing that some of them have been tampered with."

"Really?" That piqued her interest. "How?"

"By taking a ring off one bird and putting it on another. A few of the metal bands have identical plier marks, so we know there's at least one common source for some of these birds."

"Switch bands around, so an illegal bird becomes a legal one?"

"For the purpose of importation, yes."

She looked at him speculatively. "You've done a lot of this before."

"I wouldn't say 'a lot.'" He paused to sip his cup of tea and stretch his back. "I've been the ad hoc wildlife crime officer for my nick for the past year or so, dealing mainly with local egg hunters and protected birds of prey. Still not quite up to speed on parrots and exotic birds just yet, working on it."

They both turned as they heard a key in the door and relaxed as Danny Mayfield's cheerful voice called from the hallway. "Hi, it's just me, guys." When he appeared in the doorway of the lounge, he grinned over the top of a stack of files in his arms. Keen's heart sank.

"More backlog?" Keen said. This had been his third delivery in as many days.

"Yeah, some of it," Danny said. "Most of it, actually. I really appreciate your helping out like this." His boyish grin made him look even younger than he was, like a grateful teenager. "We got a ring back from RSPB. Officer there's anxious for a word. Seems there were a couple of dodgy scarlet macaws in that haul; those are on his Appendix I CITES list."

"Convention on International Trade in Endangered Species," Keen clarified for Rachel. From her expression, he realized she already knew that.

"That's right," Danny said, nodding earnestly. He stopped nodding when Keen glanced up at him with a raised eyebrow. "Anyway, he tells me scarlet macaws can only be imported if they've been bred in captivity and come with all the proper certificates, import and export documents and the like. Our birds have rings, so they're checking for a match and contacting the Department of Environment to see if any of our birds had an import permit. If they didn't, it'll get reported as an offense to Customs."

"If there's a match."

"Which is why we're checking all the databases." As Keen smiled, he amended, "I mean, *you* are. It's not one of our bigger cases, but the data entry is really time-consuming. Has to be done, though. And you've got more experience with the animal side of things than I do." He turned to Rachel, trying to sound apologetic while all too transparently doing his best to impress her. "Our lot sort of concentrate more on the people side of things. Y'know, catching bad guys."

To her credit, Rachel didn't appear overly impressed. "You don't consider people who smuggle exotic birds into the country to be 'bad guys'?"

"Of course I do," Danny said defensively. "But it's not quite in the same league as animal rights fanatics murdering people . . ."

"Really?" Rachel's eyes had widened, and Keen suppressed a smile, leaning back in his chair to watch the brewing confrontation. "You think bird smugglers are all just a harmless bunch of nutty collectors, doing it because they love animals? Do you know that wildlife smuggling is second only to drugs? More money in it than even the arms trade? And it's tied into worldwide money laundering and organized drug gangs. Last time I looked, we still called those sorts of people 'bad guys.' "

Aha, Keen thought. She had been listening to him after all.

"All I'm saying is—"

"Seventy percent of birds smuggled into this country end up dying because they've been stuffed into bog roll tubes or overdosed on Valium. Last year, some bastard was caught smuggling a couple of Lear's macaws into the country. There's only a hundred and forty Lear's macaws left, they're that rare. One of his died. You know what he could have got for them? Over fifty thousand pounds. *Each.* People are killed for less. But when you're making that kind of money, it's worth the risk and a lot of dead birds."

That hadn't been something she'd picked up from him, Keen realized.

"Okay, okay!" Danny threw up his hands in defeat. "I just meant . . . y'know."

"Yeah," Rachel said scathingly. "I do know. You meant leave the boring paper-pushing crap to the new girl and the old man, so the big boys can bugger off and do the more exciting jobs."

"Watch who you're calling an old man," Keen said mildly.

She took it as a reprimand. "Sorry, boss."

"Look, I'm not . . . I wasn't saying . . ." Danny stammered. Then he grimaced. "Goddamn it." He turned around and picked up the files off the desk again. "I'm sorry, really. Don't worry about it. I'll take care of it, sorry, it's not a problem . . ."

"Danny?" Keen said quietly.

"Yeah."

"Why don't you leave that here and go take Constable Colver out for some lunch."

They both looked at him askance. "Really?" Danny said.

"But I don't—" Rachel started to object.

"You," he said, pointing a finger at her, "are driving me nuts. And you"—his finger shifted to Danny—"are looking for excuses to be here, which is just making more work for me. So the two of you take your argument somewhere else and let me get on in peace. Take your time. As much time as you like."

"Okay," Danny said brightly, then hesitated. "Just need to get the rest of the files from the car first . . ."

Rest of the files? Keen closed his eyes and sighed as Danny left the flat. When he opened them again, he raised an eyebrow at Rachel. "You've been doing your research." She looked vaguely embarrassed, like a kid caught cheating. "Good on you. What kind of macaws again?"

"Lear's macaws. Come from Brazil, dark blue with yellow cheeks. Nest in sandstone cliffs and eat palm nuts."

"And you got all that off the PNC?"

She snorted a laugh. "No." She indicated his computer with a nod. "Off the Internet. It's called a search engine. I like to use Web-Crawler."

"Uh-huh. Just bring me back a sandwich, cheese and pickle, and a Diet Coke. And when you get back, you can show me how to use this Web crawling thing."

1 3

Lunch with Danny was the closest thing she'd had to a date in years, Rachel realized. And she was too much of a woman not to notice that Danny had a serious crush on her as well—flattering, even if the feeling wasn't reciprocal. Danny was too eager to please, too adolescent in his disposition. Sweet but harmless, and Rachel had to admit she preferred blokes with slightly more of an edge.

But Rachel came back from lunch in a better mood, with a Somerfield's cheese and pickle sandwich encased in a plastic triangle, and a squashed bag of crisps and a liter bottle of room-temperature Coke for Keen. He was still sitting behind the computer, but when she set his lunch on the desk, she noticed he was playing solitaire.

"It's okay, Mum," he said and patted Danny's stack of files. "I finished my homework first."

That made her smile. She spent the next few hours showing him how to use search engines while he ate his sandwich, drank his Coke, and asked her questions that made her certain he wasn't as ignorant about computers as he was making out to be. No more than she had pretended to be about wildlife smuggling.

Then she went upstairs to shower and change, getting ready for her first attempt at contact with Rafferty at the Blue Bull. She couldn't help the feeling of excitement buzzing in her veins, taking care to blow-dry her hair and put on her makeup. After a moment's consideration, she scrubbed the makeup off again, and applied only a bit of mascara and liner. *Less is more,* she thought.

When she came downstairs, dressed in worn jeans and a denim jacket over an old sweatshirt, scuffed boots, and her hair pulled back in a loose ponytail, she was surprised to see DI Kramer waiting for her in the lounge, sitting in the armchair as if he was Henry the Eighth on his throne, legs braced apart, hands gripping the ends of the arms. Keen sat at the far end of the sofa, leafing idly through his *New Politics of Crime Control in the Community* textbook. They both looked up as she entered the lounge and stopped in uncertainty.

"That what you wearing?" Kramer said by way of a greeting.

"Why? What's wrong with it?"

The DI looked her over scowling. "Nothing," he said finally. "Thought it might be a good idea if I came by and had a little pep talk with you before your first night, make goddamned sure you understand the ground rules."

Just great, she thought acidly. But she said, "Appreciated, sir."

"Undercover police operations," Kramer said, "doesn't mean you've got carte blanche to do whatever you fucking well please. Catching bad guys isn't enough—you gotta catch the bastards in a way that'll stand up in a court."

"Yes, sir, I know. I'm familiar with the Home Office guidelines about entrapment. No member of the police force in undercover should engage in any plans to commit a crime or act as an agent provocateur by encouraging others to commit a crime."

Kramer squinted at her. "This isn't a question on one of your fucking exam papers, sweetpea. You don't get any extra credit points here. This is how we do it for real. It's a bit of a complicated technique, so listen carefully: You go to the pub, you get a pint, then you sit down and drink it."

"Yes, sir."

"That's it. You keep your role passive, and let Rafferty recognize you. You don't try anything smart, like ask her for a packet of crisps and give her a funny look hoping that'll jog her memory. You don't drop handy hints, you don't talk about yourself to anyone there while she's listening, zip, zero, nada, *rien du tout.*"

"And if she doesn't recognize me?"

"Then you finish your fucking pint and you leave. *Comprendre?*"

Trying to mask her disappointment, she said, "Yes, sir. And if she does recognize me, I know my cover story." She glanced at Keen. "We've gone through it several times." Over and over and over.

"Really. So when were you dismissed from the police force?"

"December ninth, last year."

Kramer snorted his disgust. "And that, darlin', is exactly the kind of answer that's going to get you into trouble. Let's try it again. When did you get that pert little round arse of yours booted out the door?"

When Rachel didn't answer, Kramer hauled himself to his feet, stepped across to her and glowered into her face. "*Attitude*," he barked. "It's all about attitude. You're going to be out there, all on your own. This isn't like it is on the sodding tellie, you don't get to wear a fancy wire with half a dozen beefy lads stuffed in a van hanging on to your every word and valiantly rushing to your rescue should you balls it up. You've got to be able to think on your feet. You don't just memorize a shitload of facts; you *live* them. So—you got sacked for tampering with evidence and giving a false statement to cover up for a naughty colleague. Isn't that right?"

"Yes, sir—"

"*No, it fucking well is not!*" She blinked at his breath in her eyes. "You were *innocent*, you didn't do anything wrong, you were set up, it was the naughty colleague who lied through his teeth and tried to pin it all on you. *Right?*"

"Uh, yes—"

"Bloody hell." Kramer cut her off in disgust, turning away and dropping back heavily into the armchair. Dust puffed out of the fabric from his weight. "You know, we got a pool going on for how long it takes for you to blow your cover," Kramer said, his voice back to merely sarcastic rather than enraged. "Me, I'm betting you don't even get through tonight." He turned to Keen. "How 'bout you, Priscilla. You want in on it?"

Her blood was whooshing through her ears, and she knew her face must be blotchy with humiliation.

"Nah," she heard Keen say coolly. "She'll be fine."

Kramer snorted, then smiled at Rachel. It wasn't a nice smile. "Well, off you go, then, petal. Go prove one of us wrong."

14

Kramer waited until Rachel had left, but to Keen's surprise he made no indication of leaving. "You got anything to drink around this tip?"

In response, Keen hoisted the half-empty plastic bottle of lukewarm Coke. Not unexpectedly, Kramer scowled. "Fuck that." He reached into the inside of his jacket to retrieve a silver flask, unscrewed the top, and tipped back a mouthful. Also, not unexpectedly, he didn't offer the flask to Keen.

"I hear Danny's got you working his bird case."

"Don't mind pitching in," Keen said laconically.

"He's a bit of a twit, our Danny. Like a badly trained puppy. Never around when you want him, and always underfoot when you don't." Kramer reached into his jacket again, this time extracting a small envelope from the other side of his jacket and tossing it to Keen. "Prezzie for you."

Inside the envelope were a few dozen photographs, obviously someone's holiday snaps rather than surveillance photos, panoramic palm trees and white beaches, and all with a light-stamped time and date along the bottom corner, six months old. In the first, a group of middle-aged women stood alongside a potbellied mustachioed man evidently a local guide, with their arms held out as perches for a dozen bright-colored parrots.

"Scarlet macaws?"

"Mm-hm," Kramer said, taking another swig from his flask.

Keen slipped that one behind the rest in his hand, then examined the second, wondering what significance they held. A group of people in a restaurant, all wearing CHEERFUL CHARLIE'S CHARTERS T-shirts, raised wineglasses for the camera. The flash hadn't gone off, the shot gloomy and dark. Another showed the same group playfully threatening each other with lobsters, this one washed out with far too much flash. Keen shuffled through the photos, most of them banal shots of ocean sunsets and fake native huts, strangers in touristy straw hats and baggy shorts and garish island shirts, until he came to one that made him pause. A tanned bodybuilder in a tight-fitting Speedo sat at a bar grinning at the camera, his arm possessively around a young blond woman. She, on the other hand, was visibly giving him the cold shoulder, her head twisting away as if attempting to hide from the lens, paying more attention to her coconut-shell drink. Keen held it up to Kramer.

"Beryl Rafferty."

"Yup."

"Who's the bloke?"

"Not a clue."

"Where'd these come from?" Keen asked.

Kramer laughed, almost soundlessly. "Let's just say their provenance might not satisfy all the niceties of British law, Danny being the useless twit that he is. He's a clever computer geek and barely passable collator, but he's a lousy field agent. So you don't need to know."

Kramer's mood had darkened to a peculiar calm. "But as long as he's got you working his silly bird case on the side, check it out—see if there's any connection between Rafferty and the fancy poultry we've got in our freezer."

"Why didn't you show these to Rachel while she was here?"

Kramer snickered. "Let's just see if she makes it through the first day. Maybe I'll get lucky and be able to ship you both back to Bumfuck, Yorkshire, tomorrow morning before the two of you screw up something really important."

Keen frowned, but only said, "Any idea where these were taken?"

Kramer took a last swig, tucked his flask back in his jacket, and heaved himself to his feet. "Beryl Rafferty is a little gadfly buzzing around a big pile of shit, a pain in the arse who fancies herself Nellie Bly with a camcorder. I'm focusing my limited team resources on the big pile of shit. You, on the other hand, are stuck with the gadfly. It's all yours, knock yourself out, Priscilla."

The Blue Bull smelled of fresh paint and new carpet when Rachel walked into the old stone cottage pub, the bar just inside the front door already occupied by a few obvious regulars and a couple waiting to be seated in the refurbished dining rooms. The landlord stood behind the pumps, polishing a shot glass and looked up at her expectantly. To Rachel's disappointment, he seemed to be alone, Rafferty nowhere in sight.

"What can I getcha, love?"

Rachel quickly scanned the labels on the pumps, grinned, and said, "Pint of Bitter and Twisted, please."

The landlord pulled her pint without comment, waited for the head to subside as he gave her change for her fiver, then topped her glass. She took it and sat down next to the open fire, trying to look relaxed. After a moment, she retrieved Keen's Ian Rankin novel from her denim jacket pocket and pretended to read it, scanning the pages without taking in much of the words. Every so often, she would turn a page, look up, exchange a quick impersonal smile with either the landlord or one of the patrons quietly nursing their pints at the bar before gazing back at her book.

After an hour, she had only an inch of beer left in the glass and was ready to admit defeat when she heard voices from the little alcove behind the oak bar front leading to the kitchens. Her heart beat faster as Beryl Rafferty ambled out to escort the waiting couple to a table in the dining room. When Rafferty had seated them and taken their order, she walked back toward the kitchens. Rachel kept her focus on the paperback, then wondered if that would seem unnatural. She glanced up as Rafferty passed by, made the briefest of eye contact, and looked back at the book.

But if Rafferty recognized her, she made no sign of it. She went behind the bar and began washing dirty pint glasses, rinsing them in a sink of sudsy water. Rachel forced herself not to react, mindful of Kramer's instructions. Then, she thought, that seemed stupid as well—she remembered Rafferty all too well. Wouldn't it seem more peculiar if she *didn't* recognize her? So she sighed, sat back in her chair, put down the paperback, and practically glared at Rafferty's back. Rafferty must have sensed it, as she turned and met Rachel's gaze evenly before a knowing smile spread across her face.

"Well, well," Rafferty said. "Rachel Colver. Thought that was you. What the hell are *you* doing here?"

"Fancy that," Rachel retorted and allowed a bit of honest anger to leak into her tone. "I was going to ask you the same thing. You? Working as a lowly barmaid? How the mighty have fallen. What happened, Mummy cut off your credit cards?"

Rafferty had the grace to laugh, albeit not that pleasantly. "Actually, Daddy did. What happened with *you*—your gran finally unchain you from the basement, or did you just smother the evil old bitch with a pillow?"

"Nana's having trouble with her short-term memory, senile dementia, doctors think she might have onset Alzheimer's." *As if,* she thought. The evil old bitch never forgot a thing, especially anything she could use to dominate her granddaughter. "She won't even notice I'm gone."

Rafferty dropped some ice into a half-pint glass, poured herself a lemonade from the spigot, then crossed to sit down at Rachel's table. "I'd say I was sorry, but I suspect you aren't, either. So, is this a permanent escape, or are you taking a holiday?"

"Just wanted to get the hell away from Sandford, from Yorkshire, from everything. Been looking for a job in Newcastle, haven't had a lot of luck."

Rafferty snorted. "Yeah, that's a great plan. Go *north* to find work." Then she gauged Rachel shrewdly. "Thought you had a job, anyway. Last I heard you'd joined the police."

Live the role, Kramer had said. So she shrugged with what she hoped was cynical indifference. "Didn't work out."

Rafferty leaned back in her chair. "You're kidding, right? Little Miss Goody Two-shoes not good enough for the cops? You quit or did they sack you?"

Rachel felt her face flushing, more from being called Miss Goody Two-shoes than anything else, but it was useful, she realized. And scowled. "Just didn't work out, that's all." Which was as good as any confession. The fabricated details could come out in their own time.

"They sacked you."

"What about *you*? You give up making your silly antihunt videos for a real career as a barmaid?"

Rachel envied how Rafferty's expression didn't falter, not a flicker of anger or embarrassment.

"I still cover the occasional foxhunt as a monitor," Rafferty said amiably.

"'Monitor,'" Rachel scoffed. "What a nice euphemism for sabs."

"'Hunters,'" Rafferty returned. "What a nice euphemism for chinless toffs on horses killing harmless animals for sport."

"Oh, bullshit. You know as well as I do most fox hunters are farmers and country people, not toffs—which, by the way, is what you are yourself, y'know. Class traitor and all that."

Rafferty didn't rise to the bait. "Jesus Christ, Rach. I haven't seen you in, what? Five, six years? And we're still having the same old arguments. I'd have thought you'd have grown up since we were kids in school."

"Seven years," Rachel said. "And you haven't changed a bit, either."

A shadow passed across Rafferty's expression. "I wouldn't quite say that. So . . ." She shifted gears, brightening with a visible effort. "You seeing anyone, now that you've escaped your horrible gran's claws?"

"No." Rachel tried to keep it from sounding flat or from showing any annoyance—it was one thing for her to knock her grandmother, quite another for someone else, no matter how twisted her loyalty was. "You?"

Rafferty sipped her lemonade. "No one serious."

A heavyset farmer walked into the pub, a regular by the way he smiled and nodded at Rafferty. She didn't even ask him before she poured a pint of Guinness, set it in front of him along with a packet of crisps. He paid her in silence, then hunched over the bar to sip on his pint, neither of them having exchanged a word.

"You busy tomorrow night?" Rafferty said to Rachel, while scribbling something on the back of a page from her order pad.

"Why?"

Rafferty ripped off the page and handed it to Rachel. "I'm doing the lunch shift, off at six. Come over to my place, about seven-thirty, we'll go out clubbing and get properly pissed." Rafferty made a face at Rachel's attire. "That is, if you have anything to wear that doesn't look like you're going out to milk the cows."

"I'll try to come up with something that won't embarrass you in front of your posh mates," Rachel shot back, and wondered if Kramer would allow her to buy a decent dress on the team's budget.

"There's an Oxfam shop end of the high street," Rafferty retorted, then laughed, all the enmity in their banter spent. "It's actually good to see you again, Rach. Let's go show this northern back of beyond how *real* girls party."

16

The next day, Keen decided that it would be his turn to go out for lunch while Rachel wrote up her report on the previous evening on the computer and did a bit of Web crawling herself. After a few phone calls and a bit of orchestration, Jillie took the Northern Arriva train to meet him halfway at the Norman Arms pub on the edge of a small village fifteen minutes from the safe house.

Or it would have been, had there not been a tailback on the motorway, an overturned lorry leaking a dark viscous fluid onto the road that, by the smell and the glimpse of a few stiffened sheep's hooves, emanated from a cargo of dead animals on their way to a pyre or burial. Uniformed police waved him past impatiently, ignoring the multitude of tires tracking through the grisly spillage.

The pub was next to the railway line directly above the Tyne River, the overhead level crossings of Victorian filigreed wrought iron painted red matching the trim on the whitewashed walls of the building. A CAMRA sign out front propped up by half-barrel planters overflowing with geranium and impatiens declared this to be the Pub of the Year. He was twenty minutes late when he parked behind the train station and crossed the road to the pub. The place was busy but not crowded; locals sitting at the dark oak bar barely glanced at him as he searched the low-beamed rooms anxiously, half expecting Jillie to have walked out, believing he'd stood her up. To his relief, she was sitting by herself in a corner of the pub, nursing the half-inch residue of cider left in the bottom of her pint glass. He smiled as he walked toward her, his smile broader as she looked up, her eyes not registering him for a moment before widening in surprise.

"Jesus," she said, then stood and hugged him after a quick kiss. She had exchanged her usual academic attire of skirts and heels for an outfit more suited to an extra in *Raiders of the Lost Ark*—beige shorts with a multitude of pockets, scrunched socks over hiking boots, a denim jacket tossed carelessly over the back of the seat beside her dusty and battered.

She drew back, incredulous. "You look . . . different."

He laughed softly, aware of how rough and unshaven he looked, and ran his hand over his close-cropped scalp. "You don't like the new me?" When he saw her hesitate, not sure how to respond, he added, "It's for the job. Don't worry, it grows back." *Most of it, anyway,* he thought.

"Oh. Okay." She didn't look reassured.

"I'll get you a fresh one," he said, taking her near-empty glass. He returned with a pint of Strongbow cider and a pint of Gold Tankard ale.

The place was quiet, only the murmur of conversation rather than the usual blare of jukebox music. Most of the patrons sat at the bar or at café-style tables set into window seats. The only other occupant at this end of the room, an elderly man in a flat cap and green hunting vest, sat with a bag of crisps and a copy of the *Gazette* spread in front of him. An equally elderly dog, too heavy to have been a purebred greyhound, lay at his feet, mournful eyes watchful for any stray bit of food that might happen to drop from above. Other than a quick and quite deprecating glance at Keen, the old man expressed no further interest in either of them.

"You look different, too," Keen said as he set her pint of cider on the trestle table and took a long drink of his ale.

She colored slightly. "I got my hair lightened," she admitted, touching the mass of unruly curls tentatively. "You like it?"

That wasn't what he'd meant, but he said, "Looks great."

She looked different, he realized after a while, because she *was* different. The dissatisfied college teacher he'd first met nearly a year ago had grown from an uncertain, reticent woman into someone confident and energetic. Then, she had been distressed by the death of an old college roommate, mistrustful and wary in her fixation on solving her friend's murder, weighed down with her own troubled past, and had turned to him for help and support. After his wife, Laura, had taken his boys and divorced him, he'd found himself left adrift and rudderless, and he had to reluctantly admit a small part of his attraction to Jillie was simply one of enjoying being needed again. Now, as she talked about the new dig, he watched her face glowing with enthusiasm, her hands restless with punctuation, and felt a strange sort of loss. It was illogical, he knew, as well as selfish; she'd already embraced a new direction in her life, as well she should have, while he was still struggling with his own inadequacies and not liking the switch in their positions very much.

"You get a lot of medieval ecclesiastical buildings built directly on top of the sites of Roman forts and towns," she was saying. "Reculver in Kent and Bradwell-on-Sea in Essex, for example. A lot of them reused stone from Roman ruins; why quarry fresh stone when you've got a cheap and convenient source already, right? Up until the early eleventh century, the only structures built of stone were churches, but the weird thing about the finds we've had so far suggest this wasn't a church but a villa. So what we think we've got is an Anglo-Saxon stone structure, probably intended as a monastery or an abbey, then abandoned about halfway through, and never used as a church. Dr. Sheridan's theory is that it was later used as the foundation of a secular building, finished in timber and the standard wattle-and-daub, converting it into a rich man's country estate, if we're judging by some of the quality of the finds so far. The other interesting thing is that the original ecclesiastical building would have been on top of what would have been a Roman outpost. But the Roman stuff is pre-Hadrianic, around the second century, and almost all of it timber built." Her eyes sparkled with delight. "So, no *spolia*—no Roman stone at that depth of excavation, anyway."

"Right," he said, not really following the plot but determined to be contented with simply being in her company again.

"And yet we're finding huge blocks of *opus quadratum* stonework—"

"*Opus whatus* . . . ?"

Her hands waved at him impatiently in her excitement. "High-status Roman relief carvings, a lot of them with anthropomorphic or bestial designs. We've got architectural moldings with acanthus leaves, bead and reel decoration, dentil and cable patterns, that sort of thing."

"Uh-huh." Whatever that meant.

"Not the usual ordinary facing stone that would have been a lot easier to transport and build with; some of these stones weigh over a ton. So where did all this Roman *spolia* to build our medieval villa come from?"

"You *are* going to tell me, right?"

She laughed. "Well, that's what we're going to try to find out. Dr. Sheridan thinks that whoever built our medieval building wasn't so much interested in the pragmatic or economic side of things as they were in the symbolism. I mean, look at Hexham Abbey—that's a prime example of someone reusing ornamental Roman *spolia* to boost the prestige of the place, a sort of declaration that the Roman Catholic Church was the legitimate successor to ancient imperial Rome's authority. But Hexham Abbey wasn't built on a Roman site. It was on empty land donated to Wilfred, the Bishop of York, in A.D. 674 by Queen Æthelthryth, who was the wife of the king of Northumbria, Ecgfrith. Wilfred wanted to build the abbey directly on the Roman ruins of Coria, which is Corbridge now. But he had to take what he was given and make the best of it."

Once again, Keen had to admire Jillie's schoolteacher's ability to absorb massive amounts of obscure names and dates and facts like a sponge, even if none of those names or dates or facts held all that much personal interest for him.

"He still looted a lot of Roman stone from Corbridge, which is only four miles away, most of that just plain, ordinary facing stone, small stuff, not a problem. But a lot of it is really big stuff taken from temples along with bits off a Roman bridge across the Tyne. And carried *upstream*. They couldn't possibly have used boats, not that part of the Tyne, too shallow."

"Hmmm," Keen murmured, his stomach rumbling and his mind more on what the Norman Arms had on its lunch menu.

"The only way you could transport stone that large or that heavy is by oxcart, all along the Stanegate Roman road, taking the long way around, over seven miles. We've had a petrological survey done on the stone from our site, and quite a bit of it also comes from Corbridge as well, leftovers or broken pieces that the abbey rejected. But we've also got stone with inscriptions that Dr. Sheridan believes could be coming from as far away as twenty-five miles."

Keen didn't know much about Roman history or medieval construction methods, but his ear had been trained well enough to notice that this was the third time Jillie had mentioned Dr. Sheridan. He wondered if the sparkle in her eye was due to more than just the thrill of an unusual archaeological site, not liking his sudden twinge of jealousy, either.

"Anyway, we've just got going on it, for this year, but it's been pretty soggy ground what with all the rain. It's been making the dig harder than we expected. So far, we've only been able to excavate the backfill from last year's dig and cut a couple of exploratory trial trenches around where we think the western outlines of the villa were . . ." She stopped, examining his expression. "I'm boring you, aren't I?"

"What? No, of course not," he said hastily. "I enjoy the odd *Time Team* now and again myself." From her reaction, he was sure she hadn't seen the program. "Look, I'm starving, let me buy you lunch."

Jillie had the carrot and tomato soup with a wholemeal roll, while Keen decided he needed something a bit more substantial and ordered the vegetable lasagna.

"You given up your diet, then?" Jillie asked.

"No," Keen admitted. "But I need to fall off the wagon now and again, just to reinforce the resolution."

"So . . ." Jillie dropped her voice and leaned forward, her gaze sweeping around the room conspiratorially. "Tell me about this . . . thing you're doing?"

Keen tried to keep the wince off his face. The pub was uncommonly quiet, no television or piped music to mask conversation, only the small number and disinterest of fellow patrons keeping their privacy. But her body language couldn't have telegraphed it better had she stood on the table with a megaphone.

"I can't talk about it, Jillie."

"Not even a hint?"

He was surprised to find himself irritated, not a feeling he had experienced much whenever he was with her. Well . . . not for some time, anyway.

"It's not a game," he tried to say without reproach. "And I really can't talk about it." She took it as a rebuke anyway, he could see. He added quickly, trying to salvage the moment, "But let me tell you about something I've been working on back home . . ."

He related the story of the stolen birds of prey at the East Beck Falconry Centre but steered it away from the crime, putting his emphasis on Gerald Mitchell's picketing of the local leisure center, demanding wheelchair access to the fields for his longbow archery club. He must have done a good enough job at amusing Jillie with the anecdote, as she laughed in all the right places and quickly enough forgot her pique with his evasiveness.

But something subtle had changed between them, he realized. They picked at the remains of their lunches, sitting across from each other with awkward smiles and uneasy silence.

"You never talk much about yourself, you know that?" Jillie suddenly said, disconcertingly direct. It seemed he'd conveniently forgotten that particular trait of hers as well.

"I do," he protested, taken aback.

"No you don't. You talk about other people, you tell me funny stories, but you don't really talk about what you're thinking, what you're feeling, nothing about *you.*"

Keen sat back, gauging her. "Neither did you, when we first met, if you'll recall."

"That was different," she said. "I'd just lost a friend, and you were . . . dealing with it professionally."

"I didn't mind listening. Still don't."

"*Listening*, sure. But that's not exactly a conversation, is it? Is that a technique you learned in"—she hesitated, trying to be

160

cautious—"your job, getting people to talk to you while you never give anything away?"

"No," he said, then, "not exactly."

He'd never been much of a conversationalist with either sex, preferring to sit back and observe. True, the ability to listen was an asset in his job. The reverse was more difficult; he often found anything more complex than a recitation of facts in his police reports sticky.

"Maybe it's that I've never had all that much time to get to know you," Jillie complained. "We've had, what? A couple weeks in London and a couple weeks in Portland over the last year? A few phone calls and letters? We just always seem to end up chatting about the weather, about your kids or the cat, or my daughter, or the university and what I'm going to be doing on this dig. But now that you're doing . . . what you're doing . . . you can't talk about that, either."

It was disturbing, hearing her give a voice to his own private misgivings, his uncertainty they—or rather he—could overcome the impediments in their long-distance relationship.

"It's my job, Jillie," he said, and added—so that she would end the That Which May Not Be Spoken charade—"It comes with being a cop."

She smiled wryly, relaxing just slightly now that it was in the open. "Well, okay. Maybe it *is* the job, then—even if you're not what I ever thought a cop was supposed to be like."

"I'm not?"

"No. You're"—she shrugged—"nice."

It should have felt like a compliment, but strangely it didn't, rankling. "What did you expect? Six feet ten of testosterone stuffed in a uniform, mirror sunglasses, and jackboots?"

"Hey, you don't know L.A. cops!"

"I've read Joseph Wambaugh," he said dryly.

She blinked. "Who?"

He almost laughed, realizing that in her own way, her education was as limited as his own. "Doesn't matter. But let me ask you, how many police officers had you ever met before me? On a social level, that is?"

She said reluctantly, "Not many. Not a fair database from which to draw conclusions, I admit."

"If it makes you feel any better, you weren't what I ever expected a lady medieval professor to be, either, you know."

"A sixty-year-old prune with granny glasses and support stockings, fat ankles and gray hair in a bun?"

To be honest, he had as stereotypical a picture in his mind of a female academic as an aristocratic snob with little tolerance for any man who couldn't measure up to her standards. The temptation to set up intellectuals as cardboard figures of scorn was all too easy, as easy as it was for Jillie to stereotype police—

—or as easy as it was for bobbies on the sharp end to ridicule their gaffers as penpushing accountants. Or career officers on the force for years to resent taking orders from graduates younger than their own sons, the tribal competition between one shift and the other two, the antagonism between the Met and the provinces. The hostility between woodentop plods versus the Cunts In Drag, or even those elitists inside CID like Kramer for interlopers such as himself and Rachel. Keen wasn't immune to it himself.

"Well . . . not quite," he said. "You're too . . . pretty."

She laughed, the strain between them diminishing, then glanced at her watch. "Thanks for lunch, at least. I've enjoyed it, a lot."

"My pleasure." He felt oddly complimented, while not quite understanding why it was so remarkable, and he was reluctant to let it end. "You have to go?"

She hesitated, then smiled. "I still have time for dessert."

They ordered the sticky toffee pudding and coffee. It was delicious.

"My wife would never let me order this when we went out," Keen said, trying to find something about himself to say. "Even now we're divorced, it makes me feel guilty."

"At least you took her out to dinner once in a while. I'd have been happy with that."

"What, you and your husband didn't go out to eat much?"

"Robert?" She snorted, the derisive sound very unladylike. "After we were married, we never went out again. Anywhere."

He was genuinely astonished. "Not ever? You're joking, right?"

She exhaled ruefully. "Not ever. My ex is a rocket scientist. Really. Aerospace designer. Robert takes himself very seriously, God forbid you should call him 'Bob,' never wastes valuable time on anything he considers frivolous. He'd go to business dinners where wives weren't invited. But never just the two of us. He was hardly ever home, anyway, always working late, weekends. Too busy, too tired, any excuse would do. He's never been much of a family man." Her mocking smile turned into a strain visible on her face. "After a while, I learned to accept that was just the way he was."

Keen was quiet for a moment, disturbed that he'd been friends and lovers with this woman for nearly a year, but it was still apparent he knew so little about her.

"But you loved him?"

She glanced at him sharply. "Yes, I loved him once. I was nineteen when we met, he was twenty-eight. He was successful, smart, good-looking. Worked out every day, no red meat, no fried foods, no chemical additives. I admired his self-discipline because I never had any of my own. I was flattered someone so attractive and smart would want *me*." She seemed aware of her own self-denigration and smiled fleetingly. "Now I think he didn't want to turn thirty still single, and I satisfied his job requirements as wife and mother. At the time, that's what I thought I wanted in a man, brains and beauty. Be careful what you wish for." Her expression was more philosophical than sad. "At least I don't hate him now. But if it wasn't for Karen, I doubt I'd even see him again. So. Your turn. What's she like, your wife?"

"My ex-wife . . . ?" Keen had to think about it. It wasn't just his occupational training that had underpinned his prudence. He had been taught since early childhood that politeness didn't allow him to speak of ladies to other ladies, which, if he examined it, was more a convenience for men than for women. It certainly didn't hold true as often that good manners had stopped men speaking of women to other men, usually in lurid detail, although he had never been one of the more egregious offenders.

"Well . . . Laura's a year younger than me, looks more. She's beautiful, really she is. Green eyes, that's the first thing I noticed about her. Sounds like crap poetry, but they looked just like emeralds."

He thought hard, struggling for the words. If he wanted to become closer to Jillie, it was only fair he did his best to open up his past and his life to her. "She kept fit, keeps herself smart. She's a tough lass, works half days at an advertising firm while the boys are in school and a full-time job from home, some kind of online computer consultancy."

He hoped that was sufficient, but she waited quietly, her expression faintly amused. This was like pulling teeth. Bloody hell, what did she *want* from him?

"She still does all the cleaning and cooking herself. I don't know what she sees in Gavin, he doesn't do much to help out round the house." He caught himself, not wanting to sound like a loser resentful of Laura's new husband, and changed tack.

"Whatever the boys need, they get, but they're not spoiled. She's firm with them, not like me. Those two have me wrapped round their little fingers. I'm not around enough, more like Father Christmas than Daddy these days. But I've been lucky—I still get on with my ex-wife. She could've made it far worse on me had she wanted; the law's bloody tough on divorced men in this country, especially fathers."

He heard the wistfulness in his voice, despising it. "Don't know how she does it, really." He couldn't think of anything else to say and hoped he'd done enough.

Jillie sighed. "I'm jealous."

He nearly laughed in surprise. That hadn't been the reaction he'd expected. "Jealous of *what*?"

"Of your wife. Ex-wife. I wish I'd loved somebody that much. At least you didn't waste twenty years, you still care about each other."

That, he thought, was hardly anything to be jealous of. It might have been better had they not cared quite so much when the marriage ended.

"It's not always easy," he amended. "We still fight, mostly over the boys—we're not married now for a reason. But she's moved on. We both have. And . . ." Now he was finding it difficult, aware of unfamiliar emotions surfacing that he wasn't sure how to express. "I can't see myself being a monk living in solitude for the rest of my life, either. You know what I mean, right?"

She looked at him astutely. "I don't mind being on my own. I like my freedom. I've never had much of it before."

"Right. But should it happen . . ." His hands were suddenly sweaty, and he couldn't meet her eyes. He tried to recall how it felt when he'd fallen in love with Laura, so many years ago now. It wasn't even that he was questioning whether he was in love with Jillie, or she with him—he knew he was in love with her, but his emotions felt as fragile as a butterfly's wing, uncertain such nascent passions would ever, or could ever, lead to anything more stable than their long-distance, erratic relationship. It was only that he didn't know how to ask her, not even sure he knew himself what he wanted to know.

She hesitated for a long, uncomfortable moment. "I might consider it," she said cautiously.

Her admission gave him a curious relief. He wasn't searching for encouragement or even the promise of a future to come. But unlike Jillie, he couldn't imagine living the rest of his life alone, abandoning all hope of being with anyone else again. He knew he needed hope far more than he had ever needed love, the specter of his lonely existence stretching out like a dark road toward a blank horizon frightened him in its sudden intensity.

She reached across the table to lay her hand on his, as warm and soft as her smile. "Keen . . ."

His mobile phone rang. The moment was broken.

"Sorry," he said, fumbling to get the damned thing open. "Yeah," he snarled into it.

"Hey, boss. You busy?" Rachel chirped brightly on the other end.

"No," he lied.

"I've found Cheerful Charlie's Charters. It's on Glendowie Avenue in Gateshead."

"Great." He waited a moment, then sighed. "Good work. I'll handle it, Rachel. You just . . . stay put. I'll be back shortly."

"Okay." He could hear her disappointment through the line.

He flipped the phone closed, slipped it back into his pocket and smiled ruefully at Jillie, the delicate rapport between them already broken.

"Sorry. I've got to go," he said.

"No problem, me too," she said, briskly collecting her handbag and jacket from the chair. "Dr. Sheridan has me supervising the graduate students doing the cataloguing, shouldn't be gone too long or he gets nervous."

"Right." Can't have Doctor bloody Sheridan having a fit of nerves, he thought unkindly.

They stood up, lingering awkwardly before exchanging a quick kiss notable only by the impersonality of the gesture.

"Give me a call when you've got more time?" she said.

"Sure."

They walked out of the pub, got into separate cars, and, with a brief wave, turned out onto the road and drove off in opposite directions.

1 7

"Did you have a good lunch?" Rachel asked, sticking her head in around the door of the lounge. He'd been back less than fifteen minutes and stood looking at his desk, puzzled.

"Yeah, fine," he said, distracted.

"You want a cuppa?"

"Milk, no sugar," Keen said, holding out his used cup, still unwashed.

It was disconcerting, how easily the two of them had fallen into a routine after merely a week of living under the same roof. It certainly was easier than soul-searching conversations, their enforced companionship provisional and comfortably impersonal. But he wasn't sure he liked liking it quite as much as he was.

Then she said, "So? Whatcha think?" When he looked up, she was holding a strapless, lacy black dress on a hanger in front of her, grinning like a teenager as she swiveled her hips to make the hem swish around her jean-clad thighs. It was incredibly short, was what Keen thought. When he didn't answer, she frowned.

"I had to buy a frock. It's for the club tonight. Going out with Rafferty."

"Looks champion."

His lack of enthusiasm damped hers. "Gee, thanks, boss. I left the telephone number on your desk," she said, pointing to a notepad beside the computer monitor.

"Ta."

Any notion he was in danger of becoming too comfortable in her company had just been extinguished.

While she put the kettle on in the kitchen, he sat down, studying the top of his desk. He wasn't an overly fastidious man, not like Inspector Trumble, all squared edges and sterilized neatness. But he did have a method to his mess, and he knew someone had more than simply moved things around in the course of sharing computer time. He picked up the envelope of photographs, sorting through them enough to see they were not in the same order he'd left them in. His files were likewise not as he'd left them, either.

When Rachel got back with a fresh tea in a clean cup, he said, "You been working at my desk?"

"Yes." She looked instantly worried, apprehensive she'd done something wrong. "Only on the phone and the computer. And Danny."

He glanced at her. "Danny were here while I was out?"

"Yeah, just . . ." She rolled her eyes "You know. Checking up on me."

"Uh-huh." He studied his desk again, nothing explicitly wrong, but it left him with an uneasy feeling in his gut. "Danny have a go on the computer?"

"Dunno. Didn't notice. Everything okay, boss?"

"Hm?" He glanced up at her, taking in her anxiety. "Yeah, no worries. You remember that guy's name over at Heathrow's Passport Control?"

"Keith Metcalfe."

"Thanks."

At two-thirty, Constable Metcalfe finally returned from his own lunch break to confirm that Rafferty had been in the Virgin Islands on the dates time-stamped on the photographs, then returned via a two-day stopover in Hong Kong. Keen thanked him and hung up the phone on the desk. He picked it up again to dial, then hesitated. He set it back into the cradle and looked at it, then inspected his mobile thoughtfully.

"Rachel?"

"Yeah?" Rachel poked her head around from the kitchen archway, drying her hands on a teatowel.

"I'm going out for a bit."

"Okay."

The girl at the Carphone Warehouse in the Metro Centre mall sold him the cheapest mobile phone the shop had on offer, along with a pay-as-you-go SIM card. He paid for it in cash, put a hundred quid's worth on it, thanked her and left. Sitting in his car in the mall's sprawling car park, he punched in the number for Cheerful Charlie's Charters.

Charlie Poytner of Cheerful Charlie's Charters was out, no one knew where or when he'd be back. But the ditzy girl handling the phones assured him Mr. Poytner would call back straightaway. Whenever that would be. He drove around and found a pub, had a drink and kept trying, every half hour, and every half hour the ditzy girl likewise informed him, each time with less and less cheerfulness, that Mr. Poytner hadn't come in yet, she didn't know where he was or when he'd be in. The ditzy girl must have gone home promptly at five, when she stopped answering the phone.

Keen finished his pint, left the pub, and sat in his car, thinking. He punched another number into his new phone, one he knew by heart.

"Hey-up, Jazz," he said quietly when Jasmine answered and, before she could respond, added, "You by yourself?"

"One moment, please," she said promptly, her tone professionally impersonal. He listened to the distant sound of chairs scuffling, doors wheezing open and closed, murmured conversations in the background before it became suddenly much quieter on her end. "I'm here," she said, this time more warmly. "Whatcha need, boss?"

"It's probably nothing, just one of my gut feelings. Think you could run a few checks for me through the PNC, quietly, keep my name out of it? Without you-know-who giving you a hard time?" Last thing he'd need was Mullard sticking his nose in.

"Sure. You-know-who doesn't know bugger owt about what goes on here half the time. Too busy who-knows-where doing who-knows-what to who-gives-a-shite."

He gave her a short list, then said, "If you come up with anything, ring me on this number, leave a message on the voice mail. Don't ring me through the station."

"Okay. Hold on . . ."

He listened to a couple women's voices, oddly echoed through the line, then smiled at the sound of a toilet flushing.

"I'll get back to you as quick as I can," Jazz said finally, when the women had left the ladies' loo.

"I owe you," Keen said.

"No you don't. Cooper's stolen goods case? Solicitor was in the Costa del Sol, not Ibiza. Convinced the witness he'd taken a payoff and wasn't coming back. Got Flaky Flagler to come in as duty solicitor, looked like he'd just got out of detox, hadn't shaved, mumbling, dropped his briefcase, the usual. Thought the witness was going to have an embolism. Promptly cut a deal and rolled over on his boss, gave up a warehouse full of stolen computer equipment worth a hell of a lot more than a mere half mil." She sounded happy. "Davis gave my Halifax girl to Jenkins and put me on team with Cooper. Mullard is furious. Good thing you're getting your own nick, boss. Not a moment too soon, methinks."

"Good on ya, Jazz."

He hung up and sat in the car, listening to the sound of rain pattering against the roof, watching people juggle their carrier bags and umbrellas as they threaded their way through the vast car park. At five forty-five, Cheerful Charlie rang.

Finally.

"Yeah, yeah, my assistant left a message you wanted a word," the man was saying in a clipped, preoccupied rush. "I've just got in, been out of the country. I'm leaving again tonight, so if you want to speak to me, I'll be in the office for exactly one more hour."

Cheerful Charlie's Charters on Glendowie Avenue consisted of barely more than a shop front, set in a dismal congested clot of streets next to a betting shop–cum–off-license on one side and a Balti takeaway on the other. No one was at the single desk behind the plate-glass window plastered with travel posters. A withered palm tree in a Mexican pot slumped in the corner of the tiny shop. Three fake coconuts and a toy monkey had been wired unconvincingly to its trunk. The interior was dark, the closed sign on the door.

Keen pressed the buzzer and, when no one responded, knocked on the glass. A man Keen assumed to be Charlie Poytner appeared, frowning with annoyance. In the chill, northern climate of Northumberland, the balding man's baggy shorts and loud Hawaiian shirt seemed ridiculous, shirt unbuttoned to reveal several heavy gold chains buried in a mat of wiry gray chest hair.

"Keep your trousers zipped, mate, I'm coming," Keen heard the man grumble. He unlocked the door and let out a gust of overheated air.

"Charlie Poytner?"

"What, you were expecting Richard Gere?" His accent was heavily Mancunian, and he barely glanced at the warrant card Keen showed him, then did a comical double take. "West Yorkshire?"

"I'm up on an investigation, making a few inquiries about one of your clients."

"One of *my* clients?" Charlie Poytner said with wary suspicion, loath to find himself mixed up in any police matter. "Who? And what'd they do?"

Keen didn't like conducting an interview through an open door. "Mind if we discuss it inside?"

"Oh. Yeah, sure." Poytner let him in, then relocked the door. "We can talk in my office."

Keen followed him to a back office not much bigger than the toilet opposite the narrow hall. A large desk took up what little space there was, a Singapore Airlines map of the world behind it and a beach-scene poster substituting for a view out a window. The air smelled strongly of pine, which Keen suspected was the odor of disinfectant wafting from the toilet.

While Poytner sat down behind his cluttered desk, Keen eased into a plastic chair, twisting to avoid banging his knees.

"Can we make this quick?" Poytner said. "I've got to get to Newcastle Airport by seven-thirty. Plane full of businessmen on their way to Bangkok waiting for me."

Keen spread out several of the photographs on Poytner's desk. "Can you tell me if you recognize any of the people in these photographs?"

Poytner glanced at them perfunctorily. "Nope. Sorry." He looked up, expectant but indifferent. "That it? Can I go now?"

"They were clients of yours, on a trip to the Virgin Islands, about six months ago, I believe."

"Yeah, I got my first clue when I saw they're all wearing my T-shirts. You got any idea how many people go on holiday charters every year? I don't think I'm being unreasonable if I don't remember each and every one of them."

"No, it's not unreasonable. But you were the tour guide on this particular trip, were you not?"

Poytner rolled his eyes. "It's pretty much a one-man operation here. I got a girl to book the flights, and I go with the punters to keep 'em out of trouble." He smirked. "Perk of the job."

"Right. So you would have met everyone in these photos. Would you mind going through them to see if there's anyone you remember names for?"

Poytner's smirk turned to a scowl. "Look, I've already said I don't recognize anyone. I'm a busy man. Time is money. I don't like wasting either." As if to punctuate the conversation with his personal opinion, the man lifted one buttock to fart. Keen didn't change expression as the man muttered, "Sorry. Just got back from Manila last night. Damned Filipinos know sod-all from curry."

"Why don't you take a minute, have a look anyway." Keen's tone made it clear it wasn't a request.

Poytner made a production out of sorting through the photographs. He flicked one on the desk like a card shark discarding a deuce, a dark-skinned boy with a large fish and brilliant white smile. "Okay, here's one. That's Orazio. Don't know his last name. He's a beggar and a pickpocket and general pain in the arse. The police there should know where he lives." His tone made it clear he doubted Keen was interested in a street urchin halfway around the world.

He tossed the photo of women with the mustachioed guide, parrots on their arms. "Roberto de la Croix. Works at the St. Ursula bird sanctuary.

"And that's Marcelo Tomas," he said as he discarded a third photograph, the one with Beryl Rafferty and the tanned body-builder.

"He's not British, then, not part of your tour group?"

"Nah. Born and raised on the islands, still there as far as I'm aware. Part-time bartender, part-time gigolo. Always after the women, likes them young and European, preferably blond and rich. Has wet dreams about marrying one so he can retire to St. Tropez."

So much for Keen's theory it might have been the mysterious Rory. "I'm more interested in the names of your *clients,* Mr. Poytner," Keen said tiredly. "Like, for example, do you remember the other person in this photo, who I assume was actually one of your paying customers?"

"They come, they go, as long as they pay, who cares, I don't remembers names," Poytner complained. He glanced again at the photo and *hmphed* to himself. "She was just some posh bird Marcelo was all over the whole trip, whatsername . . ." He snapped his fingers as he thought. "Bethany, Bettna, Blythe, something like that." He looked at Keen, who looked back blandly and didn't correct him. Poytner dropped the photograph onto the pile and smirked. "Don't remember her name, but I remember *her,* all right."

"Why is that?"

Poytner laughed, dark and throaty. Then he tapped the photograph with a broad fingertip. "Let me ask you, if *you* were a woman, wouldn't he tickle your fancy? Poor bugger did everything including stand on his head to get her to notice him. Not a flicker, went out of her way to avoid him, more interested in taking pictures of fucking parrots than him. A genuine ballbuster, that one, near broke his steroid-riddled heart."

Keen suspected his views had been formed after having been rejected himself; any woman who rebuffed Charlie Poytner's sexual advances would have to be a man-hating bitch, rather than an intelligent woman exhibiting sensible taste.

"Don't you keep records of your clients?"

"Financial accounts for tax purposes, sure. But when I cash a check, I write down numbers, not names." He lifted a heavy arm to inspect a gold Rolex. "Tick-tock, Sergeant." He grinned.

"How about this plane full of businessmen waiting for you? You know any of their names?"

The man's smile dimmed. "It's a group charter. I make arrangements with hotels and restaurants and local guides. I don't need to know individual names."

"But isn't part of your job to arrange for visas?"

Poytner said warily, "My girl usually takes care of the visas, goes with the bookings."

"And neither of you keep track of passports?"

"Only long enough to make sure everyone gets their own back properly."

"Bangkok, you said?"

"That's right."

"Businessmen." Keen nodded thoughtfully. "What sort of businessmen?"

"What do you mean, 'what sort'? Businessmen. Suits and ties. How the hell should I know what sort?"

Keen shrugged benignly. "I suppose I'd assumed this was a business trip. A convention maybe?"

"That's right. A business convention."

Keen waited a few beats. "What sort of convention? They not taking their wives along, all these businessmen of yours off to Thailand for a convention?"

Poytner's scowl deepened. "Now, you look here—"

"Seems a bit odd to me," Keen interrupted, his tone mild. "A planeload of men leaving their wives at home to go off on a trip to the Far East. I know my wife wouldn't have been happy, I left her behind. That, and you not bothering with records."

"Just what the bloody hell are you implying, aye?"

Keen's eyes widened innocently. "Implying? I'm not implying anything . . ."

"I run an honest service here, and I resent your insinuations."

"Mr. Poytner, I'm sure you do. I'm sure that an official inquiry into your charter service would show everything to be on the up-and-up, not like some of those sleaze operators running sex tours into Thailand, ruining the reputations of honest tour services like yours."

The man gnawed on his fleshy lower lip. "What do you want?" Poytner demanded finally.

"If you could search through your records, just to give your memory a jog there," Keen suggested, "anything you can remember about any of the people on that trip, or this particular woman, would be very much appreciated." He handed the man his card. "Just give me a shout should anything pop to mind, won't you?"

Charlie Poytner took the card, glowering in defeat.

"Tick-tock, Mr. Poytner," Keen said and saw himself out.

1 8

Beryl Rafferty lived in a flat in not much better condition than the safe house Rachel was sharing with Keen, albeit Beryl's was closer to the city center and, thus, the clubs and pubs frequented mainly by students and the working-class young. Her flat was at the top of a flight of gloomy stairs, over a balti shop, the aroma of cooked meats and exotic spices masking the faint whiff of musty fabric and decaying plasterwork. Beryl had opened the door dressed only in a bra and lace knickers, a toothbrush sticking out of her mouth. Her belly button had been pierced with a small gold loop, a pale blue gemstone winking in the light.

"Er rate," she mumbled around the foamy toothpaste. She pulled it out of her mouth to add, "I said seven."

"You said seven-thirty."

"Who gives a fuck. Jesus, *that's* what you're wearing?"

"What's wrong with it?" Rachel said, looking down and feeling immediately defensive. Rafferty had always had the knack of making her feel somehow inadequate, no matter how well she did.

Rafferty shrugged. "Marks and Sparks?"

"British Home Stores."

"Get it on sale?"

"No," Rachel said shortly. Although she had, but damned if she'd admit it to Rafferty.

"Well, your taste in fashion hasn't changed much, either." Rafferty turned and walked to the back of the tiny flat, spitting toothpaste into the kitchenette sink. "There's beer in the fridge."

"I don't . . . ." Rachel started to say "drink and drive," then caught Rafferty's mocking look. "Yeah, okay. You want one?"

Rachel sat on the sofa sipping beer as she watched Rafferty prepare for a night out clubbing. Her father may have cut off her credit cards, but Beryl Rafferty still possessed all the trappings of a poor little rich girl: an open closet overflowing with stylish shoes, handbags, and frocks Rachel wouldn't earn enough in a year to have purchased herself. A dressing table brimmed over with costly perfumes, which Rafferty treated with as much careless indifference as if they'd been bottled water, and more cosmetics than Rachel had seen in most Boots shops. The only attempt at order in the flat was one wall of the lounge converted into a makeshift video-editing station, an assortment of video recorders on display, all of them expensive. Several were cabled into a state-of-the-art computer system and linked to a pair of monitors on either side. Rachel wondered how Rafferty had paid for all this, thousands of pounds' worth of equipment. Shelves filled the rest of the wall, neatly stacked with several hundred hand-labeled camcorder tapes.

"This all looks like it belongs to that kid in *American Beauty*," Rachel said, perusing the labels on the tapes. "Y'know, the one who videotaped everything." Rafferty must have used some sort of code, as none of the labels was remotely comprehensible.

From the open door of the bedroom where she tried on one dress, discarding it on the floor, trying on another, tossed aside as carelessly, Rafferty laughed. "Yeah, except if I ever start filming anything as boring as plastic bags blowing in the wind, shoot me."

Rafferty managed to swig down three more beers while in the process of dressing before deciding on a bright red skirt and black lace midriff jacket and a pair of toeless stiletto heels. Then, to Rachel's surprise, Rafferty shrugged on a scruffy black leather motorcycle jacket and tucked a motorcycle helmet under one arm. She grabbed a second helmet from under the bed and tossed it at Rachel.

Rachel caught it with both hands, then glared at Rafferty incredulously. "You have got to be joking."

Rafferty shrugged. "Suit yourself. It's a three-mile walk, that way." She pointed hazily in the direction of the city center, twinkling lights in the evening darkness.

"I have a car."

"You think you're going to find anywhere to park around Leit-Motif, you're dreaming. Long way to walk in heels, and they don't let you in if you're wearing trainers." Rafferty grinned, her eyes already reddened with alcohol. "Just for once, Rach, leave the good girl at home and come play with the bad ones."

Rafferty was right; parking was nightmarish around the narrow streets in the neighborhood of the nightclub, but someone had reserved space for motorcycles behind a strategically placed phalanx of skips in a back alley. Rachel had ridden pillion, sometimes just shutting her eyes rather than watching them nearly collide with other cars and pedestrians as Rafferty wove her way through traffic at breakneck speed. She was quivering by the time Rafferty squeezed the motorcycle into the last remaining slot behind the skip and turned off the ignition. Her expression must have looked equally shaken, as Rafferty pulled off her helmet, took one look at Rachel, and snorted into laughter.

"Jesus, no wonder you didn't last in the police. No guts, no glory."

The bouncers on the door of LeitMotif had adopted their fashion sense from too many clichéd Hollywood movies, Rachel suspected: three steroid-enhanced bodybuilders in faux Armani suits and wearing dark sunglasses at night, arms crossed, bald skulls so clean-shaven the polished skin reflected the neon lights. A queue snaked down the pavement nearly to the next corner, the women uniformly young, blond, skimpily dressed in black, and exposing an excess of cleavage, the men drenched in plenty of tasteless bling with baggy trousers threatening to fall off their skinny hips, and all of them laughing far too loudly, halfway to being legless before they even got into the club. Rachel followed Rafferty to the front of the queue, the subsonic thump-thump-thump of loud music rumbling from inside the building.

"Hey, Biscoe," she greeted one of the sphinxes in mirrored sunglasses. The bouncer gazed down at her without speaking. His head swiveled a fraction of an inch with robotic precision to stare at Rachel. "She's with me. Flynn here yet?"

The taciturn sphinx's head swiveled back to Rafferty. She was busy going through her oversized handbag to pull out a small camcorder, popped a cassette in it and smacked it shut as if slapping a magazine into an automatic pistol. When she looked up at the bouncer, he inclined his head ever so slightly toward the club, then reached down to lift the red velvet barrier rope.

"Thanks, big guy," Rafferty said gaily, her video camera held up to one eye as she danced in a small circle, taping the people in the queue, Rachel, the neon lights. When she swung around, she pointed it at Biscoe, the little machine whirring. "*Work* it, Bee! Ooh, you sexy beast! The camera *loves* you!"

The bouncer's stony expression didn't change. His twin opened one of the double doors to the club to allow them in and allow the wave of sound to roll over them with almost physical force.

Inside, the dance floor was the size of an airplane hangar, a long bar at the far left corner with a dozen bartending staff in matching gold and black T-shirts who served drinks with lightning speed and rigid smiles. In the far right corner, two DJs worked the sound block on a raised stage, their heads nodding like bobble dolls as they played the typical miscellany of chart and trance dance numbers. An array of amplifiers the size of refrigerators surrounded the perimeter of the dance floor, speaker cones vibrating. Blue, red, yellow, and green panels in the ceiling flashed with garish color in hypnotic beat to the music. On the dance floor, a sea of dancers surged and heaved and pulsated, arms waving like the tentacles of sea anemones above their heads. Even in the cavernous space, the heat of so many bodies already made the room swelteringly hot.

A female sentinel who looked like she could have been the sister to the three bouncers outside barricaded admittance onto the dance floor, smiling wordlessly in the din as she gestured to another woman manning the cloakroom.

"Here, hold this," Rafferty shouted into Rachel's ear and shoved something into her hand before slinging the motorcycle jacket, the two helmets, and her large handbag onto the counter. She did, however, hang on to the camcorder.

Rachel glanced into her palm, then closed it rapidly. The cloakroom girl took four pound coins from Rafferty and gave her a small numbered chip on a chain. Rafferty looped it over her neck, then glanced at Rachel.

"Well?"

Rachel checked her bag and coat, paying a pound each for the privilege, while trying to hide the small plastic bag of white pills, not—she supposed—that the cloakroom woman would have noticed, or cared if she did. As she and Rafferty were allowed onto the dance floor, Rachel shoved it back into Rafferty's hand.

Unfazed, Rafferty opened it, took out a pill and popped it into her mouth. "Have one!" she shouted, her words barely audible.

"No, thanks."

They had wriggled along the outskirts of the crowd when Rafferty stopped to eye Rachel with an air of jovial hostility. "Have one," she insisted.

Rachel took a pill and managed to put it in her mouth without swallowing, while Rafferty studied her with narrowed eyes.

"What, you want to check under my tongue?" Rachel yelled back defiantly.

Rafferty laughed, shook her head and turned away, heading for the bar. *Good,* Rachel thought in relief, and spat it out onto the dance floor where it was instantly crushed under stomping feet.

Rafferty ordered two double shots of red-tinted vodka, pushed one toward Rachel, and downed hers in one gulp before waving the glass at the bartender for another. Wherever Rafferty was getting her money from, she hadn't learned much in the way of budgeting, the drinks shockingly expensive. She went through three double shots before hooking the neck of a Bacardi Breezer and shoving through the mass of thirsty punters clamoring at the top of their lungs at the bartenders. Rachel still held on to the small shot glass, Ukrainian pepper vodka sloshing as she followed Rafferty, ignoring the appraising looks from men who intentionally brushed up against her as she squirmed past the crush of dancers.

A wide spiraled staircase led up to overhanging mezzanines where yet more thickset bouncers filtered out the chosen few from the unwashed hordes. Rafferty was apparently well known, as she didn't even need to stop to say hello before the bouncer pushed open a glass half-door to allow them through.

Upstairs, matching glass panels had been fixed to the far edge of the mezzanine, slightly buffering the music while allowing those sitting at tables drinking odd-colored mixed drinks to see and be seen. A group at one table spotted Rafferty and waved excitedly, like high school kids in the cafeteria.

"Flynn." Rafferty introduced the eldest of the group, a chipmunk-faced lad in his late twenties and—judging by the damage alcohol and drugs had already inflicted on his dissipated body—not likely to live to see forty. "Raven." This was a reedy girl with dyed jet-black hair, knife-edge cheekbones, and heroin-chic smoky-eyed makeup just a shade away from being goth. She fiddled with her drink, bloodred nails bitten ragged, fingerless black mesh gloves to the elbows. Rafferty tossed the little bag of pills at Raven, who ate one and passed it to her companions. "Pablo." A quite un-Hispanic lad: lanky mouse-brown hair, pale blue eyes, and an effeminate pursed rose of a mouth. "Stedman." Rachel wasn't sure if that was a first or last name, the boy barely out of his teens, curly ginger hair matching the mottled attempt at a goatee on an acne-studded chin. "Dagmar." The last of the group at least bore some natural similitude to her name, a statuesque woman a head taller than the rest even sitting down, dark blond hair in a thick braid down her back and cold green eyes. Rachel could well imagine her in a brass-coned bra and a helmet sporting oxen horns. She glanced at the bag of pills Stedman held out to her and shook her head. He shrugged and shoved it into the pocket of his trousers.

"Hi," Rachel said, smiling uncomfortably under their group scrutiny and unsure what—if anything—she would have to say in her report about the drugs.

"Rachel. Old mate from school." Rafferty finished the brief introductions and thumped Flynn on his shoulder with her hip. "Scoot."

The man grunted and shifted to an empty chair, allowing Rafferty to take his overlooking the dance floor. Rafferty climbed into it, her knees on the seat, and leaned over the glass partition precariously to videotape the writhing masses below.

"You go to school with Beryl," Dagmar said flatly, in a way that confirmed she wasn't British or a native English speaker. Rachel wasn't sure if it was a question or not.

"High school. Haven't seen Beryl in years, we just ran into each other yesterday."

Dagmar nodded, as if Rachel had said something portentous, then exchanged a look with Raven and the two other men. Flynn had his eyes shut, looking distinctly unwell.

"She's not one of us," Rafferty said, her eye still glued to the eyepiece of her camcorder. The group, except for Flynn who still had his eyes closed, glanced at one another before eyeing Rachel warily. Rafferty panned her camera across the crowd, then up to video her mates. Raven scowled.

"Knock it off, Beryl. We all know what we look like."

"Bloody Steven Spielberg," Flynn muttered, head drooping toward his chest as if he was about to pass out.

"C'mon," Stedman said, his voice sounding like it belonged on a ten-year-old. He grabbed Dagmar's hand. "Let's dance."

When she stood, Dagmar towered over the lad by several inches. When Rachel next spotted them, they had worked their way into the clot of dancers on the floor below, easy to distinguish by the bright ginger hair and the tall blonde.

On the mezzanine, LeitMotif staff waited tables and kept up a steady stream of alcopops in bright-colored bottles to their table—Bacardi Breezer, Glitz Ice, V2, Archer's Aqua, Screaming Mimi's, Caribbean Twist, Sputnik Schnapple, DNA, KGB, TNT, WKD, Beetlejuice, Moo Joose, Virgin ViXXen, Mother Smuckers Smoovies—*anything* but ordinary lager or beer. Rachel nursed a Zanzibar Zinger and tried not to grimace, the sugary gin-and-tonic mix in the clear glass bottle luminescent, quinine glowing with radioactive menace in the club's pulsating UV lights. Her new mates, however, chugged down the sickly sweet drinks and danced to the deafening trance music with head-bobbing, arm-flailing abandon—all but Rafferty, Flynn, and Rachel.

If this was how bad girls had fun, Rachel thought, she wasn't all that upset she'd missed out on it for so long. At nearly three in the morning, Flynn suddenly roused himself, bloodshot eyes popping open to scan the debris on the table. Rafferty ignored him, either still taping the dancers below or tinkering with the playback and editing her tapes, Raven and Pablo were snogging each other sloppily, Dagmar and Stedman pouring the dregs of bottles into glasses to see what colors and flavors would mix with others. Flynn pivoted his gaze toward Rachel, staring at her belligerently. Then he stood.

"I'm off."

That appeared to be the signal for them all, as the group's mood suddenly altered, everyone purposefully following Flynn down the stairs, collecting their jackets and bags and helmets from the cloakroom checkgirl. Outside, the air was refreshingly cool, and the sudden quiet made Rachel's inner ear ache. The entire group, it seemed, had come on motorcycles and parked behind the skips. Raven and Pablo each rode small matching Kawasakis, Stedman sat pillion on Dagmar's black Yamaha, and Flynn rode an oversized Harley Sportster, a gleaming maroon-and-chrome monster that rumbled to throat-rasping life, exhaust belching smoke.

It wasn't exactly the crew of *Easy Rider,* Rachel thought. Nor did the prodigious amount of booze or whatever the drugs were they had ingested seem to impair their ability to steer their motorcycles at top speed along mostly deserted rain-slick streets, weaving in and out between each other as if it was a game. Fortunately, Flynn didn't live far, the ride mercifully short. The cool after the club quickly became bone-chilling cold on the bike; Rachel was shivering by the time she climbed off the back of Rafferty's Honda Hornet. Rafferty's face was flushed and damp with sweat when she took off her helmet—antifreeze in the form of alcopops, no doubt.

Rachel wasn't sure whose semidetached house it was, guessing it was Flynn's. If it was his, the man was surprisingly neat: the furniture shabby charity-shop castoffs but comfortable, the kitchen cluttered but clean, pictures on the wall run-of-the-mill but hung with care.

The group plopped themselves into various chairs and settees, all quite used to their surroundings. Stedman raided the fridge and tossed out cans of lager from the doorway, held one up with a raised eyebrow to Rachel. She shook her head with a smile. He shrugged, popped it open and gulped down half in one go.

"So. Rachel." Pablo smiled at her, his little red mouth puckered up as if for a kiss. "You like hamburgers?"

Whatever other muted conversation had been conducted in the background switched off, all heads—except Flynn's—turned toward her.

"I told you, she's not one of us," Rafferty said mildly. Like spectators at a tennis match, heads swiveled to stare at Rafferty. She still had her camcorder out, but now was busy using it to review the tapes, placing stickers on small cassettes and labeling them, checking the feedback on the next before that one was marked and filed.

"What?" Pablo said with mock innocence. "I just asked if she likes hamburgers."

"Rach and I go way back. She knows I'm involved with animal rights. She even helped us out once on a hunt sab."

"No I didn't," Rachel instantly protested, then kicked herself mentally. All heads (except Flynn's) rotated back toward her. "You conned me."

Rafferty grinned evilly. "Oh, did I mention Rach is also an ex-cop?"

"Shit," Stedman murmured under his breath, more in admiration than alarm. "Really?"

"Yup, until she got fired."

"Wrong, I quit," Rachel said darkly.

"You got your epaulets ripped off your uniform, white gloves slapped across your face, and your arse tossed out onto the street," Rafferty said. Heads swiveled back in her direction. "Caught her partner dipping his hand into the cookie jar, he sang her a sad song about troubles at home, woe is me, sick kiddies, wife threatening to leave, we're gonna lose the house, and she bought it hook, line, and sinker. Covered up for him instead of dropping him in it. So they both got the sack. Lucky not to end up in prison."

Rachel could feel the heat climbing in her face, not from embarrassment over a bogus story but from the intense scrutiny of the group. Rafferty looked up from her camcorder, her eyes shrewd. "What, you think I wouldn't check you out? Or that I *couldn't?*" She laughed. "You're so *easy* to con because you're still such a soft touch."

"And you're still a bitch," Rachel shot back.

"Whoa," Pablo breathed. "Catfight. Cool."

But whatever reticence the group had felt around Rachel, it had gone, the conversation drifting into a bilateral discussion of militant vegetarianism versus McDonald's and the merits of digital versus magnetic tape systems.

"The one I bought last week has digital recording on eight-millimeter format and plays back on analog," Rafferty was saying to Stedman (who looked drunk) and Flynn (who looked asleep). "Eats batteries like a pig, though."

"The point was the message," Pablo was insisting to a bored Raven. "The Mars bars *could* have been poisoned, but they *weren't.*"

"So what good does that do, except to convince people the whole thing was all bark and no bite?" Raven said, flaking small chips of red lacquer off her nails.

"Because it's about *message,* don't you get it? If someone had actually been poisoned, it would hurt the cause, not help. It's all about hitting companies where it hurts, in the pocket, while making people *think,* not killing them."

"The new one's got a disc navigation system built in, coaxial and optical digital audio, and component video output," Rafferty said. "Five point one channel decoder, dual laser pickup, two times and four times digital zoom with graphical positioning indicator. State-of-the-art."

"Must have cost a fortune," Stedman said.

Rafferty shrugged. "Yeah, so. I'm not paying for it, what do I care."

Who was paying for it all, however, she didn't elaborate.

The sky had lightened with the coming dawn, Flynn now collapsed onto the floor surrounded by empty lager tins, Pablo and

Raven rowing quietly in a corner over the measurable IQ of a chicken they had seen trained to peck out tunes on a child's toy piano at a street fair, Dagmar morosely picking the pineapple bits out of the remains of a cold congealed vegetarian pizza she'd found in the refrigerator, Stedman still fumbling drunkenly with Rafferty's cameras. Rafferty spotted the top of the baggie of pills in his pocket, pulled it out, popped another in her mouth, and winked at Rachel.

"You ready to go?"

God, yes! Rachel managed not to blurt, and stood up. The group coalesced around her to give her friendly hugs, Pablo aiming for a wet openmouthed kiss that she managed to circumvent to her cheek instead.

Outside, the early morning air was gray, a soupy mist creeping through the tree line and rooftops. Rafferty handed Rachel the spare helmet.

"*Now* you're one of us," she said quietly.

1 9

If Keen was surprised how quickly Charlie Poytner got back to him, he kept it to himself. The connection on Poynter's end was bad, the line crackling.

"I'm on the damned plane, telephone costs a bloody fortune, you know. Hope you lot appreciate the effort," Poytner grumbled. The sound was further garbled by the noise of many people talking and the muffled hiss of airplane engines.

"We do, Mr. Poytner. What do you have for me?"

"They're dentists."

"Pardon?"

"The businessmen going to Bangkok. It's a bunch of orthodontists going to a trade fair, marketing bridges and caps and epoxy shit, exactly what I said it was."

"I never doubted it, Mr. Poytner. Is that all you rang me to say or do you have something for me?"

"Yeah, I've got something for you. I rang Roberto de la Croix. Twenty-five frigging minutes long distance to the Virgin Islands."

Keen suppressed a sigh. "We're all right grateful."

"Rafferty. Beryl Rafferty. That's her name, the woman in the photo."

"And?"

"And Roberto remembers her. She was with some sort of do-gooder fact-finding tour, I don't know, World Wildlife, Greenpeace, Friends of the Flipping Birds, something like that. Bunch of loonies nosing around asking questions about breeding endangered species in captivity, wanted to know about his scarlet macaws in particular. He told her and the rest of those fruit loops nobody at the sanctuary did any breeding or export to Britain or anywhere else, except to a few zoos they had special arrangements with. One in Cincinnati, I think. Another one in Bahrain."

"But he remembers Rafferty in particular."

"Sure, because she had a bunch of papers with her, claiming they were receipts for birds the St. Ursula sanctuary had sold under license through an import-export company to a bird dealer in London. Damned insistent about it, got him really wound up." The man laughed, unpleasant even several hundred miles up and away. "He searched her handbag for hidden cameras and found a video recorder. Thought she was one of those BBC journalists trying to stitch him up. Then he proved all her papers were total bunkum. Whatever birds the dealer had, they didn't come from the St. Ursula sanctuary."

"You've got the dealer's name?"

"Frank Eastpenny, has a shop down in London, in Mayfair." Keen jotted down the address. "You might be interested in another bit of information, just by the by." He paused, then must have realized Keen wasn't going to oblige him by asking. "That so-called import-export company? It belongs to one Byron Rafferty, now how's that for a coincidence? That her husband may be more interested in a different sort of bird in fancy knickers? Which would explain why she's gone off men—"

"Anything else, Mr. Poytner?" Keen interrupted his speculation.

"Isn't that enough?" Poytner snapped crossly.

She had flown back to the U.K. via Hong Kong, Keen remembered. She might have been visiting Daddy. Then again, the RSPB officer had also mentioned Hong Kong as a major center for bird smuggling. Was Rafferty playing amateur detective or on a shopping trip of her own?

"I'll pass all this on to Customs and the RSPB. They'll be in touch with you if they take an interest. Frankly, it's not much use to me. I'd hoped you'd come up with a few more names on those photos."

"Look, I don't *remember* any names! That's all I can do, and that's been bloody expensive enough as it is!"

"I'm sure Inland Revenue will allow you to write it off as a business expense, Mr. Poytner. Thank you for your cooperation, and have fun in Bangkok. Don't do anything I wouldn't do." He cut off Poytner's stammer of indignation. And allowed himself a small malicious grin.

May's Death Toll: 55,108 cattle, 315,668 sheep, 3,428 pigs, 485 goats, and 64 unspecified animals.

A government study funded by Britain's national environmental technology center warns the burning of livestock poses a significant cancer risk to humans from dangerous levels of dioxins released into the atmosphere. Over a six-week period, the pyres have emitted two-thirds of the dioxins produced by British industry each year. The British environment minister, Michael Meacher, responds by saying, "There is no alternative in disposal that is totally risk free."

In Northumberland, the bodies of hundreds of cattle and sheep buried at West Shipley Farm in Hamsterley, Low West House Farm, and Houslop Farm in Tow Law near Bishop Auckland have to be exhumed after the rotting corpses are discovered to be contaminating the drinking water supplied by a natural spring. At Low West House, blood is discovered dripping from drainage pipes. MAFF officials confirm the carcasses will not be burned. As several cattle were over the age of five, however, neither can the exhumed animals be reburied due to the increased risk of BSE. MAFF admits they are no closer to a resolution.

MAFF resorts to threatening commercial waste management companies with legal prosecution if they refuse to bury huge numbers of dead animals in ordinary landfills. One company, Viridor, reveals they have been forced to bury nearly 4,000 tons of sheep and pig carcasses in the dead of night in their site at Newton Abbot.

A new communication system for the North Yorkshire Police has been delayed as engineers are unable to gain access to more than half of the county's radio towers due to the outbreak of foot-and-mouth. Most of the stations are in unaffected areas, but farmers—fearing possible contamination—refuse to grant access of their land to the engineers.

Farmers' wives, all members of the Women's Farmers' Union in

Yorkshire, are posing nude for a charity calendar to raise money for families affected by the foot-and-mouth outbreak, photographed with strategically positioned horses, cows, and sheep. No pigs can be found for the photo shoot, however.

MAFF officials notify Major Malise Grahame that a vet will be inspecting his flock . . . three weeks after the army culled all 1,260 ewes and lambs on his Holme House Farm in Darlington. The animals on the 800-acre farm had been killed as a precaution after the disease had been confirmed on a neighboring farm. None of Grahame's sheep were infected.

Two hundred ewes and 300 lambs are killed in a contiguous cull on Wayne and Julie Nutall's Punderland farm in Cumbria, along with a pet pig belonging to their young sons. Only after the animals are dead do the slaughtermen realize they have the wrong address—the farm they were scheduled to cull is 100 miles away. Clive Davies, in Gloustershire, loses 225 healthy cattle due to a "clerical error." He says of the killing, "It's become a roller coaster, there's no stopping it."

Prime Minister Tony Blair runs a gauntlet of angry farmers and other countryside workers facing destitution, along with two tearful seven-year-olds who had lost their pet sheep, escaping in his Jaguar car followed by cries of: "Coward! Cumbria is being wiped out! You don't give a shit about the north!"

A virologist with the NHS and Public Health Laboratory is surprised his request to independently collect infected specimens in order to create a diagnostic assay has not only been turned down but would be considered a criminal offense. The scientist is further shocked when the senior MAFF veterinarian clearly doesn't know the difference between a protein and a nucleic acid; no one in a senior position advising the government on the epidemic has any experience in virology whatsoever.

Phil Barber, NFU Teesdale branch secretary, works out independent figures for contiguous culls after MAFF decides to discontinue issuing the count on "confidentiality grounds." His figures show that although there have been only 41 cases of foot-and-mouth, more than half of all full-time farmers in Teesdale have lost their livestock.

The charred remains of 2,000 sheep, 700 cattle, and 500 pigs in Tunstall, North Yorkshire, will have to be dug up and removed to army *incinerators after a pyre fails to properly cremate the bodies, leaving bones, skin, and wool among the ashes. Army incinerators, however, are stretched to capacity, and it is unknown how long the Tunstall remains may have to wait before being disposed of.*

In an interview in the United States, PETA founder Ingrid Newkirk has said, "I openly hope it comes here." An outbreak of foot-and-mouth disease in the U.S. would be "good for the animals, good for human health, and good for the environment."

In Toronto, Canada, an art student, vegan, and political activist is arrested after making a seventeen-minute videotape of himself and two friends as they torture a domestic cat named Kensington to death. They strangled it with a noose, attempted to cut its throat with a razor, kicked, stabbed and impaled it, and removed one of its eyes before finally skinning it alive. He later declares he intended it to be an art film protesting meat-eating. The jury rejects his claim. He is sentenced to ninety days with time served. Animal welfare and vegan groups worldwide condemn his actions.

20

JUNE

Over the next few weeks, events hovered on the edge of interesting for Keen and Rachel both without, however, ever tipping over into anything actually useful. Rachel had delved into the background of her newfound friends, discovering nothing of any major consequence. Pablo Wiggins and Andrew Stedman were flatmates, both undergraduate students at Newcastle University studying a mélange of courses loosely related to cultural anthropology. Raven (Rachel was surprised it was her real name) Morrissey worked as a part-time salesgirl in a fringe fashion boutique and lived with her mother. Dagmar Kjærgaard was Danish, living with a couple and their ten-year-old son as an au pair in High Heaton while taking English classes at a cut-rate IELTS school downtown. Only Milton Flynn had any significant criminal record to speak of, three drunk driving arrests, and a three-year-old conviction for possession of cannabis. All were known to Kramer's team as extremely low-level animal rights agitators, crowd shills during demonstrations or handing out lurid pamphlets on street corners. Time wasters, Kramer declared, including her in with his verdict, Rachel was certain.

The next time Rafferty offered her one of the mysterious white pills, however, Rachel managed to drop it into her pocket and bring it in for analysis, on Kramer's instructions. It didn't help at all when the tests came back that the little white pills—rather than Ecstasy or LSD—turned out to be nothing more than vitamin C tabs.

Keen continued with the tedious job of tracking down the origins of Danny's mysterious dead birds, while Rachel spent most of her evenings tagging along with Rafferty, either at the pub or the woman's flat or out clubbing with her friends, and her days trying to make her reports on who-said-what sound more valuable than they were, rather than the mundane ramblings of a drunken pub crawl.

Keen cleared two days off to spend with Jillie, arriving shortly before the dig quit for the day. It was a pleasant enough afternoon at the dig site, despite the sporadic shift in the breeze that wafted the stench of burning animal flesh from the pyres blazing around the clock at Avondale Farm. Then everyone would stop work and either clamp handkerchiefs over their faces or escape to the little portable hut where the archaeologists had their canteen.

But at the moment, the sky was blue, the sun was warm, and the breeze was blowing in the opposite direction as Keen watched her at work in the trenches, trowel in hand, up to her knees in mud. They'd barely shared a few smiles, a sandwich, and a thermos of bad coffee before she was called away by a tall, thin man with dark shaggy hair, a white smile in a tanned, lined face, and an in-grained air of professorial confidence. The infamous Dr. Sheridan, Keen presumed sourly, watching their body language from a distance and seeing nothing but a friendly camaraderie. But he'd never seen Jillie so happy as she was here, everything about her glowing. Even if it wasn't Dr. Sheridan who was the cause, Keen knew it wasn't himself, either. It wasn't love making her shine with contentment. She'd simply found her element and taken to it like a starving dog falling on a meaty bone.

The graduate students were busily clearing away buckets and trowels and wheelbarrows and small plastic bags with grubby bits and pieces of Roman history secured inside, already eager to descend en masse on the Twice Brewed pub. Jillie, he was absurdly grateful to notice, had turned down Dr. Sheridan's offer to stand them both a pint, preferring to return to her little B and B for a shower before investigating the dinner menu at the Norman Arms, which was rapidly becoming "their" pub.

He had just sat down next to her as she pointed out the more interesting bits of the dig. Their legs dangled companionably over the side of the trench—her legs much muddier than his—as they shared the last of the coffee in her thermos when his mobile rang.

It was the official one, the fancy flippy-open bastard buzzing and flashing away, rather than his dead-basic pay-as-you-go phone. He didn't bother to look at the caller ID when he'd figured out which bloody button to press and answered it, growling an ill-tempered hello.

"Keen?"

All that registered was that it was a woman's voice. A thrill of alarm shot through his gut.

"Rachel?"

A moment's hesitation, then: "No, it's Laura."

Laura? His heart kicked up in vague alarm as he struggled to his feet, standing over Jillie still sitting by the trench. If his ex-wife needed to contact him while he was in Northumberland, it had been arranged she would ring Weetwood who would get a message to him through Kramer's team for him to call her.

"Hold on a sec." He held the mobile to his chest to muffle the sound and said to Jillie, "Be right back." He walked away several yards before he put the phone back to his ear. "How'd you get this number?" he asked, his voice a bit too sharp even to his own ears. "What's wrong?"

"I just rang the number your DI gave me," she shot back testily. He grimaced. *Fucking Mullard,* he thought angrily, wondering if the man was really that stupid or if he was intentionally trying to sabotage Keen. "And nothing's wrong." Keen's relief was short-lived as she added, "Not really."

"Okay, so what's not really wrong, then?"

"You haven't seen the boys in over a month now. They're asking about you." Her voice was unusually irritable, almost angry.

"I explained what's going on. You know how it works."

"But for how long, Keen?"

"It'll take as long as it takes. For Christ's sake, Laura, we've been through all this before, never been a problem. So why now?"

"The kids were little then. It didn't matter as much. You were the one who's been wanting more access time, and I gave it to you—"

"Goddamn it—"

"We'll be up in Harrogate tomorrow morning, boys are meeting with the headmaster at Ashfield College. It would be nice if you could go with us, as a family."

He rubbed a knuckle against his forehead, fighting the menacing headache gathering under his skull. "I'm sure Gavin can handle whatever needs doing for that end of things," he said. "If my input into this is really needed, I'd rather meet with the headmaster some other time, once the boys are enrolled—"

"Gavin's not going to be there."

It was the tone of her voice that alerted him. "What's going on, Laura?"

She didn't answer for a long moment, only the sound of her breathing down the line, as if she was struggling not to cry. "We're having some financial problems," she said finally, her voice thick with trembling. "Gavin has had some bad luck this last year, economy's on a downturn. Things were bad enough as it was, now he's lost an important client, negotiating a multimillion-pound contract over the past eight months, a chain of luxury hotels in the Peak District. Japanese investors. It all looked great until foot-and-mouth. Two weeks ago the main backer decided to pull out, doesn't think the area is going to recover fast enough to cover his profit margins, the rest of the investors can't raise enough on their own to cover the shortfall. The deal's fallen apart."

Keen had only the vaguest notion of what an investment banker like Gavin Tremayne did for a living, but he knew whatever percentage of "multi" Tremayne earned was considerably more than Keen was ever likely to worry about in his lifetime.

"I'm sorry to hear that," Keen said. He almost meant it.

"So things are a lot tighter now than we expected. It's possible the boys won't be going to Ashfield College, not unless we can get them a bursary grant."

"A bursary grant? You must be joking." A rich man like Gavin Tremayne pleading poverty to get Keen's boys into a private school rubbed Keen the wrong way, for some reason.

"Gavin thinks . . ." Her voice clicked with tension. "Gavin and I both . . ."

"Think what?"

"It *is* a good school, Keen. I'm only wanting what's best for the lads."

"Think *what*, Laura?" he said ominously.

"It's only fair if you would . . ."

She couldn't say it, he knew. He also knew it wouldn't have been her idea to press him for money—Laura would give up sleep and food both to take on yet another job if that's what it took to pay for whatever she thought would give the twins a better shot at life than either she or Keen had had. But her aspirations for their lads were becoming an obsession.

"It's not the end of the world if the boys have to attend a state school, Laura," he said testily, his anger igniting. The apprehension he had of his lads coming out the other end of a posh boarding college with the same sort of public school accent and elitist narrow-mindedness Tremayne affected was one he'd be just as happy to avoid. "That's the big emergency you're ringing me for? Because Gavin bloody Tremayne is of the opinion I should contribute to sending the boys to an overpriced toff factory?"

"No." Her voice was subdued. "I'm ringing you so we can discuss this, you and me, because I'm sick and tired of arguing with Gavin about the boys going to a school in Yorkshire so they can be closer to you, which is what I assume *you* would prefer, instead of to Seven Oaks Preparatory in Kent, which is where he went."

He bit down on the itch to come back with something unkind; too many years of marriage had attuned him to his ex-wife's nature to realize something deeper was amiss.

"You two fighting a lot these days?"

"He"—her voice trailed off—"doesn't do well under stress."

"How bad is it?"

"Bad." She sighed. "He's had to sell the Porsche, missed some payments on the BMW, bank is threatening to repossess. He's actually worried about bankruptcy."

"I meant how bad are the rows between you two?"

"Gavin's not like that, Keen. He doesn't get physical." They both knew that conflicts didn't have to be physical to be abusive. He didn't point it out, knowing he didn't have to. "I know you think I married him just because of the money, but it's not true."

Actually, Keen was quite aware Laura had never been that sort of woman, realizing she was answering one of Tremayne's accusations, not his.

She said nothing for a long moment, and he waited in silence for her to go on when she could. "We haven't even been married a year," she said, tears now in her voice. "And it's all falling apart."

"A bursary, huh?" he said gently. "That's like a scholarship, is it?"

He heard her gulping back her emotions to get them under control. "They both have done so well this year, their marks have been excellent, Keen. Mr. Bryersworthy, that's the headmaster, says both boys could possibly qualify."

Keen exhaled and glanced over at Jillie. She was watching him, and he could clearly read the disappointment in her eyes. "So what time's this appointment?"

2 1

Elaine Mathers dozed in the chair stationed on the other side of the isolation glass, her head against her husband's shoulder as he held her upright and watched his comatose daughter's chest rise and fall in a travesty of breathing. Neither of them reacted whenever someone walked past, now too inured to the interminable waiting. A bland instrumental version of the Beatles' "All You Need Is Love" mumbled through the overhead loudspeakers, the third time that day Harry had heard it on the endless loop of music.

He hated the music, hated the antiseptic smell in the chilly hospital air, hated the sympathetic smiles of nurses every time they came to check on Izzie and jot down notes on their charts. He hated that goddamned dead rabbit for bringing its goddamned disease into their lives. He hated Elaine for being able to sleep, even if it was from sheer exhaustion. Most of all, he hated feeling guilty for hating being here at all, wanting to *do* something—anything—to alleviate this crushing sense of impotency.

He had spent long evenings in front of his computer, researching everything he could find on what might possibly be killing Izzie, educating himself to the vernacular the doctors routinely used to overawe a mere tire-fitter. The doctors, he soon learned, didn't know much more than he did, fancy medical degrees or not. Izzie had anemia and thrombocytosis; her lungs were riddled with cavitating lesions from necrotizing pneumococcal pneumonia. A CT scan showed significant lobar pulmonary liquification that kept refilling even when her lungs were drained. What that meant, Harry now understood, was that some sort of superbacteria had gotten into Izzie's blood when the sick rabbit had scratched her and was eating her lungs into Swiss cheese while she drowned in her own fluids. And none of the antibiotics had so far made any difference.

She looked so tiny, he thought, as he stared at his daughter. So tiny and fragile and oddly serene, even with the intubation tube taped to her mouth, a machine forcing air in and out of her weakening lungs. Her closed eyelids were pale blue, her fine blond hair still neatly arranged on her pillow, brushed by a nurse's aide that morning. One hand had flopped over, delicate fingers curled around her thumb, as still as a china figurine.

Harry glanced over disinterestedly as a nurse came out of the isolation room next to Izzie's, a vet's son, he knew, who'd also been infected by one of those damned rabbits. He'd seen the father a few times, a dour man in a tailored suit and tie looking more like a government bureaucrat than a vet, his Scottish brogue barely discernible under the public school accent when he spoke with the nurses. Every morning, he would stand at the window, gazing in on his son for a few minutes before walking away again, impassive, not returning until the next day. But Harry and the vet had never exchanged a single word, no mutual expression of commiseration for their shared tragedy.

Harry wondered if the government goons had paid the vet a visit as well. Had they cordoned off his house with police tape? Had they dug up half his garden, wrapped his possessions in plastic bags and carted them away? Somehow he doubted the vet's house had also been sprayed inside and out with a chemical that permeated everything with an acrid stink Harry was certain would never leach out. The vet looked like a man who wouldn't put up with that kind of thing, not the sort to be intimidated into submission. Not like a simple working sod who'd never gotten as far as sixth form.

The nurse stripped off gloves and mask, bundled them into the paper gown she had discarded, and dropped the lot into a contaminated-waste bin by the door. On the few occasions he'd been allowed to touch his daughter, Harry, too, had had to wear gloves and a mask, and a blue paper gown, not so much to prevent whatever was slowly killing his daughter from infecting him as it was to protect her weakened immune system from whatever normal, ordinary germs he and Elaine might be carrying. Bad enough she could die all because of a cute fluffy rabbit, he thought; worse if a father's kiss was the final straw.

And because there was nothing much else to do, he watched as a uniformed police officer strode down the corridor and stopped to speak to the nurse. They obviously knew each other quite well, her smile flirtatious. The officer towered over her, military-style hair-cut, painfully close shave, and a bodybuilder's shoulders giving him more an air of aggression than friendliness. They conversed in hushed voices and Harry understood more by their expressions and gestures than any stray words. Was the man in the next room able to talk yet, could he see him? No, that wasn't a good idea, he wasn't getting any better, it seemed. Was he going to die? the officer wanted to know. She didn't know, maybe, maybe not, said her look. The officer glanced at Harry, his hostile scowl quite palpably one of *mind your own business*. The nurse smiled apologetically, disapproving but unwilling to risk her boyfriend's displeasure.

Harry held the man's gaze just long enough to satisfy his own already bruised masculine self-esteem before giving in to caution and averting his eyes with what he hoped was indifference. Eventually, the nurse and the cop exchanged a quick furtive kiss and went their separate ways.

He was listening to an orchestral version of Simon and Garfunkel's "Bridge Over Troubled Waters" for the fourth time around when Elaine stirred and opened her eyes. She sat upright without a word to Harry, none necessary. It was his turn to nap, if he wanted, he knew. He knew he wouldn't.

Neither of them had moved in over an hour when Elaine suddenly squinted, then clutched Harry's hand. He flinched, startled, before realizing he'd been staring into space distractedly, not asleep but not exactly alert, either.

"What?"

"She blinked."

They both stared at their daughter, holding their breath. *She blinked.* Elaine inhaled one long gasp as Harry's heart lurched in both hope and dread. She blinked again, blue eyes opening with a confused crankiness, her little hands spasming in irritation.

"Jesus," Harry blurted. "Jesus. Jesus. *Jesus!*" He leaped to his feet, looking around wildly as Elaine burst into tears. He ran down the corridor to the nurse's station, shouting, "Excuse me! Someone! Hey!" And within moments, nurses trotted after him as he raced back to his daughter's room, where Elaine stood sobbing, her arms wrapped around herself tightly.

In all the commotion, no one but Harry noticed someone enter the isolation ward next to Izzie's, and even then Harry would later be unable to describe him clearly, his own tears of relief obscuring his vision. He wasn't sure if it had been a doctor or a nurse, or if it had been a man or woman. Not even certain anything had happened at all. But sometime during the few minutes that the nurses and the doctor and her parents scrambled into their sterile gloves and masks and paper gowns while Isabella Mathers struggled back to life, Pete Phillips's ventilation machine—all that, like Izzie, had kept his lungs from collapsing completely—was turned off.

It couldn't have been a deliberate act, the administration inquiry decided later; doubtful anyone had turned it off by mistake. Probably just bad luck, might have been a power surge, the machine was old, NHS equipment malfunctioned more often than anyone would want to admit. There would of course be compensation due, the matter referred to the Ministry of Health for an inquest. And Pete hadn't suffered, the doctors later assured the dour man in the immaculate suit and silk tie who stood looking down at the body of his son without shedding a tear. The disease had been so advanced, the bacterial necrosis that riddled his vital organs so extensive, that he would have slipped away in moments, still unconscious. It had only been a matter of time, anyway, the boy's condition almost certainly terminal; the life support had only prolonged the inevitable.

It wasn't much of a comfort to Dr. John Phillips, who buried his only child with little outward display of emotion, formally shook hands with those mourners who came to exchange the customary expressions of sympathy in the frigid country church. Then he went home to sit alone in a darkened study still reeking of whatever chemicals the idiots from MAFF—or the CDC, or the HPA, or whoever the hell they were—had sprayed in his house, despite the housekeeper's best efforts with deodorants and cut flowers. He poured himself a glass from the first of what would be many bottles of whisky and wept in private, locked in an excruciating grief and guilt that he'd never once told Pete how incredibly proud of the boy he'd been or how much he loved him.

22

Keen had made an effort, wearing a suit and tie and shined shoes. But although he'd trimmed up the edges a bit, he'd kept the stubble on his face, and his close-shaven scalp hadn't grown out enough to be any less menacing. He still looked like what he was supposed to for the job, a thug. When he arrived at the Ashfield school and got out of the car, he spotted Laura and a stout man standing by the entrance of the main building, waiting for him. The twins were nowhere in sight, but Keen could hear the sound of children shouting and squealing with laughter and guessed the lads were already busy making new friends.

The school was a modest Georgian manor house, gray stone partly buried in ivy, colonnaded porch, massive gray oak doors with black scrolled ironwork hinges, a multitude of ornate gray chimneys sprouting from the gray slate roof. Immaculate raked gray gravel crunched underfoot as he walked over to his ex-wife and the headmaster of the school, the man in a gray suit.

Laura turned, her smile automatic but her eyes widening in disbelief and not a little dismay at his appearance. Mr. Bryersworthy, on the other hand, merely blinked before thrusting out one hand to give Keen a hearty handshake.

"My ex-husband, Keen Dunliffe," Laura murmured. "The boys' father."

"A pleasure," Mr. Bryersworthy said, his voice sincere. "Mrs. Tremayne tells me you're a police officer."

Mrs. Tremayne. Keen hadn't quite thought of Laura in that way before and couldn't answer for a moment.

"Yes, I am," he said finally.

"Excellent, excellent." The headmaster beamed, then gestured toward the ornate wooden doors of the main hall, palm up, fingers pressed together tightly. "May I give you a little tour of our school?"

The outside might have seemed like a holdover from another era, but inside the place was brightly lit and modernized, the computer room well stocked with shiny new terminals, the library shelves packed with books, parquet wooden floors so polished they looked like glass. Children's artwork—all better framed than anything Keen had hung on his own walls at home—decorated the hallways, along with certificates and awards prominently displayed to demonstrate the school's academic excellence.

Laura said nothing, making much of looking around earnestly and nodding in the right places. They followed Mr. Bryersworthy up an elaborate staircase, down a hallway, around several corners, and past a hallway of high arched windows overlooking a cloister-like square where a group of children in gray blazers and shorts and pleated skirts with ties and knee socks the color of bruised aubergines played. Keen spotted the twins, dressed in matching Arsenal jerseys a few sizes too big for them over khaki cargo shorts. Although Keen had never been a fan of any particular sport, he felt vaguely annoyed his boys were wearing the insignia of a London team rather than Leeds United. The boys seemed oblivious to the adults watching them from above, too busy squealing with laughter as they played a hectic game of tag with each other and their new-found friends.

"Our preparatory school is linked directly with the college but maintains its own independent classrooms. We are proud of our exceptionally strong community spirit here and keep our class numbers small so that the children and the teachers have the best possible one-to-one liaison. Our teachers are motivated, experienced, and very committed to bring out the best in each and every pupil," Mr. Bryersworthy declared in a way that made Keen wonder how often he'd had to give this same speech to prospective parents.

"We offer a well-balanced curriculum, run to the Qualifications and Curriculum Authority guidelines, and we carefully monitor every child's academic progress."

He gazed at them both cheerfully, waiting for a reaction.

"Mmm," Laura finally said noncommittally. Keen remained silent.

They trooped behind him to another part of the school, to a cavernous hall with long wooden tables and café-style wooden chairs, a long counter with steel shutters drawn down and locked, and a vaulted ceiling so high Keen could feel the cold draft wafting through the room.

"Lunch is our main meal of the day, where we encourage conversation but emphasize polite table manners. We provide a nutritionally healthy menu, fresh fruit, yogurt, and cheese on offer. There are no junk food dispensers here, and the children aren't allowed to leave the grounds to buy sweets at a tuck shop, I can assure you."

Laura smiled wanly, while Keen said nothing.

At their lack of enthusiasm, Mr. Bryersworthy's smile broadened. "Right," he said briskly. "Let me show you where your boys would be living during the week."

They dutifully followed him to yet another wing of the Georgian house, walls and doors clean and modern but the beamed arched ceiling made of hand-hewn oak several centuries old and buffed to a warm, dark glow.

"We have six boarding houses, three for boys and three for the girls, separate, of course. Most of our boys are full boarders and stay in Burgess House. Blakeley Hall is reserved for day pupils. Boswell House is for those boys boarding on a weekly basis but one we maintain with the same quality of facilities as Burgess House, which we believe prepares the boys to make an easier transition to full board later on."

Keen's eyes narrowed, not liking this at all. Mr. Bryersworthy gazed back at him with a mild-mannered smile. He opened the door to one of the rooms seemingly at random. Inside, the room was implausibly tidy, a pair of beds made without a wrinkle in the duvets, posters of planets and dinosaurs neatly tacked to the walls, a selection of teddy bears and plush animals arranged on pillows with military precision.

"As you can see, children are allowed to bring their own toys and decorations and are encouraged to treat their rooms as a place to relax as well as study, where they can build lifelong friendships and make the house feel like a home away from home."

It looked nothing like the lads' own quite messy bedrooms, in either of their parents' houses. Keen and Laura glanced at each other, her expression vaguely incredulous, Keen was pleased to see.

"Boswell House has two dormitories, each with thirty-four boys exactly," Mr. Bryersworthy continued on blithely. "Two to a room, with a common room at either end of the hall where after the school day ends we offer structured and educational evening activities; our houseparents take pastoral care quite seriously. We also have a small kitchen where the children are allowed to make themselves cocoa and snacks in the evening with the supervision of our around-the-clock matron, which in the case of Boswell House is Mrs. Henderson, who is also a registered nurse. We also have a state-of-the-art medical center with a school doctor on call at any time."

"Mmm." It was Keen's turn to murmur evasively.

"I understand that on weekends the twins will be staying with you, Mr. Dunliffe, and holidays and school breaks with Mr. and Mrs. Tremayne, is that correct?"

"Yes." Keen didn't mean his tone to sound quite so hostile, ignoring Laura's frown.

"If, for any reason, you ever need to have them stay over at the school on weekends, they will be very well looked after, I can assure you. They will also have the benefit of informal religious classes held on Saturday nights and a proper Sunday morning Church of England service with the school chaplain."

"Right, then," Keen said flatly. "How much?"

"Keen!" Laura hissed.

"No, no, quite all right, Mrs. Tremayne. It's a fair question." Mr. Bryersworthy's smile expanded even further, showing the glint of a gold molar. "The school runs a lump-sum-in-advance scheme, which will enable you to make quite a worthwhile savings, as well as scholarships awarded to pupils starting at year three on the basis of English and maths exams. We also have partial scholarships for students showing exceptional talent in music, art, chess, IT, or sports, any of which can be supplemented by bursaries for those parents with, um, special financial circumstances. We do allow a very generous discount for those in the forces, which I believe could well extend to children of serving police officers such as yourself."

"Champion," Keen said, his voice still impassive. "How much?"

Mr. Bryersworthy inhaled slightly before he said, "For weekly board, five thousand, four hundred, and twenty-five pounds."

Keen gulped. "Per year?"

"Ah, no," Mr. Bryersworthy said with a small chuckle, as if Keen had said something mildly amusing. "Per term." His glance shifted between the two of them. "Per child."

At Keen's expression, Mr. Bryersworthy raised an eyebrow and turned his attention to Laura. "We also offer music lessons, charged at an hourly rate of fifteen pounds per hour, and we have three teachers in maths or English available for any private tutoring on a one-to-one basis at thirty pounds an hour or twenty pounds for shared lessons up to a maximum of four children at a time."

Keen thrust out one hand at the headmaster. "Thank you for your time, Mr. Bryersworthy," he said grimly.

As they shook hands, the headmaster added, "I can give you quite an impressive list of former pupils who have gone on to extremely successful careers, Mr. Dunliffe—in business, the arts, even in government. Ashfield College prides itself with offering our children the very best possible start in life, with a distinguished track record."

"I'm sure you do." He faced his ex-wife, doing his best to keep his anger from showing. "Laura."

Her face had blanched, small blotches of color speckling her pale skin. Keen turned and walked away, heading for the car park, leaving her murmuring anxiously to the headmaster. He'd almost reached his car when he heard her quick footsteps running up behind him.

"Keen . . ."

He spun around. "Not. Going. To. Happen," he said, finally allowing his anger to escape.

"It's a good school!"

"I'm sure it is, Laura. You know what else is a good school? Ilkley Primary, just down the other end of Ilkley village. It's got quite competent teachers, a decent school building, a playground, plenty of sports, IT, and anything else the lads might conceivably need. You know what else is good about Ilkley Primary? It's *fucking free!*"

She audibly gasped at his unexpected profanity, and he wondered if Kramer was beginning to rub off on him.

"Keen, please *listen* for a moment . . ."

"No, I think I'm done listening. I'm done getting sucked into your fixation with turning the lads into something they're not. They're *nine years old,* Laura. Don't you think it might be a bit soon to be worrying about their bloody careers?"

"It's important to start them off young . . ." she said doggedly, her expression hardening.

"Why? So they can be wildly successful investment bankers like Gavin Tremayne?" He didn't even attempt to soften the contempt in his tone. "God forbid the boys should grow up to be such miserable failures like their father."

"That's not fair . . . !"

"Oh, but it is." He thrust a finger at the Georgian manor behind her. "I'm not contributing one penny to sending the boys here, not one. And you want to know something else, Laura?"

Now he was scaring her—he could read it clearly in her eyes.

"Keen . . ."

"You're not sending them here, either. You're not packing the lads off to some *fucking* boarding school so that Gavin *fucking* Tremayne isn't inconvenienced." He had to admit, he thought, there was something quite liberating in unleashing such angry profanity. "I'm not having my sons growing up with housemothers and matrons and headmasters instead of parents. If you two can't provide the lads with a stable environment where they can come home every day, where *you* help them with their homework, and feed them decent meals and let them watch a bit of crap tellie once in a while or buy a bloody chocolate bar from a machine, then I can. You don't want to be a full-time parent anymore? Fine. Let *me* do it. I have a comfortable house, which is paid for, and a car, which is paid for, a steady job and no debts, no overdraft, no threat of bankruptcy or bank repossessions."

"It's not Gavin's fault!"

"I don't give a shit whose fault it is! I am *done* begging you to let me see the boys more often. I'm done feeling like I'm somehow not quite up to scratch. If you and I can't agree to sit down and make some major changes in the access schedule and a more reasonable arrangement for their education, then next week I'm going to hire a solicitor and see about getting primary custody of the lads."

Her mouth dropped open, and her own anger surfaced. "Oh, no you're *not*—"

He leaned into her face, forcing her to draw away from him. *"Oh, yes, I fucking well am!"*

She gaped at him, stunned and more than a little frightened. He had never, not once, treated Laura with such disrespect or fury; the resentment of the failed marriage, the loss of his sons, the humiliation he'd had to suffer had simmered for too long unchecked. She was close to tears, something he knew she would never forgive him for if he pushed it that far. He clenched and unclenched his fists with the effort to calm himself.

"I'm only trying to do what's best for the boys," she protested shakily.

"No, Laura, you're not. This has nothing to do with the boys," he said, his voice pitched almost to a whisper to keep it under control "You once chose the lads over me. I lived with that, I can still live with it. But now you're going to have to choose between our lads or your husband. And if you choose your husband, then I will find a judge who will listen to reason and take the boys from you. I swear to God, I will."

Suddenly, all the anger and frustration had gone, leaving him almost light-headed with a sense of purpose and determination. He opened the car door, got in, and looked up at her. "So ring me whenever you're ready to talk. We're done here."

He didn't look back as he drove away.

He hadn't quite reached the safe house when his mobile rang, his anger with Laura replaced by residual sourness. His cheapie Carphone Warehouse one. He pulled it from his pocket, thumbed it on, and put it to his ear, driving with one hand on the steering wheel and one eye on the mirror.

"Yeah."

"Boss."

It was Jasmine.

"Hey-up."

"You know that stuff you had me looking into?"

"Yeah?"

"It's been a bit tricky, sneaking this past you-know-who; sorry it's taken me so long to come back to you with anything. But there's definitely something weird going on up there."

"Hold on a sec." He pulled into a lay-by and shut off the engine. "Weird how?"

"Well, first, I don't know what it's all about, but yeah, there's a bunch of dead white rabbits been picked up and disposed of, mostly through people ringing the RSPCA. Also a bunch of live ones. My contact in the RSPCA says there's some kind of protocol in place— white rabbit gets reported, dead or alive, they're supposed to notify MAFF immediately to go pick it up, RSPCA is not to deal with it at all. After that, no record of them anywhere, they all suddenly vanish like the Cheshire cat."

Cheshire cat? Keen smiled. Ah. Alice in Wonderland and the white rabbit, of course. "You got numbers?"

"So far, fourteen dead rabbits, forty-seven live ones, all within a seven-mile radius of that warehouse explosion. Most of them end of April. But none since mid-May."

Keen jotted a note. "Okay. What about the birds?"

"Again, more weirdness. You got a lot of activity on the PNC going on with those birds, most of it generated by Daniel Mayfield. And you. That's not unexpected."

"Okay."

"But you've also got someone else interested in them as well."

"Who?"

"I don't know."

That was unexpected. "You don't know who it is?" Access to the PNC would require any officer to register their call number. "Maybe someone in my undercover team?"

"No. At least I don't think so. Could be, though, I suppose. It's someone using PNC access in at least three different stations in Northumberland, not your locale. And nearly always at night, after hours. But that's not the weird part. So far, I've got five different officers listed as the users, all retired, one of them's even dead— heart attack last November. Talk about a ghost in the machine."

"Huh."

"Some of the stuff you had me looking for? It's gone. Deleted. Other stuff looks like it's been tampered with, little things changed— y'know, dates and times, case numbers. Making it look like it's the usual backlog screwing up the works. Someone is trying to bury as much info on those birds as they can without calling attention to it."

Which explained why he'd been getting nowhere very slowly on finding out where Danny's birds had come from.

"And no way to track down who's doing it?"

He could almost hear her shrugging through the phone. "It's someone who knows their way around the PNC. So, my guess is either a cop or civilian staff, like maybe a PNC Phoenix operator. It's someone who's logging on in the wee hours, so I'd rule out civilian staff. No particular pattern to when or where, so if it isn't someone on your team playing for the wrong side, could be a PC working shifts. Only way to figure it out would be to get hold of records of who was on what shift when and where, and do a cross-check for the dates."

"Then guess what your next job is, Jazz."

"How'm I supposed to do that?" she complained. "It's not our force."

"You're a bright girl. I'm sure you'll figure out something."

There was a long moment of silence on her end. "Y'remember when I said you didn't owe me anything for this one, boss?" Keen grinned. "Can I change my mind?"

"Definitely. Any way to recover any of the information been altered or changed on those birds, run it through the system again?"

"Not on this end. You'd have to go back and redo all the data entry again." Keen grimaced, inwardly groaning. "Not that it would necessarily work anyway," Jazz said. "Not if you suspect the computer you're working on has been compromised . . ."

"Bloody hell." He thought for a moment. "Jazz, I really appreciate your help on this one."

"Uh-huh," he heard her say dryly. "Which means either 'thanks a lot we're done bye-bye,' or it means you've got even more crap for me to do in my copious free time. I'm guessing the latter."

"I'm going to photocopy as much of this stuff as I can, send you my notes. Privately, not to the station. See what you can do with that, will ya?"

"Yeah, okay. And there had better be fifteen-year-old single malt come with it as a down payment, none of the cheap stuff, I'm warning you now."

"Two bottles."

She laughed. "Mate, rate you're going, you'll end up owing me a friggin' case!"

June's Death Toll: 45,416 cattle, 213,849 sheep, 1,330 pigs, 120 goats, and 409 unspecified animals.

Residents in the tiny village of Two Law, concerned by contaminated groundwater, are suing the British government for the illegal burial of tens of thousands of animal carcasses in a nearby quarry, arguing the

Inkerman site—half a mile from a primary school—had not received a risk assessment and did not have a proper pollution license. The council also plan to file a complaint with the Environmental Commission in Brussels claiming the site has also violated European law. Children have had to be kept indoors after weekend rain flooded the quarry and enveloped the neighboring village in a putrid stink of rotting bodies, causing nausea and illness. Environmental Health authorities have been called in as large numbers of rats have continued to pour out of the burial site. Alan McClean, regional officer of the Fire Brigades Union, has issued instructions to firefighters not to cut free protesters who have chained themselves to disease burial sites in a show of sympathy with the protestors.

Seven hundred pigs and sheep are culled on Margaret and Robert Wood's farm in Bishopton, although the stock had been kept indoors for weeks and showed no signs of infection. Young pigs, normally culled by lethal injection for humane reasons, are instead shot. Subsequent tests show all the animals to be disease-free.

High Court Judge Michael Harrison intervenes to reverse the government's order to slaughter Grunty the Pig, a New Zealand Kune Kune and TV star of Pig at the Ritz, along with 11 rare sheep, because the owner, Rosemary Upton, merely visited another farm that had suffered foot-and-mouth.

More than 5,500 animals are killed in Ingleby Cross, 4,000 at Arncliffe Hall owned by Lord and Lady Bell. Gordon Chapman of Springfield Farm, one of the 13 contiguous farms affected by the cull, has lost 200 of his dairy cows. Slaughtermen broke a door and smashed a trough during the cull, and left the walls of the barns splattered in blood for two days before a government disinfecting and cleaning crew is sent in. None of the animals on the contiguous farms tests positive.

Avid foxhunter Joe Townsend, huntsman for the Hurworth Hunt in Rounton, and his son Iain are running a 10k road race in London, hoping to raise money for the NFU Farmers in Crisis from sponsors, to help farmers hurt by the foot-and-mouth epidemic.

Three small children and their parents are barred from Blackpool Zoo when they arrived for a day's outing because they live in Widdrington, next to a massive foot-and-mouth site where over 150,000 animals are buried. The zoo is blacklisting all visitors who live within six miles of any area affected by foot-and-mouth.

Hundreds of animals will have to be exhumed and incinerated after a local farmer in Devon discovered the macabre sight of bones and other remains popping out of the ground, pushed to the surface by gasses formed by decomposition. Large chunks of rotting skin from the burial site have also been found floating in the nearby Deering River, triggering fears of a public health hazard.

Two more cases of foot-and-mouth have been confirmed, one on Kelmire Grange, Thirlby, and the other at Silton Grange, Nether Silton. Two hundred fifty-one cattle have been slaughtered at Nether Silton, and three contiguous farms will lose 136 cattle and 490 sheep. Three hundred forty-four cattle have been culled at Thirlby, and contiguous areas are still being identified. One case has been found at Mill Lane Farm near Whitby, and three in the Settle and Skipton triangle. The number of animals to be destroyed has yet to be determined. Eighty-one hundred pigs have been killed on a farm in Thirsk, due to a possible "dangerous contact," although no sign of the disease had been detected in the animals.

Meanwhile, Prime Minister Tony Blair has halted decontamination programs over cost concerns, claiming the average cost of £104,000 per farm was unacceptable. The total cleanup cost to Britain is feared to be escalating to $800 million.

Already criticized for its inept management after the outbreak of bovine spongiform encephalopathy, commonly known as "mad cow disease," the Ministry of Agriculture, Fisheries, and Food (MAFF) is blamed for its failure to deal effectively with the foot-and-mouth crisis. MAFF is disbanded, and a new department, the Department for Environment, Food, and Rural Affairs (DEFRA) is created by combining part of the Department of Environment, Transport, and the Regions (DETR) with a smaller part of the Home Office, and headed by Secretary of State Margaret Beckett.

24

JULY

Summer had finally kicked in full force, the weather suddenly hot. The hope the change in the weather would help to eradicate the foot-and-mouth virus was short-lived, the culling dragging on through the summer. As was this absurd case, Keen groused to himself. Jasmine had yet to track down whoever was meddling with the PNC to suppress whatever lurked behind Danny's bird case, and Rachel had yet to glean anything of any worth out of Rafferty and her Scooby gang. Laura was apparently screening his calls, as she never answered her mobile or returned his messages, which made him both annoyed and anxious, wondering if he would have to carry out his threat to fight her for custody. He hadn't been home more than a handful of times, the house feeling cold even in summer and starting to take on that slight musty smell of desertion. He missed Thomas.

The only bright spot was that at least he had finally, *finally*, been able to spend an entire evening with Jillie, uninterrupted by either his work or her students. They'd enjoyed a wonderfully romantic dinner at the Norman Arms, the landlord beginning to treat them as regulars, after which they took a late afternoon stroll hand in hand down the footpath behind the pub. The trees were in full leaf, birds singing, cows grazing in a field with a little red barn in the distance like a picture postcard, marred only by official yellow foot-and-mouth signs posted at intervals warning walkers to keep out on penalty of prosecution—one with a postscript scrawled underneath presumably by a frustrated farmer: "or shot on sight."

The sky had deepened to an indigo blue, the air chilling, when they returned to Jillie's B and B, sneaked a bottle of White Cloud

New Zealand wine and two glasses Keen had bought that morning at Somerfield's into her room, and finished off most of it before they ended up in bed, the sex oddly comfortable if a bit too detached for Keen's liking. But he slept better that night than he had in a long while.

In the morning, they lay snuggled together, propped up on pillows, and talked in the wan early light. Or rather, he noticed yet again, he asked questions to get her to talk rather than saying much himself.

"I love the country," Jillie was saying. "I sort of grew up there."

"'Sort of'? How do you 'sort of' grow up in the country?"

"Well, it was sort of country, and since my dad was a long-haul truck driver and on the road most of the time, we sort of lived with my uncle Homer."

He remembered her talking about her uncle the last time she had been in Britain. "This being Homer of the giant ant farm fame. With all the pet goats and donkeys and pigs."

She twisted in bed, smiling up at him, pleased he'd remembered. "And chickens and guinea pigs and llamas and dogs and cats. That's him."

He remembered more now. "You and your father moved in with him after your mum died when you were . . . what was it?"

"Nine. You've got a good memory." He felt her shrug through the duvet. "But Homer was pretty much all the 'mom' I needed when I was growing up, taught me everything a mother would, how to cook, sew, that sort of thing."

"Your uncle wasn't married?"

"Nope. Well . . . he did live with Wilhelmina." She chuckled. "She was a black widow spider."

He coughed his laugh of surprise. "As a *pet*?"

"Business partner. Homer makes a living repairing optical instruments like microscopes, telescopes, gunsights, anything that uses crosshairs in the lens. He's a purist, people pay good money to have it done the old-fashioned way, with spider silk instead of metal or etching. And black widows spin the best silk for making crosshairs. Live for years, too. I think he's on his fifth Wilhelmina. He gets very attached to them, cries like a baby when they die."

"Strange bloke."

"All the ladies he ever liked thought so, too, while all the women who were attracted to him were even stranger. Besides, nobody wanted my dad and me as part of his built-in family, anyway. After my mother died, Homer and my dad built the house I grew up in, sixties hippy geodesic domes and hand-timbered framing and redwood shakes, which now I think is wonderful, but it used to embarrass me as a kid. Still there."

"In the country."

"On the edge of town, anyway. It's all been built up now, surrounded by housing development everywhere. But back then we had a big garden and a fruit orchard, and I canned vegetables and fruit to stock the cellar for winter. We had a fishpond, but the herons kept getting the catfish. One time my dad brought back live Dungeness crabs from the coast, and I felt so sorry for them I snuck them out of the house under my sweatshirt and tossed them into the pond. Dad was furious, and it didn't help the crabs any."

Keen laughed, pulling her in closer to him so he could put his face near her hair and breathe in the smell, and wondered what shampoo she used. It smelled like lavender and honey and a warm animal musk.

"We were into recycling ages before it was trendy. Homer put up solar panels so we could disconnect from the electric company. He even tried to make methane gas out of pig manure. Blew up the chicken coop by accident. Feathers *everywhere,* and man did I get tired of frying chicken every night for a month."

They laughed together, then lapsed into companionable silence. Then he yawned, stretched, kissed her on the cheek, and got out of bed. "Mind if I take a shower?" Under her gaze, he was suddenly self-conscious of his nakedness.

"Go ahead, just don't use up all the hot water."

The water was deliciously hot, and the fan in the B and B's bathroom had a squeaky bearing, both conspiring to lull Keen into easing the tension that had gripped him relentlessly between the shoulders over the past weeks. He didn't hear his mobile phone ring in his trouser pocket, didn't see Jillie grimace with annoyance, or see her grope in his clothing for his phone and switch it off to kill the ring tone. He did notice, however, when she slipped into the shower with him, stood behind him and lathered his back with soap, her hands gentle. He closed his eyes as she kissed the back of his neck and ran her fingers lower on his body, and exhaled with sheer pleasure.

One more night of mindless clubbing, drinking horrible alcopops, and popping Rafferty's vitamin C pills before heading out to Flynn's to listen to yet another tedious argument between her less-than-perfidious mates and Rachel thought she might just quit the police force for real. This was not how she had imagined undercover work would be.

"Thomas Aquinas said those who took pity on animals were more disposed to take pity on his fellow-man, 'The just regardeth the life of his beast.' Proverbs twelve, verse ten," Pablo said smugly, his legs tucked into a lotus position on the sofa as he smoked a thinly rolled cannabis joint. "The perks of a Catholic education. But one which just goes to show how completely hollow that entire argument for speciesism is."

"How?" Raven said as she reached up from where she sat on the floor to take the joint from him. She had her legs propped over Flynn's stomach, the man—as usual—passed out on the floor, an empty tin still grasped in one hand and lager leaking onto the carpet.

"Because he's saying the only reason to be against cruelty to animals is that it leads to cruelty to human beings," Stedman said, the two roommates in full swing with their habitual duo act. "Making the rights of humans more important than the rights of animals, again."

Raven's brow creased. "That's not what it means. You've twisted it totally backward. He's just saying people who are kind to animals are usually kind to people, too. What's wrong with that?"

"It's proof of how Christianity doesn't care about animal rights, even when they say they do—it's all hypocritical. I mean, look at Saint Francis of Assisi, okay? You got like a zillion paintings of him with the animals, preaching to the birds and all that. And all these Catholics are saying that proves how their religion is so far ahead of the times, how compassionate he was to animals. But he didn't make any distinction between animals and plants or even rocks; they were all the same value in the eyes of God."

"So?"

"So when everything is worth the same, nothing is worth anything. Which makes even bloody Saint Francis guilty of speciesism."

Raven squinted up at the pair of them, the corner of her lip curled with incredulous confusion. "I don't get it."

"That's because you're Jewish. Beryl," Stedman called out to where, predictably, Rafferty sat curled up in an armchair, inspecting that evening's footage and labeling tapes. "What do *you* think?"

She didn't even look up from her work. "I think that I've read Peter Singer and that you two are a tiresome pair of pretentious wankers."

Stedman gaped at her in anger, but when she looked up at him blandly, he sank back quickly enough with a scowl. "Fuck you," he muttered sullenly.

"You could try," a voice from the doorway said, galvanizing the group's attention. A muscular man with dark, curling hair to his shoulders grinned at them. "But she'd eat you for breakfast, little boy."

The man stepped over Flynn's prone body, giving it a kick hard enough to make the man groan, and leaned down to kiss Rafferty possessively on the lips. The rest of the group shifted uneasily, like children scared of the schoolyard bully. Rachel's blood whooshed in her ears, her heart leaping with a mix of excitement and intuitive fear. This was not a dilettante wannabe—the man radiated menace. He straightened and turned his stare on Rachel.

"So you're the new girl."

"Just a mate of Beryl's," Rachel said with what she hoped sounded like boredom.

"Sure." He parked himself on the arm of Rafferty's chair, one beefy arm draped over her shoulders. Beryl retained her faint mocking smile, but she'd paled and the quick glance she shot at Rachel was full of caution. "So introduce us, baby."

"Rachel Colver, we went to school together in Sandford." She inclined her head slightly toward the man next to her. "Rachel, meet my on-again off-again boyfriend. Rory Goodman."

2 6

Breakfast was pleasant enough, their morning tryst in the shower mellowing his mood as much as the crisp toast, fresh coffee, and orange juice. Guests in the countryside were thin on the ground these days, the only other diners at the B and B an elderly couple who smiled politely, helped themselves to bowls of cereal, and took a table at the farthest remove from them.

Keen set his cup down, sighed with real contentment, and smiled when the landlady—having little else to do—refilled his coffee for him, and returned to the kitchen.

"I enjoyed that," he said.

Jillie smiled. "What, breakfast?"

"All of it. Last night, this morning. Talking. Everything."

"Me talking, you mean?"

"Excuse me?"

She shook her head, biting into another piece of toast. "Nothing."

Suddenly, the mood seemed as fragile as a glass Christmas tree ornament. "I thought we had a good conversation this morning."

"We did," Jillie said firmly. "With me talking and you listening. As usual." She shrugged. "Seriously, Keen, it's okay. At least you *listen*. But that's just the way you are. That's the way a *lot* of guys are, not just you."

"Good to know," he said humorlessly.

"Oh, c'mon, it's no big deal. Men talk about concrete things; work, cars, how to run the world. Women talk about, you know . . . feelings. Stuff men don't like to get into much. Women are experts at talking, we talk all the time to each other, hardly get us to shut up. It's our national pastime, y'know."

He had to admit it; he knew she was right about him. And it was also true women *did* talk to women, far more easily than men talked to women, or even other men. It amazed him how women could talk so easily with one another, even strangers assuming an effortless intimacy. He'd listened on occasion to clusters of WPCs going at it in the canteen, although most women's talk either bored him silly or made him acutely uncomfortable. It wasn't so much what they said but how adroitly they could handle the convoluted verbal torrents.

Some years before the twins were born, he and Laura had gone to one of those awful police spring dances where he, like most of the married men, congregated in one corner with drinks in hand while the unmarried men shambled self-consciously around the dance floor with what few unattached ladies had turned up out of morbid curiosity. Bored with the routine shoptalk, stale jokes, and football arguments, he'd been drawn instead toward his wife as she talked with her friends. Words tumbled like a flock of birds all chirping away at top speed while hands weaved contrapuntal movements as intricate as Balinese dancers. No one seemed to mind the confusion, or even considered their intermingled chatter *as* confusion. It was like a curious verbal dance he had a hard time following, never mind entertaining any notion of joining in.

Nor was he expected to. While he hadn't felt excluded, whenever he'd drifted close enough to offer a minor contribution, the ladies had listened politely and even with honest interest until he was kind enough to go away and let them get on with the serious business of conversation. On the drive home, he had tried to relate this insight to Laura.

"You're just now figuring this out, are you?" She'd laughed, albeit gently enough, at his fumbling description. "Women like to dance more than men do, you've noticed? When a man leads, he isn't supposed to toss his partner about like a sack of potatoes. It's more like telling her without words what comes next. You know, guiding with your hands, little pressure on the back, that sort of thing. Men who are good dancers are usually good talkers, too. Not too many of either, more's the pity."

The late hour and the car heater had conspired to lull his thoughts into lethargy. He drove without speaking for nearly twenty minutes, the road rolling hypnotically under the tires. "I've never been much of a dancer." Glancing up at the empty road rushing away behind them in the rearview mirror, he caught her wry grin.

"We women are damned inconsistent. We like the strong silent type, too. I'm not complaining, love."

When they got home even late as it was, he'd sorted through their music, skipping her prized Streisand CDs (which he loathed) and his own random collection of Bo Diddly, Jethro Tull, and Genesis to select an old Nat King Cole. He put it on the stereo and waited sheepishly until the music had drawn her into the lounge. "What's all this, then?"

"I'm not up to boogying down to the Rolling Stones quite yet."

As Nat King Cole crooned out "Mona Lisa," he had held her close and shuffled his feet as inexpertly as any of his bachelor colleagues had that evening. "This is daft," she protested, only once, but hugged him tightly when he'd asked if she wanted, to stop. After a while, their dance evolved into one more intimate, his hands guiding her without words into what came next, naturally, wonderfully.

But in his current situation, he suspected Nat King Cole wasn't going to be of much help. He was dancing with Jillie without the faintest idea of how to lead.

He was still struggling to find the words to express this understanding to her when she suddenly looked up at someone past his shoulder, her smile brightening. Without glancing behind him, he knew with a sinking heart who it would be.

"Good morning." The jovial voice with its impeccable Oxford accent announced the appearance of Dr. Sheridan.

"Hello, Angus! You've met Keen Dunliffe before," Jillie said.

The two men shook hands, Keen not standing.

"Just in passing, never formally. It's a pleasure to meet you. Jillie's been singing your praises for months."

"Same here."

"Care to join us?" Jillie said.

"Oh, I shouldn't like to impose . . ."

"Don't be silly, sit, have some coffee." She looked to Keen for support. He managed to paste on a wan smile.

"Of course, join us, please."

Sheridan dropped the small rucksack he'd slung over one shoulder onto the floor beside a chair. "If you insist, thanks. I'll just grab a cup, be right back."

While the tall, thin professor poured himself a coffee, Jillie studied Keen questioningly. "It's okay, isn't it?"

"Sure," he said more forcefully than was needed. "The more the merrier."

Dr. Sheridan slid into the seat either side of them, slurped on his coffee, and murmured, "Oh, that's good. Fresh here, not instant. Coffee at the hostel is dreadful. *Dreadful.*" Then he put down the cup and leaned over to dig into the rucksack.

"I actually had hoped to run into you again," Sheridan said to Keen. "At the dig site, I meant, not here . . . I mean, here is fine, too." He rolled his eyes at himself self-deprecatingly. "Anyway. Jillie told me about your friend in the wheelchair, the one who's taking his local leisure center to task for not allowing his longbow club on their fields. That reminded me of something I read a few years ago, and I may have *just* found a possible solution to your friend's quandary." Sheridan busied himself with rummaging through a selection of books he pulled out of the bag and stacked onto the table, papers and yellow Post-it notes fluttering between pages. "It's in here somewhere, just a tick . . ."

Keen frowned with a clouded sense of betrayal, resenting Jillie's confiding their personal conversations to someone else. Nor did she look contrite. Then, he forced himself to acknowledge, they were colleagues. And his reaction was bordering absurdly on jealousy.

"Ah, here it is." Sheridan found the book, flipped through it to find a page before running a finger down the print. "In the West Riding villages of Bridleton, Thatcher's Hill, and Bramley Crook, a thirteenth-century royal charter requires every male villager from the age of eighteen to eighty to practice shooting the longbow one day a week in case they may be called upon to come to the defense of their king and country."

He looked up. "That law has never been repealed. Now if your leisure center happens to be located within the boundaries of those three villages, your friend can insist on the enforcement of this statute. Laws are terribly difficult to overturn, what with the cost of putting white papers through Parliament. Your leisure center will likely find it cheaper and less trouble to put in a disabled ramp for your longbow shooters. It's worth looking into, anyway."

"That's brilliant!" Jillie enthused. "What a great find!"

"Isn't English law a marvel?" Sheridan returned her smile. "That something written down eight hundred years ago could still have a direct impact on modern life in ways the authors never dreamed of."

"Yeah," Keen said quietly, his gaze shifting between the two of them, feeling like a forlorn child standing on the outside of a sweet shop looking in. "It's great."

And he knew, sadly but strangely without much pain, his relationship with Jillie was well and truly over.

2 7

The little gang broke up earlier than usual after Rory Goodman's appearance. Goodman himself had sneered as they drifted nervously away, then announced to Rafferty he had to see a man about a dog and would see her back at her flat later. He kissed her again, aggressive, hard, little affection in the gesture, before he left, giving Flynn another kick on his way out. This time Flynn woke up, glared after him blearily.

"Oh, that's great," he muttered darkly. "Hoo-ray, Rory bloody Goodman is back in town, lucky us. Who's for the chop this time?"

"Flynn," Rafferty said softly.

"What."

"Shut the fuck up."

Flynn appeared to take no offense, sitting up to scratch at his scalp, inspect the empty tins in search of more lager, then stagger off to what Rachel presumed was his bedroom, slamming the door shut.

"Jesus, Beryl. Who the hell was that?"

Beryl gave her a hard look. "Nobody you want to know that well." She stuffed her camcorder and tapes into her bag, grabbed her jacket, and stood. "C'mon. Let's get out of here."

The ride back to Beryl's flat was almost tranquil, Beryl staying curiously within the speed limit and steering the motorbike carefully. When she drew up beside Rachel's little red Polo and switched off the engine, she sat on the bike a moment after Rachel got off and took off her helmet. The woman stared straight ahead, not moving.

"Beryl?"

Most mornings after a night of clubbing, they usually exchanged terse goodbyes and staggered off on their separate ways.

"Want a cuppa?" Rafferty said finally.

"Sure." Rachel shrugged, doing her best to seem blasé. "Why not?"

The "cuppa," it turned out, was more booze; Rafferty opened a bottle of wine. They both sat on the floor, propped up against Rafferty's settee. Neither of them spoke for several minutes, only the sound of traffic slowly waking up on the streets outside, cars and people passing by. Outside, a cat in heat yowled her availability to the general feline population as a neighbor's plumbing gurgled through the brickwork.

"I remember the exact moment I wanted to become a serious filmmaker," Rafferty said finally. "Be someone who goes covert to expose the cruelty man inflicts on animals. I was about eleven years old, and Dad had just bought me my first video camera. I thought I wanted to be George Lucas, dressing up dogs and cats in space suits and making silly little movies, stuff my mum thought was cute. They loved it, showing this stupid crap off to their friends like I was destined for Hollywood greatness.

"Then one weekend I went to the mall with my dad; he wanted to look at some fishing gear, and I wandered outside where this animal rights guy was handing out pamphlets. He had a television set up behind this black curtain screen. There was a sign saying you had to be eighteen to watch the videotape, but I guess because I had a camera and said I wanted to be a filmmaker, he let me watch it."

She took a long drink from her glass of wine and poured more from the bottle into it. She didn't seem to notice Rachel wasn't drinking any of hers.

"It was showing a video where a seal is skinned alive, this poor animal staring at the camera and blinking, all its skin gone but its eyelashes covered in blood, dying so slowly. Wolves and rabbits caught in traps chewing off their own legs, strangled on wire loops, heads are crushed in steel jaws. Kangaroos being mutilated alive, and dozens of dolphins slaughtered. I was horrified. Made me sick to my stomach. I threw up on the pavement, had night-mares for months after." She laughed hollowly. "My dad was furious. Got into the guy's face and threatened to rip out his lungs."

"So that's when you got involved with the sabs," Rachel said, not making it a question.

"Yeah. I must have made a hundred videos of hunt hounds rip-ping foxes apart while toffs smeared blood on their kids' faces, rite-of-passage bullshit. Still can't get the images out of my head, never will." Rafferty was quiet for a long moment, staring out the win-dow at nothing before she turned her head to stare at Rachel, her eyes intense. "It's wrong, y'know."

"What is, foxhunting?"

"It's *wrong* to kill an animal just for sport."

"But it's okay to break out all the windows of my house and leave phony Molotov cocktails as a threat on our doorstep." Rachel heard her own voice, sounding angrier than she intended.

Rafferty blew out her breath in a soundless disdainful laugh. "You still carrying that grudge around after all this time? Jesus, Rach. I didn't do that, and nobody I was mates with then did it, either."

"Lie down with dogs," Rachel retorted.

"Believe me, I've lain down with worse." Rafferty's brief flare of anger died quickly. "Most protesters trying to stop animal abuse are perfectly ordinary, normal people. Good people. *Decent* people. Middle-class grannies who chain themselves together on roads to protest the inhumane way sheep are treated on export lorries, share their thermos of hot tea with the police who arrest them, that sort." She smiled bleakly at Rachel. "Your sort." The smile van-ished. "But the more involved I got with some of the hard-core animal rights activists, the more I realized just what sort of scum some of them really are. How much I was sucked in by their lies. Fucking *lies*."

Rachel stared at her in confusion. "What? What are you talking about?"

"The film of that seal being skinned alive?" Rafferty shook her head. "Turns out the guy who did it was this poor Inuit paid by the photographers to do it. He went to court and testified how he was told to skin it alive instead of the way the Inuits traditionally do it, clubbing it to death first. Those wolves and rabbits? They'd been caught alive and put inside a fenced compound for the filming, using illegal traps. Those men mutilating live kangaroos? Couple blokes from Greenpeace pretending to be from some hunting magazine actually *paid* a couple bastards to set up the whole thing. And the dolphins? Those poor goddamned dolphins? A film crew passed themselves off as university scientists doing 'research,' told the fisherman to butcher them alive, even gave him the knife, yelling they needed more blood, *more blood*. All to make a bunch of animal snuff films."

She drained her glass and poured more wine into it.

"But who cares if it was faked—videotape is a powerful weapon to fight your enemies—it didn't matter that the very people who were supposed to be preventing animal cruelty were doing it themselves." Her words were starting to slur with the alcohol. "It served the cause. So what if the Inuits aren't allowed to hunt anymore to feed themselves, a thousand years of native culture and tradition aren't as important as a few seals. And the U.S. Marine Mammal Protection Act didn't do anything except drive an indigenous people into poverty." Rachel wasn't sure if she'd said "indigenous" or "indigent," the wine affecting both Rafferty's mood and her ability to speak.

"Animal rights activists don't care about animals. It's *ideology* that matters, not animals. Not even people. Not even the planet. Fake fur is made from petrochemicals, but let's poison the air and the water, so long as we don't skin the poor little rabbits. They'd be against killing a single lab rat even if it meant not finding a cure for AIDS . . . although you don't see many of them out there protesting ratcatchers killing sewer rats, do you?" Rafferty giggled. "Or the fleas that live on them."

Rachel was silent, not sure what to say as the words poured out of Beryl in a long, anguished rush.

"Those pair of wankers have it all wrong, Pablo and Stedman. It's animal rights people who don't make any distinction between an animal and a rock. What they really mean when they say the life of an ant and the life of a child are morally the same, is that you can treat the child like you would an ant. Step on it, squash it, throw petrol on its home and burn it out, murder its parents, do whatever it takes for the campaign, it's only the *campaign* that matters. Kill, kill, kill to save the fucking animals."

"I don't get it, Beryl. You've been supporting animal rights for years, as long as I've known you. What's going on?"

"Animal *rights*. What a joke," Beryl said bitterly. "Look at this country, Rachel, it's a fucking madhouse. We're slaughtering millions of animals, for *nothing*. But do you ever hear one word out of the animal rights activists against it? Of course not. People like Rory don't give a shit if *farm* animals have proper food and shelter, or medical care, or legal protection so they don't suffer. They're *against* animal welfare rules—the rules just help maintain animals being used for human use, can't have that, even if it means they all have to die. Preferably horribly."

She poured the last of the wine into her glass and stared at it morosely.

"If you feel this way, why are you still working with them?" Rachel asked quietly, feeling as if she was picking her way barefoot through broken glass.

Rafferty snorted and looked up at her unsteadily, her eyes red. "I'm undercover. Just like you. Except you get paid."

Rachel's cheeks prickled in alarm. "What do you mean?"

Rafferty screwed up her face with disapproval "Oh, c'mon, Rachel. I've known you were a cop from day one." She glanced at the ceiling with bleary-eyed reflection. "Well, day two, technically."

"That's ridiculous—"

"I rang that evil old gran of yours, we had quite a long chat."

"I told you, she's got senile dementia, probably onset Alzheimer's—"

"Give it a rest, Rach. She's still as much a nasty piece of work as she ever was, but she's not senile. And she's got ears like a bloody bat, she put two and two together pretty quick, even if she thinks you're in London instead of Newcastle." Rafferty shrugged. "Besides, no way you just walked into the Blue Bull by sheer chance. Not that soon after the Richmont bombing."

It was almost a relief to give up the pretense. "Beryl, were you involved in that bombing?"

Rafferty exhaled a long, drunken sigh of impatience. "Of course I was. It's why you're here, isn't it?"

"If you're working against them, Beryl, then come with me. Tell my boss what you know, and we can help you. We can protect you, I swear."

"Yeah, right. Like you lot protected Eunice Connor."

Rachel felt her mouth go dry. "What do you know about Eunice Connor?"

Beryl's shoulder rose and fell with fatalistic resignation. "I know she was shot. I know she got careless and now she's dead. And I know that there's someone inside the police who made sure she got that way."

"Who?"

"I don't know. But it's how they knew where Connor would be that day, what flight, everything. It's how Rory got hold of military explosives to blow up the Richmont warehouse. Rory brags about his connections with the cops as being his fireproofing. But who it is, he hasn't told me."

"So why are you telling me all this?"

"Because Rory Goodman is back in town." She looked away, out the window, with desolation in her eyes. "Which means he probably knows you're a cop, too. You and me, best mates?" She shook her head. "I knew the minute you walked into the Blue Bull I was fucked. He's most likely come back to kill me. And you, too, if he gets a chance."

Rachel put her untouched glass of wine on an end table by the settee, twisted around to sit on her knees, and took Rafferty's hands in her own. "Beryl, please please please, come with me. If he's here to hurt you, let us help you."

Rafferty chuckled, deep in her chest, and grinned. "Rachel,

you're a lovely girl. And so naïve. That's why I trust you. But you *can't* help me. And I don't want you to even try because I'm not finished yet. I've nearly got all the pieces. I'm almost there. But not yet. Not. Quite. Yet. So all I want you to do is shut up and listen. Then I want you to get the hell out of my flat and run as fast and as far as you can."

28

Half an hour later, Rachel left Rafferty's flat, her hand shaking as she pressed the speed-dial button for Keen's mobile. "Come on, come on," she murmured as it rang, then hung up without leaving a message as it went to voice mail.

She parked the Polo around the corner to watch. It didn't take long to wait. Rory Goodman appeared in a dusty white Ford transit van and parked behind Rafferty's Honda, climbed the steps with several flattened cardboard containers and disappeared into her flat. He reappeared within minutes, carrying the first of a dozen boxes down the steps and slinging them roughly into the back end of the van. She ducked down in the seat, trying Keen's mobile again. Again, it went straight to voice mail. This time she left a terse message.

Goodman reappeared, without any boxes but holding Rafferty tightly by the forearm, the woman visibly drunk, staggering as he jerked her along and roughly shoved her into the passenger seat of the van.

Rachel tried Keen's number a final time, with the same result. She flipped the phone closed and tossed it on the seat beside her. *Damn it!* she cursed silently. *Where the hell are you?* Goodman climbed into the driver's side, backed out onto the road and drove off. The street was nearly deserted, but Rachel started the Polo, the engine complaining for a few heart-stopping moments before turning over. Fear thumped hard in her chest as she followed the van, making her slightly nauseous, her hands sweating. But following vehicles was not a police skill Rachel had had much experience with; she hung back so far to keep from being spotted in the meager traffic that she soon lost them. She turned back, checking side streets, searching frantically without success. Goodman and Rafferty were gone.

"Think, think, think!" she whispered to herself, frustrated with how slowly her brain seemed to be operating. Kramer? She grimaced, trying to work out whether her reluctance was due more to anxiety she wouldn't be able to persuade him or the desire to do without his help and prove him wrong about her. She exhaled against her panic, grabbed the mobile and dialed again, one hand on the steering wheel.

"Danny," she said gratefully when he picked up on the third ring. "Danny, listen. Do you know where Keen is? He's not answering his mobile. And Beryl Rafferty is in big trouble." It was all coming out in a breathless rush. "She's not involved in smuggling the birds into the country. I mean she *is,* but not how you think. She's been collecting evidence linking Rory Goodman with the JADA group in London, *they're* behind the smuggling of scarlet macaws—"

"Wait, wait, wait," Danny said, confused. "Animal rights extremists are smuggling birds into the country? That doesn't make any sense . . ."

"It does if it makes enough to fund the rest of their activities—arms and money laundering—while in their minds they're 'liberating' birds from people exploiting them as breeding stock."

"But Rachel—"

"Danny, it doesn't *have* to make sense to us. It does to *them.* And Rory knows Rafferty's got the proof to link him to JADA. He's taken her, and he's going to *kill* her if we don't get to them first."

"Okay, what do you need?"

"Find Keen. Tell him to get hold of Kramer. Tell them that Rory's probably taking her to Avondale Farm, to the foot-and-mouth pyres—"

"*Probably?*" Danny's perceptible doubt irritated her. "Kramer doesn't much care for 'probablys.' "

"It's an educated guess, okay? Just . . . convince him. I'm going there now."

She pulled the phone away from her ear, cutting off his tinny protest of "Rachel!" with a flick of her wrist to shut the mobile, and dropped it back onto the seat. Now, she thought, all she had to do was race out to Avondale Farm in time to try to rescue Rafferty from a murderous sociopath in the middle of several thousand burning animal carcasses, without backup, or weapons, or—really—a hope in hell.

Danny tried to ring her back, but Rachel wasn't picking up. He sat at his desk, staring at the computer screen unseeingly, wondering how the fuck everything had gone so wrong so fast. "Ah, bollocks," he said quietly to the empty room, stood, grabbed his jacket off the back of his chair, and was punching numbers into his mobile as he nearly trotted toward the lifts.

"Mate, we've got a big problem," he said once the man on the other end picked up. He hurriedly outlined the situation and listened intently on his way down in the lift. "Yeah, of course I know where it is," he said, ignoring the automatic smile of the woman at the desk, and headed toward the back car park. "I'll meet you there as soon as I can."

The Avondale Farm pyres operated with military efficiency; army lorries loaded with wood sleepers, hay, and coal ran a constant traffic into one end of the razor-wire compound, while farm lorries conveyed their cargo of cadavers into the other end. Once the bodies had been unloaded, bulldozers scraped up the bodies and transferred them to the waiting funeral pyres.

Hundreds of railway sleepers had been stacked into a half-dozen parallel ditches, excavated solely for the purpose of a mass cremation, each running several hundred meters and packed with several lorryloads of coal and straw bales. Eight hundred sheep carcasses, two hundred pigs, and just over seventy-five slaughtered cattle were piled onto the sleepers, the bodies then doused in oil and diesel and set alight. The huge pyres burned for days, dense black smoke and the stench of scorched flesh thickening the air for miles around. Once the fires had gone out, the ashes were scooped into skips and hauled away for burial elsewhere, leaving the scarred trenches to be filled again with more sleepers, more straw and coal, and more dead animals.

As far away from the choking black smoke as they could get, Gerald Spaulding stood with four other members of his unit, all dressed in TA camouflage uniforms, red bands on their sleeves marking them as military police. At the other end of the field, half a dozen lesser-ranking soldiers, wearing white contamination overalls over their cammies, hoods encasing their heads and filter masks over their faces, ambled through the trenches, a few with bolt pistols in well-polished holsters at their hips. Whenever the occasional spasming leg was spotted or the faint bleat of pain heard in those trenches where the animals had yet to be set alight, one of the soldiers would lean into the trench and—for those with bolt pistols—dispatch the unfortunate beast.

Spaulding spotted Danny's Mazda bouncing down the narrow rutted road far faster than he should have been driving well before the PC arrived. He spoke briefly to one of his colleagues before sauntering away toward the gate. He pointed toward a makeshift car park outside the chain-link fence, indicating where Danny should park.

Danny turned his car onto the field, mud squelching around the tires. Gerald unlocked the gate, walked through and waited, legs braced apart, his boots coated in the mire up to his ankles, as Danny got out and minced across the churned-up ground as he tried to avoid the worst of the muck on his shoes. Spaulding stood beside a large army lorry, blocking any view his colleagues might have of the two of them.

"Thank God you got here so fast," Danny said, nearly babbling. "We've got to hurry, find Goodman, find the girl before he kills her—"

"What the fuck is the matter with you," Gerald snapped crossly. "Stop panicking, for God's sake."

"It's coming apart at the seams, Gerald," Danny complained, his voice pitched high, his skin blanched with dismay. "Rory's taken Rafferty hostage, he's on his way here with her and the videotapes and the documents, *everything*. Plans to toss it all into the fire, including the girl. If he destroys the evidence and kills her, we've got nothing. *Nothing*."

"Just calm down, it's over already, everything's been taken care of," Spaulding said curtly.

Danny gaped at him. "What do you mean, it's "been taken care of"? Rafferty . . . ?"

"I mean she's fine," Gerald quickly assured him. "As soon as you rang, I immediately contacted a mate of mine in the TA, already here supervising the pyres. He rallied the troops, they were waiting for the bastard. Stroke of bloody luck, really. I got here just after Goodman did, he didn't have time to do anything, didn't stand a chance. I didn't even get much of a look-in myself—it was over so fast." Spaulding waved vaguely at the temporary buildings on the far side of the compound. "Rafferty's a bit shaken up, but she's safe and sound, having tea with the commander. Everything's fine. We got the evidence, videotapes, files, the works. No harm, no foul."

"And Goodman?"

Spaulding shrugged in a manner exuding both confidence and nonchalance. "He's not going anywhere."

"Jesus," Danny breathed in relief. "Damn, that was close. Thank God for you and your army buddies." He took his mobile from his pocket, opening it.

"Who are you calling now?" Spaulding asked. "Where's the rest of your team?"

"Rachel should be here already, somewhere—"

Spaulding glanced through the windows of the lorry, toward where the other members of his TA unit had been. They had apparently moved on, avoiding the oily black smoke drifting across the fields that further obscured them; Danny and Spaulding were alone and unobserved.

"Colver? *Here?*"

"Yeah. She's who told me Goodman took Rafferty."

"And the others? What about Kramer?"

Danny punched a speed dial and held up his phone with a triumphant smile. "They're coming, mate. Sharpish. Don't worry."

"You mean you haven't told the rest of your team, nobody else knows yet?" Spaulding said slowly, in disbelief.

"Just Rachel."

"You're here on your own?"

Danny held the phone to his ear, waiting as it rang. "This is *my* case, nobody else wanted it. Just a bunch of stupid birds, they said. I've worked it for seven months. This time, *I* get to take the credit, they'll *have* to take me seriously now. I can't wait to see their faces," he said with boyish pride. He turned away from Spaulding to speak into the phone. "Hey, Sweet?"

With his back turned, Danny didn't notice as Spaulding brushed back his jacket, unsnapped his holster, and drew the bolt pistol. In one smooth motion, Spaulding lifted the barrel to the back of Danny's head and pulled the trigger. The heavy bolt slammed into the younger man's skull with a sickening crunch, killing him instantly. Danny's body dropped to the ground at the same time as his mobile phone. Spaulding's boot stomped down hard on the little mobile, shattering it as thoroughly as he had Danny's head, driving the pieces down into the heavy clay mud to bury it completely.

Danny had signed his own death warrant the moment he'd rung Spaulding; all Spaulding needed was to know who else knew—relieved that the stupid git had been more concerned about credit for glory than sensibly calling for backup. But he'd have to move quickly, he realized. Danny had been right—it was all coming apart at the seams, all his neat, organized plans unraveling. Now he would just have to cover his tracks as fast as he could, improvising as he went, buy enough time and obscure his trail just long enough to get his money and himself out of the country.

It was too far to drag the body to the pits where it could have been expediently cremated, not without risk of being spotted. Looking around, still wary of any possible witnesses, Spaulding popped the boot of Danny's car before he reached down and grabbed the body in a fireman's lift and dumped it inside. He had to push the legs against the torso to get it to fit, brutally enough to crack several ribs audibly, but he managed to get the boot lid closed. He'd have to hope he could transfer the body into one of the waste skips later in the evening, under cover of dark, until the next convoy of lorries carried the tons of ash away to be dumped down derelict mine shafts. Chances were, he realized, the lorry driver—safe in the air-conditioned and sanitized cab, operating everything by remote control—would never even notice the body as it tumbled out with the rest of the ash and bones.

Chances were. That was just another chance he'd have to take.

Then he'd drive Danny's car to some industrial wasteland along the waterfront and torch it, before anyone noticed it—or Danny—missing. File a stolen-vehicle report, timed carefully so that it could never have been anywhere near the Avondale Farm site at the same time as Spaulding. The guys in his unit might be a little trickier to manage, having observed Danny drive up and Gerald walk out to meet him. But he was confident he could spread enough confusion to make whatever they thought they had seen useless to any investigators.

That would have to wait, perilous as that might be. He and Rory had destroyed the evidence as well as Rafferty's body, tossing it into the midst of a flaming pit, her camera, all the videos and the manila files following. Goodman had already strangled the bitch without a single pang of remorse, no doubt had even enjoyed doing it, the bruised skin on her neck dappled in a perfect outline of the man's beefy fingers. But for all his supposed hard-man toughness, Rory retched and vomited as the woman's hair and clothes caught fire, the exposed flesh obscenely white before charring black, splitting open, the fat blazing under the roil of black smoke. He was bent over, hands braced on his knees as he heaved up his guts, the mindless thug utterly defenseless, as Spaulding calmly and efficiently murdered him as well with a bolt to the back of his head and kicked the body into the pit after the woman's. Both corpses—unlike Danny's body—would be cremated into oblivion in the inferno, bone fragments jumbled and mixed into millions of others.

He had thought that would have been the end of it, all the loose ends tidied up and disposed of. But now he would have to wait for

Rachel Colver to show up and hope he could dispatch her as quietly and unnoticeably as he had the first three. He scowled. He had always prided himself on his military precision and attention to detail; he didn't like such spur-of-the-moment messiness.

2 9

When Keen's cheap mobile rang, he caught Jillie's look of surprise, wondering at it as he pulled it out of his inside jacket pocket and answered.

"Yeah?"

"Boss." It was Jasmine. "I got him. Your ghost in the machine. It's not one of your team, it's a PC in traffic, stationed out of Hexham. Bloke called Gerald Spaulding. You know him?"

"No."

"I rang his shift sergeant. He's on temporary duty with the TA unit assigned to the pyres in Avondale."

"Thanks, Jazz—"

"Hold on, that's not all. Gerald Spaulding isn't his real name— he took on his stepfather's name when his mother remarried. Gerald Spaulding was born Gerald Harmond. His real father's brother lived in London and had a son as well, Lyle Harmond. And they were both in London when that marshal was killed."

Shit. "Why hasn't anyone made that link before this?"

"Spaulding was in the FRU in Northern Ireland during the nineties, those people tend to keep secrets buried rather deep. But one thing I did manage to find out is that Spaulding didn't last long, got kicked out for—get this—being *too* violent. He pretty much went legit after that, stayed out of trouble, steady jobs, no legal or financial problems, all squeaky clean. I also had Flaky Flagler run a check on his finances, tied it into the stolen-goods case so you-know-who wouldn't start sniffing around my knickers. Flagler had a lot of trouble making any sense out of the records—Spaulding's one cagey bloke. But it seems this guy buys and sells weapons, *lots* of them. Not too clear where they're ending up. Lots of money being laundered in and out of Hong Kong. Numbers kept down low enough under the radar it didn't set off any alarms. He's got half a dozen big offshore accounts. We're talking enough for you and me and the entire nick to retire permanently to the Cayman Islands in grand style. And Keen?"

"Yah."

"He's been spending a lot of time with Danny Mayfield."

"You think Danny's dirty?"

"I don't know. Don't see it. Looks like Mayfield has been trying to use Spaulding as a resource, maybe he doesn't even realize he's been played."

"Right." *I owe you,* he bit back before he said it. She heard it anyway.

"Just go get this fucker, boss."

He punched the OFF button on the phone, reached into his trouser pocket for the fancy mobile. He futilely punched in a few numbers, wondering what he was doing wrong when it didn't work, then realized it had been switched off. He stared at it for a moment, then looked up sharply at Jillie. She winced guiltily.

"I turned it off." At his incredulous stare, she said defensively, "Every time we get a chance to get together, the damned thing goes off and out the door you go. I've been here weeks, and we've hardly even seen each other! Just one night, one whole night with you, that's all I wanted."

He said nothing as he turned it on and noticed he had a voice message. After pressing his way through the menu to get to it, he held it to his ear and listened to Rachel's scared, shaking voice.

"Damn it, pick up! Rory Goodman's taken Rafferty. I think they're heading for the Avondale Farm, there's a pyre going there. I can't explain it all now, but Rafferty's been collecting evidence linking Goodman and JADA to the murder of that U.S. marshal, and now he's going to kill her. What do I do? Do I go after them? Do I call Kramer? Jesus, Dunliffe. *Where the hell are you?*" The voice cut off abruptly. When Keen rang her number, Rachel didn't answer.

"Well," he said with far more calm than he felt while punching in the speed dial for Kramer. "I hope it was worth it to you. Because turning off my mobile may just have cost someone their life."

He got no satisfaction at all from her gasp of dismay.

"Kramer, we've got a problem," he said as the DI snarled a greeting on the other end of the line.

30

Keen pulled into the Avondale Farm car park just as Sweet found Danny's phone, the tracker device still working despite the mobile being smashed to bits and buried in six inches of mud. Sweet held the muddy instrument in one palm, then exchanged a silent glance with St. John. St. John left and returned with the jack lever from the boot of his own car. It took little force to pop open the boot of Danny's Mazda, the young tech's dead face staring up with the contortion of a smile, as if absurdly pleased to see them.

"Poor bastard," St. John murmured. He turned away, his mouth tight with anger.

"Rachel's car is parked behind some trees just past that hedgerow," Keen said. They looked at each other, then grimly tramped along the muddy track to the little red Polo. No one spoke as St. John prized open the boot, but they all blew out their breaths in audible relief to find it empty.

"So where the hell is she?" St. John said. Sweet rotated in a circle with the tracker, scanning for Rachel's mobile, and looked up to find the direction finder pointed at the row of fires burning on the other side of the chain-link fence. "You gotta be joking. Your girl has gone in there? *Alone?*"

"Looks like. She's going after Rafferty and Rory Goodman, by herself."

"Stupid bitch." Keen wasn't sure who Sweet meant, Rafferty or Rachel.

"So . . . are *we* going to wait for Kramer and armed response?" St. John asked.

Sweet stared at the huge trenches behind the chain-link fence, orange flames silhouetting hundreds of charred cloven legs pointed skyward along with the smoke seething from the pyres.

"Nah, fuck it," Sweet said. "It's going to take too long waiting around for the cavalry to show up." The three men headed for the pyres, heat already whipping across them with a force like running into a brick wall, flames growling and snapping so loudly they were forced to shout. "Who's covering what end?"

The decision was made for them, however, as Rachel staggered out of the oily smoke toward them, coughing, her face streaked where her streaming tears had cut through the soot. In her arms, she held a newborn black-faced lamb, its white wool still stained with its dead mother's placental blood. To Keen's amazement, it was very much alive, bleating plaintively as it struggled. How it had survived in the ewe's womb only to be born on a funeral pyre was a callous miracle. That Rachel had stumbled across it, and thought to rescue it while being hunted by a vicious maniac, was incredible.

"Where's Rafferty?" Sweet demanded.

"Dead . . . saw her body in the . . . I think . . . Rory, too . . ." was as much as Rachel was able to wheeze out before a fit of coughing doubled her over. St. John caught her as she collapsed, keeping her from falling.

A man in a khaki military uniform strode out from between the parallel pits, appearing through the smoke like an apparition materializing from the depths of hell. He stopped, his face diffused with dark anger and mouth tightened into a furious line, a bloodied bolt pistol in one hand down by his side, eyeing the small group with a scowl.

"This is a military operation, completely off-limits to the public," he barked out.

"We're police," Keen said, holding up his warrant card.

The man's eyes narrowed, hostile. "Doesn't matter, this area isn't within your jurisdiction. You don't have authorization to be here." Then he spotted the lamb in Rachel's arms. "And you can't take that." Before anyone could react, he pushed the barrel of his bolt pistol against the lamb's head and shot it. The impact shattered the lamb's thin skull, spattering Rachel's face with its blood. St. John recoiled, releasing Rachel as she sank to her knees. The tiny lamb jerked its reflexive death throes as she clutched it to her chest and then hung limp.

"You can't take it; it's contaminated. Has to go on the fire with the rest of 'em," Spaulding insisted again, holstering the bolt gun and glaring at the group staring at him in disbelief.

Keen spotted the name marker on the man's uniform. "You Spaulding? PC Gerald Spaulding?" he demanded. His heart was pounding against his ribs, fists spasming with a desire for violence.

The look the man shot him was a mix of arrogance and suspicion. "It's Sergeant Spaulding at the moment, and you're trespassing in a military zone. So if you don't mind, you're all going to have to leave, before I have to call in the military police to arrest *you*." He snorted his contempt and started to walk away.

"Excuse me, son. Sorry, could you just hold on there a moment . . ." Kramer called after him politely. They all turned as the DI strode past them and up to the man with deceptive calmness. Before the man could even blink, Kramer punched him hard in the face, every ounce of lean muscle behind the blow. Keen winced at the sound of bone cracking. Spaulding's head snapped back, his eyes rolling into their sockets. He collapsed to the ground, blood gushing from the mashed tissue that had been his nose. Kramer shook his hand in the air, hissing against the pain. Then he stooped and relieved Spaulding of the bolt pistol, turned and tossed it to St. John. He paused a moment, considering the stunned man sprawled at his feet, before deliberately kicking Spaulding hard in the groin. Even unconscious, Spaulding groaned, writhing feebly.

Kramer turned, his look still murderous, before he stalked past Keen. "Fuck the military police. Fuck armed response, too, useless pricks. Arrest that asshole," he said to St. John.

"On what charge?" St. John asked.

"I don't care. Breathing the same air as me. Then have that bolt pistol sent to forensics, see if any of the blood on that thing is human. Or Danny's."

Kramer squatted in front of Rachel and, with astonishing gentleness, pried the dead lamb out of her hands and laid the limp corpse on the ground. "C'mon, girl," he murmured, and brushed her hair back from her eyes with his hand, knuckles bloodied and bruised from where he'd struck Spaulding. "That's it, that's better, you'll be okay, sweetpea," he said as she looked up at him, her expression vacant with shock. Kramer scooped her into his arms, her arms around his neck, and carried her like a child away from the fires toward his car.

"Well, there goes Wife Number Six," Sweet muttered. He considered the dead lamb for a moment before he picked up the body and tossed it, albeit sympathetically, into the nearest flames. It disappeared into the pile of blackened ash and smoldering wood and charred cloven-hoofed legs pointing forlornly toward the sky where more oily smoke roiled, the stench nearly overpowering as the wind shifted, driving them coughing and eyes watering from the pits.

July's Death Toll: 21,025 cattle, 140,416 sheep, 8,948 pigs, and 137 goats.

After two months without incident in the Yorkshire Dales, 90 cows and 400 sheep are slaughtered on Leaholm Lawns Farms in Houlsyke, and two nearby farms are facing contiguous culling, raising fears foot-and-mouth is returning to the area.

Nuala Preston, a farmer in Pembroke, West Wales, receives an anonymous phone call from a man offering to deliberately infect her livestock with foot-and-mouth in exchange for £2,000. Horrified, she hangs up and rings DEFRA. Several other farmers in the area have received similar offers. The National Farmers' Union maintains the vast majority of farmers would reject such propositions. "But I think some farmers on the brink of desperation and bankruptcy might be tempted to go for it because at least they would get compensation for their animals," Ms. Preston admits. Compensation for a culled ewe, for example, is £90—more than the current market rate hard hit by the crisis.

As 14,000 animals are earmarked for slaughter in Thirsk, farmers prepare to defy the government by denying vets access onto their land. Dianne Ellis, Yorkshire coordinator for the pressure group Ground Force, is advising farmers on how to blockade their property and seek legal methods of preventing culls.

Robin Bosomworth of Marderby Hall in Felixkirk has lost his battle with DEFRA. Although no trace of foot-and-mouth had been found on his farm, 350 cattle and 9,000 pigs are slaughtered over three days, ending a dairy business established in 1938. The Bosomworth farm is notable as the place where young Alf Wight, author of All Creatures Great and Small, met his first farmer. "Before, I woke up to the sound of a farm," Mr. Bosomworth said. "Now I wake up to silence." None of the animals test positive for the disease.

Farmers refuse to allow Animal Health Minister Elliot Morley onto their land for a scheduled visit to a sheep farm during blood-testing, claiming the number of officials along with media interest could increase the risk of infection in a biosecurity area.

The RSPCA has warned that thousands of hill sheep face death from starvation if restrictions on the movement of livestock is not eased. Food stocks have run low as farmers have already used up fodder meant for the winter, and older ewes and autumn lambs will face tough winter conditions on fields already overgrazed by enclosed flocks.

Four thousand sheep on the Brecon Beacons are culled after 112 were shown to have antibodies in their blood, despite fierce protests from the farmers over DEFRA's cavalier and bewildering blood-testing policy On July 27, a shepherd on the Today show explains that the sheep had tested positive only for antibodies, but not the virus, which—as any capable virologist would know—meant that they could have had the disease and survived or been in contact with the virus but not contracted it. In either case, the sheep were healthy, not contagious, and of no threat to any other animals. Their slaughter—along with tens of thousands of animals similarly affected—is unjustifiable.

Hundreds of vets in Cumbria are facing financial difficulty as over 60 percent of their clients have lost their livestock to foot-and-mouth, while vets in the North-East have seen the loss of a quarter of their business.

31

AUGUST

The Powers That Be, Kramer had darkly informed them all once the team—including Rachel and Keen—had again assembled in the unit's bland building in Newcastle city after Danny's funeral, were not pleased. Not pleased at all. The well-cooked remains of Beryl Rafferty and Rory Goodman had been found before they had completely gone up in smoke, leaving just enough for forensics to identify the bodies. It helped, of course, that Rachel was able to recognize the small gold loop with a gemstone the pathologist identified as blue beryl as the same one she'd seen in Beryl Rafferty's belly button, once it had been cleansed of burned flesh.

The blood on Spaulding's bolt pistol was a mixture of sheep, pig, cow, cop, and villain, only the latter two being of interest to Her Majesty's judicial system. But any evidence linking Spaulding to the murders of Eunice Connor and the U.S. marshal, however, had been destroyed, nothing recovered of Rafferty's videotapes or files except melted plastic. After three years of hard work and, up to now, an enviable success rate, the team was under threat of being disbanded.

"All because of a bunch of *fucking birds!*" The fury in Kramer's voice strangled with the effort not to become a scream. "A bunch of fucking birds and a wet-behind-the-ears bint, and a fucking Tyke who decided the rest of us weren't good enough for him so he goes off on his own. And what do we all have to show for it? Three dead bodies, including one of our own, and *no fucking evidence!*"

As memorials went, this certainly qualified for one of the angriest, Keen thought. The rest of Kramer's team must have been used to it, as they sat downing glasses of whisky with little conversation or expression. The men had all dressed for the funeral in suits and ties, even Sweet clean-shaven, and Rachel wore a black skirt and jacket over a white uniform blouse without insignia.

"Not that *you* would give a shit," Kramer snarled at Keen. "Fuckheads in Home Office think you've done a right bang-up job. Congratulations, Priscilla, you're off back to Bumfuck, Yorkshire, with a promotion and a jolly little station of your very own." He stood in the middle of the room, literally bobbing with ill-repressed frustration, smacking his fists together as he struggled to force the words out. "Fucking *birds*!" he finally managed again before stomping into his office and slamming the door shut so hard the glass rattled ominously.

St. John leaned over to pour another inch of Famous Grouse into Keen's glass, then topped up Rachel's, Sweet's, and Smythe's as well.

Smythe lifted his glass. "Here's to Danny."

The others raised their glasses and murmured in unison, "Danny."

"He'll live on in our hearts," Sweet said, his tone sepulchral.

"We'll never see the likes of him again," Smythe said with equal solemnity, but a furtive smile twitched in the corner of his mouth.

"He touched all of our lives," St. John intoned with theatrical gravity.

"Fucking birds!" Kramer bellowed, the sound muted behind the glass.

The three men snorted, trying hard not to but collapsing into helpless laughter.

"It's not funny," Rachel insisted. She looked over at Keen, cross. "He's *dead*. That's not funny."

"No," he agreed quietly. "It's not."

Shamefaced, the three DCs choked back the laughter, shamefaced and bleary-eyed. "Sorry," St. John muttered, wiping at his eyes, then exhaled through puffed cheeks and loosened his tie. "Sorry."

Kramer had been growling down the phone to some poor unfortunate soul. He banged the handset back onto his desk, heaved himself to his feet, and whipped open the door to his office to glare at Rachel. "You!"

Surprised, she put a hand to her chest in silent inquiry.

"Yeah, *you*! Drag your pert little arse into my office. *Now*."

The four men outside Kramer's office didn't budge from their chairs, drinking steadily while watching Kramer hunched over his desk and snarling unintelligibly at Rachel. She sat ramrod straight in front of his desk, answering whatever questions Kramer was demanding of her so softly not even the tone of her voice leaked from the glass office. Kramer finally swiveled away, kicked over his rubbish bin, and flung a pencil across the room in exasperation. Rachel flinched but stood up calmly and left his office, closing the door behind her.

"Okay, Rach?" Keen asked her sympathetically.

"Yeah." Her expression was perplexed rather than upset. "He's offered me a place on the team."

"You're kidding," Sweet said, stunned.

"This team," Smythe said, pointing at the floor. "Here?"

"With us?" St. John added.

"Yeah."

The three colleagues broke into huge smiles, knocking glasses together in a sloppy toast, whisky sloshing. "Hot damn!" Sweet said gleefully.

Rachel looked around at them all with amazed gratefulness. "You're really okay with that?"

"*Shit,* yeah!" St. John said. "Means we're not being disbanded after all!"

So much for the welcome committee, Keen thought as her face clouded.

Keen dropped Rachel off at the safe house to pack and headed out for a last drink at the Norman Arms. The interior of the pub was deserted when Keen arrived, despite the time of day. The landlord wordlessly pulled him a pint, then returned to his spot at the open window. In the distance, near the red barn at the far end of the field, half a dozen men dressed from head to toe in white decontamination suits glided through the long, ungrazed grass of a paddock like pale specters. Keen flinched as he heard a shot, even though it was no more than a muffled pop. After a long moment's silence, there was another. And another, the gunshots unevenly ticking down their deadly count.

"You should see 'em," the landlord said to no one in particular. "They just stand there watching, the cows do. Looking at you with wide eyes like they're asking you to explain." He turned, his own eyes cheerless. "Don't even moo."

Keen nodded and drank his pint faster than he would normally, suddenly just wanting to be gone, throw what was left into his bags and drive as far away as he could.

Preoccupied with his bleak thoughts, he'd opened the door on the Vauxhall when Jillie startled him.

"Thought I might find you here. You've been ignoring my phone calls," she said from behind him.

He turned around. She wore her hair pinned up, but her hand brushed back the wisps of rebellious curls that had escaped to tease her eyes. She was still in her Indiana Jones archaeologist's gear— bare legs now tanned under her multipocketed beige shorts, a well-worn archaeologist's trowel hanging from a loop, the tops of socks scrunched down around the ankles of dusty workman's boots, and a close-fitting army-olive T-shirt that fitted her body nicely. It might have been even nicer had she been smiling.

"I'm not a big fan of mobile phones," he said, offering her a smile of his own. When she didn't smile back, he added, "I've been busy."

She frowned. "Thin, Keen."

"Still true. For both of us."

"I just want to tell you again how sorry I am about what happened. It was selfish and thoughtless, and I'm just so relieved no one was hurt."

Which would remain the official story. Jillie would never know about Rafferty or Goodman or Danny or Spaulding or any of the others caught up in the mess. It wasn't just that she had no need to know; she'd had enough turmoil in her life and now that her luck was finally turning around, he wasn't sure how well she could have dealt with the guilt. He'd carried the can for massive acts of stupidity he'd committed himself with terrible consequences on more than one occasion. This time, he could shoulder her share of the blame as well.

Her eyes flicked back and forth appraising him before she glanced away and said, "We're winding up the site for this year, we'll be done end of the week."

He nodded. "What's next for you, then?"

She shrugged, the gesture apologetic rather than uncertain. "I'm thinking of going on this dig in Israel with Dr. Sheridan's team."

He considered it. "If that's what you want." That wasn't quite the answer she'd hoped for, he could tell. He took a breath and lowered his head. "Listen, Jillie—"

"Don't," she cut him off. He looked back up. She held her hands up as if to ward off his words. "It's not working out with us, I know that. We're just . . . too different."

"Worlds apart." He smiled again, the effort forced. "Half a world, anyway."

Her frown deepened. "I'd just hoped we could still be friends."

"We are still friends." Studying his shoelaces again, he said quietly, "But don't use me."

She laughed, shocked, a strangulated sound. "*Use* you! Christ, how the hell could I *use* you?"

"Easy. I'd let you, and you know it. I'm asking you not to. Enjoy your freedom. Go to Israel, if that's what you want. Dig up half of Jerusalem. But do whatever it is you want because *you* want it. Don't use me for an excuse." He raised his eyes to brave the indignation rolling from her like a wave of heat. "Because you're quite capable of doing anything you set your mind to without it."

Her lower lip jutted in an expression he knew was her way of fending off hurt. He waited until it softened. "So we're okay?" she asked, uncertain.

"Yeah. We're okay." He almost meant it.

Her angry energy had gone. "Maybe I'll see you later, here, if you'd like? We could have a last drink together, maybe . . . talk?" she said. He knew she knew he wouldn't be there, there was nothing left to say.

"Sure."

255

They stood awkwardly together in the car park.

"I gotta get back to the dig," she said finally and smiled wanly. "Cheers, love."

He made no effort to kiss her goodbye, and after a moment, she turned and walked away, her slim, strong figure losing none of its femininity in baggy shorts and boots. It didn't make him feel any better.

Both Keen and Rachel had what little they had brought with them packed and ready to go by the door when someone knocked. Keen opened it, expecting someone from Kramer's team, mildly surprised when it was a Parcelforce courier. The middle-aged deliveryman, with pale blue eyes and a Tom Selleck mustache so black Keen suspected he must dye it, gazed at him intently, then shifted a large padded envelope under one arm to check the name on his clipboard.

"There a Rachel Colver here?"

"Rachel," Keen called out.

She was equally as surprised and puzzled as he was but signed for the package. "Thanks," she said distractedly as the courier handed it to her, then closed the door. She looked at it, turned it over, then turned it back again.

"Who's it from?"

"Dunno." She scowled, eyeing it suspiciously. "Just hope it's not some sort of stupid windup, y'know, 'let's have a wheeze getting one over on the new girl' initiation bullshit."

"Want me to open it, just in case?"

She hesitated, then grimaced. "Nah. Let's just get it over with."

She sat down on the battered sofa and ripped open the top of the package with a show of bravado, peeked in, then tipped out the contents onto the cushion beside her. A dozen small camcorder DV tapes, two fat notebooks held shut with rubber bands, and a thick padded Jiffy envelope. Rachel picked up one of the videotapes, looked at the label on the edge. Her face went round with shock as she stared up at Keen.

"They're Beryl Rafferty's tapes."

"Holy shit."

They had no way to view them at the safe house, but a phone call (on Keen's cheapie; he'd already handed in his fancy mobile) to Kramer had them back in Newcastle town center and upstairs in Kramer's office with Symthe setting up a tellie and a camcorder hooked up to playback.

Kramer crossed his arms across his chest, cigarette smoldering, as he squinted dourly at the screen.

The only tape that hadn't been labeled in code was simply lettered "To Rachel."

The camera had recorded the interior of Rafferty's flat, picture shaking for a moment as it was turned on and focused. Then Rafferty sat down on the sofa and faced the lens, taping herself.

"Hi, Rach. If you're watching this, it means I'm dead." Rafferty laughed, seemingly amused. "That has always seemed like such a bogus line in the films, y'know? 'In thirty seconds this tape will self-destruct.'" Rafferty sobered, her expression wry as she shrugged. "Doesn't matter. Hopefully you'll never have to see this, but I want some insurance that what I've been doing . . . trying to do . . . for the past year isn't going to be for nothing. I know you've always thought of me as a bitch, and maybe I am, a little. But you're not. I know *someone* in the police is dirty, though. I don't know who, not yet. If I just give all this to the cops, I can't be sure it won't get 'lost.' But one thing I do know is that you're one of the good guys. If I send this to *you,* I know you won't stop until you get the bastards, all of them. You always were a kiss-arse pain that way."

Rafferty swallowed hard, licked her lips. She glanced away, her eyes glittering wetly. "All I ever wanted was to *be* someone, to make films that made a real difference. If I'm dead . . ." She rolled her eyes and tried to smile to lighten up her words. "Well, guess that means I'll never work in this town again. So please." The smile faded. "Do the right thing by me, Rach."

Rafferty looked as if she wanted to say something more, then laughed at herself softly, got up, walked out of shot and turned off the camera.

Rachel, Keen, Kramer, and Smythe sat for the next twelve hours watching the dead woman's tapes, taking notes, making phone calls. They hadn't gotten through half before Kramer stood, grunted with pain as he stretched and cracked the vertebrae in his back. "Go home, get some rest," he said to Rachel, his customary anger dampened. "I want you back here at seven sharp tomorrow morning."

"Yes, sir."

"And you. Priscilla. Just go home."

But he held out one meaty hand and shook Keen's courteously.

3 2

The Man From VAT, six uniformed police, and an RSPB officer had paid a quiet late-night call on Frank Eastpenny's pet shop in London, well after it had shut for the evening, while four other officers woke Eastpenny from a snooze in front of his tellie, the Raquel Welch in fake caveman furs on the late-night BBC One film mixing pleasantly with his dreams. Over a hundred birds were seized, including five scarlet macaws along with papers declaring them to be registered siblings legally bred and raised in captivity. Anticipating this, they took blood samples, which were rushed to Lambeth where two SOCOs and a lab technician waited. Thirty-two minutes exactly before Eastpenny had to be charged or released (when he could immediately alert any of his confederates in JADA), the test results came back: None of the birds were related to each other; the documents were bogus. Once his solicitor had hammered out a deal, Eastpenny became more cooperative in a large-scale covert operation now set into motion.

Within twenty-four hours, 117 riot police had bashed their way into five separate houses in a predawn raid, four in London, one in Kent, arresting nine suspects, eight of whom were charged with varied and multiple counts of murder, attempted murder, extortion, terrorism, criminal property damage, live animal smuggling, fraud, and anything else anyone could think of that might be levied against them. In Kent, Lyle Harmond was dragged naked and struggling out of bed while the lovely young woman he'd been snuggled up to wept hysterically and babbled in incomprehensible Ukrainian.

The one suspect not charged, a petrified seventeen-year-old university student, cooperated with police inquiries with enough information to lead the Metropolitan forensic team to a stash of weapons, one of which—a short-barreled black machine pistol— tested positive as the gun that had killed Eunice Connor and U.S. Marshal Kim Prescott, and crippled DI Vic Sanders for life. It had been wiped clean of fingerprints. Who exactly among the other eight suspects had actually pulled the trigger would take several years for the legions of solicitors and barristers of Her Majesty's courts to decide.

In Northumberland, Stedman and Pablo were arrested on suspicion of aiding in the Richmont bombing, and quickly worked out deals to grass on anyone even remotely connected to Goodman, including Flynn, the son of an extremely wealthy businessman married to the unhappy Ukrainian lady in Kent. Dagmar got on a plane to Denmark before she could be questioned and promptly went to ground, while Raven testified against her erstwhile clubbing mates without being charged with any offense herself, afterward shaving her head and joining a Buddhist sect in Cornwall.

Byron Rafferty arrived at his corporate investment offices in the City to find his secretaries and clerks clotted in the corridors with worried expressions as a small swarm of police raided his files and carted away his computers. Beryl's brother had been genuinely stunned by how easily his baby sister had exploited his firm to cover up the bird-smuggling cartel, filtering money with his company through channels in their father's commercial property developments in Hong Kong. But Byron junior and Byron senior cooperated fully and were absolved of any criminal involvement.

Beryl Rafferty's tapes, carefully edited, got their fifteen minutes of fame on the national news within days. ITN would later produce an award-winning three-part documentary on the young and courageous free-lance undercover investigator murdered by extremists, which both Keen and Rachel were sure Rafferty would have loathed. But at least she wouldn't be forgotten, Rachel was satisfied to see.

In the meantime, Keen returned to Weetwood to turn in his resignation, accepting the post as acting inspector at Sandford station effective immediately. He made a quiet offer to Jasmine, asking her to come with him, but all the WPC would say was she'd think about it. Keen didn't suppose she'd thrive as a big fish in a small pond, however, the little piranha quite capable of taking big bites out of big fish and liking it too much.

Rachel Colver found a flat on the outskirts of Gateshead—not too unlike the safe house she had shared with Keen—that would allow her to keep her dog, returned to Sandford to pack up what few belongings she owned, and left her grandmother's house without a pang of regret, or much of a farewell to her nana. She stopped by briefly to Keen's new nick to say goodbye to her old workmates, who wished her well. She would be fine, Keen was certain.

Sid the Yid, on the other hand, would mope for weeks before her replacement arrived, a gangly six-foot-three rosy-cheeked constable fresh out of police school who followed Sid the Yid around with puppylike devotion, much to his annoyance.

Laura finally rang, and—to his amazement—offered him a deal: She would voluntarily give him primary custody of the lads for a year, but only a year, mind. They could go to Ilkley Primary and live with their father full-time, traveling down to London every other weekend to visit their mother and stay every holiday. Now that he was working regular nine-to-fives instead of shift work, he could give the boys the stability of routine they needed, while the time away would give Gavin the chance to get back on his feet without distraction, she said. At the end of the year, well . . . they'd have to see where they all stood. So in a fortnight, he would be picking up the lads at the Leeds train station, bag and baggage.

Jillie sent a postcard from an archaeological site in Israel, camels and sand dunes on one side and a chatty "weather is here, wish you were hot" message on the reverse. She seemed happy.

All things considered, life didn't seem so bad, he thought as he finished his first month as inspector at his new station and drove home through the early autumn chill. The pasture around his house seemed oddly vacant, and it took Keen a moment to realize why. There were no sheep in his fields.

He parked his car in front of his house and followed the narrow track pressed into the earth and grass by generations of sheep toward the low stone wall between his land and Derek's, his heart thudding with a sense of resigned dread. He stopped briefly at a tuft of wool that had snagged on a corner of one of the stones, a small white flag waving in surrender on the breeze. Plucking it off the wall, he rubbed the softness between his fingers before holding it to his nose and inhaling deeply, dragging the animal's scent into himself, into his soul, into his blood. He held the smell of every sheep that had ever been born, lived, and died in these rolling green Yorkshire hills for a thousand years, and the smell of all the men and women who had bred them, earned their livelihoods from them, and loved them. His throat tightened in a sorrow so thick he couldn't breathe for a moment before he put the bit of wool into his pocket.

He stopped at the gate, now uncharacteristically locked, waiting for Derek to walk down the empty path toward him.

"It's done," he said simply once he'd reached the locked gate. He made no motion to open it and let Keen in, instead folding his arms across the top of the metal rail, his hands laced together so tightly his knuckles were bloodless. "Came about noon yesterday, had a dozen police show up with them. Kept us locked up in the house, wouldn't even let us make a phone call while the bastards shot the lot. They're dead. Every one." Derek looked away, his gaze intent on the far side of the pasture.

"Joanne?" Keen asked.

Derek's momentary silence said more than words could. The woman would not have had her husband's ingrained stoicism. "She'll be all right. I'd invite you up," Derek finally said reluctantly. "But she's not too keen on your lot at the moment. G'her time, she'll come round."

Keen wanted to say how sorry he was, but the words died in his mouth, massively inadequate.

"Be crowded right now anyway. We've got the vicar and his wife and half the congregation going in and out like a bloody train station. Tea and scones and Scripture-quoting. Don' do no harm, I s'pose. She just needs a good cry."

Keen recognized a suicide watch when he saw one. The two

men stood without speaking for a long moment, the loss for words more than the usual Yorkshire reserve.

"Listen to that," Derek said quietly, his voice hushed as if he was in a church.

Keen canted his head, curiously. He heard only the wind shushing through the grass. "What?"

"The silence. Never heard nowt like it afore," Derek said with a harsh exhalation that might have been confused with a laugh if his smile wasn't so desolate. "E'en the birds have stopped singin'." His throat convulsed as he swallowed and glanced over at Keen before pushing off the gate and stepping away. "Ah'll sithee."

"Aye," Keen said softly, but it was to the man's back as Derek walked off without a glance back, shoulders hunched and his hands buried in the pockets of his coat. "Sithee."

August's Death Toll: 17,603 cattle, 92,213 sheep, 1,271 pigs, and 47 goats.

In the space of five hours, David Dugdale loses 271 cows, one bull, two calves, and thirty years of work building up his pedigreed herd of Friesian and Holstein cattle on his farm in Crathorne near Yarm. He is angered by the government's suggestion that farmers like himself are profiting handsomely from compensation claims, and their decision to review the amount of compensation being paid out. At an average cost of £1,000 per head of lost cattle, many farmers like Mr. Dugdale will struggle to rebuild their stocks and businesses, as well as repair and replace buildings damaged by the cleanup. Elsewhere, Weardale farmer Dennis Craig has been ordered to pay the £830 bill for a set of traffic lights he was required by DEFRA to install in order to disinfect that part of the A689 road crossed by his 30 head of cattle when they were moved to fresh pasture.

Despite tough restrictions in the biosecurity "fortress" area around the Thirsk, North Yorkshire, two new cases of foot-and-mouth have been discovered. Animals at Griffin Farm, along with those at neighboring Sandhill Farm in Bagby and Glenside Farm in Kepwith will be destroyed. All livestock on the Horsehouse Farm near Whitby are being slaughtered.

A leaked document has exposed the government's contingency plans to cull a further 4.5 million animals, sparking alarm and anger across the country. Anne MacIntosh, MP for Vale of York, said, "If true, it confirms we are looking at a meltdown of the livestock industry." Durham Council, Wear Valley Council, and Derwentside Council have vowed to fight government plans to reopen the Inkerman mass burial site in Tow Law to cope with the additional 4.5 million animals. Residents of Tow Law are further angered after Gordon Kingston, Newcastle Disease Emergency Control Centre chief, is transferred after only two months. Town Councilor Sid Worgan said, "He would speak to you and he was frank. Now we will probably return to lies, lies, and more lies."

Andrew Keighley, father of two, has committed suicide on the family's Manderlea Farm in Poole-in-Wharfedale. He had been laid off from his job with the Wharfedale Farmer's Auction Mart in Otley after its closure due to foot-and-mouth. Although fastidious about disinfection, Mr. Keighley had become distressed and worried he would be blamed for the spread of the outbreak.

Chaos ensued in the small village of Bagby as a cull was carried out on the nearby farms of Monk Park, Bagby Hall, and a small freeholding in the village. Horrified villagers were unable to leave as lorries congested the narrow road through the village and animal carcasses lie in full view in fields along the roadside. The noise of the cull continued from noon until eleven that evening, distressing many, including children with pets among the culled animals who watched as their animals were killed. The villagers blame DEFRA for incompetent handling of the cull and lack of communication with local police.

Northern pig farmers are worried as a new disease, postweaning multisystemic wasting syndrome (PMWS) is moving north and has reached the York area. The disease, which has a far higher mortality rate in young pigs than foot-and-mouth, is spreading rapidly due to movement restrictions and cramped conditions imposed by DEFRA foot-and-mouth regulations.

Peter Hutchinson of Westwick Hall, North Yorkshire, has been ordered by DEFRA to disinfect the road that separates his grazing pasture from his milking sheds each time he moves his herd of 60 dairy cows, a process that takes ninety minutes, twice a day. The Environmental Agency, however, have expressed concerns over the disinfectant polluting a ditch connected to a stream that runs into the river Ure. "I feel very depressed," Mr. Hutchinson said. "I'm in a catch-22 situation."

A valuable Swaledale ram, Mossdale Nuggett, is killed by vets along with 1,000 other sheep and 225 head of cattle on a Wensleydale farm. Friends Eric Nelson and Robbie Cowperthwaite had saved for four years to buy the pedigreed ram for $50,000, sharing the ram's breeding between their two farms. By an unfortunate twist of fate, the ram was at stud on Mr. Cowperthwaite's farm when his entire stock had to be culled, while Mr. Nelson's farm at nearby Clatham remains disease-free.

Dr. B. Dixon, European editor of the American Society of Microbiologists, warns that ignoring vaccination during an epidemic such as Britain's has created "the perfect scenario for disaster." Professor Midmore, an economist at the University of Wales in Aberystwyth, releases a study predicting the cost of combating foot-and-mouth as well as compensating farmers for their losses will reach £5 billion by the end of the year. The report also said that vaccination rather than culling would have saved the taxpayer at least £3 billion.

The government promptly rejects Professor Midmore's figures.

POSTSCRIPT

At five to three in the afternoon, on the eleventh of September, 2001, while the rest of the world was transfixed by the attack on the World Trade Center in New York, Jo Moores, a PR spin doctor working for Steven Myers, secretary of state for Transport, Local Government, and the Regions, sent her boss an e-mail.

"It is now a very good day to get out anything we want to bury," she callously suggested. Among the buried news that went nearly unnoticed, the foot-and-mouth epidemic was officially declared at an end.

On the same day the foot-and-mouth epidemic was pronounced over, however, a case of the disease was confirmed in a flock of sheep in Swaledale, another in Palliard in South Stainmore, and one more in Brough, County Durham. Other cases were discovered over the following months, and the cull went quietly on for the rest of the year. Rural Affairs Secretary Margaret Beckett told the Commons in late October that another wave of foot-and-mouth was expected to flare up again before the end of the year, saying it would be "almost a miracle" if it did not.

The RSPCA considered legal action against government officials for animal cruelty after documenting complaints from farmers in the North-East and North Yorkshire of animals that had had their throats cut without being stunned, live animals buried with dead livestock, and knives poked into the still living animals' eyes to check if they were dead. Allegations were made of newborn piglets crushed with a shovel one by one as they were born, lambs held underwater and drowned, injured cows shot by slaughtermen still crawling on the ground in distress as they were clubbed to death with lorry spanners.

The Tow Law mass burial site reopened yet again to take thousands more dead animals from all over the country, infuriating villagers already fed up with the constant smell of putrefaction, water contamination, and obfuscation by DEFRA officials.

The number of rats in urban areas rose sharply, in some places by 30 to 50 percent, causing health concerns. The high number of farms where livestock had been culled no longer stocked feed on which the rats survive, forcing them to migrate in search of food.

Mike Cooke of the Border Collie Rescue took in 211 British border collies, all working farm dogs rather than pets, trained to herd sheep in areas where there were no longer any sheep to herd. Mr. Cooke collected one of them belonging to a five-year-old boy on his birthday and was politely given a cup of tea and slice of cake by the lad before he took away the family's dog.

DEFRA continued to investigate numerous allegations of biosecurity violations, lorries leaving contaminated areas covered with ash from pyres, rubbish bags with blood-spattered protective suits from a cull on a confirmed outbreak dumped by the roadside, drivers annoyed by long delays avoiding decontamination stations by sneaking through back roads into restricted areas.

Delegates at a major mental health conference in Bristol heard that the number of suicides among farmers was expected to rise over the winter, with increasing cases of depression, family violence, drug and alcohol abuse among the farming communities affected by the outbreak.

In October, Jackie Stephenson of Butterknowle near Bishop Auckland desperately petitioned to get movement restrictions lifted to shift his 50 head of dairy cattle to 113 vacant acres of lush pastures, as the seven-acre paddock where the cows were confined had been stripped of grass and turned to a quagmire of mud. Mr. Stephenson's 220 healthy sheep had already been slaughtered on humane grounds, as they likewise had no access to nearby grazing due to movement restrictions.

In November, organizers of bonfire-night firework displays in the North-East canceled events to prevent the spread of foot-and-mouth, still considered a grave danger in the area.

In December, Michael and Sarah Thompson, six and four, of Saltburn, East Cleveland, wrote to Santa with concerns that movement restrictions imposed on reindeer would prevent him from delivering presents to farms afflicted by the foot-and-mouth epidemic. Officials at DEFRA instructed the Disease Control Centre to issue an exemption to S. Claus, with the stipulation he must adhere to the traditional rooftop delivery system. The special license was officially granted.

And the Rural Rebels, militant countryside campaigners, brought traffic between Scotland and England to a standstill with a blockade of tractors, lorries, vans, and cars on major motorways to protest the government's continued refusal to hold an independent inquiry into the foot-and-mouth epidemic.

In September, 11,729 cattle, 79,227 sheep, three pigs, and 22 goats were slaughtered; 383 cattle, 3,033 sheep, and two goats in October; one cow and 625 sheep in November; and four sheep in December. After a sheep near Hexham, Northumberland, was merely suspected of exposure to the disease, an additional 2,100 sheep were slaughtered in January.

The government's official total of animals culled from 2,030 farms where foot-and-mouth disease had been found, as well as 5,000 neighboring farms "cleansed" in precautionary culls, was 561,802 cattle, 3,489,114 sheep, 146,145 pigs, 2,577 goats, and 932 miscellaneous animals. The Meat and Livestock Commission later confirmed independent estimates that included animals government statistics chose to overlook—4 million lambs and 150,000 calves killed with their mothers, 1.6 million sheep, 169,000 cattle, and 288,000 pigs, all healthy animals destroyed on "welfare grounds" because they couldn't be moved during the livestock transport restrictions, and half a million healthy "light lambs," small mountain breeds raised in Scotland, Wales, and the moorlands of England, culled simply because there was no longer any market for them.

Only 2,030 cases of foot-and-mouth disease were ever confirmed in Great Britain.

In all, the final death toll was just over 11 million animals.